Bitter Sweet

Bitter Sweet

a novel

Hattie Williams

BALLANTINE BOOKS
NEW YORK

Ballantine Books
An imprint of Random House
A division of Penguin Random House LLC
1745 Broadway, New York, NY 10019
randomhousebooks.com
penguinrandomhouse.com

Published in the United Kingdom by Orion Books, London.

Hardback ISBN 978-0-593-87420-2
Ebook ISBN 978-0-593-87421-9

Printed in the United States of America on acid-free paper

987654321

FIRST US EDITION

Book design by Mary A. Wirth

The authorized representative in the EU for product safety and compliance is Penguin Random House Ireland, Morrison Chambers, 32 Nassau Street, Dublin D02 YH68, Ireland, https://eu-contact.penguin.ie.

For my daughter, Astrid Snow

What happens in the heart simply happens.

—TED HUGHES

Bitter Sweet

Prologue

It took years for me to stop looking for Richard.

With just a few clicks, if I wanted to, I could find some update on him. There'd be a new interview to read or an article that he had written himself, sometimes a television appearance to watch back. That kind of access to someone who is no longer a part of your life is just plain unhealthy.

Well-meaning friends would message me when he won an award, or had a big publication, saying things like *I hope you are ok,* and, *Thinking of you.* When they did, even years later and after I had started to turn away rather than look into his light, it would prompt me to go online and search his name to see what they were referring to.

There were times that he would catch me off guard—a picture of his face in a newspaper I was reading, there looking back at me as I turned the page, or, worse, his voice on the radio, suddenly like he was in the room with me again. His mouth next to my ear.

He could not ever be contained, because he was famous. He permeated the bounds of our own relationship and our direct connections.

It must be a small club to be a part of, to have loved and then lost someone whom the whole world has a piece of. Maybe that's why no one ever warns you.

CHAPTER

One

2010

Richard Aveling stood to the left of me. I had been so distracted by thoughts of the man that I hadn't even noticed him as I'd fumbled a wet thumb over the wheel of my lighter trying to get a spark to light my cigarette. I had been watching this day move closer in my calendar for months, knowing it would be the day that I would finally get to meet him. He was as tall as people said, and broader. He was older than the photos printed on the inside of the covers of his books by perhaps ten or even fifteen years.

"Do you need a light?"

"Yes, please," I said, my heart hammering against my ribs. I pushed my hood back, realizing in horror that I was standing in the alleyway at the back of the Winden & Shane office in my old blue waterproof jacket and a fake leather skirt, smoking a roll-up in front of a man who had lived inside my head for over ten years. I'd planned my outfit for today so carefully, but my heels were upstairs waiting for me under my desk. This wasn't how I had imagined it. Not at all. "I don't usually smoke this early in the morning."

He lit my cigarette, positioning his own between his lips as he did. One hand shielded the flame from the gray drizzle that was falling quietly around us. The attraction was immediate.

"Neither do I. But I have an insufferably boring meeting this morning so I thought I would allow myself one." His voice was deep, and the soft northern corners of his accent were more angular than when he spoke on the radio or television. He looked me straight in the eye, drawing heavily on his own cigarette. There was a spot of rain on the white paper and the end burned gold around it.

The meeting he was referring to had been booked in since before Christmas. I had felt like it might never really happen. As I'd shaken my umbrella off outside the office building that morning, I'd thought, *How did I get here?* I had felt elated, excited for everything. This was my adult life. I felt proud of myself. The shelves of books that lined the walls in Reception only confirmed to me that I had moved seamlessly into the majestic, distinguished literary world of publishing. Now, though, I didn't know what to say.

"Richard Aveling." He presented the hand he wasn't smoking with.

"I know who you are. I'm Charlie. I'm Cecile's assistant." I surprised myself by saying it in a tone that implied that it was just a silly job and I knew it, this job that I was so proud to have, that I defined myself by. I took his giant hand, shook it, and leaned back against the wall so that we were standing opposite each other. The concrete was cold and wet through my thin coat. I regretted this move immediately but committed to it. I tried to look confident.

"What happened to the last one—Kate, was it?"

"Katy. She got a job at Simon and Schuster. I joined last spring. I'm going to be helping Cecile with the PR for the new book."

"Are you now?" He raised a thick, dark eyebrow and took another long drag on his cigarette, which he held like a dart, eyes never leaving mine. "And what is it exactly that are you going to be doing?"

I stuttered. This was not something I should have said to him. He was celebrated as one of the best British authors of the last century, famous far beyond the confines of publishing. He was certainly the biggest and most important author that we published. He was guarded like a secret by everyone who worked in his team. This was unthinkable.

"I just mean helping her with admin, booking trains, restaurants, mailing books, that sort of thing. I won't be doing anything important, I'm just the publicity assistant. You probably won't even see me again." I tried to smoke my cigarette but a raindrop had put it out. He said nothing. Then—

"Well, I hope that's not the case." A half-smile equally reassured me and made me feel uneasy. "It's nice to have someone new here. It becomes quite tedious working with the same old lot of them every time. They mean well but they do fuss. It wears me out." He flicked his cigarette to the ground, ignoring the ashtray. "Would you be so kind as to let me back in this way? I left my umbrella in Reception." A twitch at the side of his mouth. *I* wasn't fussing, it said.

I punched the code into the keypad and the door clicked open. He moved past me and I could smell the smoke on him, and something else that I half recognized: something expensive. He nodded and headed in, familiar with where he was going.

A little while later, I was sent to Reception to collect Richard and his agent, an important and serious man called John Cormorant, and take them up to the boardroom on the top floor. I had recovered myself and without the blue raincoat, and with some lipstick and my best heels—a pair of black suede boots that had cost close to a week's pay—I knew that I looked good. I was thin and young and with that, I was powerful.

When I introduced myself formally, Richard made no acknowledgment of our earlier meeting, which I liked very much.

CHAPTER

Two

I'd interviewed at Winden & Shane in the spring of 2009, the year before I met Richard. I was twenty-three, and it was my second job out of university. I had dreamed of working in publishing since I was a teenager and my mum had explained to me that publishers existed. I hadn't really thought about it at all before then, presuming a writer wrote a book and it magically appeared on the shelf.

The interviewer had asked me what I liked to read. I'd said that I loved Richard Aveling's writing, but I'd been careful not to say how much in case I'd seemed too intense, or like a fangirl. When I'd gone back for a second interview with Cecile, who was to be my boss, I told her, too, thinking this would be a positive. Her follow-up question caught me off guard.

"If you are successful, you would be working with Richard and his team directly. I'm sure you have seen the news that he has a new book coming next year. With such a long gap since the last one this is naturally going to be our focus for 2010. Can you tell me about a time when you've managed a very high-pressure situation at work?"

I faltered badly and left convinced I would never hear from Winden & Shane again. In all honesty, I had no idea how I would hold it together in front of this man whom I privately, quietly idolized with religious fervor. But despite my fears, I got a call later that week to say that I had got the job. At the time I was working as an assistant at a women's magazine, making a lot of coffee and processing a lot of expense receipts, very occasionally writing filler copy. When I told them I had another job they said I didn't even have to work my notice and that I could just finish up the week, which told me everything about how replaceable I was. Maybe it was because London was overrun with graduates desperate for badly paid, entry-level jobs. Maybe my lack of enthusiasm had showed.

So, it happened. The following week, I started at my new role as a publicity assistant at Winden & Shane. On my first day I sat in that big, arterial reception, which felt like some magnificent library, thinking about how this was the very real beginning of something. *This is where I belong,* I thought to myself. *I am seen, finally, and understood.* My hair, previously streaked with pink and green, and, for a short time, blue, was now a respectable brown. I had a new dress on, a new handbag, new shoes and even new tights, with no holes in the toes. I felt like the person I always dreamed of becoming. A smart, young, professional woman living independently in London.

Cecile came to get me herself and we sat down in the large basement that served as a breakroom for a cup of tea, to talk about my first duties and what the week would entail. I wrote notes in my best cursive in a brand-new blue notebook, specially bought from Paperchase like it was the first day of term. I smiled and nodded, hoping she wouldn't see how nervous I felt on the inside. I thanked her again for the opportunity. She seemed distracted, as she always did, too busy for small talk. The longer I worked there, the more I realized this was often the way with the older staff. They wanted to get out on time at the end of the day and to do that, when the workload was so massive, all pleasantries and social chatter needed to be cut. They were terrifying, and I was honored to be terrified by them.

Winden & Shane was the smallest of the big publishers, and the biggest of the small publishers. It was always talking of its "independent spirit," which really just seemed like an excuse for the office being a mess and the email server always breaking. There was a constant feeling of disorganization, and everything was always urgent, or late.

The office itself, which was near King's Cross, was totally chaotic and looked nothing like the modern glass-and-chrome building of my imagination. Instead, it consisted of two enormous and very grand Georgian town houses which had been knocked through to create one interior. There was a wide staircase, which branched off to the left and right at each of the four floors, and a lot of dark corridors peppered with small, dimly lit meeting rooms that were impossible to identify. Every door in the whole building seemed to be made of oak and took the full weight of a body to open or close.

Each department had an open plan floor with a kitchenette and individual desks, which enjoyed ample light from the tall, slim windows at the front of the building. Desks were piled high with newspapers, books and manuscripts, and there were cardboard boxes on the floor around every corner waiting to trip someone up. In winter, a draft ran through the whole place, so we'd sit in coats and hats at our old Dell computers watching the little egg-timers on the screen turn until we gave up and held down the power button with a gloved finger, mourning the loss of an hour's work.

Our managing director was the most feared of all. She was an ice-cold woman called Allegra Evans-Milberg. Allegra was American English, extremely thin, and had white-blonde hair cut into a sharp bob that was professionally blow-dried every morning at her home, or so it was rumored. She wore thick, red glasses on a beaded chain that jangled when she walked, and huge decorative earrings that hung below her hair. Allegra paid the junior staff almost no regard. If you erred and sat too close to her at any of the meetings she chaired, she would look at you with such quiet intensity that you would immediately give up your seat and scuttle to the back of the room and sit on the floor, or, if you were lucky, a filing cabinet. Allegra had an elderly terrier called Woolf (after Virginia) with bad breath and worsening incontinence, and she needed to be taken outside regularly. Care of Woolf during the day—which included cleaning up accidents—fell to the assistants, or whoever was on work experience that week. It was your only chance to be noticed and have your existence acknowledged by Allegra, though, so it was worth it.

Quickly, and subtly, I'd started to feel some sort of difference from my peers. For as long as I could remember, I had felt like an outsider, sometimes for reasons I could give words to, but more often not. I'd been so sure that now, as an adult, in the gorgeous world of glittering books and brilliant minds that could be as easily lost in made-up worlds as mine, I would finally find a place where I could fit in. But it had not been anything like I had imagined. Everything about publishing was different from what I had expected, but mostly the people.

Before I'd started working at Winden & Shane, I had never thought anything much about how I had grown up. I hadn't thought that we were exactly poor, but we lived modestly. I had never even known the kind of wealth enjoyed by my colleagues existed for what were apparently regular people. The way I spoke started to change without my meaning it to. I developed new mannerisms. I was creating a version of myself that would better fit in, but I was racked with anxiety, eternally self-conscious and worried I would break the veneer I was forging for myself. There was only so much I could pretend. Almost all of the other juniors seemed to have a flat or house in London that they or their parents owned. They were Oxford or Cambridge or Durham graduates, and had a relative who was an author or worked at the *Guardian* or *The Times*. Everyone seemed to me to be connected, existing in a web that I had no knowledge or understanding of. I had a degree from Sussex University and, when I first joined, lived in a damp single room in a shared flat near the notoriously grim Hornsey Lane bridge in Archway. I flushed when one of the aloof, beautiful young publicists mentioned she had been a student at the private school where my dad taught PE. I said nothing, and later felt bad about that.

Despite this, which was a part of how I felt about my life at work but not all of it, I found kindred spirits and best friends among the junior staff. There was a group of us who would eat supermarket sandwiches on the canal at lunchtime when it was warm enough, but it was out of hours that we came into our own. We'd drink cheap wine after work in the many pubs of King's Cross, somehow always still waking early and fresh enough for work. I smoked roll-ups and at home ate almost exclusively plain pasta. I wore ballet pumps or lace-up, pointed boots, short skirts and big necklaces over tunic tops. Sometimes I slept with men I met in pubs or at parties on weekends, fell in love with them immediately, and scared them away just as quickly. Sometimes I took ecstasy and kissed my friends in the corners of dark rooms in strange houses with no idea of how I'd get home. We'd indulge our comedowns the next day with Bon Iver and Bright Eyes, dreaming of the kind of love those men felt, and wondering if we would ever find anything so iridescent and beautiful. Nothing was permanent.

I'd never had friends like Ophelia and Eddy, and they fast became my closest confidants. At the time, they both worked as assistants, too—Ophelia in the editorial department and Eddy in the publicity department with me. When Ophelia's housemate moved out that first summer, I moved into the beautiful, sparsely furnished house in Stoke Newington that her parents bought for cash as an "investment" some years before. We quickly decided that Eddy should move in as there was another empty room, and so a few weeks later he joined us.

It was a tall, terraced house built of red brick on a quiet street lined with silver birch trees. The house was set across four floors and the attic had been converted into an extra bedroom with an ensuite, which Eddy took, because Ophelia rightly said that you should never share a bathroom with a boy if you want your friendship to last. Ophelia had the main bedroom, on the floor below, and below that was my room and an office, which her parents used for storage. There was even a spare bedroom, which they kept in case they needed to stay, but she said they never did. They only lived in Cambridge.

It was a great house. None of us would be able to afford to even rent a room in such a house as this on our tiny publishing salaries; we paid rent far below what Ophelia could have charged us. Given just how comparatively badly paid publishing was, I was confused by the fact that everyone who seemed to work with us had so much money.

"It's because they can afford to live on such shit wages," Ophelia explained to me as if she wasn't talking to me from the other side of a ravine. "It's a job you do for the love, not the money. If you want to make money in PR, you go into finance, politics or the charity sector. That's what my dad always says."

Ophelia Devereaux was stunning and rich and generous. She had received a world-class education at a very prestigious private school known for its "hippie" campus and relaxed teaching style, before studying English at Oxford and walking out with a first. She was effortlessly vibrant, extremely well read and ate even more rarely than I did. Everything about Ophelia seemed to me to be perfect; her dark hair that never had a split end, her enormous brown eyes and spotless golden skin. She was radiantly gorgeous and I loved her. Eddy Carnegie—Eddy being short for Edwin, which amused us endlessly—was from Edinburgh but puzzlingly spoke with an English accent. He was rich and beautiful, and beautifully gay. Taller even than Richard, Eddy wasn't just "publishing hot" (a phenomenon that occurs in which even the most mousy or mediocre man becomes suddenly desirable and handsome when they work in publishing, due to the dire lack of men in the industry). Eddy was *hot* hot. He was slender with thick, dark-auburn hair and russet freckles scattered like stars on his skin. For a redhead, he was very tanned. Eddy had a 2:1 in comparative literature from Cambridge and wanted to be a writer, but was very insistent that this be kept secret. Back then, nothing was more embarrassing than working in publishing and having aspirations of a literary career.

Both Ophelia and Eddy had complicated relationships with their families, which they talked about a lot. Ophelia's mother, Clemmie, would pop by regularly, filling up the fridge with organic fruit and vegetables and other expensive things from Whole Foods when she did. She always seemed perfectly nice to me, if a little absent. Like Ophelia she was beautiful, with the same big eyes and a tiny frame, but her hair was a shocking white. She wore a lot of silver jewelry, which she made herself in a studio built on their Cambridge property. Shortly after I moved in, I found her arranging lemons in a bowl on the kitchen island. The leaves were still attached, which I had never seen before. Her silver bangles chimed against each other as she hummed something I didn't recognize. I watched her from the door before sneaking away back to my room. She was lovely, this mother. I felt very sad imagining how my own mother would have filled the fridge for us, taking me to the supermarket and then maybe for a glass of wine before I put her on the train home to Dad. How would she have greeted him—a baby in his arms, Laura in her house, in her space? It was easy for these fantasies to jumble with reality before smoothing themselves out as being strange parallels that could never coexist.

Ophelia's mother's childhood best friend's older sister from her years growing up in Switzerland was the former sales director at Winden & Shane, recently retired at fifty.

Eddy was much more coherent when it came to explaining his family situation. He was so rehearsed and clear in his arguments that he must have been relaying them for years to various crowds: the boarding-school boys, then the university lot, now us and really anyone who would listen after three large reds on a Thursday night. His father believed that men should be "proper men." His mother had left his father shortly after the financial crash and now lived in Malawi with a younger man. Eddy's three older brothers—two of whom worked in the City making disgraceful amounts of money and one who worked as a scuba-diving instructor in Thailand—were much less of a disappointment than Eddy, whom they nicknamed Nancy from a young age.

"The most frustrating part of it is that Barnaby is as gay as I am, and he has always been the meanest of all of them." Eddy would lean forward and confide this, teeth stained with red wine. "He can parade around with Pandora or Penelope or whatever girl he is currently fucking, but he is one hundred percent getting dick on the side. Everyone at school knew it and at Christmas I borrowed his laptop—cock pop-ups everywhere! But Dad just acts oblivious and off they all go to the shoot, parading their masculinity like a bunch of peacocks."

Eddy's godfather was the former literary editor at the *Telegraph*.

The feeling of intimacy I had with Ophelia and Eddy was completely new to me. It was intoxicating in the best possible way. They were tactile and open about everything. They would take baths with the door open, asking for a top-up of wine or for you to pop in and put a towel on the radiator without batting an eyelid. Ophelia would often crawl into my bed at night when she was drunk or upset or both, curling an arm around me and sighing something sweet into my ear about friendship and forever. Eddy would bounce onto me like a lovely Tigger while I sat on the sofa, asking me to translate any potential subtext to a message from whichever boy he was chasing that week.

I was completely and utterly in love with both of them, and understood really nothing of either of them. I had no idea what they saw in me, but they did, for whatever reason, seem to love me back.

CHAPTER
Three

At work we all did our very best, getting in early and working late. Work never ceased to give us hours of things to talk about, mostly disbelief or disgust at how badly our bosses were treating us or how unfairly other people were being promoted.

Ophelia and Eddy had been at Winden & Shane longer than me and were probably owed a promotion. They had this way of talking, like the world was going to come to them eventually, so why shouldn't it just hurry up and do it now? They were frustrated with my more passive approach to my career and abilities, which almost certainly stemmed from having absolutely no idea what I was doing. I was just constantly surprised, each and every single day, that I had this job, that I'd not broken this wonderful dream in half. I loved the work. I loved every day of it. I was hungry to learn and hungrier to please and for the most part I was fairly efficient. There was something about my naivety that Cecile liked in those early days.

Cecile was, like all our bosses, the subject of much interest and speculation. She was in her mid-forties, I'd guess, and she was very petite with a head of spectacular, dark ringlet curls that bounced when she walked. I didn't know much about her life and how she had grown up, other than that part of it had been in France. A little trace of an accent could be heard in her voice, and she sometimes swore under her breath in French. She dressed beautifully—"Just like a Parisian," everyone would say. I had no idea what that referred to, having never been to Paris.

Cecile was famous for her speed. She spoke quickly, worked fast and walked at a remarkable pace for someone of her stature. Even though I towered over her at five feet and seven inches, it was hard to keep up with her and I wore flat shoes when we were out of the office for this reason. She was always highly caffeinated. A voracious coffee drinker, Cecile was very particular about her coffee and where it should and shouldn't be bought from. Cecile had been at Winden & Shane for over fifteen years and was the director of publicity. She was very well known across the industry for being the toughest, and the best. Journalists feared her. There were stories of authors throwing hardback copies of their own books at her and her ducking without even blinking, and of magazine editors being reduced to tears on the phone for posting an early—or worse, bad—review.

Our favorite rumor about Cecile was that she had a huge portrait of herself in her own hallway, but I'd never heard that from anyone who had actually seen it. She didn't seem to be the sort, but then if there was a sort, I'd have been the last person to know. I didn't notice any vanity in her other than that she looked amazing each day.

"I bet she's naked in it, with just a red silk sheet covering her modesty," Eddy had said on one of our first trips to the pub as a trio. He and Ophelia were thrilled to be relaying all the office legends to my virgin ears. We were smoking with our glasses of wine balanced precariously on the brass windowsill, the air heavy with exhaust and pollen. I was listening to them with rapt attention, giving the exact right amount of shock and awe at each revelation.

"No, I think it's classier than that," Ophelia replied. "Like, in her Barbour, and a flat cap, holding a shotgun with a brace of pheasant. Or in a toga with a shield! Hah. Yes, I bet that's it. She's such a tiny *Boudicca.*"

"Well, she certainly married a king," Eddy said with glee. From the way Ophelia laughed too it must have been a joke that related to an education that included classics. I went along with them, hoping they wouldn't notice I was totally lost. "Charlie, you must have heard about this—it was the biggest scandal in the industry for years. You've heard of Matthew Ridgebrook, as in Ridgebrook & Co.? He's, like, the biggest literary agent—or he was until about ten years ago because he is ancient and although he apparently refuses to retire, he does less these days. Anyway, he was married to Elouise Linden, who was one of the directors over at Bloomsbury back then. You know Cecile used to be at Bloomsbury before she joined Winden & Shane? Well, she left there around the same time that Matthew left Elouise and now they are married and live in a Regency mansion in Islington and have twin boys."

"She had an affair with her boss's husband?" This shocked me, but I knew I should add a good mix of delight in with it, so I did.

"That's what everyone says. This industry is absolutely rife with scandal. I can't get enough of it."

None of us could. Like a captor we had fallen in love with, it didn't seem to matter how many times publishing kicked us, we would excuse it and then come back for more.

In my life, there are things that have happened to me, and things that I have done, that have proven to be moments with a clear before and an after. One of those moments, perhaps in some ways the biggest, was the day that I met Richard Aveling for the first time.

A first meeting is important, and this was the first time that Richard met me. But I'd first come across Richard when I'd just turned twelve. Our English teacher had been the one to introduce him; one of Richard's poems had been on the English syllabus. It explored the idea of infinite time through the metaphor of a tree. Every child in the country read it. Richard was a great poet—he had published three collections of poetry—but he was much better known for his novels. It wouldn't be for another year that I would pick up one of those. When I did, it was his first, *The Road Goes Only Back.* I loved him immediately. This handsome and dark-eyed man with round, wire-frame spectacles gazing back at me from the back of his book. Floppy, dead-straight black hair falling across his face. I studied that photo intensely, feeling some stirring of something new. It was not like the crushes I had on the boys at school. He was an adult, he was un-silly. The relationships in the book were full of sadness and rejection and longing and sex and things I was only just starting to understand, and I felt like he was holding out a hand to me from the other side of adolescence, saying, "I will not patronize you, because I understand how grown-up you really are." I became obsessed with this feeling, and with him. The inescapable sadness that arrived with my teenage years started to cloud my vision and I could indulge it deliciously when I focused on Richard's books.

These were the days before the next thing to do would be to go to the internet to find out more about someone. The first of his books that I read belonged to my mum, but she only had the one at the time, because she said you should always pass a good book on. So I went to the library, as I did every Saturday, and I borrowed all of the fiction he had written, which was, then, two other books. The librarian looked at me quizzically, no doubt because of my age, but I read them all in a few weeks, then borrowed them again and again until I eventually owned copies of them myself. His poetry collections I understood less, but nonetheless loved.

We were so happy then, the three of us in our little suburban family bubble. We lived in a small 1930s ex-council house on a quiet cul-de-sac, overlooked by an uneven row of firs. Glass doors at the back opened onto a modest garden with a sunken pond. There was a rope swing that hung from a willow tree. It was just us for the most part, and various cats. We were all completely unremarkable and our life was simple. We found color in all of it. I was quiet and bookish, loving choir and swimming, and walking the South Downs at weekends hoping for a glimpse of a horse or a dog. With the encouragement of my mum, I entered poetry and creative-writing competitions at the library, the local newspaper and even *Blue Peter,* and I sometimes won, and often came runner-up. Nothing made me happier than a new box of colored pencils. But, even then, when I was small and far from adolescence, I'd started to think that something wasn't right. I would be easily overcome with feeling, at a harsh word spoken by a classmate, the death of a pet, a glimpse at the evening news from behind the sofa when I should have been in bed. So overcome that I would be rendered inconsolable and dumb with the feeling of it all, because there was just so much of it. I remember so clearly my mum wrapping her arms tightly around me, my own pinned at my chest, as she rocked me on her lap, whispering that everything was OK while I shook and wailed and screamed. The force of her arms, of her love, was all that could calm me. More than once she was called to school to collect me when I became hysterical and physically sick with it. Sometimes it came differently—on the morning of a day when I was due to sing a solo at assembly or present a project, or that there was a class party that meant we could wear our own clothes and not school uniform, I'd wake up white with fear, knocked into utter submission and unable to speak. I'd sit on the floor of the bathroom in my pajamas, unmoving, eyes fixed on the wall. Mum would try to coax me into the world again, reassuring me that it was OK, and Dad would look on, not knowing what to say, pacing with his hands behind his head. On those days she would call us both in sick and we'd spend the day on the sofa, or in the garden, or baking—there had to be an activity to distract me and it was often cooking. She'd then put a hat on me to disguise me in case we were seen out on a sick day, and then she would take me to the beach and get me to put my bare feet in the sea, even in winter, I suppose to shock the life back into me and bring me back to my body. She always knew how to break my sadness, how to cure me in a few hours. She was a magician in that sense, and because of it we had no need for doctors or therapists.

When I was older and we started sharing more of her interests, she would cut out any reviews or interviews that she thought I would like from the big newspapers she read on Sundays across the kitchen table from my dad. It was from these articles that I learned what books Richard liked and then read those, even Henry James and Philip Roth; all men of course. On summer weeknights sometimes we'd drive to the beach and I'd happily wander off to look in the rockpools gifted by the low tide as Mum and Dad sat on the stony shore, arms around each other, unpacking their days. Because they both worked at a school, we had long summers stretched out with trips to Norfolk or the Devon countryside, and once we even went to Spain. If it sounds idyllic it's because it was, those precious and innocent years of my life that I try to keep close.

By my mid-teens, my moods shifted and although I could still easily short-circuit at the right stressor, my response was less dramatic and less external. What I found instead was that my mind wandered to the darkest of places when I least expected it, to thoughts of oblivion and emotional apocalypse. These intrusive thoughts bothered me but I could contain them; I could function knowing that at the end of each day there was safety at home, and that every five days I didn't have to worry about school and friendships and lessons and teachers and boys and all of the awfulness that came with them. That I had two blissful days at home, with Mum and Dad, at the library, at the supermarket, at the beach or on the Downs, watching films with microwave popcorn, Mum and me in matching slipper socks.

I was sixteen when my mum died.

It happened the week before I'd received my GCSE results. At the funeral, I'd read one of Richard's poems. Two years later, after some of the worst years of my life, I'd written about Richard in an essay for my English A-level, comparing him to Richard Ford. In my loneliness a few years after that, in the small room I had taken near my university campus one hundred and fifty miles from the wooden urn holding my mother on a bookshelf in our living room, I'd read the first of his books again, remembering how Mum and I had talked about it and how she'd enthused over it. How she had said, "He's terribly handsome," looking at the photo of him on the back cover.

I would return again and again to the adult worlds that Richard had built for me, long before he even met me. I found comfort and safety there in among the melancholy of his words, which nestled next to each other on the soft paper in their own unique and alchemic order. Why words worked as they did when he instructed them so was impossible to pinpoint. He was *a remarkable talent, a once-in-a-generation writer, incomparable,* so said the quotes on the back of his books. He was famous in the way that so few authors were; he was recognizable outside of the literary world.

A few years after Mum died, Dad met Laura in the queue at the post office. She was much younger, only in her thirties, but it didn't seem to matter to either of them. They hit it off and she moved in with him. In my last year of university, Dad came to see me to tell me that they were going to have a baby, but that it would never change the fact that he loved me and my mum more than anything, and that he would always be there for me. I told him affectionately that he was far too old, and that it would kill him, but that I was still happy for him. Mum always said that a baby is only ever a good thing, which I also reminded him of as I felt bad for pointing out his age. He was fifty-one when Noah was born.

With Noah's arrival, I was, without any real intention, moved into that strange space that was Dad's "before." When I first held Noah, it was with the kind of distance that you might hold a bomb. He screamed and screamed until Laura took him back, reassuring me that he cried with everyone, although he calmed immediately in her or my dad's arms. We had nothing in common but chance, I thought to myself on the train back to Brighton that day. He wasn't even my blood because Dad wasn't my real dad. I had known it my whole life but I had never felt it before, not until Noah arrived.

CHAPTER

Four

As a publicity assistant, a day's work consisted of endless expense receipts, budget spreadsheets and book mailings. It could be dull, but I didn't mind that at all. The days were interesting and there was always something exciting to look forward to in the week ahead. I'd felt that the curtain had been lifted for me and that I was a part of it, this big literary engine. Accompanying Cecile with authors to talk shows and breakfast radio, holding their handbags and getting their coffee, pouring warm white wine into dusty glasses in the bookshops of central London on Monday evenings, all of this felt wonderfully important. I didn't mind that the authors were demanding and needy, suddenly unable to buy themselves a bottle of water or locate a toilet once in the presence of a publicist, or that Cecile would call me late at night or even on weekends when something small came up or she had an idea. I didn't even mind clearing up after Woolf, such was the strength of the enchantment this world held me in. But my favorite thing about all of it was getting to read the books that were being considered for publication, and then watching them be discussed by the more senior staff each week. Reading these books long before they were shiny and polished and spellchecked and typeset and bound into a book with a cover sitting on a bookshop table, it was a privilege. To see what they were before they became books just gave them more magic.

The new manuscript by Richard Aveling arrived that October. Everyone was talking about it and desperate to read it, but it was being kept under lock and key for fear that it might be leaked. This only fed the excitement and speculation in the office.

"We're not sending this out widely," Cecile said to me from across her desk. "But you can take a look; I know he's your favorite. Here's a watermarked bind-up. For God's sake don't leave it on the Tube or something stupid, Charlie. We'll be discussing it in the meeting this week. Obviously we'll be publishing it, but they'll want to hear some thoughts on it from the junior staff, it being Richard. We need to bring in younger readers with this one before his entire audience dies off." Cecile pushed a large brown envelope toward me and I tore it open, dropping the contents into my lap. There it was. I ran my hand across the type on the front page. *Altitude at Sea,* it said. *By Richard Aveling. Uncorrected proof. Not for resale or quotation.* I looked up at Cecile and she smiled.

I skipped lunch with Ophelia and Eddy that day, and the pub after work, and most of the night's sleep. The book was about a young man called Seb, a corporate lawyer, taking a leave of absence from his high-pressure London job and returning to the small Scottish island he grew up on to dry out, wean himself off what he considered a mild heroin habit and say goodbye to his dying father. The father, a cold and bitter former fisherman who had never shown him any love, was dying of dementia in the family croft, and, in the fug of his withdrawal, the son was soon drawn into his father's delusions and strange reality, remembering his own abusive childhood with a mix of his memories and his father's. It was a story of the cycle of abuse, a father-son relationship, how time and class could separate a single generation, madness and what reality means to each of us. At six hundred pages it was a beast of a book, and I loved every word. This was Richard's great novel.

His editor at Winden & Shane, Markus Lloyd-Dewson, was delighted by my enthusiasm. He was probably well into his sixties, if not older, and had the look of a caricature of a well-to-do elderly gentleman as he always wore a bowtie and braces with a tweed suit.

He worked only a few days a week and was rarely in the office, spending the rest of his time in Suffolk, gardening, caring for his quince trees and reading. Working together for so long, Richard and Markus had built such a close author-editor relationship that the company seemingly paid him a full and rather fat salary just to work on Richard's books, even though Richard only wrote one at best every five years.

Altitude at Sea was discussed in that week's meeting to unanimous noises of positivity. I stood at the back of the room with the other assistants, some perched awkwardly on filing cabinets, others on the floor, while the more senior staff fought for a chance to speak, none really listening to anything anyone else had to say. You could see their prepared comments being rehearsed in their heads, all hoping to say something more insightful and clever than anyone else, searching for obscure literary comparisons that would prove them to be the best read person in the room. Everyone would "mmm" and agree with the best comments.

"It has the cool realism of Updike," said a young editor to a few mutters of agreement. I saw her neck flush red.

"There is the expansive epic of Hardy," said another, greeted with a less enthusiastic response. He didn't seem bothered. The men in the office were, generally speaking, more confident and this particular editor was never shy in speaking up, happy to take any credit going for either his own work or someone else's. *A slippery fish,* as Ophelia once described him.

"It leaves Amis comparisons in the dirt," said another young man from the foreign-rights department. Everyone really liked that one.

Literary peacocking, I thought, doodling a feather in Biro in my notebook. Whoever said university didn't prepare you for real life was wrong. This was essentially a study-group discussion with a checkbook.

After comments were concluded, Allegra, who seemed uncharacteristically quiet on the subject of the book, said in her strange, Anglicized, upper-class New York accent, "Richard will be in London in February, so we'll need to be ready to present marketing and publicity plans then. Sales, I'll also need you there to talk through the retailer strategy. Cecile, can you find a time for him to come in?"

I had something clever to say too, but I wasn't really going to say it, I told myself, feeling the weight of six hundred pages and two hours' sleep suddenly hitting me. It was only 10:45. But by midday I perked up. In my inbox was an email from Cecile asking me to confirm the meeting details with everyone, listing the names and email addresses I was to add.

There it was: r.aveling1954@aol.com

The world was opening up.

CHAPTER Five

I had made good friends before Ophelia and Eddy.

In primary school, and all through secondary school, I'd had a handful of friends, mostly from choir, that I would meet up with sometimes on weekends or after lessons.

Sixth form was different. I stayed on at my school for sixth form rather than go to the local college with my few friends—we decided together as a family that it was better for me to stay at a place I knew, so that I could focus on my exams and getting into university. But then I lost Mum that August, and when term started some five weeks later, I found myself back at school and completely lost.

What happened then was that because my mum was dead, I became the subject of much interest at my school, and a group of more popular and glamorous girls sort of adopted me, like a curiosity.

What I understand now is that teenaged girls are often fantastically bored and frustrated by not being allowed to experience the real, adult world. Parents and rules and laws insist on keeping them children until they turn eighteen. Much of their understanding of the adult world comes from pop music and films and television, all riddled with tragedy and drama. And because I was living at the center of more tragedy and more drama than they had ever been privy to, this particular group felt that I was suddenly special and, honestly, I enjoyed the attention and the distraction. This new group of girls seemed much more mature than my old friends were. They were smart and studious as well as pretty and good at sport, and although they had never disliked me, until this point I had been of little interest to them as the bookish and quiet girl who would forget her PE kit on purpose almost every week. But I was out of my depth, in every sense, and I made a mess of everything by misunderstanding a situation with a boy, the brother of one of the girls in the group. So when, after a year in their inner circle, the friendship group spat me out like an unexpected maggot in a mouthful of apple, I lost all hope of ever making friends again and fell into a bad depression. It was like the gates were opened and I was submerged in grief, unable to see the surface, to move or breathe without the weight of it, like an ocean above me, pinning me down. I was finally feeling the loss of Mum and I missed weeks of school, unable to get out of bed. When Dad, who wanted so much to help but had no words that could reach me, finally took me to our family GP, I was put on antidepressants. I never came off them. I was never offered any counseling, or a follow-up appointment.

I finished sixth form quietly, without ceremony, and without the grades my teachers predicted two years earlier when Mum was alive and well and the future was something I felt excitement for. Back then, they had said that I could get a place at Oxford or Cambridge if I worked hard enough, even though I went to a state school. As it turned out, I didn't get anything near what I needed for that. Instead, I got a place at Sussex University in clearing to study English literature.

I was so desperate to escape the misery of my life and the home I shared with my mum's oppressive absence that I would have taken anything. But my problems followed me, as problems do, and I found university even more difficult than sixth form, and friendships especially hard. After the loss of not only my mum and my old friends, but also my new friends, and the catastrophic way it had all blown up at sixth form, I was withdrawn, insecure and increasingly self-medicated. I couldn't talk to people without half a bottle of white wine and then I walked a knife-edge to either crying in the toilets or being sick in them. I took a lot of photos with my little digital camera, but, looking back on them late at night in my bedroom in London when I couldn't sleep, I didn't recognize half the faces or for those I did, I couldn't tell you their surnames. I had some intense, transient friendships and disastrous relationships, walking the lanes of Brighton in bootcut jeans with the waistband cut off so as to make them as low as possible, digging through the vintage shops for mothy old dresses to wear with strings of beads and ballet pumps, drinking bottles of the cheapest white wine with whoever would drink with me. I took a book with me wherever I went so that I felt less alone. I worked in cafés and bars and clothes shops; jobs were like friends, temporary. Sometimes I'd find someone who would stick with me for a while and I'd move into a room in their house, lugging my duvet, pillows and three boxes of belongings up and down the many hills of Brighton, to a grand total of ten different houses or flats in the city in three years. I'd move on when I found something better or the friendship or living arrangement turned sour, which it inevitably did. One friend took particular care of me for a while, even getting me signed up for some CBT through the university, but I found it patronizing and overly simplistic. Then, despite all the kindness she showed me, or perhaps because of it, I slept with her ex-boyfriend and that was the end of that.

Christmas was always the worst. I'd go home to Dad for a few days, but it was horrible without Mum, and awkward for us all when Laura moved in. As soon as the trains were running again, I'd head back to Brighton, telling Dad I had a load of parties to go to or some other lie and sit in whatever miserable moldy flat I was calling home, alone and too broke to put the heating on, waiting desperately for New Year's Eve to arrive and with it, hopefully, some housemates to talk to. I was called unstable and chaotic a lot. On more than one occasion I was told I was "a nightmare." I fell for men who were not available and let them sleep with me, and then, desperate for their attention, cried for days when they didn't call me or reply to my texts. None of my boyfriends stayed around for more than a few months because I was so clingy, even with the ones I didn't even like. I was drawn to anyone off-limits but was always surprised when things didn't work out. I was at once determined to find security in a boyfriend who would ease some of my loneliness, and unable to make the choices that could ever lead to a meaningful relationship. I had no roots, no anchor. I couldn't take care of myself—I didn't know how to. I took a lot of drugs; we all did.

These periods of destructive behavior were punctuated with chunks of time spent in strict sobriety. This was usually after some devastating argument with a friend, or a boyfriend breaking up with me. I'd vow to myself that I would change. I'd do meditation and yoga classes at the Buddhist Center, the only place that I always felt welcome, immersing myself in the practice for as long as the phase lasted. I would go for long runs in the biting cold along Brighton seafront, tears streaking into my hair as the relentless, restless wind blew me every direction except for the one I was trying to run in. I'd sit and read in vegan cafés, eating side salads as mains, using up some of the calories I regarded as having "saved" on sugary soya milkshakes. As the weight fell off me, I would start feeling some control over my life, over my body. But it was always short-lived.

I studied enough to get through the first two years, and relentlessly in the third year, and somehow walked out with a degree and first-class honors. Dad and Laura, who was by then heavily pregnant, came to Brighton for my graduation. They took me for lunch at Pinocchio's, which was a budget Italian favored by the students of the city, and ordered a bottle of Prosecco that they could only have a sip of. Dad told me how proud he was, and he was, and Laura was happy for me, too. They had to get off straight after the bill came as Laura was tired and feeling uncomfortable and not looking forward to the long drive home. I found some of my university friends to drink with and that night we sat on the stony beach, feeling disconnected, listening to the waves in the darkness and wondering what on earth was next, what was out there for us.

Two months later, the investment bank Lehman Brothers collapsed and with it so did the economy. Ophelia, Eddy and I would talk about that day, what we had all been doing, where we had been when the news started coming in. They had a very different experience of the crash, naturally, because money and the stock market were much bigger things in their lives.

I wondered, sometimes, if they would have loved me if they'd known me back then. If they would have stayed by my side and carried me through the mess of those years. I thought they would.

That second Christmas living in London, my first working at Winden & Shane, had been the happiest I'd known in the six years since my mum had died. With the first Christmas lights and first overheard playing of "Fairytale of New York," I'd felt the ache of my loss keenly, as I did every year. This was the hardest time of year for me, but that Christmas I was carried through the holiday season on the shoulders of Ophelia and Eddy. They took extra care of me, distracting me when they saw I was sad, making sure I knew I could talk to them about how I was feeling and reminding me of that fact often. One night I broke down to them in the smoking area of a pub near Leicester Square after a lovely Christmas party in our favorite London bookshop, but it was just the once, and they didn't mind. After releasing some of the building pressure, I felt much better and we carried on with the rest of the night, staying out far too late and barely making the last Tube home.

I had been given some extra responsibility at work in the form of getting some of the more beautiful hardbacks and special editions of classics that we published into the Christmas gift guides that ran in all of the newspapers and magazines. I'd been surprisingly successful, which Cecile had been delighted with, and, thanks to the conversations I'd had with journalists, as well as Ophelia and Eddy's vast network of connections across the city, we'd had invites to Christmas parties every night of the week through all of December. London looked beautiful with all the lights and the decorations. A huge Christmas tree appeared in the reception at work, decorated tastefully with carmine velvet bows and a myriad of gold, twinkling lights. Gift-wrapped packages were scattered below it, but we discovered that they were just empty boxes after popping into the office for a shoe change late one Thursday evening. Clemmie dropped off a treasure trove of Ophelia's "party" clothes from Cambridgeshire and we'd get changed in the work toilets every evening, curling our eyelashes and straightening our fringes with Ophelia's beloved mini, portable ghds. No one seemed to mind that we'd drift in a little after 10 A.M. the following morning because it seemed that everyone was equally hungover.

Eddy left for Christmas on the twenty-second of December, taking the sleeper train to Edinburgh to stay with his grandparents, who were hosting. Eddy's father came from a long line of the dying upper class and was in fact landed gentry. Despite inheriting millions in very grand but disintegrating properties he found himself in dire financial circumstances after the crash, which exposed some poor business decisions. He was now on the brink of ruin and barely keeping his head above water. When Eddy, his youngest and outwardly gayest son, decided on a career in publishing, it was a bitter pill to swallow. Fortunately for Eddy, he was granted access to a large trust fund when he turned twenty-one, much of which he was now spending in east London pubs. I think he was quite looking forward to parading his ever-evolving campness and ever-dwindling bank balance to his broke father and tormenting Barnaby and the other brothers. His grandmother adored him.

The Devereaux family were, as usual, spending Christmas in Switzerland, and Ophelia invited me to join them. I couldn't ski, I explained, but I was very happy to spend the days that they were on the slopes reading at their family's chalet, which sounded absurdly glamorous and had "staff," which Ophelia said meant a maid who also cooked for them, and a cleaner. Dad seemed relieved to not have to deal with me as well as Laura and the baby, and he gave me some money toward the airfare as a Christmas present, but Ophelia's mum booked our flights and waved me away, bangles jangling, when I tried to give her the money back. I bought her a mug and packet of really nice herbal tea from Liberty—packed in a purple paper bag—and gave it to her on Christmas Day when no one else was around. She looked embarrassed, and I flushed as I realized how silly I was. A woman like Clemmie didn't need a mug and tea from Liberty—she could buy the store. She brought me in for a short-armed, bony hug, patted my hair and mumbled something in French, pinching my cheek and floating off to her bedroom with the bag. I was mortified.

The snow was thick when we arrived, and Ophelia described it as being "powder," which was great for skiing, apparently. Her dad, Claude, collected us from the airport in a shiny black Mercedes four-by-four with heated leather seats. I sat in the back while Ophelia chirped away to him in the front, flicking between radio stations and warming her hands on the air blower.

The chalet was far more impressive than Ophelia made out. This was something she always seemed to do, downplay how nice her things were. It was a beautiful and opulent log cabin, four stories with wraparound balconies and a pitched roof. It looked like a Christmas card. Ophelia was richer even than I had imagined.

The inside of the cabin was lit with a warm yellow glow and smelled of Christmas trees, because there were no less than three in the house. Each of the main rooms had a gas fire encased in glass and was a mix of exposed stone and wooden pine cladding to match the outside. Corner sofas were covered in soft pillows and furs, and deep-pile rugs were littered about. It was like a magazine, or a Christmas romcom. It was extremely comfortable.

Ophelia and I shared a room with an enormous bed and an en-suite bathroom. We had our own balcony, which was exciting to me, but I guess Ophelia was used to it, so she shrugged off my happy surprise, skipping out of the room shouting for her mama and in search of Baileys, her long, dark hair bouncing against her white knit jumper-dress. It was the twenty-third of December and it was just getting dark. Snow was falling softly and again, I thought to myself, *This is where I am now. The world is opening up.*

That evening, we drank Baileys over ice, and then red wine, and played cards in the living room with Ophelia's little brother, Sam. Sam was eighteen and in his first year at Cambridge "reading" economics. He was much nicer and more charming than any eighteen-year-old boy I had ever met. Like Ophelia, he had big, dark eyes with long lashes and thick, dark hair. He was going to be gorgeous in a few years, I said to Ophelia in bed that night.

"Yeah, and he knows it," she replied with a chuckle. "He'll be prime minister one day."

For all of the screaming and crying and fast-talking arguments in French they often had, her family life seemed absolutely perfect.

I'd learned a lot about the Devereaux family that week. Clemmie and Claude had met at the Swiss boarding school that they had both attended, married and had children young. They weren't even fifty and looked fantastic, athletic and well groomed. They had a mix of old family money and new, hedge-fund money. Claude was some kind of banker, following in the footsteps of his father, and this meant that he worked a lot of hours and had to make a lot of private phone calls, even at Christmas. He wore frameless spectacles that he liked to take on and off a lot as he moved his attention from one person in the room to the next. He had a head of hair that my dad would have killed for, and he probably would have told him that.

For the most part they spoke English when we were all together but as conversations would start between them, they would sometimes slip into French.

"Did you not study it?" Claude asked me on the first evening, taking his glasses off and sipping at his Scotch.

"Well, a bit, in school, but I didn't take it as an A level. I got an A star at GCSE, but I really can't do much more than ask where the swimming pool is or order a croissant."

"Remind me where you went to school?"

"Er, West Grange. Comprehensive. It's in Hampshire."

"Oh. I don't know it."

Of course he didn't. Thankfully Ophelia tuned her ear into our conversation and jumped in to save me.

"Papa, please don't ask people where they went to school. It's such a gross question. I've told you this a hundred times. Fine in the elitist old-man clubs or wherever you go to with the suits, but nowhere else and *especially* not with my friends." She took my hand and lifted it up into the air. "We're going to smoke," she said and danced me off up the stairs. I gave a bemused Claude an apologetic smile and shrug.

On the morning of Christmas Eve the Devereauxs left for the slopes early and I stayed in the chalet. With Ophelia gone, I stretched out across the whole of the super-monster-king-sized bed and dozed until 10 A.M., when my curiosity about the house and hunger propelled me up. I padded upstairs to the kitchen to investigate the fridge. I was shocked to find a very small, stocky woman in an actual maid outfit, minus the hat, cleaning the oven. I presumed she must be Marcy, the Devereaux's Swiss maid.

"Oh, hello, miss! Can I make you some breakfast?"

"No, no, no, not at all, I just wanted . . . a glass of water, if that's OK . . . No, no, I can get it . . . Oh, thank you, Marcy. And maybe just a banana; I'll grab that one from the fruit bowl, no that's fine, thank you . . ."

I quickly returned to the bedroom and flopped back onto the bed feeling horribly awkward about the whole interaction.

A maid, I thought, laughing to myself. *What is this world I have found myself in?* My phone buzzed. It was Ophelia, telling me to eat whatever I fancied, and that Marcy would cook for me if I wanted anything. There was a pixelated little photo with it, a selfie of Ophelia in her snow goggles, rosy-cheeked on a ski lift. I closed the phone. I couldn't afford to text abroad.

Although I had other books that I should be reading for work, books that I would be working on the following year, my focus was fixed on Richard. I had *Altitude at Sea* with me to give it a second, more leisurely read, and also his first and then most recent novels just so that they were really fresh in my mind again before the new year. I tried to read but I couldn't concentrate and, an hour later when I heard the back door close, I crept back upstairs to the kitchen to find the moka pot and make some coffee and toast. The house now empty, I made myself comfortable under a heavy blanket in front of the living room fire and read all day, occasionally breaking to smoke a cigarette on the balcony.

I decided to start with *The Road Goes Only Back,* Richard's first novel and general reader favorite, which had won him the Booker Prize when he was just twenty-seven. The book was about a man who couldn't escape the grief and trauma of the unexplained suicide of his first wife, something that he believed he caused and should have prevented. Although he tried to move on with his life, remarried twice and moved from Yorkshire to America, events kept drawing him back to the fateful night of her death, and the irreplicable love he felt for the woman he lost. Only after he found out many years later that she was having an affair with his best friend, and that was why she killed herself, was he able to understand her secret world and her unhappiness and that he was not the cause of it. In a fit of anger at having wasted his life grieving for her, he killed himself. It was beautiful and sad. The copy I brought with me had originally been my mum's. The battered old hardback, with its tea stains and smudges and an old bus-ticket bookmark, was one of my most treasured possessions. She'd written her name at the top of the first page, in her neat handwriting that I knew so well. The swirls of her lettering were like a time machine, flinging me back into a world where she still existed as a physical being. How impossible it felt now that she was ever really here, flesh and blood and bones. I wondered if her fingerprints marked any of the pages or whether a loose crumb from a biscuit was buried in the fold of the spine. Running my thumb across her name, feeling the dent from the pen, I could almost imagine the scratch of the nib across the page, almost feel her here with me.

I can still remember the moment when she first pressed the copy into my hands. I was sitting on my bedroom floor trying to tape a song off the radio; it was a Sunday afternoon and the chart show was on. I remember her words exactly:

"I think you are ready for this. It is very grown-up and has lots of things we should talk about, but it is my favorite."

I didn't have many memories of Mum that I could remember this clearly, but every one that I did, I kept catalogued in my own memory, going back to them often to make sure they stayed fresh. My favorite was something she said once at the beach on a beautiful summer's evening, the pink sky reflected in the warm shallows of the water where we stood in our bare feet. "These are the kind of moments I will remember for my whole life. Will you try to remember this one, too, Charlie? Then we can remember it together."

I thought about Richard. The way he wrote about grief and loneliness was more emotionally vivid and poignant than any other writer. I flipped the book over and looked at the little black-and-white picture of him on the back cover. He was only four years older than me when it was published. He was on the television enough that I knew what he looked like now. It was indisputable that he had aged incredibly gracefully, retaining the handsomeness of his youth, much thanks to the fact his hair was still dark and thick. He'd be fifty-five or fifty-six now. It sounded old but it wasn't really, a bit older than Claude. I felt another bolt of nervous excitement go through me—I'd be meeting him in a couple of months, I'd be there to talk about his new book. It was truly thrilling to think about.

Ophelia took my love of Richard's writing to be very sweet and typically studious of me. She was familiar with his books from studying them at school like me, but she called his writing "too male" for her tastes. She was excited for me though, as was Eddy. Eddy called Richard's books "the type of books the boys at boarding school used to bash me round the head with."

I told them so much about my life and my inner world, but I didn't tell them everything about my infatuation with Richard. I didn't want them to make me feel stupid—or worse, weird—if he ended up crushing me by being a disappointment. *Never meet your heroes,* as the saying goes. If he was rude or cold to me, it would be devastating. I would rather not meet him than have the image of him that I held so dear shattered. I didn't want to lose the feeling that I could only find when I read his words.

I wished I could call my mum and tell her about all of this, about work, about my life as an adult. She'd be so enthusiastic about it all. Me working with Richard, sitting in this beautiful house in Switzerland, my friends—all of it. But, as usual, this ache, this urge, tried to form into a fantasy of a reality and got stuck around the cogs of Dad and Laura and the baby. This time, it was how we would explain to Laura that Mum wasn't actually dead at all, though we couldn't explain the funeral. Then the spell would break, and the truth of the situation would flatten out in my mind like a crumpled page of a book, the reality obvious.

The Devereauxs had come home tired, happy and hungry at about 4 P.M. on Christmas Eve. Ski clothes had been dumped in the lobby as they'd talked over each other in a mix of French and English, laughing. Marcy returned and presented a feast of heated cast-iron bowls of raclette and buttery potatoes. There was a roast duck, breads of all sorts and a selection of meats laid out on the table in the kitchen. There were figs and grapes, and a bowl of salad, which no one except Clemmie touched. Champagne was opened and everyone helped themselves, Clemmie and Claude leaning on the kitchen island deep in conversation. You could tell how in love they were from just watching them.

Ophelia and I stuck with Sam, playing cards and drinking until the day's excursions had worn them out and we all went to bed. As Ophelia softly snored under her pink silk eye-mask, I lay in the warm, comfortable bed and watched the digital clock click past midnight. It was Christmas Day. Dad would be asleep in bed, Laura next to him, Noah in his room with a pillowcase full of plastic crap, chocolate coins and a satsuma at the end of his crib. They'd be having smoked salmon and scrambled eggs in the morning with some cava and orange juice. In the darkness I felt a wave of homesickness hit me. It wasn't homesickness, though, it was sickness for the past, for days that were so far away that no physical trace remained. The kitchen we would spend Christmas morning in as a family was ripped out and replaced. The sofa set was gone and a new one moved in; the carpets changed. The curtains swapped for blinds. The TV, even the kettle, everything old moved out for the new. My room was now a guest room, although they never had any overnight guests. Laura's family all lived nearby so they had no need to stay and Dad, like Mum, was an only child so there were no aunts or uncles or cousins. The only family we had were Sally and Amber, my much older stepsisters from Dad's first marriage. They came for dinner sometimes, but they didn't stop for the night. *The walls are the same, and the window frames and the doors,* I thought. Something of Mum must still live in those, the vibration of her words must have imprinted somewhere, knocked a particle next to another in some infinitesimal way, still unchanged.

I'd called home in the morning from Clemmie's phone. Dad had sounded happy and exhausted, as always, and distracted with half an eye on the baby, who'd been chatting away wordlessly in the background.

"Happy Christmas, Charlie—thanks for the presents," Laura had yelled.

"Same to you," I said, and Dad said to her:

"Charlie says same to you." Then to me, "Thanks for the lovely gifts. The baby loves the truck. And Laura is very pleased with the aftershave you got me—she says I needed an update. You know she says I always smell of Lynx Africa because the kids at school spray it everywhere. How's Switzerland? What are you having for breakfast?"

Dad always wanted to hear about food.

"It's really nice; thanks again for the money for the airfare. Um, it's all very Swiss, so I think croissants and cheese and stuff."

It was croissants and cheese and stuff, but the stuff was French toast made with brioche with syrup and bacon or berries and cream, huge plates of fresh fruit, jams and marmalades, as well as smoked salmon and trout, more meats, Marcy on hand to make eggs any way you liked them, and coffee, juice and more champagne.

"Do you want eggs?" asked Clemmie when I returned her phone.

"No, I'm fine, thanks, Clemmie."

"You know, Marcy is paid more in the five days we are here than we are in a month," Ophelia whispered to me, taking a piece of melon from a plate. "Have the eggs, Charlie."

And so I had the eggs, and I had my first Christmas away from home.

With the exception of Christmas Day itself, The Devereaux family skied every day we were in Switzerland, and I read, feeling very at home in my new surroundings and wishing that we could stay forever. Time off the slopes was a blur of food and booze, and other than a tipsy Sam trying to awkwardly kiss me on our last night, fairly uneventful. I didn't tell Ophelia about this until we were back in London. She howled with laughter, dramatically rolling off the sofa with tears streaming down her cheeks and a smudge of makeup under each eye, but she did eventually promise not to tell him she knew.

"I can't promise I won't ever say anything because it is just too deliciously good not to torment him with, but, yes. I pinkie swear. For now, my lips are sealed."

Ophelia and I both felt that being back in London was a huge anticlimax after the excitement of Christmas and the trip abroad, and we were glad that Eddy was back in time for New Year's Eve. Not a night I had traditionally had much success with—the pressure to have a good time had more than once left me crying in a gutter, friends lost and no way to get home—but we were determined to make the welcoming of a new decade a good one.

It was, though, just like any other night out in London. Eddy,

Ophelia and I had got drunk before we'd even left the house, hopped around bars in Shoreditch and spent too much money. Eddy had some cocaine left over from Christmas, so we took turns on that in the loos to perk us up when we felt too drunk. Ophelia bumped into an old university friend at a bar she had insisted we go to and disappeared with him at around 2 A.M., leaving Eddy and me to share an eye-wateringly expensive taxi home, which he paid for.

"You know, Charlie—2010 is going to be your year." We were downing glasses of water in the kitchen. He kissed me on the cheek and stumbled off to bed.

2010. A new year, a fresh start. Things were about to happen, I felt it, although I had no idea just what was coming.

If you'd told me then, I would never have believed you.

CHAPTER
Six

Of all the before-and-after moments in my life, none was more catastrophic, as world ending and new world beginning, than the moment that my mum had a massive stroke in her car outside Sainsburys.

She'd been there for about six hours, they thought, before the alarm had been raised. All of those people who had parked up next to her, who'd wheeled their trollies past her—they must have thought, *There's a woman taking a nap in her car.* I've never been able to stop thinking about that. How if one of them had knocked on the window earlier and realized, called an ambulance there and then, that maybe she would have survived. I was told it wouldn't have made a difference, and she wouldn't have had any symptoms or pain, but I will never be able to shake that thought.

That evening, on the day that it had happened, Dad had been worried sick and had called me back from a friend's house after Mum failed to come home from work. A phone call to a colleague from the school had revealed she'd not come back after lunch. She'd just been going to do some admin, and had complained earlier of a headache, so they thought nothing of it. It had been another few hours before the police turned up. When we'd seen the police car park up outside the house in the dark, Dad had said, and I will never forget this, "Oh, my dear God, please don't let it be."

She'd popped out at lunch to get a few bits and had lost consciousness in the front seat of her car. I don't know if she'd gone in to get her shopping and it had happened after she'd packed the car, or if it had happened before she'd been in. I don't remember anyone bringing the car home, or seeing it again after that day, or what had happened to the shopping, if she'd had any. When I think of it, she isn't slumped over the steering wheel, her head is back against the headrest. Her mouth is closed.

We'd gone to the hospital that night. She was almost certainly brain-dead, we were told, but because she was young, they gave us the option of surgery to try to relieve the swelling caused by the bleed. We insisted that they try. We knew we'd never forgive ourselves otherwise. So, they sent her to another, bigger hospital and they tried it. The operation took seven hours. The longest seven hours of my life. After it was done, we were able to see her again. She was in a private room on the intensive care unit, a nurse positioned at the end of the bed with a screen and charts. Her head was shaved; it hadn't occurred to either me or Dad that they would do this, and we were both very shocked and upset. She didn't look anything like Mum. Her beautiful auburn curls were gone. She was gone. There were staples in her head and a tube in her throat. Her hands were soft but so very cold. The nurse encouraged me to rub them with moisturizer. Two days after that, we agreed to take her off the ventilator and the tube was removed. She died an hour later, at nine o'clock in the morning, just as the school bell would have been ringing. It was slow and it wasn't peaceful. It wasn't like on TV, with a heart rate that became a flat line. The line jumped about, started, restarted, tormenting us in the cruelest way imaginable until a doctor came in and turned the screen off, looking furious with the nurse for leaving it on.

I didn't want to see her at the funeral home, but Dad did go. He said she looked very peaceful.

"Like she was sleeping?" I said through thick tears, inconsolable.

"Just like that," he said.

Two days after she died, I'd collected my GCSE results. I'd gone to the school to collect them late in the day, because I'd known everyone would have been and gone by then. The piece of paper with my grades blurred in front of my eyes; ten A's. But I felt no joy. A lot of people came to the house in the first few weeks. Then we had a funeral for her, which I got a new dress for, followed by a wake at a local pub, and then people stopped coming over and I started sixth form and the new world order was established.

It was August when she died, and it was so hot. All I wanted was gray skies and rain, but every day the sun shone and the flowers bloomed and the birds sang in defiance of my wishes, and I was totally powerless in all of it. I was newly sixteen. A few months before, it had been my birthday, and we'd eaten cake and I'd been allowed some wine with Mum. Mum and Dad gave me a necklace, a tear-shaped aquamarine stone on a delicate silver chain. I thought it was the most beautiful and sophisticated thing I had ever seen.

"To go with your eyes," Mum said as I hugged her. "Sixteen! I can't believe it. My baby girl. All grown up."

When she died, I felt as if my world stopped turning. As if I was frozen in time. In the years and weeks and days since, when I'd think of her, I'd feel like a little girl, not a professional woman, not an independent adult. Every heartbreak, every flu, every birthday and Christmas, it would hit me, and it would, I guessed, for the rest of my life. *I am a child, and I want my mum.* But she was gone.

At first, I didn't ever talk about it, then it became all I could talk about. In the immediate aftermath, people were desperate to be the one I would open up to. My few friends, my mum's friends, my friends' mums, even the priest that officiated her funeral, all of them were there for me in those first weeks. To my friends I was a fascination, a girl marked by real tragedy rather than the drama that we, as teenage girls, applied to our own lives at every opportunity. I was completely unanchored. These offers of support, of an ear or a hug, they were there only in the first weeks. When I didn't immediately offer up my insides and accept the hugs and handholding they were offering, they soon drifted back to their own lives. I suppose they didn't want to feel sad about her dying all the time. They had that choice, and lives without her that they could go back to.

Dad didn't break down in the clichéd way people do in fiction. He didn't descend into a world of alcohol and painkillers. His grief was quieter than that. It was angry. Before she had died, he had been a sweet and soft man, this bald and aging PE teacher who adored his wife. He didn't ask me if I wanted to talk about it, or tell me he loved me and that everything would be OK. We moved around each other like ghosts, like we were the ones who had died, not her. We didn't really say anything at all, except maybe, "Did you double-lock the front door?" or, "We need milk." The house was always tidy; he made an effort there, but her absence was enormous. He never thought to turn the lamps on and the overhead light off when the sun started to set, so the living room was never cozy. Neither of us could bear watching the Saturday-night television shows we used to watch as a family, so we'd skip them altogether.

I never felt that we were not biologically connected until she died. For as long as I could remember, he was Dad. But without her, I felt it so deeply that I became internally obsessed by it, that he had his own real daughters and now he was stuck with me, a cuckoo in his home. I had no right to any of it. I looked so much like her, too, except for my hair, which was dark. Everyone said so at the funeral, all these people I'd never met before. And I think that was especially hard for him. He didn't come to me when he heard me crying at night and I didn't go to him when his sobs made their way into my room through our shared wall, my hand pressed against it, cool and hard. When everything came crashing down on me the following summer, at the start of my A-level year, we were so independent of each other I don't think he noticed at first. It was a really terrible time in my life, and I try very hard not to think about it too much.

I'd come to understand later, from my dad, that my real dad had been difficult. That us leaving him had been the first big before-and-after moment in my life. I'd missed out on the relationship I would have had with my mum where she would have told me about it, he said. They'd never really talked about how they would explain it to me and because of this he'd been reluctant to give me any details of what had happened in my first five years beyond that word. *Difficult.* There'd been so many conversations I'd missed out on, about her life, about my life, and when she died that history had been erased as there'd been no one to tell it. There'd been days back then that I would have exchanged my sixteen years with her for another mum who was still alive. But that was just in the depths of grief, when you will do anything to change your unchangeable situation.

As I'd got older, I'd moved out of the absolute darkness of the shadow of my grief into a place where, although it was always with me, there were more days that I could see it only on the periphery, my vision no longer completely obscured by it. Rather like a familiar, it hovered just above me, shitting on me on occasion without any warning or apology. Only later, after time had offered some relief, had I felt differently, and that in fact I wouldn't change anything about her because she had been just perfect.

And she had been mine and mine alone.

CHAPTER

Seven

January 2010 was cold and wet and dark like no other January before it. The burning excitement of November and December was wet ash in the January rain and we'd limped through those first weeks of the year with a lot of early nights and sluggish mornings.

Cecile was in a particularly difficult mood. Her nanny hadn't come back from Spain after Christmas, quitting without giving any notice, and her children had seemed to be in a rotating dance of colds and flu that meant she'd been called out of work to collect one or both from school on an almost daily basis.

"Call my husband for once," I'd heard her scream down the phone as she'd kicked her office door shut with a four-inch heel. A minute later she was rushing out of the door with her laptop bag and coat saying she was on her mobile if it was urgent.

Under a staggeringly large pile of Christmas expense receipts, more order forms and travel arrangements for elderly authors who apparently couldn't buy their own train tickets, thanks to a lot of encouragement from Ophelia and Eddy I was quietly plotting my future. The next step in my career was, I knew, a promotion to the coveted role of junior publicist. After making a fortuitous comment about "younger readers" in a catch-up with Cecile, I was given a small but momentous project—to come up with ideas for reaching that audience for Richard's new book. It wasn't to distract me from my main responsibilities, Cecile said, but if I wanted to pull some notes together then she'd have a look at them and they might even possibly, and that was a *big* possibly, be included in the publicity plans. It was the first time I had something that wasn't admin or caretaking to work on, and I was determined to be brilliant. I was starting to take on more and more extra responsibility, which meant that I would, surely, soon be able to step up and out from under Cecile and pass the assistant baton to the next person.

Spending so much time with Ophelia and Eddy gave me a new confidence. I was now starting to speak up more, picking apart the bad decisions or bad behavior seen in my colleagues during the day, and agreeing with their complaints over cups of flavorless herbal tea at night. We were trying a January without any booze at all, but only Monday to Wednesday after the first week.

I spent all of January waiting for February to come, and all of February waiting for the twenty-third to arrive; the day Richard would be coming into the office. I finished rereading his entire back-catalogue and I was so deeply immersed in his world that I started to phrase my thoughts in his voice. The view from the bus, revealed as I wiped a fist through the condensation in the morning dark, would become a moment of absolute poetry. I'd rehearse exactly what I would say to him if he asked me about the book, and how I would say it. I bought and returned clothes to wear, and finished all of my other work as quickly as possible to be sure that nothing could distract me from being in the meeting.

And sure enough, the day came. It was a Tuesday when I first met Richard Aveling in the alleyway behind the Winden & Shane office and the third of those before-and-after moments in my life happened.

Late on the Friday afternoon of that week, Cecile waved me into her office from behind her desk, her phone between her ear and her shoulder.

"Hold on one sec . . ." I turned to leave again. "No, not you, Charlie, sorry. I need you to take some copies of *Altitude* to Richard's flat. He's there for another hour. Can you go now? Just drop them in his post cubby and leave—don't go up. Yes, yes, I'm here. Sorry . . ." She shooed me out, gesturing at me to close her door.

I had not stopped thinking about him in the days since I had met him, delighting in every second of our interaction, then cringing at things I had said, replaying it all over and over as I fell asleep at night. I sat back down at my desk and took a very slow breath out, and in, and out again. I double-checked his address on the computer, although I knew it by heart, picked up three copies of his book that had been printed out in our post room and bound with plastic covers to protect them, put them in a Jiffy bag, got my coat and bag, and, saying to Eddy, "Back in a bit," in the breeziest voice I could muster, I left the office and headed for the Tube.

After the meeting on Tuesday there had been an email chain and a few responses, including one from Elaine Aveling, Richard's wife. Cecile had explained to me that Elaine looked after his diary and some of his financial matters, mainly his expenses.

"He can't—or won't—do it himself. He rarely replies to emails so if you need something done, it's usually Elaine you'll have to ask. I thought she might have joined us for the meeting but she's away a lot at their place in France. Look, it goes without saying that I expect absolute discretion from you on everything, but it's an odd arrangement. They've been married for years, but live quite separate lives. Anyway, you'll meet her at some point soon because she comes down to the Covent Garden flat quite a lot."

Richard had three houses, as far as I could tell—a large farmhouse called Stone Heap House that was his main residence in the Yorkshire part of the Peak District, a flat in Covent Garden that was his secondary residence, and some kind of old chateau in the Languedoc region of France that Elaine liked to spend a lot of time at. Cecile had been many years ago, but I couldn't glean much more from her than that. It seemed there had been a golden age of publishing that I had missed by a few years—trips abroad, lavish sales conferences, opulence and glamour, and a fair amount more misbehavior than we had even now.

In the carriage of the Piccadilly line train to Covent Garden I checked my makeup in the cracked compact mirror that had belonged to my mum, which I carried with me everywhere. I carefully put on some red lipstick, taking care not to get any on my teeth, and smudged it in to look more natural. I gently brushed my thick fringe with a little fold-up brush, and refreshed my eyeliner. An elderly woman opposite looked at me with such disgust for my public vanity that I felt momentarily foolish. But I smiled at her, a big brazen smile, and she looked back down at her newspaper.

By the time I got through the lift at Covent Garden, it was raining. My sad little blue rain mac that Dad had got me had a hood, and in my haste to leave I had forgotten my umbrella, so I pulled the mac on over my coat and headed toward Seven Dials, dodging puddles. It was 4 P.M., but the strange, fast-fading light had the quality of dawn.

The flat was not as I'd expected it to be. It was in one of the grand old buildings that line all of the streets of Covent Garden, with large, uniform windows that now house mostly offices. I counted five stories. At the front, on the street level, there were two shops, and not the kind that I could afford to shop in. Around the back, on a corner by an alleyway, was the entrance. There was a fan of terrazzo steps that led up to a heavy wooden double-door with brass fixtures and a buzzer with a camera. Before I had a chance to press 8a, his flat number, the door swung open and there was Richard, who was on his way out. *Again with my horrible raincoat,* I thought, heart racing a little less at this meeting than my first. He held the door open for me to come in, and there was an awkward moment where I realized he didn't recognize me and was just letting me into his building.

"Richard?" I pulled my hood back.

"Ahh! It's the smoking publicist. With her famous blue raincoat. Got my books?"

He stepped back into the hallway to let me in. The building was so grand from the outside that I was surprised at how scruffy the hallway was. Post was piled up above overstuffed mailboxes and takeaway leaflets littered the floor. There was a strong and distinctive floral smell of an industrial cleaning product that I've never smelled anywhere else since.

I presented the package to him, and he took it. He was so tall. He seemed even taller than he had at the office three days earlier. I nervously patted my fringe, willing it to look straight and neat which it never, ever did.

"Thank you, erm—"

"Charlie."

"Yes. Charlie." He paused and looked at me. He was wearing a brown peacoat with the collar turned up. His hair was still thick, but thinner at the temples than in his photos and streaked with dark gray. He had a day's stubble on his chin and his round, tortoiseshell glasses had started to steam up a little. He was magnificent and again, I felt a sense of awe at how impressive a man he was.

"Have you read it, Charlie?" He tapped on the laminate cover of one of the books with a perfectly manicured nail.

"Of course I have," I said, taken aback. "Twice, actually." I felt my cheeks flush. He looked at his watch.

"Would you mind staying for a cup of tea? Do you have time? I want to pick your brains about the book. As a younger reader."

"Yes, I'd love to." Cecile had said not to go up, but he had asked me to, so I could hardly decline. It would be rude of me to refuse Richard Aveling when we all worked so tirelessly to please him. "Were you on your way out, though?" I slipped off my raincoat hoping it might disappear, trying hard not to be as graceless as I felt in his presence. He'd made a reference to a song my mum liked—"Famous Blue Raincoat." She'd have loved to hear about this.

"That can wait. The flat is on the top floor and the lift is broken, I'm afraid. Can I take your bag?"

"No, no," I said. My armpits sweating grossly into my dress, I followed him up four long flights of stairs.

He removed his boots at the door, and so I did, too, but he kept his coat on. The ceilings in the flat were high and ornate. The floors were all wooden and the walls all white. A small lobby led into a wide corridor with a kitchen, a bathroom, a bedroom, his office, and, at the end, a huge living room. It wasn't shiny or showy. It was airy and bright and elegantly understated. The whole place felt literary, with piles of books and newspapers and wall-to-wall bookcases. There were framed graphic posters from exhibitions and plays, and some modern oil paintings and pencil drawings. The kitchen surfaces were a dark oak and there was an Italian espresso machine next to rows of mason jars of sugar and tea and rice. A huge butler sink stood in the middle of the room and a ceramic bowl full of slightly sad lemons, with leaves, sat next to a pot with three newly emerging daffodil bulbs. Everything seemed to me to have a story. This was not just stuff, this was a life.

A little radio was quietly playing Radio 4. He indicated for me to perch on a stool at the kitchen island. The rain was drumming hard now on the vast sash window, and it was almost dark.

"Coffee? Tea? Whisky? Rye? What can I get you to drink, Charlie?"

I wasn't sure if he was joking about the whisky, so I went with tea. He made two cups of dark tea with no sugar and while he did, asked me questions like how long had I been at Winden & Shane; when had I graduated and where from; what had I studied at university; what I was reading now; in particular which writers people *my age* were into.

I crossed and uncrossed my legs and tried to sound casual in my answers. I didn't know what to do with my hands. Under his coat was a soft, caramel-colored jumper. Sometimes he'd pause as he looked for a teaspoon or a teabag and sweep his hair back. The intimacy of these moments was overwhelming, and I felt myself blush. I wasn't able to piece together the thoughts that would allow me to work out if this was a very normal thing to be happening, or if it was a *something*.

"So, Charlie," he said, sliding the cup of steaming tea toward me from the other side of the kitchen island. He was leaning on his forearms, looking at me with such bold confidence, I had to fight not to look away. "You, it seems very obviously, are younger than most of the dusty old furniture in that office, and so may have some ideas about how we might get people of *your* age to read this book. I ask because you have read it not once but twice, which I hope means you like it, because they don't, I expect, pay you to read. So, just between us, I wonder if you might tell me what you think of it."

I recovered myself a little and in doing so found I could look him in the eye with the same directness, if not height, that he did mine. His eyes were somewhere between green and gray, but dark at the edges. I cocked my head slightly to the left and paused, playing the part of someone else. No one at work had actually asked me what I thought about the book itself, only what I thought about how to sell it. No one had really cared about my opinion or asked me about my ideas on his prose or his themes or anything like that. But he had.

"Well, I think it's the best thing you have ever written, naturally." He smiled and lifted himself off his forearms, looking a little quizzically at me. "It's different from anything else you have written stylistically, which is obvious, but it's not a huge departure thematically. What is most interesting to me is that it ends with some sliver of genuine hope, whereas I don't know that your previous books have done. And with Seb, you have written a young man with more affection for his faults and failings than you have done with any of your other protagonists."

"So, what you are essentially saying, is that I'm getting soft in my old age?"

"Maybe," I said, surprised even by myself. I smiled and sipped my tea. He smiled back at me. "I actually thought it would end differently," I said, almost at once regretting it. His eyebrows furrowed slightly.

"Go on," he said.

"Well, at the end, when Seb is on the boat back to the mainland, it feels so resolved. I thought that maybe he would find the boat couldn't reach the shore. That he would find himself sailing back to the island again, stuck in a loop or something. That it would be revealed it was all a fantasy from his own deathbed. That the cycle of familial abuse and memory loss was in fact endless, that he was destined to experience a similar death to his father's." Richard was silent, and perfectly still. I didn't know where this had come from and I couldn't tell how it had landed, because he somehow looked both angry and impressed. "But don't listen to me. I don't really know much about anything when it comes to publishing—I'm only just starting out. And I only work in PR. The book is perfect. I think that it would be something that my friends would love, the ones that maybe haven't picked up a Richard Aveling before. I really think it's your great novel."

He had been frozen, but he shifted suddenly, liking this. He seemed to like everything I was saying, and I liked it, too. He looked as disarmed by me as I felt. There was a long pause before he said anything else.

"If it is, if this is my great novel, then what comes next? I was told by a lot of people that my first novel was a great novel, and maybe I've not written anything as good since that, until now."

"I don't know. Maybe your next novel will be better, maybe every book you write after this one will be better."

He walked around me to the bay window next to a small fold-out dining table covered with plants in various states of opulence and death, and he pulled the sash window up and open. He took a cigarette from a pack on the table and offered the carton to me. I stood and took one, and he lit it for me. I was careful not to stand too close, taking a spot on the other side of the table, blowing my cigarette smoke into the London evening. Rain sprayed back into the room and onto the plants. We didn't speak, standing there in his kitchen, smoking his cigarettes.

I told Ophelia about my trip to Richard's flat as soon as I got home, unable to hide my excitement. I'd been worried about how long I'd been there, and that I'd come straight home rather than going back to the office, but it seemed like no one had even noticed my absence.

Ophelia wanted me to relay every detail. She asked what brand the espresso machine was, but I'd not been able to remember. "How old is he, do you think?" she said from the other end of the sofa. We were eating packs of instant noodles from the corner shop.

"Fifty-five, or fifty-six, but he doesn't look that old at all."

"That's older than Claude," she said. She often referred to her parents by their first names when they weren't around. "You don't think he's, like, a creep? Inviting young assistants up to his flat . . . it's a bit *creepy,* don't you think?"

"I don't think so," I said a little defensively. "He wasn't creepy at all. He just wanted to talk about the book." I cringed, remembering what I had said.

"What? You've got that look you get when you think you've done something stupid."

"I can't believe I did this, but I talked about the ending, about how it was all a bit neatly wrapped up. Remember how I was saying it would be better if it turned out at the end that it was all actually a fantasy of his own making, like, a sort of memory? That he was stuck in a cycle."

"No—did you actually tell him that?" I nodded, reeling at the memory. "What did he say?"

"He didn't really say anything. He just sort of looked at me, and then changed the subject. He was really lovely, Fee. Eurgh. I can't believe I did that."

"Oh, don't worry, it's done now. I'm sure he'll forget about it and I doubt he'd tell on you. Especially if he *is* an old creep and he fancies you." I spluttered at that.

"There is no way he fancies me! It's just how it is with these authors, right? You know the stories about how much time you end up spending with them. Cecile says the whole team used to go to France, to his house out there. I'm sure if he was a creep we would have heard about it, someone as famous as him. Don't you think?"

Ophelia just shrugged. I hated her talking about him like this. I hated that she thought the only reason he would want to spend time with me was because he was some lechy old man. Of course she didn't get it, Ophelia with her doe eyes and pale, skinny boyfriend with his City job. The university friend from New Year's Eve was, anyway, close to being elevated to boyfriend status, but had not yet made that commitment to her. She stayed at his place a lot, in his new-build apartment on the river, with a gym in the basement. He was standoffish to both me and her, and spoke with such a ridiculously plummy accent I found it hard to really listen to a word he ever said. He wore an expensive suit and ordered Grey Goose vodka. I'd been out with them twice and decided that was enough.

I changed the subject after that. Talking about Richard out loud had flattened the excitement of my afternoon with him. It was better to keep him to myself and hold on to the feeling that maybe, just maybe, something exciting was happening in my life. Something felt different—I felt different. He had listened to me, to what I had to say. I had earned a role in his life and his work because of my job. I had, finally, friends that understood me, a house I loved living in and a job that could contain me. Nothing had happened between Richard and me, but in the way you can smell snow before it falls, I could feel that something was possible. That maybe my life could work out better than I expected, and that he, this man I worshipped, would have some small part in it.

I didn't want anyone else to find out about my time with Richard, especially not Cecile. He was so much older, and much more important, so to be spending time alone with someone so young and junior might be misunderstood. Especially after Cecile had told me not to go up to the flat at all. But I wanted more time alone with him and I didn't want to do anything to sabotage that. Surely it was a sign that he liked me, that he found me interesting and valuable, I told myself. If he did find me attractive, I couldn't see why—there was nothing about me that would be attractive to a man like him. All I had was my age.

I was surprised to bump into him at work the following Monday. I had no idea that he was due to be in the office, but it occurred to me that I wouldn't know unless it was for a meeting that Cecile was expected to join. He was sitting in Reception, waiting for Markus, when I came back in from picking up lunch with Ophelia.

Richard was sitting on one of the big chesterfield sofas in the lobby. The receptionist, Saskia, whose heels were usually kicked off under the desk, was sat up very straight, her legs crossed and shoes firmly on her feet. This was what Richard did to women, young and old. And it wasn't just women. There was a scared-looking man whom I didn't recognize as an employee on the sofa opposite, clearly starstruck by Richard, and doing a terrible job of hiding it by pretending to read his book, which was upside down.

"Charlie," he said to me. I hadn't been sure if I should say anything to him or if he'd even remember me, but I had hoped he'd notice me and he had. "Nice to see you again."

Ophelia stood by me, but he didn't acknowledge her at all. I could feel her making herself taller, and hoping very much to catch his attention, but he ignored her completely. She was desperate for an introduction.

"Hello, Richard."

He didn't get up, but he leaned his giant frame forward so his elbows were resting on his knees. "Would you mind letting Cecile know that I'll come by her office after I've met with Markus?"

"Of course. She's out at a lunch, but she'll be back by two-thirty. Do you need me to get Markus for you now?" I was surprised that he had been left here waiting like this, so exposed. Saskia looked up at me with a furious expression that said, *I have this under control, thank you very much.* A part of celebrity, I was learning, was that everyone wants to be the one to help.

"I'm early. He'll be down soon. Nice to see you again."

It was my cue to leave. I could feel everyone's eyes on me: Saskia's, Ophelia's, the poor greenhorn in the corner. Richard knew my name and had paid none of them any regard.

An hour later, Cecile returned from her lunch meeting flustered and smelling a little of wine. She was holding a large paper coffee cup. I followed her into her office and pulled the door shut.

"Cecile, Richard is here—I bumped into him in Reception. He asked me to tell you that he'll be coming by after his meeting with Markus. He didn't say what time—do you want me to clear your afternoon? There's nothing that can't be moved."

Cecile flopped back into her chair and let out a sigh. "Yes, I think you'll have to. I have to be here if he wants to speak to me. Did he say what it was about? He's rewritten the end of the book, you know. We were just about to go to print. He sent in another chapter this morning. Markus is having kittens. This will be why he is in. You and I will need to catch up later on the implications for those who already have a copy for review. This is a huge headache. He is oblivious to how much difficulty this will cause. It has real potential to damage the whole publicity campaign—the whole publication. But obviously not a word about this when you see him."

I went back to my desk, internally panicking. I thought about messaging Ophelia but I had to hold it together until after work, or certainly until Richard had left the office. I could speak to her then. I put away the morning's empty coffee mugs and threw the paper bag that had housed a croissant in the bin. I sat up very tall in my chair and tried to look as natural and important as I could, but I couldn't concentrate on any of my work. Had he possibly changed the ending because of what I'd said? If Markus and Cecile found out I'd be in big trouble, I was sure of it.

An hour went by before he came down and although I was in a heightened state of anxiety, by then I was distracted and caught a little off guard. He appeared next to my desk, his fingertips resting on its edge. He had lovely hands. I looked up at him. Cecile's door was closed and her blinds shut.

"Is she in there, Charlie?"

"She is." I tried to behave like a graceful host at a dinner party rather than a tangle of nerves, turning away from my computer and standing up to escort him to Cecile's office. Everyone was looking at Richard over their computers, quiet and listening out for what was being said. I went to her door and knocked lightly. Cecile called for me to come in. He moved past me and greeted her with a formal peck on the cheek. She was so tiny next to him that it was almost comical.

"Thanks, Charlie." Cecile motioned to Richard to sit in the armchair opposite her and I went to leave.

"Actually, perhaps Charlie might be of help here. If she has a moment."

Cecile looked surprised but motioned for me to sit. I popped back to my desk to grab my notebook, closed the door and pulled out a chair from the corner, nervous to hear what this was about or if he would mention the previous week at the flat. But he didn't. And to my great relief, he didn't mention anything about the ending of the book, or what I had said about it.

What Richard wanted to talk about was who we should be sending early copies of the book to. The usual old guard, Julian Barnes, William Boyd, Colm Tóibín, were all on the list. But he wanted younger writers, and some women, that maybe hadn't already been thought of. Naturally this was something we had already spent much time thinking about, but Cecile was very deliberate in not saying so in such terms. She listed the writers we planned to send copies to, careful not to say anything about the last-minute change to the book and how many people we had already sent it to. He nodded and looked thoughtful, his fingers laced across his chest as he sat back and proposed some of the names that I had mentioned to him at his flat. Zadie Smith, Helen Oyeyemi, Rachel Cusk, Jennifer Egan. I noted them down like it was the first time I was hearing them, tilting my head and nodding in a way that said, *Oh yes. Good idea. I'll get right on this.*

I kept my good posture and calm demeanor for the duration of the meeting, which lasted about ten minutes, but internally I was doing backflips. I knew that it was me who had put the idea in his head, who had suggested many of these writers to him, and that was why he'd asked me to be in the room. He didn't mention our conversation—and Cecile knew nothing of our discussion in his flat the week before. But *I* knew. It was a wonderful feeling, to be listened to and respected by a man like Richard. I was desperate to read that last chapter, to see if anything that I had said to him had gone into it. Even the possibility of it made me feel sick with excitement.

After the meeting ended, Richard said he needed to see another colleague to collect some letters that had been sent to him care of Winden & Shane. Cecile asked me to take him. They parted as they had greeted, with a peck on the cheek. I walked him out through the office, which had gone deathly quiet the moment Cecile's door had opened. I loved walking next to him, showing the whole office that I was in his inner circle. I was just an assistant, sure, but I was trusted with Richard Aveling. We collected his post and I walked him to the top of the main stairwell. We were alone.

"I know the way from here, Charlie, thank you—I've been coming to this office for years. Probably since before you were born." He said this with a smile. I found it hard to meet his eye. He was standing very close to me, closer than he had in Reception or in the main office. "It was good to see you again. Thanks for those suggestions about who to send copies to. I hope you don't mind that I took them as my own, but I assumed you might not have told Cecile about our chat and I didn't want to get you in trouble."

I nodded. I didn't mind at all, I was flattered. But right then, I was hit by how strongly I felt that I didn't want him to leave. I wanted to ask him about the new chapter, about his weekend, about his day. It might be weeks before I'd see him again.

As if he'd seen this thought pass across my face, which he may well have done, he leaned in and said, with his mouth very close to my ear—

"I'll see you again very soon, I'm sure."

And off he went, down the stairs and away from me and my racing heart.

I didn't hear from Richard again until that Friday morning when he emailed me directly to ask for a desk number for Markus's assistant, which was very odd as it was on the bottom of all of the emails Markus sent. But then at 3 P.M., Cecile called me into her office, and I understood. He was checking that I was in.

"I'm sorry to do this to you, Charlie, but I need you to go to Richard's—he has asked for bind-ups of the book with the new chapter by the end of the day. The new chapter is all typeset now, and I have some already printed in the post room; you just need to collect them. We won't get them there on a bike in time in Friday traffic. Obviously, you don't need to come back to the office, but don't stick around at Richard's—drop them and go. Do you understand? I would do this myself, but the twins have their school play and I can't miss it so I need to leave in the next twenty. Thanks for everything this week; you've been great. See you on Monday. Drop and go, yes?"

I'd not been given the extra chapter to read—I wasn't important enough for that—but I had gleaned from conversations in the office that the change was strikingly similar, although not identical, to the suggestion I had made the previous Friday. When I'd told Ophelia that he had changed the ending, her jaw had dropped.

"You absolutely can't say anything to anyone," I'd said.

"And neither can you, Charlie—you'd be in big trouble. God, imagine if he has used your idea for the ending?"

I was sure that I wouldn't say anything to Richard about it when I saw him. That would really be an overstep.

Because it was a Friday and we were going for the usual after-work drinks with the other assistants, and because I'd hoped for a replay of the previous week, I'd worn a really good office outfit—a hip-hugging tartan skirt with a little black polo-neck tucked in, and my black wedge boots. There would be no horrible blue raincoat today; I remembered an umbrella. I think that I had known, really, that he would find a way to call me back to him that week, but I hadn't dared to let myself believe it because good things rarely happened to me. I had thought of little but him, of what it might feel like to kiss him, to feel his hand on mine. They were the innocent, fairy-tale fantasies of a teenage girl, never veering further.

The streets around his flat were busy with Friday afternoon drinkers in suits, their collars unbuttoned, ties discarded. It was still overcast but it was a little warmer and this slight change in temperature had the city feeling like we were on the edge of spring. When I arrived at his flat, he buzzed me in and told me, through the intercom, to come straight up. The lift was working again and as the doors opened at the top floor, his floor, my heart skipped a little faster. He was waiting in the doorway of the flat for me, arms folded, shoes off, smiling. I had a little distance to walk to him in my heels. I felt horribly self-conscious as he watched me.

"Hello, Charlie. Will you come in?"

I nodded, ignoring Cecile's words in my head, and carefully unzipped my boots while he stood over me, slipping them off and dropping three inches in height as I did. He was more casual than the week before, a dark denim shirt rolled at the sleeves and worn-out cords with a few white paint splatters. He had red socks on. I followed him into the kitchen. On the counter was a beer bottle, sweating from the fridge. He shrugged at it as he took the copies of his book from the package and set them on the side next to him.

"Will you have one? It's Friday afternoon, after all. Surely Cecile doesn't expect you back."

He handed me a beer from the fridge, popping it open, and gestured for me to follow him into the living room. It was a stunning room. There was a dark-red velvet sofa, with neatly folded blankets placed at each end, and a mahogany coffee table on which sat a half-drunk cup of coffee, a skin forming on its surface. There were built-in bookshelves that reached to the high ceilings, filled with books. There must have been thousands of them. On the other side of the room was a long dining table covered in more books—some I recognized as being new books that he had been asked to quote for—and then piles of neatly folded linens and newspapers next to two typewriters. I imagined dinner parties at the table, with writers and actors and critics all sitting around drinking red wine and smoking as Elaine spooned food onto plates in flickering candlelight. The sorts of dinner parties that you would dream up in the pub.

There was a record player, too, by the window, and stacks of records. I could see some I recognized, records my dad had on CD—the Beatles, stuff like that. "Leonard Cohen," I whispered, picking one up that was next to the player. The album was called *Songs of Love and Hate,* and there it was on the track listing: "Famous Blue Raincoat." Now I knew. This was truly, actually, *something*.

There were three huge bay windows along the front wall. It was dark outside now. Richard opened one and took a cigarette from a pack on the table and offered it to me. I loved this—a pack of cigarettes in every room. I carried my one packet of tobacco around for a week at a time, picking out the sticky crumbs in the days before payday. I sipped my beer, then took a long, deep drink, and smoked my cigarette. Radio 4 was playing in the kitchen.

"Is Elaine staying with you at the moment?" I asked, stroking the burning end of my cigarette in the ashtray.

He smiled at this.

"No. She's in France. We have a house there. She hates the winter in England so she's there most of the time. Our house in Yorkshire gets very cold. It's not for the fainthearted, winter on the Peaks. I love it. She wants me to put central heating in through the whole place, but I won't have it. We have stoves and open fires."

"It sounds wonderful," I said, hoping it didn't sound like I wanted an invitation.

"It is. It couldn't be any more different from this. Elaine inherited this flat from an aunt about thirty years ago. I hate to think what it's worth. It's an obscene luxury to have a place like this but, as we didn't buy it, it doesn't seem so crude. Another?" He pointed at my empty bottle. "Or something else? There's wine."

And so went the afternoon. I almost asked him about the new ending, but it just didn't feel right. We smoked, and drank beers at a gentle rate, and then we had some white wine—delicious, crisp, dry wine, so unlike the stuff I bought from the bottom shelf of Sainsbury's—and then a pizza. I sat on the floor and looked through his records, and he sat on the sofa, occasionally getting up to play something to me. The famous Richard Aveling from the small black-and-white photo on his book covers melted into something completely different. I never forgot who he was, not for a second, and the strangeness of the situation hit me more than once. Ophelia was wrong, though—he wasn't a creep. We had plenty of authors that were, ones that everyone knew about. The youngest female staff were generally shielded from those men, with all steps taken to avoid them being left alone with them. Once you got more senior, it was just expected that you were tough enough to deal with their wandering hands or disregard for personal space. They got away with it because the author's happiness was more important than anything else. It was just the way things were.

When I noticed the clock on my way back from the bathroom, it was gone 8 P.M. and I remembered myself. I told Richard I had to be getting going as I was meeting some friends. He looked a little surprised.

"Of course. You are young. The night is young. How old are you exactly, Charlie?"

"I'm twenty-four next month," I said. I walked to the hallway and pulled my boots on in as delicate a manner as I could. Richard held out my coat to me, which I liked. I turned and slipped each arm into it, then turned back to him again, scooping my hair out from the collar as I did. "Well, good night," I said. "I hope I didn't outstay my welcome."

"You didn't," he replied. His hand was on the door handle, blocking my exit. He didn't open it. "You are welcome here any time you like."

Then he bent to me and kissed me on the cheek. It was a goodbye kiss, a polite but affectionate kiss, not the kind of kiss you would give a junior who worked on your book. He didn't pull away after, and so I turned my mouth to his and he kissed me again, his mouth staying firm on mine. I put my arms around his neck and pushed back against him and he lifted me up, his hands on my thighs, holding me against the wall. I was drunk, and so I'm never sure if I remember it right, but that's how I think it happened. We hardly moved; it was a slow kiss, almost chaste. Then as quickly as it happened it was over and I was smoothing my skirt down, balance a little off. I laughed and he laughed back. With a sudden and unexpected confidence that felt a little like recklessness, I went into the kitchen and took a pen and notepad that was on the side next to a white plastic telephone, and I wrote down my email address and mobile number with a little *x* underneath.

"That's my non-work email," I said. "I'm guessing you aren't much of a texter." He took the piece of paper, looked at it and folded it in half.

"Have a good weekend, Charlie," he said.

I messaged Eddy. He was still in the work local with Ophelia and some of the others from the office so I went to meet them. Ophelia had been out at a "team-building" session all afternoon, so my absence had not been noticed.

"Where have you been?" Ophelia looked utterly miserable.

"Oscar is ghosting Ophelia again," Eddy said with a furrowed brow, looking at the floor.

"I'm drinking through the pain."

"Oh, honey. Not again." I hugged her. "Sorry I'm late, I met a uni friend in town."

"Who was that? You smell like expensive aftershave."

"Just a friend from uni! You don't know him."

"Oh, good. No one you fancy, I hope, because you have a whole peppercorn stuck in your front teeth."

CHAPTER Eight

No amount of willing an email from Richard to appear in my inbox would make it happen. As the weekend went on, my hopes dwindled and I started to feel depressed in a way that I hadn't for a long while, longer than I could even remember. Sunday came and there was a storm alert across the country, so Ophelia, Eddy and I hunkered down and made stew and dumplings, an elaborate process that took most of the day. After a while, they stopped asking me what was wrong and trying to cheer me up. I was dreading the next day, of having to email him or his wife about something stupid and inane. The week before had been the best of my life. How had I ruined it? Had I forced myself on him, desperate for his attention? Had I created the whole thing, the feeling of ease between us? Was it the peppercorn in my teeth? My newfound confidence was slipping away and I felt silly and anxious.

The week dragged on much the same. Nothing appeared in my inbox. I was obsessed by thoughts of him. By Wednesday I had just about given up all hope. Then Cecile called me into her office. *This is it,* I thought. *I'm finished.* Richard must have called her and told her that I had humiliated myself by making a move on him, a married man. Everyone would find out. Of course they would—in this office, this industry, nothing was secret. Stories like this followed people forever. I'd never find another publishing job, not after this. I would lose everything.

"Charlie, are you all right? You've been very quiet all week. And you look ill." Cecile was eyeing me with a vague hint of disgust, like I might be contagious.

"I'm fine," I said, my shoulders dropping as I realized this wasn't going to be the conversation that I had been fearing. "I used to get migraines. Maybe I have one coming on, I don't know."

"Well, do go home if you are unwell. Migraines are seriously ghastly. Anyway, maybe this will cheer you up. Do you fancy coming with me on a little press trip? One night next week. Wednesday. Sheffield. Richard is accepting an award at the university, and we'll have the BBC there doing some filming bits for the documentary coming later this year. I could do with some help. We'll get the train up on Wednesday and come back on Thursday morning. I might even buy you a glass of wine. What do you say?"

Cecile's perfect eyebrows were raised, and she was smiling, leaning in to me. She was looking at me with such care and warmth that I thought I might cry. What I wanted to say was that I had ruined everything, ruined it all. That this should be so exciting, but instead I was dying from the embarrassment of my behavior and that I couldn't possibly face him. I had emotionally started to let go of his writing, of Winden & Shane, and imagined myself out of a job, humiliated. In a particular moment of internal melodrama, I had started planning a disappearance; I'd move to Scotland and take a new name.

But I didn't say anything about any of it. Instead, I thanked Cecile and went off to book our travel. Then I opened a browser window in the corner of my screen and went to my Hotmail account. I'd write to Richard myself, put an end to this unknowing and misery. Anything was better than this feeling of limbo, of purgatory.

Dear Richard,

I fear that I have made a fool of myself with my behavior on Friday night. I wonder if you would please forget the whole thing.

Very best, Charlie

I hit send. This was the best course of action. Face it and move on. I'd have to leave the country, change my identity, or just die. At least I'd know my fate. But twenty minutes later, his name appeared at the top of my inbox.

Charlie. Don't be ridiculous. Come by the flat tomorrow eve if you are free. If you want, spend the night. R

I had felt so utterly hopeless before his email. The relief was so intense it felt physically pleasurable. I wanted to laugh, to tell the Charlie of five minutes ago how silly she was. But after it had settled enough for me to look at it, I saw that the relief had come with a realization: I was stuck in this. Swallowing back tears, I quietly slipped out of the office and down through the back door to the alley where I had first met Richard. I lit a cigarette and kept walking, keeping my feet moving in tempo with my heart, imagining the feeling of arms wrapped tightly around me, slowly pulling myself back together.

Somewhere among all of this relief and realization was something less easy for me to understand, something that had the shape and smell of fear. He had asked me to stay, so I could be pretty confident that he wasn't asking me to come over so he could humiliate me. I had slept with plenty of men, and some women, but never anyone much older than me. He was handsome, although his age made him slightly alien. Would I be a disappointment to him, would I be enough and know what he needed? If I had been this devastated when I'd thought things had ended after two evenings and one brief kiss, where would I be left after sleeping with him? And what about his wife? I knew that their marriage was unconventional, but not where I fitted into that, if I fitted at all. Would she walk in on us at the flat? All of these questions were smart and should have led me toward a decision that would protect me, but lust, boredom with myself and my love for the Richard on the page were all more powerful than good sense, and so when I got back to my desk I replied to say yes, that I'd come by at about 8 P.M., and I started to make my plans.

I told Ophelia and Eddy that I was going to Brighton after work on Friday for the night and wasn't sure if I was staying all weekend. Ophelia asked if it was the same friend that I had seen the previous week. She knew I didn't really keep in touch with people from university. I had talked less about the years between school and meeting her, fearing that it would put her off a friendship with me if she knew how I had been back then. I said it was and that it was this friend's birthday, and we had a night out planned at all of the old clubs and bars we had loved in our university days. A friend from university *had* recently copied me into a group email inviting me to a birthday party in Brighton, so it wasn't a complete lie.

I knew I could tell Ophelia when I was ready, and when I knew what there was to tell. But still, it felt like a betrayal. We told each other everything, about the most mundane events of our days. Things as huge as sex and relationships were talked through in great detail, shared with care and attention, interrogated and updated on hourly, sometimes. But I knew that she wouldn't understand this. That she would try to stop me, that Eddy would, too, and I didn't want to be stopped. No matter how else I rationalized it, with thoughts like, *I don't have to tell them everything* and *it is to protect his privacy* and *I want to keep this for myself,* it came down to the fact that I didn't want anything to get in the way of what was about to happen, because I wanted it so much.

I had a glass of wine with them after work, just to loosen up a bit, then took the Tube to Covent Garden. London was busy with crowds of tourists dressed for the theater, as well as the usual suits. I'd packed my best matching underwear into a tote bag with my toothbrush, phone charger and a change of clothes. Humming through every part of my body was that pleasurable feeling that comes with the possibility of new love. *Remember this,* I said to myself.

Richard was leaning in the doorway of the flat when I arrived, as he had been the previous week. He was wearing jeans and a T-shirt, two items of clothing I was surprised he owned. He looked great and I felt a rush of physical attraction. When I got inside and he had closed the door behind me, he kissed me, hard, and I opened my mouth to him this time and felt the wine on my breath mix with the coffee on his. The kiss lasted less than a minute.

"It's very, very good to see you again, Charlie," he said, a hand still on my waist.

I was still a little angry about his not contacting me, but I smiled, and said, "You, too."

We went into the kitchen, and he poured us both a glass of white wine. Radio 4 was playing, and the overhead lights were off, with the room lit with the warm glow from the under-cupboard lighting. It was tidier than I had seen it before.

"I was very pleased when you got in touch, but, Charlie, I must ask, what was all that about? I'm going to infer from you coming over that you want to be here. Did I give you some impression that I hadn't enjoyed our time together?"

"I didn't hear from you, so I presumed it had been a mistake."

He laughed at this. "Oh, Charlie. Is that how young people do things these days? Send an immediate message after a kiss? I didn't hear from you, either."

"No, well, of course you didn't," I said with a little more hurt than I meant, because I felt suddenly silly and small. I was drunker than I'd intended to be because I'd not had any lunch.

"Well, I don't see what the difference is. Things are a little—uneven, here, with me being a bit older than you and such. I didn't want to make you feel pressured or uncomfortable." I shuffled my feet and sipped my wine, feeling foolish. "Well, let's just forget it," he said after a moment, more gently. "Shall we go into the living room?" He touched my face briefly, sweetly.

In the living room, Leonard Cohen was playing on the record player and two of the three sets of voluptuous floor-length curtains were pulled closed. It was tidier in here, too, but I found it hard to imagine Richard Aveling tidying up.

"The cleaner came today, so naturally I can't find anything," he said, as though he had read my mind. "If you see a pair of dark-green reading glasses, I'd be very happy to be reunited with them." He smiled at me, and I couldn't help but smile back.

I sat on the end of the sofa, curling my legs underneath me, trying to look as petite and at ease as possible. He sat next to me and moved his hand to my leg, finding the tiniest of ladders in my tights on the back of my thigh. It tickled.

"The Tube. A pair don't last a week in London," I said. He moved his hand so his palm was between my legs. He was rushing things. It didn't feel like the kiss had felt last week—that chemistry and excitement was absent, maybe because I knew now what was coming. But what could I do? I was here, in his flat. I wanted the feeling of the week before, when we had talked for so long.

"Oh, I brought you a book. I mean, I didn't buy it—it's a proof someone sent me. It's that one I was telling you about." I reached down into my bag and handed him a slightly dog-eared proof copy of *A Visit from the Goon Squad* by Jennifer Egan. "I loved it. It's not like anything I've ever read. The way she structures it is so clever." He took the book and ran a hand over the cover, studying it, before placing it on the coffee table in front of him. I felt suddenly very childish, like I had when I'd given Clemmie her Christmas gift a few months before.

"Thank you. I'll take a look." His hand returned to the space between my thighs.

If he read it or not, I don't know. He never mentioned it to me if he did, but, then, looking back, I'm almost certain he would have hated it.

"Do you mind if I smoke?"

"Of course. You are my guest."

I got up and moved to the window, trying to slow things down as much as I could.

"Can I have one of these?" I took one from the pack on the table before he had a chance to answer. He nodded. I was being skittish, I knew it. I was suddenly so nervous of what was coming. If I had told Ophelia, she would have talked me out of it. I should have told her. *But I want this,* I reminded myself. *That is why I am here.* There was only so long I could delay things before he would question what was going on and honestly, what had I been expecting? Long, lingering looks across the dinner table? Hand-holding and confessions from the deepest and most private recesses of his heart? He was married. I saw myself, suddenly, as he must see me. Some naive young thing, hanging on his every word, ready to open her legs at his instruction and take all of him inside her, because I was desperate to be consumed by this great man. I shook the thought out of my head. No. It wasn't like that. He had taken my suggestions and written them into his actual book. He had asked me to come here. I had been the one to kiss him, not the other way around. Richard liked me, he wanted to hear what I had to say. There was a real connection. I couldn't look at him, but I knew that if I did, I would see Richard Aveling, handsome, magnetic Richard Aveling, sitting on his sofa, looking at me. He did want me, but where I fitted into everything was not clear.

"Elaine," I said after a little while, blowing out a plume of smoke.

"What about Elaine?" He was still on the sofa.

"Does she—I don't know how to ask this. Does she mind? Does she know? Do you have an open relationship or something?"

"I'm not going to talk to you about my marriage, Charlie."

I blushed again. It hadn't landed as I'd wanted it to. I pinched my brow in an insuppressible response to my embarrassment. Richard got up and stood next to me, taking a cigarette and lighting it.

"You don't need to worry about Elaine. She's not going to walk in here unexpectedly, if that's what you are concerned about. You've not told anyone that we have spent time together, have you? I place a lot of value on my privacy, more than on many things in my life. I like being with you alone without anyone looking in. I don't think everyone would understand. I've been thinking a lot about you, Charlie, since I met you in that alleyway."

I looked up at him. This small offering of affection eclipsed everything else he had said. It was enough to make my heart hum change to song, and to settle my nerves. He leaned in to kiss me again and I kissed him back. Richard Aveling wanted me. He thought about me. He could have me.

"I've not told anyone. Don't worry about that."

"Good. Now, shall we go to the bedroom?" He put his cigarette out.

"I need a moment first, if that's OK? Can I use the bathroom?"

Every part of me felt overcome with emotion, with excitement and with fear for knowing that once this was done, it couldn't be undone. How could this be really happening? In the privacy of the bathroom, I changed into my matching underwear—a black set with a lace trim that I had bought in Marks & Spencer—and cleaned myself up a little. I swilled toothpaste around my mouth and checked my teeth for peppercorns. I looked at my reflection in the huge bathroom mirror that reached from the floor to the top of the high ceiling. I was very pale, but I hadn't really eaten much in the last week so at least I looked skinny. I had a dark bruise on my shin from bumping into my bed at home. I lifted my long hair over my shoulders and pulled a face at myself. I could just say I didn't want to have sex with him yet, that I wasn't ready, but then would he think I was immature, or that I didn't really want him? I did want him. I wanted him more than I had ever wanted anyone. But I didn't feel turned on by him today like I had last week. The evening hadn't been how I'd imagined, how I'd hoped it would be. But it was OK. It wasn't a big deal. It was just sex. It was, ultimately, what I had come here for.

The bathroom was opposite his bedroom, and I opened the door a crack. I could see him sitting on the edge of the bed, his profile to me, hawkish. He was fully clothed and motionless, staring at the wall. I'd not been in this room before.

I walked into the bedroom and round to him, trying very hard to look confident. I stood in front of him, hoping he didn't notice how self-conscious I felt. He put his hands on my hips and pulled me into him, kissing my stomach. I could feel the shortest bristles against my skin. I ran my hand through his hair. It felt waxy and smelled of coconut. I pushed him back onto the bed and climbed on top of him, but he flipped me around so he was on top of me. We pushed against each other, hands, mouths, everything. At six feet five, he was nearly a foot taller than me and almost twice as wide. I was physically overwhelmed by the size of him.

He took his T-shirt off. His body was much softer than I had considered it might be. His nipples and chest were softer than I'd expected, so was his stomach and his back. The skin on the backs of his arms felt almost papery. It was the first time that I had noticed his age and been so aware of mine, but, despite this, he was somehow still the handsome young man in the black-and-white photo on the back of his books, eyes alive with brilliance, jaw sharp and hair black. A man whom everyone wanted to be close to. He took his trousers off, and his boxers. He moved slowly but firmly, unhooking my bra and slipping my knickers off. I held his face in my hands as he kissed me, but he took them and held them above my head on the bed. I wasn't really there with him, I was performing, I was someone else pushing back against him. He stroked me briefly before pushing himself inside me with a groan that made me, for a short moment, want to laugh.

"Are you on the pill?" he asked, looking at me. I nodded. I'd wished he'd worn a condom, but it was too late now, so there wasn't any point in saying anything and I desperately wanted him to like me, to enjoy it. It hurt more than it felt good, and I had to work not to cry out with the pain of it, but I wrapped my legs around him and submitted, faking an orgasm, and then he came quite quickly, after just a few minutes.

He kissed me after, more gently, and ran his hand along my collarbone. The weight of him on top of me meant I couldn't really take a deep breath and fill my lungs, but I didn't want to spoil the moment, so I ran my fingertips along his shoulder, feeling the sparse wiry hairs there, and he laid his head in my neck.

"You are beautiful, Charlie, do you know that? So beautiful." I kissed his ear. After a few more minutes, I arched my back, and he came out of me. I don't know why but the situation suddenly felt undignified for both of us.

"I have to use the loo," I said. He moved off me and onto his back. I was self-conscious walking naked across his room. I peed and noticed I had bled a little. When I came back into the bedroom, he had put his boxers and trousers back on and was pulling on his T-shirt.

"Come here," he said, reaching out a hand for me. I covered myself and went to him. He moved my hands away and put his arms around me. He kissed the softness above my hip with his big mouth. "Look at you." I teased his hair and smiled.

"I can't find my underwear."

"I don't think you should ever wear clothes. Do you want this?" He handed me the caramel-colored jumper he had worn the other day from the wardrobe. It was huge and soft and smelled of him, and I slipped it over my head with pleasure, feeling a little better as I did. Richard was on my skin, in my hair and I was in his clothes, in his bed. He had liked having sex with me, and that's what I'd wanted. It would get better.

"I'm getting some more wine for us," he said and headed out of the room. I could hear the background noise of Radio 4 in the kitchen, and, from the living room, the needle on the record player clicking through the speakers like a heartbeat.

We had sex again that night, although I was so sore from earlier I didn't enjoy it in the way I had wanted to. We pushed against each other again, and then I submitted to him again when he was inside me and I knew that he liked that. I didn't feel really aroused by it, even when he went down on me. I'd feel little flashes of who he was, and I liked *that,* but, otherwise, it was in all honesty quite disappointing. I couldn't explain it. Maybe it was his body, the way this perfect man was suddenly older and more real, that we hadn't really talked that much that night. I was so small physically, and emotionally small in the whole situation. I wanted to please him, this giant, I wanted to be the best he had ever had. But for me, sex wasn't the most important part of being with him.

After we'd had sex the second time, he fell asleep on his side with his hand on my stomach. The bedside light was still on and so was the radio, and I waited a long time, listening to his breathing slow as sleep engulfed him, before I got up. I went to the kitchen and drank a glass of water, then refilled it from the tap and drank another one. I turned the radio off but left the lights as they were. I brushed my teeth and took off my makeup, turned off his bedside light and slipped into the bed next to him. The sheets were so soft and heavy, like hotel sheets, and there was a luxurious, dark-orange comforter on the bed, which I pulled up. Richard stirred and slipped an arm around me, pulling me into him. I was surprised by this. I nestled into him, finding a shape that fit to his. Usually when men had had enough sex, they wouldn't be affectionate so as not to give the wrong idea.

I replayed the conversation from earlier over and over in my head. What had he meant by keeping this private, by not telling anyone? Would this happen again? This extraordinary man wanted me, *me.* By sleeping with him, I was giving something to him. It was something that he liked, and that made him like me. It became clear just how terribly deep I had fallen for him. There was no way back now; if he woke in the morning and asked me to leave, made his excuses now he'd got what he wanted, if it was over, my heart would be completely broken.

I didn't really sleep much that night. Richard, on the other hand, slept deeply and noisily. He was so warm that the heat seemed to radiate from him, sticky and damp, and I longed for some space in the bed but he was heavy on me; there was always a leg or an arm that I was unable to extricate myself from, as he would just pull me in closer when I did.

I must have fallen asleep eventually, because when I woke at 10 A.M. the bed was empty and the flat was delicious with the smell of coffee. I slipped into the caramel jumper again and nervously stepped out of the bedroom. Richard was in the kitchen reading the *Guardian* and eating toast. A cafetière of coffee sat next to him on the small table.

"Good morning," he said looking up from his paper and smiling at me. He had found his green reading glasses. "Would you like some coffee? And toast?"

"Yes, please. Sorry I slept so late." Ten A.M. wasn't actually late for me. I could easily sleep till one on a weekend, but I didn't want him to know that. Grown-ups didn't do that.

He got up to get me a coffee cup, running his hand around my waist as he passed me in a way that felt familiar and comforting. He took two slices of bread from a paper bag and put them in the toaster. Richard Aveling was making me toast.

"I'm always up early. I didn't want to wake you. Did you sleep well?"

"I did," I lied.

"Do you want the *Review*? The *Weekend*?" He pointed at the newspaper supplements on the table, indicating for me to sit. "Help yourself—I've read them."

So, there it was. Richard and I eating toast with marmalade and drinking coffee, reading the Saturday newspapers, like it was the most normal thing in the world.

I expected Richard to make his excuses and ask me to leave, but he didn't. In fact, he took me back to bed for some of the morning and then asked if I had anywhere to be. He had to pop out to run an errand or two, but asked if I would stay around and he would make me dinner, if I liked. I could sleep some more while he was out, or read, or have a bath. He showered, dressed and left, and I took a long bath in the big clawfoot tub.

He was gone much longer than I expected, so long that I wondered for a while if he would return at all. He didn't come home until five-thirty, by which time it was dark. We ate seabass and green beans and potatoes that he'd cooked beautifully while I sat, perched on a stool, smoking and talking him through the workings of Winden & Shane from the point of view of an assistant. He laughed at my characterizations and even feigned shock at the few new office romances that were rumored. He told me some good stories about the older staff that I swore to take to the grave, including that Allegra's real first name was Cheryl. I didn't talk about Cecile, although he asked, as they had known each other a long time and I thought it best to not blur any of those lines.

We didn't have sex again that night; Richard was tired, and I was grateful. He kissed me in the bathroom after I had brushed my teeth, circling the small of my back with his giant thumb, and asked me if I had enjoyed myself. I kissed him back harder, slowly and deliberately, and he kissed my neck. We fell asleep on our own sides of the bed and I slept much better. I dreamed it was the summer, and that Ophelia was a tiny fairy and I had to get her to London by carrying her in a tin in my pocket.

In the morning Richard woke me to have sex, and we ate a breakfast of eggs and bacon and toast. We talked about our work engagement in Sheffield the coming week. It would be terrible for both of us, but, Richard explained, much worse for me, if anyone was to find out. I would almost certainly lose my job. This shocked me back to reality with a sharp snap.

"You won't tell anyone, though," I asked him anxiously. We were standing in the kitchen and he was showing me how to use the espresso machine. "I mean, I know you won't, but maybe if we just agree that we don't tell anyone at all, then we know it can't come out."

"So, not even your best friends? Cordelia and Ted?"

"Ophelia and Eddy." I corrected him with a smile. He smiled

back at me affectionately in a way that made me wonder if the slip-up had been a little joke.

"That's what I meant. But would you be able to do that? To not tell them?"

"Of course. I don't tell them everything about my life." This was a gross lie. "I don't think they'd understand. And they work with me, don't forget, so it is just too risky."

"If you are sure you can keep that promise, then I think we will be OK." I hadn't mentioned a promise, but I didn't say anything. "No one will hear about us from me. Over the years I've had to learn to keep my private life very private. But you must understand that I will have to behave differently with you at work. You might not like that, but I have known Markus and Cecile for a long time and so any slip-up, no matter how small, might be picked up on."

"I understand. Don't worry about that." The conversation was terrifying me but I didn't want to let on how much. I wanted him to think of me as being breezy and low maintenance, not the nervous people-pleaser that I really was.

"It's not all bad. It does add some element of fun, don't you think?" He slipped a hand around my waist and pulled me into him playfully. There wasn't any excitement in it for me. I was just worried that I would lose my job. I pushed that thought aside. No one was going to find out.

Richard said he would try to ring me in the hotel we were both staying in after the award ceremony, if it seemed like we might be able to meet when Cecile had gone to bed. Then, at around one that afternoon, I said goodbye as he was going back to Yorkshire, and I made my way home across London, full of secrets and experiences beyond my wildest dreams.

When I got home, there was an email from Richard.

Dear Charlie. I am writing to you in case you need reassurance, in which case, you should feel reassured. See you on Wednesday. xR

CHAPTER Nine

When I got back to the house that Sunday afternoon, I was glad to find that Ophelia and Eddy were out. I decided to go for a run. I would go through long phases of running, and long phases of not running, and more recently it had been in the latter. I had hated sport at school but running was different. Running made me feel good. When I was running, I could quieten my brain without trying to. I liked the way it hurt and the way I could push through the pain if I wanted to, intensifying it until my legs screamed and my chest burned. The pain felt healthy.

It was warm and springy and overcast, and the ground was still wet from the night's rain. I ran along Church Street, up through Clissold Park and then along the back streets around Rectory Road. The pubs were full of groups of friends eating Sunday roasts and drinking pints of cold beer, and the usual army of pushchairs were in tandem, dads in Bretons and mums in raincoats. I watched them all with fascination, popping out an earbud to pick up a line of conversation here and there as I rushed past them, imagining their lives.

I was listening to a mix of rock and indie bands that I had loved in my teens and university days on my iPod. It reminded me of feeling so disconnected from the world, from my friends. Desperate for something, anything to happen to me that would make me want to stay alive and take me outside of myself. I had been so horribly unhappy. I wanted to reach backward through time to that girl, that version of me, and tell her everything would be OK, that there were things beyond her imagination lying in wait for her, that her life would not be sad and ordinary. It was something like that feeling I'd get at night when I tried to really think about the stars, and the universe, and how incredibly small I was, and how my experience of everything was all there was, and how strange that was. *How strange it is to be anything at all,* Jeff Mangum sang in my ear. Yes. How strange, I thought. My feet seemed to get further and further away from the rest of my body. It was as though I didn't even need to tell them to run, they just knew to do it. I wondered if Richard was thinking about me.

When I got home, I realized my foot had been bleeding into my shoe for the whole run. My nail had dug into my big toe and gone dark purple. I hadn't even felt it.

A couple of hours later, Ophelia burst through the door, blotchy-faced and very upset. I calmed her, surprised at how much her distress affected me, and we cuddled up on the sofa with cups of tea and one of the good blankets from her room. Once she was ready to talk, I told her to start from the beginning and it went like this: her almost-boyfriend Oscar had asked her to come round the day before, but when she got to his flat, she had found him doing cocaine off his glass coffee table with two of his banking friends, and he'd clearly not been to bed. She'd nonetheless stayed and, after the friends had gone home a few hours later, he'd tried and failed to fuck her, and had fallen asleep. She'd been furious and had left, but a string of texts on Sunday morning and an invitation to meet him for a boozy lunch at the pub—just the two of them—had been enough for her to forgive him. Only it had all gone wrong again. After several Bloody Marys and a bottle of red wine, she'd "opened her big mouth" and asked if she was his girlfriend, to which he'd replied that he wanted to take things slow.

Given they'd been seeing each other for a month now, not to mention hooking up lots of times all through university, Ophelia told me between hiccupping sobs that she wasn't really sure how much slower they could go, and that she didn't know why she was putting up with it, but she just liked him so much that she couldn't bring herself to break it off.

Knowing there was nothing I could say to change her mind, and that if it did work out with Oscar and I had tried to put her off him that it would be remembered forever, I supported her in this decision. I didn't have a leg to stand on when it came to relationships, but I felt very glad to finally be out of the world of dating useless man-children with commitment issues and casual drug habits.

Not telling Ophelia about Richard was harder than not telling Eddy. She knew something was going on in my life but, fortunately for me, Oscar continued to keep her preoccupied and any time conversation veered into murky territory where I felt a confession coming on, I could just steer things back in his direction. She was lovesick, which was absolutely baffling because he seemed like such an idiot and wasn't even hot, and she was so gorgeous and interesting and lovely to be around.

Over the next few days, she tried to catch me out a few times, but I was on high alert. I badly needed to talk to someone about what was going on, but I knew I couldn't. I'd notice her looking at me over her computer screen, brow slightly furrowed, sipping on one of the five Diet Cokes she drank each day. I didn't like keeping this big thing that was happening to me from her. I had taken Richard at his word that there was no issue with me staying over, but I wasn't really sure how I'd explain the situation with Elaine to Ophelia. I wasn't even totally sure how to explain it to myself.

I presumed that Richard and Elaine must have some kind of arrangement in their marriage. I'd never heard any rumors of Richard having affairs, or behaving inappropriately with staff. He was so famous, surely people would know if he had. Everyone knew about all the affairs that were going on at work. Sometimes you even felt as if people were flaunting their behavior. Everyone knew about Cecile's affair, for example. And, just last December, Xander, the director of the international sales team, had been caught with the team assistant, Meghan, in the toilets at the end of their Christmas lunch. He was married, too. There were more examples than I could count.

Although Ophelia and Eddy were from the same world as the older staff, they were nothing like them. They were more connected to the reality of London life. Every now and then they'd say something about quince or Tuscany or couture that meant nothing to me, but it was different. Publishing had institutionalized many of the older staff into thinking that appalling behavior and very outdated or out-of-touch views were completely acceptable.

Often, the cause of an outburst of bad behavior would be directly related to technology. I'd been screamed at by one older publicist for pressing print on a document when she'd been loading headed paper into the "hateful machine." Her archnemesis, another publicist who had sat opposite her for almost twenty years, had laughed from behind her computer. There had been a cup of coffee thrown—it had been cold and missed her by a mile—and each of them had complained to HR that the other was guilty of "bullying." HR had long ago refused to deal with either of them after making it very clear that they should both face disciplinaries for their behavior. Allegra had said that there would be no such action taken and that was the end of it as far as they were concerned. And so, the feud went on.

It was completely and utterly bonkers but, as I was regularly told, just the way things were in this industry. It was very hard to tell the difference between affectation and eccentricity, especially with the older staff, and I had no idea if the madness of all of it was normal and what everyone experienced in the workplace, or if it was quite unusual. Sometimes it felt impossible to deal with because you couldn't rationalize much of the behavior and attitudes. On occasion, though, it could be funny, and on those days we would delight in it.

At work, Ophelia, Eddy and I kept our behavior outwardly professional, trying very hard not to descend into fits of giggles as we emailed each other with various bits of office news and gossip, or a commentary on whatever mad thing was happening in the office that day. Over the last few weeks, we had seen more of Eddy at work than we had at home. Unlike Ophelia, Eddy had been extremely successful in his love life of late and was seeing not one but three men across the city, and getting a lot of very varied sex. He had an older man (thirty-eight) in Farringdon who had a stunning apartment, a delightful miniature schnauzer, and an even better bank account. He bought Eddy lovely clothes and had kinks that would be too much for our straight ears, he told us. There was a financial lawyer (thirty-three) who was heterosexual, but called Eddy when he was drunk every few weeks and cried after sex but had a lovely cock. And his favorite, a tall and tanned Chilean doctor (twenty-eight) who worked in the emergency department at the Homerton Hospital and kept unsociable hours, so that wasn't ideal.

I loved how Eddy moved between them, and his job, always happy and always so sweet. When he did appear back at the house, he'd cook for us and cuddle up on the sofa to relay his adventures with such glee that for entire evenings, we didn't even turn the television on. His friendship was warm, and he made me feel so loved. Both of them did. It was as close to having a family as I had felt since Mum died, and I drank in every little detail of them. Every mannerism, every bad habit, every misheard song lyric, every stray hair in the bathroom was proof of our closeness. I had been deprived of this feeling for so long and I didn't take it for granted even for a second.

I'd talked to them quite early on about my history of depression. It was the same night that I'd told them about losing my mum. Ophelia had cried with me as we'd sat in the living room, buzzing slightly with the tail end of the rush of a dab of MDMA at a club night at KOKO hours before. The sun had been coming up and I'd felt empty and hollowed out. I'd told them I would never take drugs again, except for the ones I was prescribed. They'd listened with great attentiveness but had not been fazed by the conversation that followed.

"I mean, who hasn't been on antidepressants at some point," Eddy had said with a comforting arm around my shoulder. "I took them in my last year of university. Dad has been on them since the crash. It's not a big deal, darling."

"My mum took them after Sam was born." Ophelia nodded encouragingly. "I'm so glad you told us, but it's really nothing to be embarrassed about."

I slept in Ophelia's bed that night. We lay, shivering under the sheets, wishing for darkness and willing sleep to come quickly and lift us out of our comedowns.

"I love you, Charlotte Turner," she said to me in a whisper so quiet I could barely hear her.

"I love you, Ophelia Devereaux," I whispered back after a few minutes, but she was already asleep.

At 11:49 A.M. on Wednesday, Cecile and I boarded the train from King's Cross to Sheffield. She bought us a Marks & Spencer picnic and coffees for the train, and sat opposite me hammering at her giant, geriatric laptop with her index fingers—she only used the two fingers for typing—for the whole two hours it took to get there. She had been offered an upgrade by the poor, desperate IT department-of-one almost weekly for the last two years, but she refused on the basis that she had only just learned how to use this one and it had all her passwords saved. I was reading a short-story collection that Richard had lent me: *A Time to Keep* by George Mackay Brown. It was quiet and very beautiful writing. I loved it.

"One of Richard's favorites, you know," Cecile said, pausing her frantic typing, her hands in position as though pointing.

"Oh, I didn't know that," I said very naturally, trying not to show much interest, or how much I *did* know.

I had trawled through absolutely everything I could find online, hoping for some clue that could explain Richard and Elaine's relationship. I'd checked interviews and articles going back years, and had even started looking through the folders of press cuttings that we kept in the office archive after the rest of the team had gone home. But I could find nothing more about them, or about her. His books were filled with characters who were unfaithful, but I could not intuit anything that fitted Richard and Elaine's situation, and, anyway, I knew that looking for truth in his fiction would lead me nowhere useful.

What I did know was this: they'd been married for nearly thirty years—since before I was even born. He had, briefly, been married to an American folk singer who had had some success in the UK in the late 1970s, but that relationship had been short and they'd been divorced within a few months. Richard's debut had immediately made him a literary celebrity and he had won the Booker Prize. He had married Elaine a year later. Her father had been a prominent Labor MP so that had been of significant interest to the press. She was a champagne socialist and a playwright—or had written two plays back in the 1980s, both of which had been very well reviewed. I couldn't find anything more about her and he didn't mention her anywhere—there was not even a passing reference to a wife in the biography in the back of his books or in his acknowledgments. They didn't have any children, I knew that, but not why.

I had googled Elaine, too. There were lots of pictures of her, and many of them together at the premieres of his two biggest film adaptations in Los Angeles, and even some on the red carpet at the Oscars, in what were now very dated clothes. But the one that I liked the most was an old photo of her scanned from a yellowed newspaper. A headshot. She was quietly beautiful, with dark hair which she had worn in that very 1980s bouffant style, slim shoulders, looking intensely at the camera, unsmiling. I couldn't stop looking at it.

We headed to our hotel to drop off our things, then went on to the university to meet the BBC team who were going to be interviewing Richard. When he arrived for the interview, they'd do some other shots around the city with him before the award was presented that evening at a gala dinner. Richard was to give the keynote speech that would open the city's literature festival. I'd replied to the email he'd sent on Sunday, but we'd not spoken since then. My heart felt open and happy. I was enjoying this feeling with some curiosity, feeling into the corners of it, letting the brightness of my mood warm me, feeling it expand and grow and then pop in little bubbles of joy. I was determined to be extra professional and to show Richard just how assured and capable I was. I wanted him to see that I was just as good at my job as he was at his.

All of it melted away, though, when he arrived at the university library with his wife.

He looked harassed and miserable, as did she. She was taller than I'd expected, taller than me—maybe five feet eleven—and much prettier in person than I had thought she would be. Her slim frame was wrapped in a beautiful tan rain mac, which, I knew, from a flash of the lining, was Burberry. She wore an enviable pair of black leather boots with a Cuban heel and at her throat, a simple red silk scarf. She even *looked* expensive. That face from the old cutting was still very recognizable, sharp cheekbones and deep-set eyes. Cecile was as surprised to see her as I was but ran over in the usual master-of-people way she had about her, and embraced her like an old friend whom she didn't really like very much. Unexpectedly, it was envy rather than guilt that I felt pulling at my insides. Envy not just because she had Richard, but for her whole life. Her houses and her money. Her clothes and her sense of style and her beauty. Her whole place in the world. Richard looked at me briefly, then went straight across to the journalist from the BBC and shook his hand. They clearly knew each other, too.

Regardless of the situation, I would have felt awkward in this moment. No matter where I stood it seemed that I was in the way of the crew as they moved their equipment about to set up in a corner room adjacent to the library. Everyone was so busy, or chatting to someone they knew. I tried very hard not to stare at her, or at him, and busied myself by looking through the documents I'd brought that were stapled neatly and arranged in a slim plastic folder. Why hadn't he warned me? I checked my email on my phone, but there was nothing from him. Why wouldn't he get a mobile phone like a normal person, instead of relying on email? I wanted to run out of the room, but the very best thing I could do for him—for us—was to act completely normal and unfazed and do my job. To show him I could handle all of it. He looked magnificent in his coat and boots, towering over everyone. I comforted myself with my secret. Some part of this man was mine.

Elaine didn't bother to introduce herself to me, or, in fact, in any way acknowledge my existence. We all stood to the back of the room while Richard was interviewed about Sheffield, the literature festival, and the award, which was for his contribution to literature in the county. Elaine looked at her BlackBerry, switching her weight from one leg to the other, and I noticed she looked older up close, with makeup sunk a little into the creases around her eyes. It was impossible to ignore, though, that she was very attractive, and very impressive. I felt small and childish next to her in my cheap clothes.

After the interview, Cecile asked me to go and get coffees for everyone while they set up the next shot. I was grateful when she handed me her Amex—often we were expected to just pick up expenses, which was a constant source of anxiety for me given how close I was living to the edge of my overdraft.

"Can I get you a coffee, Richard?" I asked, trying very hard to be normal. I'd approached him while he was alone for a moment, Cecile and Elaine in conversation with the producer and the interviewer.

"Yes, please. Charlie, isn't it?" He didn't even flicker a smile. The producer's assistant was within earshot. "Black, no sugar. Thanks." He walked over to join them. I had known it would be this way, but it still it hurt, although no more than a papercut.

I got their coffees—Elaine wanted a macchiato but the coffee shop staff looked at me blankly and I wasn't exactly sure what it was myself, so I got her a cappuccino instead—and spent the rest of the afternoon trying not to get in the way, hoping for some glance from Richard to say sorry or let me know it was OK, but there was nothing. He hardly spoke to her, either. He was in a "malaise" as Cecile described it later when we left the hotel for the dinner. I could smell spearmint toothpaste on her breath as we talked in the taxi. We'd both changed into something a little smarter—it wasn't black tie or anything—and had freshened up our hair and makeup. I was wearing my favorite black shift dress over a vintage white shirt with a long, pointed collar that I'd found years ago in Snoopers Paradise, a flea market in Brighton. Cecile looked stunning in a silver sequined jacket over tight black trousers and her trademark heels. I was certain none of her things had come from a flea market.

I'd be on a table at the back with some other guests, I'd been warned. It turned out to be some booksellers from some of the local independent bookshops, a couple of librarians and a teaching assistant from the university's English department. There was also a high-school student who had won a creative competition, and one of the prizes was to attend this particular evening. The food was OK, and I was very careful not to drink too much.

After dessert, Richard was presented with the award and gave a ten-minute lecture about the literary importance of Yorkshire and the city of Sheffield's impact on him as a writer. I sat upright when he started speaking, turning my chair so it was facing him to show just how attentive I was being. He spoke in the way he did in interviews, slowly and deliberately, putting emphasis on the ends of words in a way that made everything he said sound lyrical. He loved performing like this and he was a truly exceptional public speaker—everyone said that they could listen to him talk all night. Much of his lecture was recycled from older interviews and talks, which Cecile and Elaine would know as I did, but it was unlikely anyone else would. I suppose someone who spoke in public as much as he did couldn't be expected to come up with something new to say every single time.

My mind started to wander into fantasy toward the end, thinking about his hands on my neck, feeling little flushes of enjoyment at the thought. But then I would remember Elaine, and I would be pulled back into my chair at the competition-winner table, the kids' table. I could just about see the back of her. She'd changed and wore a simple, long-sleeved black dress that must have been tailored to fit her, and elegant heels. She sat with an arm across her body, a hand on her elbow, her narrow shoulders slightly hunched in on herself. At the end she clapped, but they didn't kiss when he returned to his seat. She said something inaudible to him and he nodded without meeting her eye. I couldn't stop looking at them. I was so distracted that the other people on my table had given up trying to converse with me. How odd it was to be jealous of someone so old.

After it was all over, Cecile offered to buy me a glass of wine in the hotel bar, but I said I was tired and went to bed. Richard had left the dinner in a taxi with Elaine, nodding goodbye and saying thanks to me almost as an afterthought. We had booked them a room at the hotel, but they had decided not to stay. Watching them drive off, I could feel all the air in the balloon of my chest leave with them.

I lay on my bed utterly deflated and checked my email on my phone again. There was nothing. After a little while I went out of the hotel into the street. There was an off-license I'd spotted earlier, and it was only 10 P.M. I bought myself two miniature bottles of white wine, went back to my room and drank them both. I fell asleep and dreamed of nothing good—Richard slipping into the shadows whenever I tried to catch up to him, my mother in her nightdress at the top of the stairs saying she felt very unwell, and other sad and anxious things that disappeared in the morning with the sharp cracks of light that broke through the heavy curtains as my alarm sounded me awake.

CHAPTER Ten

I didn't hear from him until the following evening. I'd felt morose all day traveling with Cecile. My head ached so much I was starting to fear that it could even become a migraine, although I'd not had one in years. No doubt sick of the sight of me and my bad mood, she sent me straight home and told me she didn't want to see me until Monday. She sort-of patted me on the back when she said it, though, so I knew I wasn't in any trouble.

The house was very still. It felt odd being there in the middle of the day on a weekday, like I was intruding on its privacy. I took some painkillers, which eased my head, and slept on and off but only lightly, repeatedly pushing myself into the waking world to check my email on my phone.

Charlie, I'm coming to London tomorrow (Friday). Can you come by the flat after work? xR

Well, this is probably it, I thought. It was over. It had already become too complicated, or he had changed his mind about me, maybe coming to his senses when he'd seen me standing next to his beautiful, put-together wife. But then that little *x*—maybe it wasn't? I thought about waiting a while to reply, but the message had been there for an hour already.

I don't think I'm going to go in to work tomorrow, Cecile gave me a few days off. So I can come whenever really. Cx

I hit send and put my phone on the pillow next to me and stared at the ceiling. Bright spring sunshine filtered in, watery in the darkness of the room. I wanted it to rain. I always wanted it to rain. I checked my phone again. Nothing. I tried to sleep more but couldn't. It was only 2 P.M., but I poured myself a glass of Ophelia's white wine and lay on the sofa with the curtains drawn, watching old episodes of *Twin Peaks,* the only DVD box set we had. I wanted that weather, the clean air, the clear water on the stones, the firs. To be far away from here.

Ophelia and Eddy didn't come home after work. Ophelia texted me, asking where I had got to. She had a book launch to go to but said she wouldn't be home too late. She asked me if I needed soup or anything picking up, because her instinct was always to care for me. It reminded me to eat. I pulled on Eddy's giant winter coat and shuffled to the corner shop to replace Ophelia's wine and get something to fill the emptiness in my stomach, then returned to the sofa with cheese on toast and finished the wine. I must have fallen asleep because suddenly it was almost dark and the DVD logo was bouncing about on the TV screen.

Can I telephone you?

Was all the message said, in its old English way. *Telephone you,* not *call you.* My insides seemed to shift position. *No,* I thought. *No, you may not, if you are going to tell me you don't want to see me.*

Yes

I rinsed my mouth and my face with cold water from the bathroom tap. My phone vibrated on the side of the sink. An unknown number.

"Hello," I said.

"Hello, Charlie." His big, deep, northern voice, in my little phone. I felt my eyes start to sting with tears as I sat down on the edge of the bath.

"Hello, Richard."

"Is everything OK? You didn't—tell Cecile anything, after yesterday?" It felt like days ago.

"Of course I didn't," I said, surprised by my pointedness. I softened my tone. "I wouldn't do that, ever. Don't you know that?"

"It's just you said she had given you some time off . . ."

"I had a headache this morning on the train back, and I get migraines. Or I used to. I told her I wasn't feeling well and she said I had been working too hard and to take a few days as next week is going to be so busy." There was a long pause.

"I only wondered—I'm sorry, Charlie, how are you feeling? Are you quite well?"

"I'm fine, really. It was just a bad headache. It didn't turn into a migraine. I slept a lot today and feel much better for it."

"Well, then, as you don't have to work tomorrow, I could pick you up on my way into London and we could spend the day together—it would be at about ten in the morning; I presume your housemates would have left for work by then."

The little, tiny ember of hope that was still burning somewhere in my heart grew bright with his breath. A fat tear fell down the side of my nose into my mouth.

"Yes, OK. I mean, they won't be here. How long will you be in London for?"

"I can't stay long but if you want, make your excuses for the evening and spend the night with me. Would you like that?"

"Yes," I said, quietly, not wanting him to know how much. "Shall I email you with my address?"

"Yes. And, look, I've got a mobile phone. I'll write to you with the number. Don't expect me to start texting—I'm far too old for that and please don't ever call it unless we have arranged for you to do so. I'll phone you when I'm outside your house. Charlie—I'm sorry. About yesterday and it all being so awkward. We'll talk tomorrow when I see you."

After we'd hung up, I cleared up the mess I'd made nesting in the living room, washed up the dishes and my wineglass, drank a pint of water and showered, scrubbing every inch of skin until it burned pink, little beads of blood appearing on my thighs. I covered myself in moisturizer, which, on my raw skin, stung in a way that I liked.

Feeling my new, smooth skin, thinking about how nice it would feel for Richard, I fell asleep with my hair wet and the bedroom light on.

Ophelia must have come into my room because when I woke up, the curtains were drawn properly, the light was off and my book was neatly on the bedside table. The house was quiet, already empty for the day. I had two hours until he arrived, and I felt light. That little flame was burning again like a pilot light, promising that things were OK. I had coffee, did my makeup and hair, paying extra attention to my fringe, dressed and packed a bag. I tidied my bedroom, in case he came in, arranging my books with the best and most interesting visible. But my room was suddenly callow. The room itself was beautiful, with a huge sash window that overlooked our garden and the still-bare sycamores at the back of it, but my things felt silly and cheap, nothing like his beautiful flat where everything felt so sophisticated and weighty. There wasn't much I could do other than hide a few things: my teddy bear, a few Polaroid photos of Ophelia, Eddy and me, a string of fairy lights which had, with my new eyes, become hideous. I left the framed photograph of my mum, though, taken on holiday in Devon the year before she died, smiling and shielding her eyes from the sun in a blue-and-white-striped linen dress. I wanted him to see that.

He called a little before ten, but wouldn't come in. He was parked down the street in a muddy, battered old black Land Rover, the kind you see in the countryside, not the kind you saw in Stoke Newington. I caught his eye and waved. I felt very exposed walking toward him, unsure where to look, at the pavement or at him. Getting into the car felt so intimate, this little space, this normal space that was such a part of everyday life. It smelled of cigarette smoke and although it wasn't dirty inside, it was scruffy. He leaned over to kiss me very briefly.

"This is publishing heartland," he said, looking out at the street from below the sun visor, which he had pulled down as some kind of camouflage, clearly worried he'd be seen. He shifted the car into gear, and we roared down the road at such a speed I almost lost my balance putting my seatbelt on. "And, before you ask, the reason I have this car is because where I live it can get very muddy, and snowy, so you need a big car. And I don't very much like the train. I'm too tall to be comfortable on the train."

"I like it," I said, spreading my hands on the warm dashboard. "I like the height."

As we drove across London, Radio 4 on low in the background, he'd move his hand from the gear stick to my thigh every now and then. His eyes were fixed on the road, and he swore frequently at other drivers, cyclists, pedestrians. I had to try hard not to laugh because if it had been anyone else, I would have had to point out how funny it was to be so cross. We talked about things on the radio, about London, about traffic, about the car. He'd stayed the night before in Oxford with a friend and had a hangover from too much red wine.

He parked in a private underground car park near the flat.

"I'm sure we won't bump into anyone, but if we do, Charlie, just go along with whatever I say. Is that all right?" He leaned over and kissed me on the mouth, letting me know he was sorry to say it. His lips were chapped and felt rough on my own.

"Of course."

We didn't bump into anyone he knew, and no one seemed to even recognize him, probably because of the rain. I had longed for it so much the day before and it had arrived, and everyone was rushing about, looking down, newspapers or umbrellas over their heads. That smell that London pavements gave off when it rained filled the air, a scent that's somewhere between the countryside and tar. It was so romantic, running into his building and to the lift, dripping wet, slipping off our coats, and then him lifting me up in the hallway like he'd done when we'd first kissed in that same spot. His mouth tasted like a hangover and coffee, but I didn't care; I wanted him, all of him. He felt better to me than he had before.

After, as I lay under him on the bed feeling warm with him, his wet hair across my face, it became real, him and me. He hadn't taken off any of his clothes and I still had my bra on, my shirt open, but otherwise naked. I let out a little laugh. His big hands were holding my backside where he had wanted it. He was still out of breath. He lifted his face to look at me and smiled.

"Am I forgiven?"

I bit my lip, looked at the ceiling thoughtfully, trying to be coquettish.

"You are forgiven." He kissed me very slowly, very deeply, and I kissed him back. "You need a shower," I said to him, my confidence renewed.

"Good God, I really do. Will you make some coffee?"

He handed me the caramel jumper I liked so much, and my underwear. I made coffee using the espresso machine, remembering what he had taught me, feeling my way around his kitchen, feet bare on the tiles.

He'd left the bathroom door open and called for me to bring his coffee in to him.

"Get in here with me," he said through the steam, and I did. He washed my hair, and ran his hands over every bit of me, making me come for the first time as I leaned back against him. He was forgiven.

I told Ophelia by text that I'd gone to my dad's for the weekend. Richard and I slipped into stride with each other. He still wanted sex more than me and I didn't always like it, but him wanting me gave me more pleasure than anything else could.

"Tell me about your family," he said on the Saturday afternoon. It was still raining, which was fine because we couldn't go out anywhere anyway.

"I've told you about my family," I said. We were on the sofa, my legs across his lap as we read the paper, a blanket covering my feet. It was unnaturally dark for the time of day and we'd already opened a bottle of wine.

"Not really, you haven't. In fact, I can tell you precisely what you have told me. Your father is actually your stepfather, you don't speak to your biological father, and your mother died. You don't have any siblings."

"Ah, but I do have siblings—two older stepsisters, and a baby stepbrother. Although my dad isn't married to his partner, so I guess he's not even step. He's not anything."

"OK, well, there you go. I don't know much. Indulge me."

I put my paper aside. "What do you want to know?"

"I want to know what your family are like. What growing up in your family was like. I want to know more. I want to understand your childhood. If you don't tell me, I'll join all sorts of dots and create a story for you. That's the trouble with being a writer. Much of real life becomes fiction."

I paused. Something in me felt suddenly out of depth, like I was swimming in open water and the ocean floor had disappeared. I didn't want to talk about these sad things, for them to pollute this place where I didn't have to think about the past.

"It was happy." The wine had gone to my head. "I mean, as far as I can tell. My memories start at the age of five, which is late. And I think that things were a bit tricky when Mum and Dad first got together because they were both married to other people. They met at the school where they worked—Mum was the receptionist. My real dad moved to Spain after we left him, I don't even remember him, and we've never had any contact at all. He could be dead for all I know. My dad—my stepdad, that is—already had two daughters who were much older than me, that's Sally and Amber. They hated each other even more than they hated me and Mum, and we were in a really small three-bedroom house, so I remember their visits being . . . fractious. But then Amber went to uni and didn't have to come and stay anymore, and Sally was nicer to me when Amber wasn't around. She'd bake fairy cakes with me sometimes, paint my nails, stuff like that. But after things settled down, it was . . . it was *happy,* I think. It was peaceful. I loved my parents. We didn't have very much; I'm not like other people in publishing. I don't advertise that. Because although we didn't have much money, we weren't exactly poor—Dad taught PE at a private school. I feel like people think that you have to be posh to be cultured or something. My parents voted Labor and Mum taught me about books and politics and art. They nurtured my hobbies—writing, choir. Then my mum had this heart problem and had to have minor surgery and things for the first time in my life were scary, but she got better quickly. And then one day, about a year after that, she had a stroke in her car in a supermarket car park. She died a few days later. It was completely out of the blue. And it was indescribably terrible." I reached across the coffee table and took a big sip of my wine. Richard was quiet. He lit a cigarette and handed it to me.

"How old were you?" he asked quietly, gently stroking my foot.

"Sixteen." It felt like telling it for the first time.

"I didn't mean to upset you. But I don't think being upset is such a bad thing when you have had something really dreadful happen to you."

"I'm not upset. It happened like seven years ago."

"That's nothing. What was she like, your mother?"

I was taken aback by this question. People usually followed up asking for details of the death, or by offering sympathy and saying, "I'm sorry," like it was their fault.

"She was lovely. Really lovely. Kind. A great mother. She didn't ask anything of me, except to be honest with her. We were very affectionate. I didn't go around telling people how close we were, or that we were best friends, but we were. She was very protective of me, of my . . . sensitivity. She always said I was sensitive, and that I was trusting. Not *too* sensitive. Not *too* trusting. That's what she meant, but she didn't put it like that. I had some troubles managing my emotions when I was younger. I would get sad and overwhelmed and sort of short-circuit. I didn't really have many friends because I didn't know how to talk to other kids, or how to be with them. I never had that problem with adults. Mum knew exactly what to do when I got into one of my moods and could pull me back to myself, get me level again. She understood me better than anyone, she loved everything I loved. I wasn't ready to lose her." It was like reading lines of a monologue, a story not my own. I wasn't sure where the words were coming from.

"Everything changed after she died. I guess it's the obvious end of innocence, but it was more than that. Our life as a family was gone along with her. It was such a huge shock. I can't even get my head around it now, telling you. She just didn't come home from work one day. I have these fantasies that she's not really dead, that she comes back. And we have to try to explain everything to her, explain my dad's girlfriend and baby, where her stuff is, explain why we had a funeral. Explain to people that she's back." I paused. I had never told anyone about these imaginings. I sounded deranged.

"She liked your books. She used to cut out your articles and reviews from the paper and save them for me." I blushed and immediately regretting telling him this. I had been very careful to never have him think I was a fan.

He smiled and chuckled a little. "That's very endearing to hear,

Charlie. I'm glad you can talk to me about these things." He wasn't looking at me, but he kept his hand on my foot through the blanket.

"What about yours?" I asked. I knew some but I didn't want to let on to that.

"My parents? Well, I'm sure you have read something in those articles your mother saved for you. My father left when I was young. He was an alcoholic and he was physically abusive. He died about twenty years ago. My mother lives in a home in Yorkshire. She has Alzheimer's and doesn't know who I am anymore. My stepfather died years ago, around the time my mother started showing first symptoms. She was cold and emotionally distant, but she—and my stepfather—provided all I needed. He was more well-to-do, richer than we had been. Which wasn't hard. When she married him, I was nine, and they sent me away to boarding school almost immediately. They started a new family. I had—I have, I should say—an older brother, but we are estranged. And a younger stepsister, and she sends Christmas cards and calls on my birthday, but we are not close. Being sent away was the best thing that happened to me because in that hateful school I received an education, and the world of books was opened up to me. Without that, I don't know if I would have become a writer. Maybe I would have, maybe it was inevitable. I don't know."

"Can I ask why you didn't have a family? I'm not asking about your marriage—I know that's off-limits."

He frowned.

"Elaine couldn't, can't have children. She had some health issues when she was young that I won't get into. Before we married. I always knew. At the time it didn't bother me, but later—it bothered both of us. And before you ask, we didn't want to adopt; my desire to procreate was firmly rooted in ego, to create another that was built from pieces of me. My passions, my hairline." He smiled.

"You do have a wonderful hairline," I said, stroking his hair, which was so straight and abundant, such a dark gray, and always felt waxy. It was thinner in the middle, but you only noticed if you were really close. "For someone of your age." I hoped this would lighten the mood, but instead, his face hardened.

"If you have a problem with my age, Charlie, you should probably tell me now."

I couldn't tell if he was joking. The shift in him was so small but the room had gone cold.

"I don't, obviously, I was just joking."

He went back to his newspaper. He wasn't stroking my foot anymore.

"I was just joking," I whispered, leaning into him.

"It's fine. Don't make a fuss."

He didn't look up. I took myself to the bathroom because I thought I might cry and I didn't want to do that in front of him. After a while I heard him call me from the kitchen. I dried my face and rinsed my mouth with cold water from the tap. I opened the door and he was standing down the hall, smiling from the kitchen doorway, asking me what I fancied for supper.

CHAPTER

Eleven

We saw each other a lot over the following weeks, on weeknights when Richard was in London. We didn't have any whole weekends. He was very busy and preparing not just for the publication of the book here in the UK, but in America, too. When he was in Yorkshire, he would call me some nights out of the blue and we'd speak for a while on the phone.

Ophelia was driven mad by not knowing where I was, and who I was seeing. All of her patience had been used up. We had lived so closely, so truthfully, that it wasn't possible to just separate myself from her, especially about something as monumental as whom I was having sex with. She wouldn't let it go.

On top of this, there was the issue of my twenty-fourth birthday.

Ophelia and Eddy had been on me for weeks to arrange something to celebrate. They'd tried multiple approaches, from a quiet dinner at home with just the two of them to a proper party at the weekend. They'd even suggested buying tickets to see Foals, a band I adored that I knew neither of them had much love for. In the end, I had agreed to some quiet drinks after work with the two of them, just in the work local.

I didn't like to celebrate my birthday. Like Christmas and Easter and Bonfire Night and all other recurring calendar events, my birthday had become another moment to feel, really feel, how my life should be different. To feel my grief lucidly, in a way that contrasted sharply with how it felt most of the time, which was more distant. Birthdays were especially hard as with each passing year I moved away from the person that I had been when I had last seen my mum.

I'd drunkenly explained this to Ophelia on the bus home the week before, her warm hands squeezing mine and her eyes filling with tears. I'd told her about how Mum had always made my birthday morning special before school, making me French toast with strawberries and cutting the bread into the shape of a heart.

On the morning of my birthday, a Wednesday in early April, I had been rudely woken by the two of them bounding into my room with balloons and a *Happy Birthday* banner, singing along to Stevie Wonder who was blaring from a laptop. Eddy had been wearing an inflatable crown that he'd placed upon my head and declared that breakfast would be served to the second biggest queen in the house shortly. There'd been pancakes and pastries and even a bottle of Prosecco, which we'd had a little sip of with orange juice, even though we'd had to go to work. No French toast—Ophelia was far too thoughtful for that. Instead, she had carefully cut a large strawberry into the shape of a heart and placed it on the edge of my plate. It was the most perfect birthday gift I could have asked for, and, although I couldn't say it, I'd given her a look that let her know.

I gave in to her questioning that night and gave up a small part of my secret world for the first time. Maybe it was the strawberry that changed my mind, maybe I was just tired of keeping it all to myself. We were outside the pub smoking, just the two of us. I'd been waiting for Richard to call and confirm he was back in London, which he'd expected to be that day, another reason I hadn't wanted to make any special birthday plans although I would never admit that. This is how it was. I wanted to be with him all the time, so I kept my personal schedule clear so I could drop everything easily if I heard from him.

When my phone rang, Ophelia tried desperately to get a look at the screen, craning her neck around me as I took it from my bag and scurried away from her to answer. He asked me to come over immediately, so I made my excuses there and then, draining half a glass of wine in one go.

"Oh my God, Charlie, you absolutely have to tell me what is going on. Secret phone calls and then rushing off into the night—

this is madness! What if you get murdered and the police ask me where you were? What would I say? What kind of friend would they think I was?" She was half joking, but there was a desperation in the way she spoke. She was really reaching for new arguments to persuade me.

"He isn't the murdering type."

"But they never are! That's what they always say. 'He was such a nice man, kept himself to himself . . .'"

"Look, it's complicated, and I will, I promise, tell you about it when I'm ready. Soon. I don't want to jinx things right now and I am begging you, Ophelia, as your best friend, please let it go. I will tell you. It's nothing exciting or scandalous. Please trust me. And please, for fuck's sake don't tell anyone else."

"So he *is* married, then?"

"Ophelia . . ."

"I knew it!"

"It's not that straightforward. You need to give me time to get things sorted, then I can explain everything to you. In all of the glorious detail you want. I would tell you if I could—you know I would."

She pouted shamelessly but did eventually stop asking.

That night, for my birthday, he gave me an early copy of *Altitude at Sea,* a first edition, signed:

For my dear Charlie. All my love, R

I read it over and over, that inscription, and hid the book underneath my bed where it would not be found just as he had told me to. A piece of him in my room. All his love.

Eddy was interested in my "secret lover," but, unlike Ophelia, he respected that I didn't want to talk about it and so he didn't press me. We were getting excited about the upcoming literature festival season and the trips we would be going on. Wilton-upon-Avon in July, Cheltenham that October, and maybe even Edinburgh. It was a perk of working in publicity that you got to go to the festivals and big summer events, whereas Ophelia, who was in Editorial, would be stuck in the office.

Eddy was working on some of our other big books of the year, but nothing as exciting as *Altitude at Sea*. As a man in publicity, Eddy was a rare phenomenon and so assigned to work with all the male authors on the list who couldn't be trusted with the younger female publicists, because they'd get "handsy." Because of this, Eddy got to work on some bigger campaigns than an assistant would otherwise, but also got stuck at a lot of events with unpleasant older men who barely hid their disdain at not being assigned someone else—someone young, green and female. It was unfair, but just the way it was.

Work was busy and, given the rhythm of publishing, although it was busy for Eddy and me, it was even more so for Ophelia, who was preparing for the annual London Book Fair, one of the biggest publishing industry events of the year, which would take place the following week. She was reading new manuscripts on submission until the small hours every night and barely made an appearance in the pub. She moaned about it, but we knew she was loving every minute of it. The busier you were, the more important you were.

Richard would be in London for the week of the fair. Winden & Shane was hosting a drinks reception for his foreign publishers, who rarely got to meet him, at a very fancy pub near the huge conference center in Earls Court where the fair would take place. I was needed to pour Prosecco and hand out books and tote bags.

We were in bed in the flat the Thursday before the week of the fair when I asked him if I'd get to see him the following week. He was sitting up working through some queries from the person who was translating *Altitude at Sea* into German, reading glasses perched on the end of his nose, and I was curled around him on my side reading an Ishiguro novel he had lent me.

"I don't know. Elaine is going to be in London at some point in the week. So I probably won't be able to see you other than at work. And you know how I have to be when I see you at work. Do you understand, Charlie?" He put a hand to my face as he said it.

"Does she know about me?"

"I believe that she knows that I have a friend who I meet sometimes in the city," he said carefully. I waited for him to say more but he didn't.

Elaine wasn't at the drinks reception, but a lot of other people who pretended to know Richard very well were. Everyone wanted to talk to him—his publishers from everywhere from South Korea to Iceland were there. They all reminded him of previous meetings over the years, of funny or clever things he had said, hoping it would prompt his memory of them. They all wanted to show him how familiar and close they were. It was the sort of sycophantic behavior that I knew he hated.

A beautiful young woman working at the bar asked Richard to sign a proof I'd given her—she was a big fan. It felt nice to be able to give her that, to be able to give someone else a little piece of him. I had much more of him than she or anyone in the room knew. He didn't seem to take much notice of her, although from the way she behaved with him it was clear that he could have had her if he liked. He gave me one glance that night that said, *Hello, Charlie, I see you.* It felt like electricity.

I was desperate to speak to him alone. Cecile had told me earlier in the day that one of the junior publicists was leaving for a job at Random House and that there would be a vacancy, and that she expected me to apply for it. I had been doing a few smaller campaigns for books that no one cared about, and she had been very encouraging about my work. I knew Eddy would want to apply, too, so we'd have to talk about that. She hadn't told me I'd got the job or anything, but, still, it felt like an invitation, and I was very excited. It would mean a bit more money and bigger campaigns of my own, but, most important, an end to Cecile's admin. I knew Richard would be happy for me, but I didn't know when I'd next see him or have a chance to tell him.

After he left and we were about to clear up, I slipped out for a cigarette despite Cecile's tuts—she hated me smoking and regularly lectured me on the damage it did to "young women's bodies." It was a warm evening and west London was leafy and fresh and smelled of the promise of summer. The sky was darkening, and I thought

Richard had already gone, but then I saw him on the pavement under a streetlight, smoking. I tried to catch his eye, but I couldn't, so I chanced it and went up to him.

"Where did you come from?" he said.

"I was just smoking, I thought you had left."

"I'm just waiting for a taxi that Cecile supposedly called me." I was sure to keep a good distance from him. In this situation he felt like a stranger. "Charlie . . ."

"I know. I just wanted to say good night. When can I see you next?"

"I don't know; Elaine is in London. Look. I'll call you. You know I'll call you. All right?"

A black cab pulled up and he got in. I wanted him to kiss me, to ask me about my day. But the cab just drove off, taking him to his wife and their second home, and I was left to get the Tube across to the other side of London and fall asleep alone in my bed, the excitement and pride I had felt at my job news completely gone, siphoned out of me by his coldness.

Eddy didn't apply for the job in the end because, when it came down to it, he said he couldn't face going any deeper into the belly of the beast that was Winden & Shane. He instead applied for an editorial job at Penguin, and he got it, and I got the junior publicist promotion at Winden & Shane, and so everyone was happy except Ophelia, who was the only one of us still stuck with "assistant" in their job title.

Eddy had somehow managed to skip a few steps in his career, as was often the case with the men in publishing, and, despite having no editorial experience, he'd been tasked with deputizing on the running of a small literary fiction list, with two direct reports and a significant pay rise. Ophelia and I discussed how ridiculous and unfair this was when he wasn't around, but it wasn't his fault he had been so successful, so we could hardly be angry with him about it. It was just another injustice of the industry for us to bond over. Really, we were mostly just devastated that the three of us were being broken up.

I, on the other hand, got a huge amount of extra responsibility and a very small pay rise. We had some warm white wine in the office to celebrate my promotion and Eddy's leaving, followed by even more white wine and shots in the pub next to work with the wider team. We were all horribly hungover the following day, but it was a Friday, so we managed to coast through with no grown-ups in sight, helping Eddy pack his things into a selection of miscellaneous tote bags that we found in the marketing department's store cupboard. Considering how tight the company was when it came to our salaries, it was a mystery to us that they could afford to print so many tote bags and postcards that ended up in boxes under piles of more tote bags and postcards in store cupboards, never to be seen again.

That night, Richard opened a bottle of champagne for us and cooked steaks with dauphinoise potatoes while I had a bath. Time with him over the previous six weeks since the book fair had been limited, although our phone calls had increased in frequency, and we now spoke almost every day. I loved the closeness of these calls, thinking about him in his study in the old stables at Stone Heap House, in the very room where so many of his books had been written. His voice sounded gruffer late at night, and his accent was stronger when he spoke from home. He slept in the room that adjoined his study most nights because it was easier to keep just one part of the house warm. I guessed from the times of the calls that Elaine did not sleep there with him, although I had no idea if she was in Yorkshire, London or France. I didn't ask and he didn't volunteer information.

This was the first full weekend in months that we could spend together, and we had talked about it for a while. He laughed at my hangover when I arrived, which was a relief because for some reason I thought he might be cross about it and tell me off. It was that creeping anxiety sort of hangover, but much of it floated away once I'd seen him. He kissed me deeply, brusquely. He hadn't shaved. I knew he'd had a drink while he was waiting for me to arrive. It felt so right, him cooking to the radio on a Friday night, me arriving like I was coming home.

I told him I loved him that night. We were on the sofa and I was drinking red wine, because there is nothing better than good red wine on a certain kind of hangover. I was relaxed and full and warm and clean and tired, and I had said it in my mind so many times, I just let it slip out. I just pressed my vocal cords together and the thought was given sound and entered the world where it would exist forever. "I love you, Richard." No fuss, no big moment. Just, "I love you, Richard."

He didn't even look up at me from his book; he was reading poetry, Ted Hughes, whom he referred to as "the other Yorkshire Man." He just said that some things exist perfectly without being spoken, and that I knew that. I knew that what he meant was that he loved me, too, that saying it out loud was not something he was going to do. It was probably because it was a betrayal too far.

When we had sex that night, I felt outside of myself and full of sadness. This was what I had wanted, all I had wanted—this extraordinary man whom I loved so much loved me back. He hadn't said the words, but that was what he had meant—what else could it have meant? But I couldn't see it, I couldn't feel it. I had disconnected. I wished I could take my words back.

"Are you OK?" he asked me after. The lights were all off in the room, which was good because I was upset and I didn't want him to know.

"Yes. I'm really happy."

"You're crying because you are happy? That's not very . . . Charlie."

"I'm not really crying."

"OK." He paused, tensed. "Sometimes when we have sex, I feel like you're not really here in the moment with me. Tonight, for example. Am I not doing something you want, or you like?"

"No. Not at all. I'm sorry. I don't know how to describe it. I always feel like that. With everyone I've been with. Outside myself." I'd never in my life found words for this.

"Do you know why that is?" He was on his side, his hand on my stomach. He was being very attentive to me, and I understood that it was because he had not said he loved me back, even if he did feel it.

"Nope. Just always . . . it's always been like this."

"Did anyone ever hurt you?"

"Sexually? No. No, I don't think so. My first time was a complete disaster, and it blew my life up, which maybe didn't help."

"What do you mean?"

"It's a long story."

"I don't mind long stories. Have you seen the size of the books I write?" He was trying to make me laugh but it landed flat, and I tensed even more. I didn't want to talk about it, but I didn't want to ever withhold from him.

"So, after my mum died, a lot of the kids at school took an interest in me and I guess I got moved into the more popular group. They were smart and pretty; it wasn't the airhead stuff from American films. But they took me in, and I loved the distraction and feeling so . . . interesting. Without my mum around, I needed other company, and I went in hard. They were so different from the friends I had before. Sleepovers always involved booze and sneaking out of the house to the beach to meet up with boys. This was all new to me.

"There was this one girl, Cassie, and her older brother, Lee, was just a year above us and we all liked him. All of us fancied him, though Cassie didn't like it that we did. She was the center of the group and had known the rest of them since nursery, or whatever. A real queen bee. Anyway, in August before our last year of sixth form started, she had this party and I drank too much and had to lie down, and Lee said to sleep in his bed. I was dressed stupidly in this tiny skirt and push-up bra that I'd borrowed from Cassie. I thought maybe he'd kiss me and put his arm around me, and we'd spoon to sleep. And we did, but then I woke up and he was, well . . . I was so out of it. I kept moving his hands back to my waist, but he kept on and on, pushing it further and further.

"I mean, he knew I fancied him, so I guess we just kind of did it. It's weird, because he didn't even kiss me. I thought it meant I would be his girlfriend. But it wasn't like that. He told everyone the next day and none of the girls would speak to me. I didn't even want to go all the way with him. As soon as I woke up the next morning and he asked me to get out of his room because he wanted to sleep, I knew that it had been a terrible mistake. He never spoke to me again, either. The group closed up around me; it was like they had never known me. They were so fiercely, blindly loyal to Cassie, who always insisted on this kind of thing from her friends. She wasn't someone to cross. She would pass messages through her friends on MSN telling me to leave her alone and stuff like that, but that was it. She wouldn't talk to me. I tried to apologize for the first few weeks, I even wrote her a letter, but she wouldn't read it. She just put it back in my locker unopened. So then I just gave up.

"I was so depressed I don't know how I got through my last year. I missed the first full month of term and got put on antidepressants. I had no friends. My few old school friends from before, all of them had moved on to a sixth-form college rather than stay on at school, and they were hurt that I'd not confided in them or kept close with them after Mum died. They had known her, and I think looking back many of them were really upset that she had died. I made a mess of everything."

Richard was silent, but he was breathing hard.

"Did you tell him it was OK before he had sex with you?"

"I didn't say anything. I didn't expect it to be the night I'd have sex for the first time. I didn't tell him no, exactly, I tried to move his hands, but I was so shocked I just went cold. I was wasted. It wasn't how I'd ever imagined it. I froze, I guess, and then once it was happening, I just went along with it because I was too embarrassed to ask him to stop."

He said nothing, but even though it was dark I could see his face was screwed up.

"I know you are thinking he did something wrong, but he didn't. I was in his bed. I fancied him. I wanted something to happen. I could have stopped it, I'm sure. I'm probably not explaining it right."

"He raped you, Charlie."

"No, that's not it."

"If you didn't want it to happen and he did it anyway, that's what it was."

I thought about the first time I'd had sex with Richard. About how it had moved quicker than I'd liked, how he had asked if I was on the pill as he'd pushed himself inside me, how he hadn't asked for permission. I'd wanted him; so surely that was consent. I didn't move him off me. Maybe back then at school, that hadn't been the case. But in both situations, I had let it happen.

"You're oversimplifying things."

"Because this is a simple thing."

I couldn't talk more after that. We didn't say good night, but at some point we must have both fallen asleep. The next thing I knew it was morning and he was on the edge of the bed, dressed, holding a cup of coffee. It was early, I could tell from the light. I felt like he was calling to me through quicksand, that I was falling deeper and deeper, my ears filling with it. My head was throbbing sickeningly behind my right eye. I was asleep but aware of the pain, stuck in it. I tried to wake up and to sit up, but I couldn't. The light was so bright. I covered my eyes and groaned.

"Charlie, I'm sorry to do this but I need you to go. Elaine is on her way down from Yorkshire. A friend in London is unwell and she wants to see her. I'm so sorry to . . . Charlie, are you all right?"

I tried to remember how much I had drunk the night before. Nothing, maybe two glasses of wine. So this wasn't a hangover. This was the worst possible timing.

"I have a migraine. This hasn't happened in so long. Shit. I don't have my medication. Please, please can you turn out that light."

"What can I do? Can you get up?"

"Do you have any paracetamol, ibuprofen, codeine, anything . . . Oh, God. I think I'm going to be sick." He quickly bought the bin over to me, emptying the bag out. I retched. "I'm so sorry."

If I hadn't felt so dreadful, I would have been embarrassed. He got me water and some strong painkillers that he had left over from a back injury, and a cold compress. I wanted nothing more than to die, for the pain to stop. Wondering how I was going to get across London in this state was causing consternation in my muddled brain. Surely he would make an excuse. I couldn't move.

But he didn't. The painkillers helped a little, enough for him to get me downstairs into the lobby, where I slumped against the door until he brought the car round. I was still wearing his caramel jumper, and he'd packed my things into a carrier bag. Elaine was a few hours away, so he was going to drive me home, or to a hospital if I wanted. If I needed to go to A&E, he would wait with me until one of my friends could get there. He asked again and again who he should call, holding my phone in his hand. He was genuinely concerned, panicked, although how much at my illness and how much at Elaine's surprise visit I couldn't tell. He helped me into the back seat of the car where I could lie down, covered me with a blanket and handed me a bin bag to be sick into if I needed to. My thoughts were jumbled and slow, flashes of pain and nausea rolled through me. The drive must have been less than an hour, but felt somewhere been two and three days. I tried to recognize where we were by the turns he took, the sounds from the street, but I could have been anywhere. I had never felt so wretched. I couldn't stop crying.

When we got to my street, he asked me if I could make it inside on my own. I said I could, knowing I couldn't, and was sick in the gutter as soon as I stood up. Migraines always made me sick like this, but I knew if I could get to my tablets, which were in the house, it would be eased in less than an hour.

"Will . . . Look, Charlie, I need to get you to your door, I want to get you to your bed, but if your housemates see me in their house at 9 A.M. on a Saturday morning with you in this state, that's not going to be good for us, for us being together. Do you understand, darling?"

I nodded and rubbed my face, my hot tears mixing with the cold sweat on my forehead. He had never called me darling before.

"Key . . ." I pointed to my handbag. He got it out for me. I leaned on him. "They won't be up. Help me to my door and help me with the key, then go. Fuck off."

He said nothing but did as I asked. The door clicked open and I pushed into the hall. The house was silent as I knew it would be at that time.

"Charlie, are you sure you are all right? You don't need to go to hospital?"

"Go," I said. He dropped my bags next to me in the hallway and went to put his arms around me, but I slammed the door. I heard him saying he'd call me in a few hours. Then, after a few minutes he left, and I heard the old Land Rover roar off down the street at speed.

I took my tablets, which were over a year out of date, and managed to keep them down. Then, miraculously, I fell asleep, which is the greatest relief you can get from a migraine.

Sometime later, Ophelia woke me very gently, her small hand stroking my hair. She looked very worried. She was sitting on the edge of my bed, holding a glass of water.

"Babe, are you OK? You look dreadful. Are you sick?"

It took me a few minutes to realize where I was. My head hurt much less, but the pain had been replaced with heavy fog.

"Don't worry, Fee, it's a migraine, that's all. God, it's been years since I had one. I forgot how bad they are. I feel a little better now. What time is it?" I could see light coming in through my curtains, but it could have been Monday for all I knew.

"It's five . . . on Saturday."

I sat up very slowly and took the water from her and sipped it. I'd been sick in a bin next to the bed. I didn't remember that happening. She was looking at it, trying very hard not to be disgusted.

"I'll just sort this out. OK?"

I must have fallen asleep again before she came back.

CHAPTER
Twelve

Around noon on Sunday, I surfaced. The migraine had run its course but had left me empty and feeling very strange. My legs felt weak under me as I pushed my weight through them, and I found that I couldn't think about what had happened with Richard, or indeed the whole previous forty-eight hours. Every time I let my brain go toward it, it was like an elastic band snapped me back into the moment. Migraines always left me feeling raw and nervous.

Ophelia was in the kitchen, dressed, drinking coffee. The French doors were open and our neglected garden was alive with insects. She got up when I came in and put her arms around me very gently, like I was brittle and would break at her touch.

"How are you feeling?" She stroked my back. She was so little, I thought.

"Weird. Very weird. But it's over. Please make me get a GP in London so I can stock up on medication. I never want to go through that again."

"Charlie . . . Charlie, your mobile was ringing off the hook yesterday. I didn't hear you come in, but you left your bag in the hall. I know I shouldn't have but you were so out of it you didn't even seem to be aware I was there, and I was so worried, and I just sort of panicked and I answered it. But I think I knew as soon as I saw the screen. Even though it just said *RA*. Everything clicked. I knew exactly who it was."

Pollen and dust were swirling slowly in the dim light of the kitchen, which was broken with sharp beams of sun that fell through the mossy skylight above. When had it become summer? It had been pouring with rain on Friday, and cold. But it must be June. My feet felt freezing on the porcelain tiles.

"Look, Charlie, I know. I spoke to him, to Richard. He was worried you had died or something. He told me you had been very ill, and asked did I know if you still had migraines. I did, of course. But not how ill they make you—Charlie, it was awful seeing you like that. But, anyway, I kept checking on you and gave you another dose of those pills; I looked them up on the internet. And then I called him later to tell him you were OK and sleeping, and he said to say he'd call you tonight, Sunday night. I think we need to talk about this, Charlie . . ."

"Not now. Please. I feel . . . when I feel better."

I could hear her words, but they were like scattered pieces of a jigsaw puzzle. They didn't make sense as she said them. It took a moment to put them together. She knew. She had spoken to Richard.

Fuck off. Go. That was what I had said to him.

"OK, when you are feeling better. I love you, Charlie, I just want you to be happy." I said nothing. "You need to eat something." My stomach felt as empty as the rest of me, sick with emptiness.

"I don't know if I can."

"Just have some toast. You need something inside you."

And so I sat there, dirty and thin and empty in my dressing gown, as Ophelia made me toast, and cut up little pieces of fruit, gently coaxing me to eat like I was a toddler.

Summer arrived in London that Sunday. That night, we sat on the sofa watching television. My mobile, which was on the coffee table, buzzed with his initials and for the first time, I didn't try to hide it. For the first time, I didn't answer.

Ophelia said nothing.

I called in sick on Monday, and was told to take all the time I needed. Richard called again twice and sent an email.

Charlie, please, call me back. I won't keep calling.

I found a doctor's surgery that was taking new patients and explained to the receptionist about my migraines and the severity of the attack I had just experienced. A GP called me in the same afternoon. She was young, maybe just a few years older than me. It seemed amazing that anyone my age could do anything as important and specialized as being a doctor. She looked into my eyes with her little torch, and checked my blood pressure.

"Any idea what brought it on? It can often be exhaustion, stress or anxiety. Do you know what your triggers are?"

"I have no idea." I let my mind slip back, for just a moment, to the conversation I'd had with Richard the night before it had come on.

"Any family history of migraine?"

"My mum didn't get them. I don't know about my dad. I don't really know anything about him at all. We left him when I was really little, and I've had no contact with him since." She made a note of something on the computer.

"And how's your mood?"

"Fine," I told her. "Just that work has been a bit stressful."

"What do you do?"

I told her and she seemed impressed, saying it must be very glamorous. I told her it wasn't.

"And your meds—are you happy with them? I have your notes from your previous GP in . . . let me see . . . Brighton. It looks like you've been on antidepressants for . . . hang on, it's here . . . about seven years."

"Yes, that would be about right."

"Have you explored any talking therapies? We have some available here."

"I tried CBT; it didn't help. My mum died when I was sixteen. I've been on them since around then."

"I'm really sorry to hear that, Charlotte. That must have been very traumatic. I see you are on a high dose. Not the highest, but, still, I'd consider it high. A side effect of these SSRIs can be migraine. If you ever want to explore therapy, I'd be really happy to give you a referral to the brilliant team here in Hackney. I firmly believe that antidepressants work best alongside talking therapies. So maybe we could book in another appointment for next month when you are feeling better and chat more about what we have available here. Waiting lists are long but that's not a reason not to explore this as an option."

I told her I would make an appointment for next month but walked straight out with my prescription for a fast-acting migraine-relieving nasal spray. I went to the pharmacy, feeling the warmth of summer breaking through the leaves of the poplar trees, watching the world as it must exist every weekday when I was usually at work.

I slept a lot and watched daytime television.

I didn't know what to say to Ophelia, or to Richard. Ophelia tried to talk to me about it again after work on Tuesday, but I told her I wasn't feeling right again yet and she dropped it. She was being a wonderful friend considering all I had been keeping from her. She didn't have a cross word for me. I had thought she would have exploded with the drama of it, but she was measured and solid and endlessly kind, making me supper and leaving me lunches each day, all of which went in the bin. She even did a load of laundry for me that she found in the overflowing basket in the corner of my bedroom, folding everything into perfect little parcels and laying them neatly on my bed, which she made with boarding-school precision. I didn't deserve her.

By the time I woke up on Wednesday, I was starting to feel sick of my own misery and ready to try to pull myself back into the world, so I found a yoga class locally that was listed online for that lunchtime and took myself out. It helped to clear my head, the breathing and the slow movement, the smell of incense and the cold mat under my forehead. After, I got a coffee and a croissant from one of the bakeries on Church Street and went to the park. Everyone around me was so connected to the world. People were walking in couples, with their friends, with their children. I was the only person alone.

I wanted to erase Richard from myself as much as I wanted to marry him. But I couldn't erase him, and I couldn't leave him—I had neither the strength nor the will, let alone the sense. Every good, golden strand of my life could be traced back to him. I could see no way back. I didn't really want any way back.

We were, I realized with both delight and horror, connected to each other now. This relationship would be something I would be trying to recover from for the rest of my life, whether we ended things now or in twenty years. But it would end, because everything ends. And Richard Aveling was not someone that you could ever just part from. There would be no one else like him for me ever again because he was an extraordinary person, and I loved him in a way that was different from how young people loved each other. He was from another world, another time. He was a giant in every sense of the word, and I was nothing. I had given him everything of myself.

In that moment, a part of me wanted to take it all back, the talks we'd had about my mum and the sadness that had occupied me for so much of my life. Although we were connected, I had no idea, truly, if he could break from me and forget about me, and, feeling nothing, just move on with his life.

I ran through my options for survival. Even if I left Winden & Shane, if I moved to another publishing company, I would still see him at events, festivals, book fairs. I could try to avoid him, but I knew I wouldn't be able to do that. But most painful of all was the one-way connection I felt to him through his books. For so long his words had been building worlds in my imagination. I had relationships with his characters, I had memories of their imagined lives imprinted on me. Those memories, in turn, connected me to my younger self, to my mum. They were almost more precious than anything else about him.

The grass was slightly damp from the dew, and I could feel it slowly seeping through my leggings. I put my earbuds in and cycled through my iPod, looking for the saddest song I could find. I stopped at the National. I lay down and closed my eyes.

Elaine. I had never asked Richard for anything. I had never wanted to ask if he saw any future for us. I hadn't even really allowed myself to imagine a future where we were together because it was so unlikely. Such fantasies would bring me no pleasure—they would instead indulge a realization that I tried very hard to keep away from. If he planned to leave her, he had never said so. But then I never saw any evidence of his affection for her and he didn't talk about her. There was never a trace of her in the flat. It was too soon to ask about those things, anyway. It had only been four months.

Had I imagined the intensity of it all? Was it really so different from Ophelia and her useless banker boyfriend who wouldn't commit? Of course it was. This was a real, adult relationship, complex and with consequences. It was also the first relationship that I had been in where I had felt real intimacy, I realized. I had talked about things with him that I hadn't been able to give voice to before. I had accepted his faults, his occasional coldness with me, I had let that be, and I had shown him mine, bared it all and he hadn't rejected me. I had been so unwell in front of him, I had told him to fuck off, I had told him about things that had happened to me that I hadn't understood and he had given them a narrative that was probably more accurate than anything I could have done on my own. And all of that intimacy, that closeness, had collided with being thrown out of his flat onto the street because of the stark reality that he was married.

He had a wife.

I had a choice, I suspected, if I really wanted one. I could walk away from him, from this great love, and live an unhappy life with his shadow always just a step ahead, above, or around a corner. Or I could accept that the situation was less than perfect, that the future would remain unknowable, and I could be with him in the way that I had been. I could drink in every minute of it while it lasted and then, if I needed to, when it ended, I could die if it hurt too much.

I let the restless shadow of the horse chestnut tree above me mottle the sunshine over the dark yellow of my eyelids. I lay like that for a long while, breathing deeply, accepting my decision, oscillating between relief and panic. Sadness was inescapable for me. Even where I had found happiness, really for the first time since I was a child, it was there in everything I touched.

Hi. Let me know when to call or if you want, call me whenever. I'm in the park, on my own. Cx

Richard phoned me ten minutes later and asked me to come over straight away. Elaine had had to go to France to oversee some building work on the house and wouldn't be back for a few weeks. We sat in his kitchen that afternoon, as we had done the first day I had set foot in the flat all those months ago, and we drank coffee, hardly talking, my face bare and my unwashed hair tied messily in a bun. He asked me if I was better. He didn't say if he meant the migraine or the rest of the emotional mess he had been exposed to. I told him about my doctor's appointment, the yoga class, about my conversation with Ophelia and that I was going to have to tell her what had been going on because really, she already knew. We were at each end of the little table with the sash window wide open, the hot air, thick with pollen and pollution and truth perfectly still between us. We had lasted a whole season.

"I share a part of my life with Elaine. That's not going to change. I've never said otherwise so I'm sorry if you thought so."

"I know. And you didn't."

"I won't keep you here if you don't want to be here. You can go anytime. But I don't want that. I like you being here."

"I know that, too."

"But things aren't going to change much. It's hard to explain to someone so young but certain parts of my life have been lived, and lived with her, and I'm not going to blow my life up now. How we are together, how this feels, is very separate from her and it doesn't make it less . . . important. Do you understand what I'm saying, Charlie?"

"I do. I do understand. I don't want this to end."

"Neither do I."

We looked at each other then for the first time that day. He looked so tired. He was wearing his decorating clothes again, which I now understood he wore when he felt low. I went to him and put my face into his chest, and he put his arms around me and we stayed like that for a long while.

The next day I went back to work. Richard decided to stay on in London for a week and I spent every night with him.

Things did get a little easier after that. As I had promised, I sat down with Ophelia and a couple of bottles of wine and told her everything. We sat in our kitchen after work with the back doors open. She was concerned—that was her initial angle anyway—because she didn't want me to get hurt by him. She didn't want me to lose my job or to have this end my career in publishing; sleeping with authors wasn't acceptable until you were much more senior.

"What if it gets out?"

"But you are the only person who knows."

"But you could get seen. Elaine could see an email or a text or something."

"That won't happen. We are really careful. And she is hardly ever even with him."

"But it could happen, Charlie. Even if you are careful. These things do get out. And then what would you do? You could lose your job, everything."

"It won't get out. And if it does, I guess we'll cross that bridge when we come to it."

Honestly, I had no idea what we would do. But I knew the risks. She swore that she wouldn't tell a soul, not even Eddy. As the evening wore on, and the first bottle was finished and we opened the second, the light started to fade and she started to become less supportive and grew angrier, a side of her I had never seen before.

"What about his wife?" she said. She was drunk. "You are making a fool of her. You could ruin their marriage. And he just took the ending of the book from you. Did he even ever thank you? Or acknowledge it?"

I became defensive and we exchanged the first cross words of our friendship. But another half a bottle down and we were back to being the best of friends ever in the history of friends and nothing could break us. We cried and held each other. By the end of the second bottle, we had come to a place where I understood she didn't like it, she didn't feel good about it at all—in fact she thought he was a piece of shit and an old creep—but she loved me and because of that she would stay true to her word and support me if that's what I wanted. I knew that she was coming at this from a place of love. That she wanted to protect me. And I told her that.

What I didn't tell her was that I loved Richard so much that without him I would probably die.

CHAPTER
Thirteen

By mid-July I had become so used to the light lasting late into the evening and the weather being warm that winter seemed like science fiction.

The city had shed its winter skin and was almost unrecognizable from the London of February. Londoners had abandoned the city and been replaced by tourists. As a result, everything seemed to move at a different pace. The pavements were slow with groups of people with maps and cameras, and those markers of familiarity—red telephone boxes, the men shouting, *"Standard, Standard,"* in their cockney accents waving the free newspaper at passersby, zebra crossings—all became caricatures in this otherwise living city. Central London felt like a film set.

The Tube and bus were quiet in the mornings and evenings, and the heat made it hard to sleep. I didn't enjoy summer in the city—it made me long for the countryside and the beach back home. An acrid smell of rubbish rotting in wheelie bins hung about in the air, mixed with the fumes from the traffic. The heat was unrelenting, bouncing from the buildings and the pavement with no breeze or respite to be found. I wanted soft grass and cornfields, sticky, salty hair and sand between my toes. I wanted the shade of generous oak trees. Whenever I could, I retreated to a park to read and drink warm tins of gin and tonic, finding some relief in these green places where you could almost shut out the noise of London if you really tried.

The senior staff at Winden & Shane were all taking long holidays in Tuscany or Sicily. We'd have to pick up the panic of their own vacation-inflicted deadlines, but, other than that, work was quiet and slowed into a sort of fug that we all enjoyed immensely after the furious rush of the previous six months.

I felt a new distance between Ophelia and me that was impossible to ignore. There had been a brief moment of relief after we had talked it through but it had been short-lived. I had to censor myself just as much, even with her knowing, because I knew how much she disapproved of Richard. So eventually, I just stopped talking about him altogether. She was also spending more time with Oscar and his friends, and she knew that I wasn't very fond of Oscar either, so we found a new rhythm in our friendship and living arrangements that felt uneasy to me but was safer for both of us. I wasn't surprised that this was happening, but I felt very sad about it, so much so that I put my hackles up to soften the blow that was surely coming. My friendships were always temporary, I reminded myself, so why would this one be any different? I presumed this was just the beginning of the inevitable.

Instead, I focused on other things. Namely Richard. My thoughts, my work, my life, all concerned Richard.

At work I was extremely careful not to give anything away. I practiced pausing before saying anything aloud, so that nothing slipped out that would lead to the affair being discovered. I was so rehearsed in this that it became second nature. Everything was consumed by him; I counted down the days we were apart, wishing them away and him back to London. Sometimes it would be a week, ten days even on one occasion, but the night before we were meeting, I would preen and go to bed early so as to wake up on a day when we'd be together again. If he was doing the same, if he was self-censoring with Elaine as much as I was with everyone, I had no idea because we did not ever speak about her, or his life with her.

I tried to take every day, every moment with him as it came. It felt good and real when we were together, but when we were apart I would obsess over every minute he was not in contact with me, wondering if our latest meeting would be our last. The insecurity and anxiety of it affected me physically. I lost my appetite, and running was the only way I could quieten my mind when he was away. I was thinner than I had ever been, which I liked, although if he noticed he didn't say anything about it.

Nothing but Richard mattered. This secret was my most treasured thing.

People asked if I had a boyfriend, as people do to young women. Dad even tried on the phone one night, almost certainly prompted by Laura. We had been speaking less and less. He used to call every Sunday, an unofficial arrangement but one which we had kept for the last few years. Since weekends were so often reserved as my time with Richard, we had stopped and now we just spoke when I felt like answering my phone.

"No, Dad, there's no one special. I'm focusing on my career at the moment."

In many ways this was true because I was working very hard, and with the new focus I had found in Richard, I was less chaotic and more consistent in this area of my life. Cecile was giving me more and more responsibility and I'd started speaking up in meetings, all the blood in my body rushing to my face as I ventured a thought or opinion while trying not to pass out. But no one laughed or flinched in embarrassment on my behalf. They all acted as though I had always talked in meetings. I was finding my feet and getting my balance.

Although he would never use the word, with his first publication in eight years looming, Richard was becoming anxious. He was distracted and quiet and sometimes short with me. He'd always apologize and tell me what his reasons were afterward. I accepted that what I could do to support him was to be understanding. Because we only ever spent time together in the privacy of the flat, everything was contained. I had become so used to it that it felt like a second home. There was another Charlie who came alive once the door closed and I was safely inside. The best part of my life existed there. I got to know which floorboards creaked and which curtain would always fall open, the sound that the fridge made late at night, the click of the neighbor's chain being bolted on their front door. I'd stopped worrying that Elaine would walk in any moment, but I couldn't leave anything there—Richard was clear with me that I must be very careful about this. No toothbrush, no mascara, and absolutely no underwear. If I did slip up, it could mean that we wouldn't be able to meet there anymore.

Since the migraine, I'd not mentioned Elaine at all. As a result we were closer and more easy in ourselves. He would talk about her only if it related to his travel plans, and then it was in purely practical terms. Her name would pop up in my inbox every now and then, and when it did, I would feel a rush of cortisol-soaked panic disperse in my chest like an injection of ink into water. Fight or flight mode would be engaged. But that was it. I didn't see her, and I didn't really think about her, not as a woman anyway. She was some hangover, some complication that I wanted gone so much I hoped that by just pretending she wasn't there it might manifest as the truth. If only, I'd think to myself, if only she would die, or leave him, whatever. Then we'd be together. I was cruel to her in this respect, and for all my faults I wasn't usually a cruel person, but she had done nothing in her life as far as I could tell to warrant my kindness or understanding.

It didn't occur to me that there would have been other women, and other affairs. He had told me that she knew he had something going on, so it should have been obvious to me. But I saw only what I wanted to see, because I was blind with love for him and high on the feeling of importance that he gave me in return for all the sex he wanted. For the first time in my adult life, I felt validated. I could hardly remember my life before him.

Richard certainly hadn't tired of having sex with me. If anything, he wanted me more and more. It had taken me a little while after our conversation about what had happened in sixth form, and he was surprisingly patient with me. We didn't talk about it specifically, that subject was closed and off-limits without me having to tell him as much. But I started to feel his frustration and I hated it, so I pushed past the discomfort, as I had done with men before. I just unhooked my brain and disconnected from my body, which knew to move in the practiced way he liked, saying all of the right things, making all of the correct noises until he came, momentarily powerless over me, and then he would be softened and kind with the pleasure of it.

Sex with Richard was unlike sex I had had with anyone else. When I wasn't with him, I'd think about him constantly. I'd come before I fell asleep every night just thinking about him, touching myself in the lightest way. Whenever he was on television, which was more and more frequently, I'd watch him and be overcome with lust to the point that I would physically ache. But when I was with him, I'd feel far outside myself.

His body was beautiful to me because I loved him. Although he was in no way fat, he didn't take very good care of himself or do any exercise as far as I could tell, and he was so much older at fifty-six. I had started to notice other runners on my route sometimes—young men, lean and tanned and firm-bodied. It was so hot that many ran shirtless, and I would want to place a hand on their chest or their stomach, just to know what it felt like. I hated myself for being so shallow. Richard was good to me, and he was decisive, and that gave me the confidence and the energy to do whatever I could to make things pleasurable for him. He loved my body, the shape of it, the firmness of it. He would touch me like a doll, sometimes, telling me about the bits he liked best, stroking and playing with me even after sex was over, me lying naked on my back or on my front next to him, him leaning over me on his side. It made me feel good about how I looked in a way that I hadn't ever before. So I let him dominate me, I let him think he was giving me deep and intense orgasms, when the truth was that he rarely did. But I didn't mind. The pleasure I got from sex with him was something else, something more powerful. It connected me to him, to be so disconnected, it allowed me to see things from above—it wasn't something I could give words to, even if I'd had someone to tell.

That July we went to the Wilton-upon-Avon Literature Festival, one of the biggest events in the literary calendar. Richard was doing a special preview event for the book, discussing it with a popular academic-turned-television-presenter. We'd been in situations like this a few times now and we were getting very good at it. We couldn't fake unfamiliarity anymore as we were working together so closely.

We had a façade that we slipped on and no one seemed to notice a thing. But then why would they? No one would suspect that I, an ordinary person and a junior publicist, could have the attention and affection of the great, brilliant Richard Aveling.

Wilton-upon-Avon was a market town just outside Bath known for not much more than the festival. It was small and picturesque with narrow, cobbled streets and an ancient stone church. It was a typical, affluent rural town and usually quiet, save for the summer tourists that came to see the remarkably well-preserved ruins of an early medieval monastery nearby. But, for a week every July, Wilton-upon-Avon would transform into the center of the literary world, alive with media, authors and publishers. And this year, for the first time, I was one of them.

Our team, including Richard's agent, John Cormorant, were all staying in the same hotel. John Cormorant was one of those people whom you only ever referred to by both names. Markus and Cecile were with us, too. After the event we were going for dinner; it was far enough from London, and enough of a special event, to warrant staying overnight. I had been looking forward to all of it for months. The festival was famous, and it was exciting to be a part of it, but more than that I loved seeing Richard work. The way he carried himself when he knew he was on display, the way everyone looked at him in his beautiful, pristinely pressed clothes—he was at his most attractive to me in situations like this.

The festival itself took place on a field adjacent to the river Avon which edged the town, in huge white marquees with stages and bookshops and bars and food trucks. Richard's event was late on a Friday afternoon and the tent was completely packed with five hundred in attendance. I stood at the back, watching him, listening to his deep Yorkshire drawl as he rolled out the lines he had repeated again and again about the book and his writing. He kept his long legs crossed and leaned back in his chair looking so at ease and so comfortable, yet it was so completely different from how he would sit at home. The interviewer raved about the new book and the event ended with some questions from the audience that were, as usual, not questions so much as statements intended to show off just how much the reader understood.

About halfway through, Cecile's phone silently lit up in her hand.

She whispered, "Charlie, anything he says that gives you any red flags, anything unexpected, write it down. I have to take this—it's the nanny."

As it turned out, the nanny was calling to say that the twins had fevers and were really quite unwell. Cecile's literary-agent husband, Matthew, was also somewhere at the festival with an author and couldn't leave, and, although Cecile couldn't either, she did.

"Stay, Charlie, go to some events, enjoy the hotel. But don't join them for dinner, that would be awkward. They'll want to catch up and have a lot to talk about. But do get yourself dinner and expense it. Didn't you say Eddy was here? Why don't you meet up with him instead? But use your own card; I need the Amex. I'll see you on Monday."

After the event had finished, I found John Cormorant and Richard and told them that Cecile had had to go and that I had some friends I was meeting for dinner. I pretended that I had not been going to join them in the first place, and I said goodbye. Richard and I had planned to try to meet up later at the hotel. He was excited about having sex with me somewhere other than the flat, and I was excited to have sex with him in secret, to feel the weight of him, this man who had just held the audience captive, to have him to myself. Everyone wanted a piece of Richard, but it was me that he wanted.

I was disappointed about the dinner, but I knew that Eddy was at the festival somewhere and we'd planned to try to meet for drinks that evening anyway. Since he'd left Winden & Shane, and the shift between Ophelia and me had happened at home, I'd not really seen much of him; we were always at home when the other wasn't. I'd loved that brief period, which was really less than a year, where we'd all been so close. I'd never felt that kind of love before. It made me ache to think about it, but there was nothing I could do to change it short of breaking things off with Richard and there was no way in hell that was going to happen.

Eddy and I met at a pub in town and found a table outside in the garden. It was still early, and that dreamy kind of summer evening where it was exactly warm enough to sit outside. I ordered a bottle of Prosecco and some crisps that I hoped I could expense in place of dinner, and we drank and smoked and caught up like we'd never been apart.

Eddy loved his job but hadn't found friends there in the way he had at Winden & Shane. Despite this, he had endeared himself to everyone, naturally, and set about buying some books, which he was very excited to publish. I promised to read everything. We got light-headed on the Prosecco and told each other how great the other was and how much we loved and missed each other.

I got up and went to the bathroom, and when I came back, Richard and John Cormorant were sitting at another table in the pub garden. I caught Richard's eye quite by accident and he lifted a hand to wave. John Cormorant turned around, but he didn't acknowledge me. Markus must have left. They were well out of earshot and the pub garden was buzzing with conversation. Richard was smoking, drinking a pint of something dark, and looking serious, probably complaining about the ineptitude of his teams across the world. I sat down with Eddy, my back to them.

"So that is Richard Aveling, is it? I've never actually seen him up close. He's much taller than he looks on TV."

From the way he was looking at me, I knew then that he knew. "Please don't say anything that might be overheard, Eddy, I'm serious." My happy mood had disappeared. Ophelia! She had promised.

"Obviously I'm not going to do that." He paused and took a drag on his cigarette. My heart had escaped my chest cavity and seemed to be lodged in my throat. Daylight was almost completely gone, and the garden was lit with strings of tiny lanterns, which shone warmly, making everything look like it was in soft focus. "And before you go sending furious texts to Ophelia, don't. I figured it out all by myself. I saw him sitting in his car on our road that day you were ill. I was coming home early that morning. I told Ophelia and she said it couldn't be, but when I talked to her about it again, well, I don't know if you have ever seen that girl try to lie but it is absolutely tragic. And given that I know you have a secret, older, married lover, and the way you reacted when you came back from the toilet and saw him . . . well. You are well and truly fucked, Charlie, if anyone else finds out."

"They won't."

"You know we can't sleep with authors until we are much more senior."

"I am aware. Look, can we drop it?"

I turned and looked over my shoulder. Richard caught my eye again. It was funny seeing him in a pub beer garden, smoking. He seemed so out of place.

"Is this the reason things are so weird with you and Ophelia?"

"They aren't that weird. And if they are, she made it that way by being so judgmental about it." I was half whispering now, but I was angry with her. With Eddy knowing too it felt like control of the situation was slipping from my fingers. It wasn't her fault; I knew that really. I just wished she could have tried harder to cover for us. Mainly, I hated the thought of the two of them talking about me.

"Judgmental how?"

"She called him . . . a creep. She thinks I'm wrecking their marriage and setting fire to my career. That he's going to hurt me. She doesn't get it. It's not some stupid fling. We're together, properly together. He has an agreement with his wife."

"What kind of agreement?"

"I don't know the details. It's not my business."

"Don't you think if there was an agreement, he would have told you about it?"

"I don't want to talk about it."

Eddy was quiet, looking at his cigarette, thinking about what to say next. I'd never been cross with him before.

"Look, Charlie. Ophelia is just looking out for you. She loves you like a sister. And she hasn't got a mean bone in her body. You know that."

"Well, I was just looking out for her, telling her that I think Oscar is a dick, but she didn't like that at all."

"Oh my God, Oscar is such a dick." I smiled and he smiled back, the tension eased. "Charlie, you've got to do you. But I think in all honesty you are smart enough to see why Ophelia might think some of those things, and it's not because she's judgmental, it's because that's what it looks like from the outside. I won't tell a soul, but you need your friends. You know you get dark sometimes, and if you're in this . . . thing . . . with him . . ." He clucked his tongue and glanced in Richard's direction. "Things have the potential to get *dark*. Which could be double-dark for Charlie. And if that happens, you'll need a friend like me, and like Ophelia. So I promise to not be judgy, and I'll talk to Ophelia. Maybe then we can all go out and get wasted like we used to, with no slimy bankers or creepy old men, unless they are with me. How does that sound?"

As we talked, I saw Richard getting up to leave. Eddy and I ordered another bottle of Prosecco. An hour and a half later, I called Richard's room from the phone in my room, and he invited me to come and see him. He told me to be very careful not to be seen. He'd put a spare key card under my door.

When I got to his room he was already in bed, sitting up, shirtless. He looked far too big for the bed.

"Are you drunk?"

"A little." I was trying to be cute and it wasn't working.

"Who was that you were with?" He closed his book. It was something obscure that I didn't know. He was wearing his reading glasses and looked stern.

"That was Eddy." He looked blank. "My housemate. He used to work with me." I was surprised he didn't know who he was. Eddy was one of the closest people in my life. I talked about him all the time. Was he jealous, mistaking him for someone I might be interested in?

"He doesn't know about us? You didn't tell him?"

"No, of course not." A lie. "Only Ophelia knows, and you know why."

There was a long, uncomfortable pause. Then he said, "Have you slept with him, too?"

I was leaning against the door, and I let out a laugh so loud I instinctively covered my mouth.

"Eddy? I'm not his type. Being female and all."

Something about Richard felt off. He didn't react to this at all. He didn't even blink. I wasn't sure whether to turn around and go back to my room or go to him. He said just nothing, holding his book very tightly, looking hard at the cover.

"Come here," he said, finally, and gestured at the bed, peeling the duvet back. I wished I'd brushed my teeth before coming down. I kicked my shoes off and went to him, lying on my side facing him. "I know it's hard not telling your friends."

"It's not hard." Another lie. "I don't mind. I just want you. I don't need to share this with anyone." Maybe it was the Prosecco-and-crisp dinner, maybe it was the gorgeous evening with Eddy, but it hit me just how untrue this was and how much I missed my friends. I pushed that thought down and looked at him submissively, knowing he'd like it.

He put his book on the table next to him and turned to me, pulling me down the bed with surprising force so he was on top of me. He was naked under the covers, which surprised me for some reason, and he was hard—I wondered if he had been before I'd even come in. I had never really thought about his private sexual world, what he thought about, if it was me or Elaine or other women. He held my wrists above my head with one hand and pushed my skirt up so it was almost at my rib cage. He didn't kiss me, but he kept his face very close, eyes fixed on mine. He pushed my underwear to the side. It was too fast, he was moving too quickly and it hurt so much I yelped, which seemed to spur him on more. I couldn't seem to get outside of myself and yet I didn't want him to stop looking at me like that, like I was the only thing in the world. He was letting go of control. It had never been like this before, so cold.

After, I wanted to cry.

I slept in my own room that night. Richard had checked out by the time I made it down for breakfast. I sat alone at a table in the hotel restaurant with a copy of the *Guardian* and a pot of mediocre coffee while people moved around me, up and down from the buffet, globs of congealed yellow egg and edges of unripe melon discarded on the sides of their plates. Snatches of conversations about hangovers and surprise guests and silent mode and ineffective air-conditioning and inconsiderate 2 A.M. smokers brushed my ears as my focus moved in and out of my own head. Picking at a tiny pastry dotted with raisins, all I could stomach, I checked my emails, hoping to find something, anything from Richard that would make the night before feel better.

I had to leave early, meeting a friend in London for lunch. Come to the flat this afternoon, I'll be back at around 4, staying on a few days if you want to come and camp out. xR

CHAPTER
Fourteen

I didn't go to Richard that day. It was the first time I said no to him. I told him that I had plans with my friends, and that felt good. Eddy had a lunchtime event, but I didn't fancy it, so I spent a few hours walking around the festival site, exploring the tents and drinking coffee.

I felt very strange, which was in part the hangover, but something else, too. The night before had been unpleasant, but I took some solace in the extreme intensity of it, which seemed to radiate through me. I could still feel Richard's jealousy vibrating quietly in my bones. So much of my experience with him was disorientating and new. For the first time, there had been a switch in the power he had over me. He had shown me a weakness. Finally, I had seen a crack in his armor that gave away something of how he felt for me. I wanted to hold on to it, and I was sure that the moment I saw him again, it would flip back to how it had been. Submissive little Charlie. He would get bored with her.

I met Eddy at the train station, and we bought crisps and tins of gin and tonic for the journey. Eddy had been in touch with Ophelia, and it had been agreed that we were going to have a night together like we used to and talk it out over drinks. I didn't know what had been said and how much of our conversation the night before had been relayed back to her, but Eddy's positivity was infectious, and I wanted to mend things with Ophelia and to return to how we had been: an indestructible little unit. I missed her and it had taken me until now to realize how much, because it was easier not to.

It was so hard for me to back down, to find my way back to people once something had been broken. I didn't like this about myself, and I didn't want it to be like that with Ophelia. I wanted things to be better with us than with the trail of broken friendships I had left behind me over the years. Maybe that would take me facing her and our disagreement, rather than running from it. Certainly, it was a risk worth taking for a person like Ophelia because friends like her didn't come along very often. My evening with Eddy, and then with Richard, had left me longing for her in a way I had only ever longed for one person. My mum.

We got back to the flat at around 5 P.M. Ophelia gave me a slightly cautious hug at the door. I was grateful for Eddy's undivided attention for the evening. It immediately defused things—although I had a hard time looking Ophelia in the eye. I wanted to go to her and wrap my arms around her, but I wasn't sure how she would react if I did.

We opened a bottle of wine and sat in our little garden, which miraculously caught the evening sun. Eddy had put our Spotify playlist on his laptop and the tinny little speakers choked out the nineties songs we remembered so well: Coolio, the Cardigans, TLC. The mood was good, and the white wine tasted great in the summer evening air. My hangover was morphing into a new buzz. The plants in the courtyard had grown wildly in the last few weeks, thanks to a few afternoon visits from Clemmie and the gardener, and it was lush and green. I felt the soft tendrils of one of the hundreds of ferns between my fingers and breathed the evening in, making a mental note to spend more time out here. Ophelia was golden brown despite spending all the hours of daylight in the office and she looked beautiful, her slim legs stretched out in front of her, and her hair perfectly straight. Even in an old T-shirt and pajama shorts she looked glamorous, like she was in some teen sitcom. I looked down at my own pale body. The annual crop of ugly dark freckles had started to appear on my forearms, knees and hands. I pulled a shirt over my shoulders in a hopeless attempt to stop them in their tracks.

Richard hadn't replied to me, and I had decided with Eddy on the train back to London to stop checking my inbox for the day. I'd even put my phone in my room to remove temptation. So far, we'd not mentioned his name, or Oscar's, but I knew later we'd have to talk about it. For now, I was enjoying the company of my friends. I wished Richard could see me, happy and sociable with these beautiful young people. I wished he could see my life beyond his flat.

We drank wine and talked about people from work, and then we got changed into real clothes and headed to the pub. The streets smelled of barbecues, and you could hear laughter and the sound of music from people's back gardens. Ophelia linked her arm through mine and I squeezed it and kissed her on the top of her perfect little head. Our ballet flats slapped the pavement in time.

We found a seat outside the Rose and Crown, and Eddy went in to order a bottle of wine, leaving Ophelia and me sitting opposite each other on the picnic bench. I felt suddenly shy, and like I would do anything to keep her as my best friend. All of the bravado and anger I had felt was gone, replaced with something much warmer. I rolled a cigarette for something to do. We didn't speak, though, and I was relieved when Eddy retuned with a silver ice bucket and a bottle of pale rosé.

"Right. Let's get this over with, shall we? You two are the best of friends and this whole thing . . ." He gestured at us, filling our glasses with wine and digging about in the bucket for ice. "Is just too sad. And I get it. Charlie, Ophelia feels that you are being cold and distant since you have been with, well, you know who." He looked around, checking the tables next to us for anyone we might work with, which was smart given this part of London. "She also thinks you don't like Oscar. Ophelia, Charlie feels that you are being judgmental about her relationship, which we have talked about, and I think she now sees where that might be coming from. So, I think it's best if we just talk about this and get it all out so we can get back to being friends that drink too much together. Charlie, do you want to go first?"

Eddy was amazing. He was wasted in publishing. He'd be great in hostage negotiations, or the UN or something. I looked at Ophelia, really looked at her for the first time in weeks, and tears suddenly, uncontrollably, welled up in my eyes. I realized I was actually quite drunk.

"I just don't feel like you even tried to understand." The words sort of fell out of me, unchecked. "We talked it through, and I thought we were good but every time after that, when I mentioned his name, I could see you flinch. I know you so well, Ophelia," I said, choking. "That I knew you were judging me, him, the relationship—that you didn't really support me even though you said you did. So that's why I stopped talking about him with you."

Ophelia was crying, too. Eddy was sitting next to her, and he was stroking her back and holding my hand across the table very tightly. "You just looked at his age, and the fact he was married, and I get what it looks like, but it's so much more complicated than that. He's helped me to . . . There are some things that even you don't know about, Ophelia, and he is really helping me to work them out." I wasn't entirely convinced by myself on this, but I couldn't stop myself from talking. "And I know what you think of him and it makes me feel like you think the same of me, and now I can't tell you anything and it makes me really sad, because you're my best friend. I love you so much it hurts. I don't have many people, Ophelia. You and Eddy are my people. I can't lose you, too. I want to tell you stuff and get your advice. But I just feel like the whole time you are thinking it's going to end badly, and it will be all my own fault."

I wiped the tears from under my eyes with my thumb. Little clumps of makeup floated in the sticky wet of my vision.

"God, I'm sorry, Charlie." Ophelia was almost whispering, looking at me with such love and understanding that it made my heart hurt to think of the weeks of her friendship that I had lost because of this argument. "I love you so much. I do think I've been a bit judgmental, and not completely supportive. But you didn't tell me anything and it was going on for so long and that really, really hurt. That you couldn't—didn't—trust me with it. I know you've got good reason to not trust people, but I thought that with me, it was different."

For the first time I saw it, just how much the secrecy had impacted my two best friends, and I felt sick about it.

"I'm so sorry. I should have told you."

She sniffed. "Yes. You should have. It's OK. But the way you have been about Oscar—I have to say this to you both. Yes, you, too, Eddy. I know you both hate him. You don't get it—he's so nice to me when it's just the two of us. You didn't even give him a chance. Just because he works in finance, you think he must be awful. But he's not. Not everyone has to be an arty Lefty to be a good person, you know."

She was right. We hadn't. I looked at Eddy.

"OK, I'm guilty here, too," he said, holding up his hands. "I'm sorry, Fee. Look, maybe we all need to start afresh. I promise to try to get to know Oscar better."

"Me, too," I said, recovering a little from the emotion of it all. "If you can try very hard to give me a bit of a break about Richard. I know if I could talk to you about it more, you would understand things better."

She looked doubtful for a second, but then a smile spread across her gorgeous face. She got up and came around the table to sit next to me. She pushed her wet face into my neck, and we held each other very tightly, crying and laughing at the same time while Eddy rolled his eyes and lit another cigarette.

"Look at us," Ophelia said. "Crying like drunk girls in a pub on this beautiful summer evening. Let's just forget all of this business, OK? I promise to be open-minded from here onward about Rich . . . your relationship. I have been judgy and I don't like it in myself. And I'm really glad that you are going to try to get to know Oscar better. In fact, I have something I wanted to talk to you about that relates to that. Next month, he's going to France with a few friends and one of them—this lovely guy called Finn—his parents have a villa. It's nothing fancy but Oscar has invited me to go out there for a bit, but said it's only going to work if I bring a friend to keep balance in the group, otherwise it's all these boys that are school friends and little old me. So, I suggested that I bring both of you. There's a spare double room and you could share. I've looked up flights online and a return is pennies. We don't have to pay for accommodation, just car hire as it's in the middle of nowhere and I can get that, or we can split it. If we get a little banger and go for a week or five days, it won't be much each. August in the office is dead and we all have loads of holiday to take . . ."

And so it happened that we were going to go to France, the three of us, the following month. We spent the evening discussing details and getting excited, drinking more and more until the temperature dropped and the cool air caught our skin. We went home, all of us together, and Ophelia slept in my bed with me, like she used to. The next day we booked our flights online over coffee.

Richard emailed me early on the Sunday morning, asking if I was coming over. His message was short, and I could feel that he was less than happy, but nothing could dampen my mood. Feeling lighter than I had in weeks, I packed a bag and caught the Tube down to Covent Garden. Ophelia and Eddy seemed to be genuinely happy in wishing me a lovely Sunday, and it made me feel so good that they did. Everything looked bright and fresh—even the smell of the bins and traffic tasted less bitter in my throat. The Tube was full of Sunday travelers, in pairs or groups, talking and laughing. I even made eye contact with a few people and smiled, a cardinal sin on a weekday.

I practically skipped into the flat.

"You're in a good mood," Richard said, heading into the kitchen without my usual greeting of a kiss at the door. He was clearly not.

"I am," I said. I went to him and kissed him, then put my arms around him and rested my head on his chest, breathing him in. The flat was hot and stuffy despite the windows being open, and he gently leaned back to look at me. I kept my arms around his waist.

"I was disappointed that you didn't come last night. I thought you would have wanted to see me. I'm not going to spend much time here over the next month." I knew by now that when Richard was in a bitter mood like this, I should be as quietly sweet to him as I could be and he'd shake it off. I wasn't being passive, I told myself. Just managing him.

"I know, I'm sorry. It was important to me to spend some time with my housemates. We're actually going away together next month to France. For a week." He let go of me and turned his attention to a loaf of sourdough bread on the counter, cutting a slice for each of us. Something I had learned since moving to London was that the harder the bread was to actually eat, the more it would cost you. I plucked a greasy olive from the plastic Waitrose tub next to him. He didn't look up.

"I'll be in France next month, too. Didn't I tell you that? I'm sure I did. I don't know why—August there is unbearable. You'll hate the heat. Where are you going?"

"We're flying to Béziers. It's an hour or so north from there; I don't know the exact place."

"Béziers." He corrected my pronunciation.

"Is that near your house?"

I knew that his house was somewhere in the south, that he flew to Béziers, and that he would be there for a chunk of August, because he had indeed told me.

"I think you know it is. Well, I don't know where you are going, but my house is about an hour southwest of the airport. But we won't see each other, obviously. You'll be with your friends." The way he said "your friends" was subtle but enough for me to know he was cross I'd not come to him the night before.

"I'm sure I could get away for an afternoon or something, if you wanted." The thought of an afternoon with him in France was so wonderful I could barely let myself imagine it.

"I doubt it will work out. I will be with Elaine."

His mood was so stubborn and dark, I knew there was only one way to get him out of it. He tried to resist initially, saying he was too hot, but I climbed on top of him on the sofa and, braless because of the heat, I slipped my dress off over my head. That quickly persuaded him.

He softened with me after we'd had sex, as I'd known he would, and we spent the Sunday afternoon reading and drinking cold beers. The sheets felt cool when we went to bed. By the evening, the sky had become loaded and dark gray, preparing herself for a night and day of thunderstorms.

"I wish I didn't have to work tomorrow," I said. He opened his arm out and I moved across the bed to him, resting my head on his chest.

"It does seem unfair. Why don't you call in sick and spend the day with me. It's going to rain all day."

So that's what I did.

CHAPTER Fifteen

Even at short notice it was fine for us to take a week off in August, as we knew it would be. It was even encouraged—better to take your holiday when there was no work to be done and most of the publishing industry were offline somewhere between Marseilles and Tuscany.

We'd booked early morning flights from Stansted. Ophelia insisted on paying for a taxi to the airport, which I very much appreciated as we had to check in at 5 A.M., and it would have meant taking the last train and sleeping there.

I'd bought a new black swimming costume, a big wide-brimmed straw hat with a black bow and a few dresses from H&M and Primark. Ophelia had lent me a few of her things for the trip, knowing that I was broke and self-conscious, and not equipped with a wardrobe suitable for the south of France in August. She'd even taken me to get a pedicure with her at one of the nail bars near our house, something I had never done before. I loved sitting next to her in the big chair, chatting and laughing as twenty-four years of callouses were razored from my feet. It was like having new skin. I had not known it was possible to be vain about your feet, but there it was.

I felt so good in my new dress, a dark-green linen smock that came down to my knees, sipping coffee and reading my book next to my best friends, my toenails glistening red in my flip-flops. Things between the three of us were better than they had ever been since we'd ironed out our issues. The love I felt for the two of them was so intense it could feel unwieldy. I didn't know what I had done to deserve them, but I was starting to believe, at last, that I did. Things would be different with these two. We would always be like this. Friendship this strong would last a lifetime.

It turned out that the place where we were staying, a tiny village in the Languedoc region, was more than a two-hour drive from Richard's house, in the opposite direction from the airport. This had left me feeling disappointed and taken away the edge of the excitement I'd felt for the holiday. I had hoped we might get to spend some time together, that once I got to France we would make plans to steal a few hours away, or even a whole night at a little country hotel or something, but it was probably too far. It was a long time to be apart and although I was dreading time away from him less since everything between Ophelia and me had been resolved, I still ached when I thought about the days stretching to weeks without him.

He'd flown the same route, though, I knew that, although he had left a week earlier. I liked thinking about him sitting in this same chair at the gate, waiting for boarding to be called. I'd asked him if he flew first class, but he laughed at that, although he told me later he always booked the extra legroom seat.

Since he'd been gone, he'd called me almost every night, describing the light and how day changed to night, the buzz of the crickets and the shadows of the bats ducking through the sky feasting on mosquitoes. The heat was extreme, and he spent the days inside in the cool stone interior of the old chateau he owned, although he said it was more of a farmhouse. On the nights he didn't call, I'd not hear anything from him, not even an email, but I knew Elaine was there, and that they had friends coming and going. There were lots of expats in the village he lived in, who unlike him, didn't speak a word of French. He found this community oppressive and wished for solitude and to be left well alone, but his celebrity meant they felt some ownership of him, and were overfamiliar and intrusive, dropping by uninvited for cups of coffee or sundowners.

We'd opted not to pay to choose our seats, so we were flung to far ends of the plane, but it was such a short flight we didn't mind. As we broke through the cover of clouds and the blue sky opened up all around us, I marveled at it all. I'd only flown a few times before and hadn't ever had a window seat like I did now. It still seemed like magic to me, to be this high up and to feel so peaceful and quiet. I had my headphones in, and The Shins were playing. I felt like I was in a film. I wouldn't see Richard, but at least I'd feel closer to him.

It was horribly humid and pouring with rain when we landed. The heat hit us like a wave when the plane door opened. Big drops of rain steamed on the tarmac, and we covered our heads with our bags as we dashed into the tiny airport. It was only just 9 A.M., but it felt so much later, as we'd been up for so long. Ophelia had rented a car for us, which she was going to drive as Eddy had never driven abroad and I couldn't drive at all. We shoved our luggage in the boot, and I called shotgun. Eddy stretched out in the back. We'd printed off directions from Google Maps. The rain cooled on us as the air-conditioning kicked in. Ophelia pulled her seat in so that she was almost under the steering wheel. She was so small she could barely see over it.

"Sunglasses, co-pilot," she said, holding out her hand.

We had to circle the car park a few times for Ophelia to get used to the car, but I was amazed by her driving. She was always good at things. To me, the thought of driving a back-to-front car on back-to-front roads seemed to be some kind of superpower, yet, here she was, weaving in and out of the other cars on the motorway, chewing gum like she did it every day of her life. "Always hire private-school girls. They know how to talk to adults," I'd overheard Markus say to Cecile once, and it had stung so much that it had stuck with me. But looking at Ophelia, I had to concede there was some truth in it. Ophelia knew how to "talk to adults."

The drive was made longer by me missing a key exit, but no one minded. Once we'd left the motorway, we took a series of smaller roads winding higher and higher into the countryside. The sun had burned off the clouds and it was a beautiful day. The fields were awash with sunflowers and lavender, and then there were vineyards—miles and miles of vineyards.

"Vin!" Ophelia said every now and again, pointing at them.

"Vin!" we'd say back to her.

Once we got to the village, which Eddy said was more of a hamlet, Ophelia called Oscar and he came on foot to meet us. We stood outside the car, smoking in the shade of the huge poplar trees, taking it all in. There was a little stone bridge with a noisy stream below, clouds of mosquitos rising from the water. All of the houses were quiet and their blue shutters tightly closed to keep the heat out, Ophelia explained. Oscar greeted Ophelia with a kiss. She threw her arms around his neck and he lifted her off the ground, her feet dangling and a sandal falling off, even though he wasn't much taller than her. I'd never seen him be so affectionate with her, and I felt a little pang of sadness in my own heart. He wore swimming shorts that came down to his knees, a baggy T-shirt and flip-flops, and hid his eyes behind big aviator sunglasses. He gave us both a peck on the cheek and apologized in advance for the state they were all in. They'd been up drinking and playing cards until 3 A.M.

I jumped in the back of the car with Eddy, and Oscar took my seat next to Ophelia, directing her up a small side road and past two terra-cotta villas to a big iron gate, which he opened with a key fob.

The house was beautiful. It was an old stone farmhouse with dark-green shutters, set over three floors and nestled against a hill. The basement level opened at the front of the house onto a paved terrace where we parked the car, and it had two bedrooms and a big games room with a table-tennis table. The middle floor, with the kitchen and living room and dining room, opened to the back onto another terrace, which then led out to a turquoise swimming pool with loungers and parasols. From here you could look out onto the valley and the surrounding mountains and forests and vineyards. A spiral staircase at each end of the house took you to the top floor, which had another two bedrooms and a bathroom. That was where our room was.

The house was quiet because the others were still asleep. Oscar went to put on coffee while we put our things in our rooms. I put my swimming costume on under my dress, checking my profile in the mirror and sucking my stomach in as much as I could. I'd covered myself in fake tan the night before and it was streaky on the backs of my thighs, and the tops of my feet were significantly darker than the rest of me, but Ophelia had assured me one dip in the chlorinated water of the pool and it would even itself out.

The inside of the house was what an estate agent might describe as rustic. It smelled deliciously of old woodsmoke from the fireplaces. It wasn't grand like Ophelia's chalet in Switzerland, but it was lovely and felt homey. I much preferred it. There were colorful oil paintings of jazz musicians hung on nails without frames, and piles of books and interior-design magazines dating back more than a decade. The sofas sagged and were covered with a multitude of brightly colored mismatched throws and pillows. Old farming scythes and forks and wagon wheels, probably found in the surrounding grounds, framed the doorways.

On the back terrace, Ophelia was perched on a white plastic garden chair, tearing apart a croissant. She was already in her bikini and had a big white cotton shirt over her shoulders that I'd never seen before. Oscar had laid out more croissants and chunks of ice-cold cantaloupe and a bowl of fat, orange apricots alongside two cafetières of coffee and a box of little brown sugar cubes. I was surprised by him. Perhaps I had been quick to judge. I made a point of thanking him warmly, and Ophelia gave me a look that said, *Thank you.*

After breakfast, Ophelia and Oscar disappeared to his room and Eddy and I headed to the pool. The sunlight cracked into discs and rippled on the surface of the water, which was a shade paler than the blue of the sky. It would be too hot to be in the sun soon. We sat on the side of the pool with our legs hanging in the cool water, then slipped down and submerged ourselves into the quiet of it. When we came up for air, we laughed out loud at how utterly gorgeous everything was and how great the week was going to be.

I was sitting in the shade of a parasol on my sun lounger reading an early Martin Amis novel that Richard had lent me, when the first of the group arose. My hair had almost dried in the heat and I'd pushed my fringe to the side as there was no way it would behave in this weather. Eddy was snoozing next to me, headphones on with his hands resting on his chest, unafraid of the sun. I could hear the treble of John Grant coming through them, an album called *Queen of Denmark* that he was obsessed by and that we had listened to twice in the car from the airport.

"Tiny French beer?"

Sunblind, I couldn't make out any details of the man standing over me, but he placed a cold bottle in my hand. He pulled a lounger next to me with a scrape and sat on the edge of it.

"I'm Finn. This is my parents' place. Welcome!"

Finn was so good-looking that he could have been an actor. That was my first thought. He had the kind of body that clothes seemed to be designed for. He had a beautiful tan, the kind I could only ever dream of, and I'd guess he spent a fair amount of his time doing something that involved exercise. He was wearing navy-blue swimming shorts that sat neatly against his body. Stubble shadowed his jawline. There was a fine silver chain around his neck. He popped his Ray-Ban Wayfarers onto his head, pushing his perfectly wavy brown hair back as he did, and I noticed then that he had stunning pale-blue eyes. He opened his beer. I sat up, suddenly self-conscious. He didn't speak like Oscar, or Ophelia, or Eddy. There was a looseness to the end of his words that reminded me of the original East Londoners who drank in the Wetherspoons near our house.

"Thank you. Sorry, I was on another planet. I'm Charlie." I moved my arm quickly across my waist to cover my stomach, which was bloated from the coffee and the flight. Eddy was still fast asleep, oblivious.

"Sorry we weren't awake to greet you. We got a bit carried away last night. Hence, hair of the dog."

"Don't worry about it. Thanks for having me. Us. This place is amazing."

"It's great, isn't it. My parents bought it before I was born so I've been coming here a few times a year my whole life. It's a lot of upkeep because it's so old. I actually prefer it here in May or September. It's too hot at the moment. I'm driving to the supermarket to get some stuff for lunch before everything closes. Do you fancy a trip or are you too engrossed in your book?"

I went back to my room to change into a camisole top and some cut-off denim shorts I'd been wearing since my first year of university. When I came back downstairs, Finn, now in a T-shirt and running shorts, was resting his hands on the shoulders of someone called Ciaron, who was on the sofa sipping a soluble aspirin for his hangover.

"Right, last call. OK, come on, Charlie." He said my name like he'd known me for years rather than ten minutes.

The seats of the car burned against the backs of my thighs. It was an old red Citroën that belonged to Finn's parents and the air-conditioning wasn't great, so we opened our windows and I leaned into the cool air as he drove the winding hill roads out of the village. A cassette tape was playing *Graceland* by Paul Simon. I watched his hand move from the gear stick to the steering wheel and felt something I wasn't sure I liked. I was drawn to this man, in the part of me that I kept for Richard.

We walked around the supermarket picking out different colors and shapes of tomatoes, unfamiliar cheeses, pear-shaped glass bottles of Orangina, crates of beer and bottles of red and rosé wine. Finn confidently ordered steaks and cuts of meat from the deli counter in French, and I was quietly impressed. Like Ophelia, he had an air of confidence like the world was just there, waiting for him to come and interact with it. For me it felt the opposite, like I was intruding in the world, always waiting to be identified as an imposter and dragged off to where I really belonged.

Before we went to the queue, Finn grabbed five big bags of ice and a box of lemon ice lollies from the freezer. At the till, I tried to give him a handful of euros, but he waved me away, saying I was a guest and this one was on him. Everyone always seemed to have more money than me. The price of the shop was close to my budget for the whole holiday.

He put the meat and cheeses into silver-lined bags with the ice in the boot of the car and threw me an ice lolly. The heat inside the car was intense and it melted faster than I could eat it, sticky, sugary lemon dripping down my fingers and wrist.

Finn said we should stop in town and get bread because it was better from the bakery than the supermarket. We parked up in the shade of plane trees with their paint-by-numbers bark in a sleepy town a few miles from the villa. Just a few cafés and bars were open, bright plastic awnings still in the absent breeze. We walked a little way, Finn pointing out where the market was on Wednesdays and Sundays, the best place for ice creams. At the bakery, which was just about to close, he ordered bread in French, chatting with the young girl who worked there as if they were old friends. I noticed her looking me up and down, wondering how it was that someone as ordinary as me was with someone who looked like Finn.

We stopped for a beer on the way back to the car, and I went to the little *tabac* to buy skinny French cigarettes for Ophelia and me. When I joined Finn at the table, he toasted my glass with his and we took long sips of the ice-cold beer. It was delicious in the way beer sometimes is in the heat, on holiday in beautiful places, with new people.

"So you do the whole book thing with Ophelia? Publishing or PR, or whatever?"

"Publishing, yes. We work together. Although Ophelia isn't in PR with me, she's in editorial. What about you?"

"I'm an architect. Or more precisely I'm training to be an architect."

"I thought you were a banker like Oscar."

"Well, first, Oscar isn't a banker. He's a broker. And secondly, nope. Never had an interest in finance. Oscar was in the year below me at school. Our parents are friends; we grew up on the same street. I've always been set on being an architect. It's long training but I love it."

"What kind of buildings do you design?" This was the most intelligent question I could think of and I recoiled internally in embarrassment once I'd said it.

"I'm working at my dad's firm, so it's mostly private houses. Y'know, extensions, loft conversions, but for really rich people, so it's these mad houses. Sometimes we design homes from scratch. But not tower blocks, or amphitheaters. If you see what I mean."

"You live in London?"

"I do. Peckham Rye. My family live in Richmond—that's where Oscar and I grew up. You?"

"I live with Ophelia and Eddy."

"Ah, yeah, I think I knew that. East, right?"

"Stoke Newington."

He nodded at me, dragging on a cigarette, and playing with the condensation on his glass.

"Are you from London?"

"No, Hampshire. Near the coast. I'm not from the same world as Ophelia and Eddy. I grew up in a three-bedroom semi and went to a comprehensive school. And I didn't go to Oxford or Cambridge." I didn't know why I was saying this, why it was so important that I separated myself from them. Whenever I met someone who I thought might have come from a background like mine, I had to point out just how different I was from my beautiful, clever, privileged friends, as if that shared background might offer a connection that would otherwise be lost. I had judged Finn entirely by the way he spoke, but it occurred to me that if he had grown up on the same street as Oscar, it was unlikely to have been in a three-bedroom ex-council house.

"We have that in common. I went to Edinburgh."

"Sussex."

"Well, we both still went to excellent unis. So, Charlie, from the three-bed semi, what do you think of this little corner of France so far? I'm glad you're here. It was getting a little boring with just those two for company." His leg was touching mine under the table, but I couldn't tell if it was deliberate or not.

"Seven whole days. I'm happy to be here."

"Did you go in the pool yet? As soon as we get back and I get this unloaded, I'm in. Fuck. It's so hot. We'd better get going before the meat cooks itself in the car."

He left a ten-euro note under his glass. As we walked back to the car, his hand guided me along at the small of my back. I was flirting with him, I realized. Tragically, poorly flirting with him. Resting against my guilt, supporting it, was playfulness, and a stirring of excitement. There was no harm in flirting, after all. It's not like I could cheat on Richard. We'd never talked about me and anyone else. I didn't know if he still slept with Elaine. I tried very, very hard to never think about it. But I also presumed that I was the only other person for him, and I guessed he had made the same presumption of me.

When we got back to the house, the ice had melted but the food was cool and not ruined. Oscar and Ophelia had reappeared, and we pulled the table-tennis table outside into the shade of the front terrace, drinking little bottles of French beer and smoking endless cigarettes. At around 4 P.M., we went back to the pool to swim and read and relax. Finn brought out a pack of cards, but no one else wanted to play, so he and I played round after round of Shithead, keeping score in a notebook with a little stub of pencil.

"You look so French in that hat and black swimsuit and big sunglasses. Are you sure you're not French?" Finn was looking at me playfully.

Eddy overheard this and rolled his eyes.

"We'll never hear the end of that. Usually she just gets told she looks Irish."

"In the winter I wear a black turtleneck and a beret. I read only existentialist poetry in cafés. I drink only espresso. And I smoke only Vogues."

"Those little cigarettes do look good on you."

I knew that the feeling I got from his compliments was nicer than it should have been, but there is nothing like being told you look French to gladden the heart.

We played cards late into the evening. The rest of the group went to the house and made dinner. I felt like I'd known Finn for years, not a single day. When we went to bed that night, I realized I'd neither heard from Richard nor missed hearing from him.

"Finn is hot for you, Charlie," Eddy said to me as we lay in our huge brass bed that night, drunk on sunshine and beer. A little fan blew the hot air sadly and noisily around the room. "You should go there. He is one of the most beautiful men I have ever seen in real life."

"That's never going to happen. I'm not interested, even if he was interested in me, which he isn't."

"You mean, you're in love with Richard?"

"Yes. I am in love with Richard. Obviously."

"Well, I don't think that should stop you from having hot holiday sex with Finn. Sex doesn't have to be love."

"I know that! Anyway, even if he did like me, it just wouldn't feel right. I'm with Richard."

"Charlie, he's married. I'm not going to get on at you about that, but I don't think you need to keep yourself all for him. Has he asked you to? That wouldn't really be fair."

"We've never talked about it. It's unsaid. If I really wanted to, I would sleep with someone else. But I don't."

Eddy sighed. I wasn't getting anything past him.

"He is gorgeous, though, isn't he." I giggled.

"He really is. I want to know what's in those little swim shorts. Please. Do it. Just for me."

I was so excited for what the next day would bring, and it was so hot in our room, that I couldn't fall asleep for a long time. But when I did, I slept deeply and dreamlessly.

The next couple of days were much like the first. I spent a lot of my time with Finn, and we found a rapport that was both playful and tactile. We finished our drinks at the same time and wanted snacks at the same time. He called me French Girl, and threw me in the pool more than once. We played table tennis and cards and even briefly Scrabble. We did supermarket and bakery runs together, stopping off at places along the way. He asked me if I was single, and I told him it was complicated. I asked him if he was single and he told me he was, and that it was uncomplicated.

On Tuesday, we decided to go wine tasting at a nearby vineyard and all piled into the two cars. It was the first time Ophelia, Eddy and I had been alone since we'd arrived on the Saturday and there was much to be discussed. Eddy and I were pleasantly surprised by Oscar, who was much sweeter than we had given him credit for. Ophelia was delighted by this. Their relationship was becoming serious, and she was happy. Secretly, Eddy and I had talked a lot about how we couldn't see what she saw in him. He was skinny and small, and his unapologetically pompous accent still made me want to laugh out loud, but at least he wasn't being nasty to her anymore. I was happy for her, even if I didn't understand it, and I hoped she felt the same for me about Richard.

The conversation quickly switched to "what was going on" with me and Finn.

"Nothing! I promise you! Absolutely nothing! It's not like that." It was exactly like that, but I'd been very careful to make sure that I'd not crossed any lines.

"I knew you'd get along, Charlie! He's great. I love Finn. By far my favorite of Oscar's friends. He's single, you know, and not stuck on any exes or anything. Architect in training, lives in London, twenty-seven, he couldn't be more perfect for you." Ophelia had taken it too far, veered into a place where I knew exactly what she was really saying, and it was, *He's not an older married man, he's age-appropriate and available and we want you to be with him instead of Richard.* She must have seen my thoughts flit across my face. "I didn't mean . . . Shit. Sorry, Charlie. He's just so gorgeous and I love seeing you happy and messing about with him. You've laughed more in the last few days than you have in a while."

"I know," I said, eyes fixed out of the window. I reached a hand across and squeezed her thigh to let her know that it was OK, and she squeezed my hand back.

Wine tasting was fun, but it was oppressively hot. Ciaron, who was paler even than me, got sunstroke and was sick in a hedge, so Finn and Oscar took him back to the house. Ophelia, Eddy and I went on to a wild swimming spot we'd read about in a guidebook at the house. We parked up and walked downhill to a cove beside a beautiful, clear river that was flowing slowly. A group of French families were together with their children a little way along, set up with blankets and towels and tents for the youngest ones. We slipped off our shoes and waded into the cool water. The stones were smooth under our feet. An old viaduct further upstream bridged the river with its arches pressing into the water like stilts.

"This is like a dream," I said to my friends.

I'd been in Finn's company solidly for three days and without him around, I missed him. As I floated in the water, listening to the sounds of the world below the surface, I thought of Richard and wondered where he was in that moment, if he was nearby. If he was thinking about me. He'd tried to call the night before, but I'd not had my phone when he rang. I'd emailed him to say he could call tonight, and he had replied that he was looking forward to it. I missed him, that was true, but there was a part of me that was so happy in this little group, in this place, that I didn't want to be taken out of it by the sad reality of my weird relationship. Being here was giving me some clarity. Even if I wouldn't admit it, our relationship was impossible to explain to anyone because it made very little sense when you tried.

After our swim, Ophelia and I lay on the sand, drying again in minutes. The heat was gentler now the worst of the day's sun had passed. Eddy was still in the water, talking to a young guy about our age.

"I think Oscar might be the one," Ophelia said to me, leaning on her side, her head resting in her hand. "I've never felt like this about anyone. I've always had this feeling about him, even since uni."

I sat up to give her my full attention. "That's great, Fee. I'm really happy for you." I was, but I also felt suddenly very sad. "You seem very happy. I'm glad things are working out."

She smiled at me. Her left canine always poked out a little when she smiled closed-mouthed.

"Do you think that's how it is? I mean, I know it's really romcom. But that there is a 'one'?"

"I don't know. Maybe." I paused, thinking. "For some people, sure there is. But look at my dad. He was married, then divorced, then married and widowed, and now he's got another partner. If there's only 'one,' I feel sad for him and for the other partners that weren't his 'one.' Maybe he was their 'one,' even if they weren't his." I thought for a moment before I said anything else. "And I mean, with Richard. He has been married to Elaine for so long, but then he has me, as well. And he was married before her. So, is Elaine his 'one,' and, if so, does that make me his 'two'? Because if I am completely honest, which I said I would be with you, I can't imagine for a second being with anyone else. I can't imagine loving anyone else. I can't imagine what I would move on to after him, if it ended."

It was the most honest I had ever been about him, and it felt a little less heavy in my chest once I'd said this truth out loud to my friend. Ophelia placed a hand on mine in that sweet, kind way that she had about her. "I hope you get everything you want, Charlie. I really do. And if he is what you really want, then I hope that you get him as fully as you want him. I've loved the last few days, though, seeing you so happy and at ease with Finn. Which you have been. I don't know if it's him, or this place, or what it is, but you seem . . . you seem easy in yourself."

I looked out at Eddy and thought about what Ophelia was saying. I had felt free and happy the last few days, but I was on holiday—of course I had.

"He has made me feel more, I don't know . . . normal. He's great and we obviously get on very well. But that's OK, isn't it, to be friends?"

"I don't think he is focused on friendship, honey. He told Oscar he likes you."

"He did? When? What did he say?"

Ophelia rolled onto her back and laughed. "I knew you'd like that! I don't exactly know what was said, but enough to know he really likes you."

I lay back down. "I just don't think it would feel good. I'd feel guilty. We've never talked about what the rules are, or if there are any rules, but I know Richard wouldn't like it if I was sleeping with someone else any more than I'd like it if he was sleeping with someone else. Other than his wife," I added quickly, lightly, with a little laugh, just to stress I knew this was both ridiculous and silly. I'd never been able to be lighthearted about my relationship with Richard, and it felt good when Ophelia laughed with me.

Ciaron was in bed when we got back, and Finn and Oscar took it in turns to take him cool compresses and iced drinks. Ophelia prepared a meal for everyone, salads and chicken marinated in lemon and thyme cooked on the BBQ until it was crisp and charred at the edges, and we drank rosé until we were heady with it. At 10 P.M. on the dot, my phone vibrated on the table and I saw Richard's initials. Finn looked at my phone but tried not to let on he had, lighting a cigarette and asking anyone if they wanted anything from the fridge. I took my cigarettes and lighter and excused myself, heading down the hill and away from the house.

"Hello, Richard."

"Hello, Charlie. I've missed your voice. I've missed you. Funny to think we're in the same hot evening in France, isn't it? I almost can't imagine you here, out of London."

We talked for about half an hour. I told him a little about what we'd been doing, careful not to mention Finn in more than passing, which was hard because I wanted to talk about him. Richard had had some friends out for the weekend and was delighted they had left. He was looking forward to getting back to England, and I couldn't think of anything worse. He was sick of the heat, and sick of Elaine. Everything she said and did was grating on him. He'd never spoken about her this much to me, and, although in part I delighted in how awful she was and how miserable she was making him, I found myself longing to get back to the group and away from his domestic situation. He was lifting the corners of the happy and carefree mood I had worn like a cloak for the last few days, and I didn't want him to.

When I got back to the house, everyone was playing cards. Ciaron had emerged and was sipping iced water, looking very sunburnt.

"Hello, you," said Finn, moving up to make room and dealing me into the game. Then he whispered, "Was that who makes things complicated for you?"

"Mmmhmm." I tried to be coy. "Don't ask."

We carried on drinking and playing until everyone but us had peeled away to bed.

"Dip?" suggested Finn. We were quite drunk.

"Now?"

"Come on. It's beautiful in there at night."

The water did feel amazing. I'd let myself get a little burnt and for the first time in my life I had tan lines, something Ophelia and Eddy had fallen about with laughter at when I'd told them earlier. I had no idea why it was funny.

Finn and I trod water, moving in circles around each other, giggling and splashing each other like a couple of teenagers. He caught my hand and pulled me over to him. He lifted my legs around his waist and I looped my ankles together and locked my arms around his neck. It felt electric being this close to him and when he kissed me, I kissed him back before I'd really thought about it. He was gentle with me, more so than I'd expected. His mouth felt so different from Richard's. He pulled away.

"This isn't just a holiday thing for me, you know. I want to see you when we're back in London."

I was taken aback by this. But then, that was what he would say, I thought. I didn't move away from him, though. The lights below the water reflected up on his lovely face.

"Finn, I don't know what I'm doing. I can't—I can't sleep with you."

"Some married guy? Is that right?"

"I'm not going to talk about my relationship with you." In some way I knew that I was imitating Richard when he had said all those months back that he wouldn't talk to me about his marriage.

"OK, I get it. I thought maybe something was going on between us. Did I misread things? I mean, you're in my pool, with your legs wrapped around me, so I can't have totally misread things." He said it with a smile, just teasing, not accusatory. Why was I still stuck to him like this? He felt so good. He liked me, this gorgeous, available, smart human being wanted me. He kissed me again and I kissed him back in reply. He pulled me closer into him and I could feel that he was enjoying it, and I knew I was, too. But he didn't push things further. We must have been out there for a while, because my fingers were pruning.

"I'd better get to bed," I said, and he moaned, moving his mouth to my neck, scooping my wet hair out of the way. I uncoiled myself from him.

"Are you sure you won't sleep in my room?" he asked. I shook my head. When we got out, he wrapped me in his towel and we walked back to the house. The lamps in the living room were on and we moved silently together to close up the house for the night. He brought me a glass of water. His room was on the bottom level, the master with an ensuite. His parents' room.

"You know where I am if you change your mind."

"I won't."

"That's OK, too."

I kissed him good night for that.

Eddy didn't stir when I got into bed. I thought about going down to Finn, but something was stopping me. I thought back to Richard and the flat, to his bed, to being in his bed. I thought of him on his sofa in his reading glasses, studying some dusty old book, foot tapping along to a record. I thought of the coconut smell of his hair and how he'd said he missed me. I fell asleep somewhere between all of those thoughts and woke to him calling me. It was morning—10 A.M. according to the little bedside alarm clock.

"Charlie? Good God, are you still asleep? Look. Get ready. I'm coming to pick you up. I'll be there in about an hour. I'll call when I'm in the village and you can walk and meet me. I need to see you. I'm sure you can make your usual excuses."

CHAPTER
Sixteen

Ophelia was in the kitchen making breakfast with Oscar and Eddy when I came down. She was wearing one of Oscar's shirts open over a different bikini than the one she'd been wearing the day before. I was dressed in a white cotton dress and flip-flops. I'd got ready as quickly as I could, dreading this moment and telling her what I was doing, knowing it was probably wrong. But what choice did I have? He was already on his way when he'd called. He needed to see me—needed to. I couldn't say no.

"Fee, can I speak to you for a second?"

She looked concerned and followed me into the living room. Oscar and Eddy didn't seem to notice me at all, deep in discussion about the process of making coffee.

"Richard called and he wants to take me out for the day. He's on his way to collect me now. In fact, I think he's maybe already here. You don't mind, do you?"

She looked hurt and I hated it. "But we're going to the market today, and then for lunch and kayaking—we've been looking forward to it all week."

"I know, I know. But he just called, and he is already on his way. I didn't plan this. I'll be back this evening. Fee, I've not seen him in weeks and I really miss him. Can you explain to Eddy and make excuses?"

"What about Finn? I thought last night . . . He told Oscar you two had kissed. What's going on, Charlie?"

I was mortified. Of course he had told Oscar.

"I was drunk, and he kissed me, is more how that went." I felt myself getting defensive and I wasn't sure why. My phone vibrated in my tote bag. I took it out and saw that little *RA* that usually stoked such happiness in me. Ophelia looked at it and crossed her tanned arms in front of her body defiantly, shutting down the doors on her sweetness.

"Do what you want, Charlie. See you later."

She walked off back to the kitchen. I wanted to go after her, but I knew she was right to be angry and I didn't want the confrontation, to see her angry at me, or to have to face Finn and what had happened the night before. So, instead, I hurried out of the house and down the hill to the village. I ran away.

Richard was waiting for me, leaning against his car, which was an old khaki-green Jeep that was in even more of a state than his car at home. He was wearing a panama hat, tennis shoes, a linen jacket and trousers, and a plain T-shirt, looking like he had just walked off a film set. He was more tanned than I'd ever seen him, and for the first time, relaxed around me outside of the confines of the flat. I felt a flood of joy rush through me, momentarily washing away the dread that the conflict with Ophelia had brought. He kissed me so hard his hat fell off. The thought of Finn's mouth intruded, making me feel sick with guilt.

"Hello, Charlie," he said as he put me down.

"Hello, Richard. You look like Cary Grant." He smiled and tipped his hat to me.

There was a place he wanted to take me for lunch. A tiny restaurant that tourists didn't know about in a village about an hour away. No one would recognize us there. I didn't tell Richard about the bad feeling with Ophelia, I didn't want it to seep through the boundary of my life with him, this place that felt so good again now that we were back together. I felt terrible for the thoughts I'd had about him, about us, in the previous few days. Now that I was back with him by my side, it was clear how little it mattered that I couldn't explain this situation to anyone else. Everything made sense again.

I did send Ophelia a text, because I felt horrible about any bad feeling with anyone, let alone her.

> I'm sorry if I've upset you. I couldn't really say no when he was almost at the house to pick me up. I didn't plan for this to happen. I'll make it up to you and Eddy. xx

On the drive we listened to music, and I talked about the holiday. He had been in France for nearly two weeks now. They had had a steady stream of visitors and the heat was starting to feel intolerable. He was keen to get back to work. While he'd been away, we'd had the news that *Altitude at Sea* had been longlisted for the Booker Prize and we'd not really spoken about it yet. He was dubious about it, as the same writer rarely won twice. He was sure it wouldn't win, but he didn't want to deal with the humiliation of being dropped at the shortlist. He was getting more nervous, I could tell, although this just manifested as frustration at various people not doing their jobs correctly, Cecile included.

The sky grew overcast the longer we drove, and the air felt thready with the threat of thunderstorms. We parked on a poplar-lined road and walked up a steep hill into a quiet village with narrow streets, which seemed to weave into a tight web. No cars would have been able to get through—it must be very old, older than any other place I'd seen while I'd been here. Many windows and doors were left wide open, but we didn't see a single soul. A cat stalked past us, flopping in the dust as we approached, fur waxy and dirty. I stopped to rub its belly, but Richard hurried me on.

By this point the sky was so dark that the light had taken on an eerie quality that felt too dark for the time of day. As the first drops of rain fell and thunder rumbled aggressively in the distance, echoing off the mountains, Richard ushered me through the door of a small restaurant that was so well hidden in the wall that it was a wonder anyone ever found it.

We were the only customers other than two elderly gentlemen who sat in a corner. The tables had red-and-white-checked tablecloths and little glass milk bottles with red carnations. The walls were plastered roughly and painted white with old watercolors and newspaper articles and reviews framed and hanging at odd intervals about the place. It was charming, I agreed. Richard pulled out a chair for me like we were on some old-fashioned date. It was a while before anyone who worked there appeared. The other couple didn't say a word to each other; they just sat in silence, eating soup.

"The food here is second to none. I've been coming here for twenty years and never found a better meal in all of France, let alone the UK."

The owner eventually appeared from the back through saloon doors and greeted Richard as an old friend. He was about Richard's age and had an enormous belly and a thatch of dandruffy white hair. They spoke in French, so I couldn't really understand what was being said.

"This is my friend, Charlie."

I understood that much. The man kissed my hand and then carried on speaking to Richard about, as far as I could tell, food and wine. We were to eat whatever the chef prepared for us, paired with wines chosen by him. This made me nervous, but I didn't want to show Richard that I was too fussy about food for such an arrangement.

It was so odd, sitting at a table in a restaurant with him like this. So odd in fact that I found it hard to relax. Ophelia hadn't replied to my text and my skin was sunburnt and itchy on the wicker chair. I took a big gulp of my wine to try to relax, but it went straight to my head. I'd not eaten since the night before. We talked about the restaurant, mostly, and the meals he'd eaten there over the years. How France had changed and how it had stayed the same.

The food, as it turned out, was incredible, and I had the best meal of my life. Sweet baby artichokes, rabbit cooked with dark-brown lentils and tomatoes, a burnt crème brûlée, all served on mismatched china plates and eaten with mismatched cutlery. The chef came out at the end of the meal but again they spoke in French, so I didn't really understand much of what was said, beyond the fact that the food had been brilliant and the chef was delighted to be complimented. We had coffee and Richard paid the bill.

It was almost 3 P.M. and the sun had broken through the clouds. Everything outside was fresh and still a little damp; all of the plants looked a little greener, the houses with their half-moon terra-cotta tiles a little redder, and the sky a little bluer. Richard collected a blanket from the boot of the Jeep and we headed downhill to the river. We walked alongside it for about half a mile out of the village to a secluded grassy patch with trees. We said little, full and feeling the warming effects of the food and wine. We lay down next to each other on the blanket. It was quiet except for the sound of the water below us. Richard perched his hat forward on his nose, his arm bent behind his head as a pillow.

"I didn't expect to see you, let alone to be with you like this. In public."

"I thought you'd be happy about it," he said, not moving. I lay my head down on the blanket, facing him.

"I did. I do. It's just unexpected. You are usually so worried about us being seen."

"Too worried, probably. I don't know why. Out here it is so different from the situation in London. I feel on show there, in a way I don't here."

"I thought it was because of Elaine."

"It is a bit of that, too. I don't want her to be humiliated. But maybe I worry about that more than I need to. She's a grown woman, more than grown really. She has her own life and her own secrets, and I don't interfere. To be completely honest with you, she has been hateful company the last few weeks. In private, that is—when we've had people stay, she has been charming. She's like that. She can switch it on and off when she wants to—I find it to be an extremely unattractive quality, such falseness that you can change your mood to suit the room."

Because he never really talked about her, and I was so curious, I said nothing, hoping he'd say more.

"You're not at all like that, though, Charlie. You are so purely yourself. It's like you have no exterior. I see all of you, all of the time. I can read your mood by the way you walk on any given day, the way you hold your head. It's enchanting and quite the opposite of her."

His words had several effects on me at once. I was so flattered to be thought of by him at all that I wanted to ask him to marry me on the spot. I was also surprised by this interpretation of me, which I saw as being so untrue that I wanted to tell him that he was wrong. But I was so enamored with the idea of being the poetical person he imagined me to be that I couldn't think about much else. For some reason I said—

"Have you fallen out with her? Is that why you called and we've had this day together?"

He lifted his hat off his eyes, but he didn't look at me. "We have fallen out. But that merely prompted me to do what I wanted to do, what I have wanted to do since you have been in France, which is to call you and come and get you, and to take you to a place that I love, that I wanted you to see. Things aren't as black and white as you want them to be, Charlie. A marriage is not just two people who love each other and live their lives intertwined. That is a version of marriage, and I know what you grew up with. But marriages can look very different. Reasons for staying together can be complicated, too complicated to explain to anyone outside of the marriage. My marriage does not lessen the connection that I have with you. The two things exist in very different spaces. You must know that I love you."

I kissed him, then. He had told me what I wanted to hear more than anything else in the world. I rested my head on his chest as he dozed in the shade of the tree, breathing him in, thinking that no matter what was to come, this was a moment I would remember and hold dear to me for the rest of my life.

I let him rest for a little while, but, as much as I wanted the day to last forever, I knew that I needed to get back. Ophelia had sent a text saying that dinner would be at eight, but there were no kisses or pleasantries. It's not like we could spend the night together and I wanted to make good with her and Eddy. Finn was another matter, and not one that I had the headspace for out here with Richard.

He insisted we made a stop before we left, at a *brocante* in the village he said I'd love. He was right. It was like a cave, filled to the rafters with antiques. Nesting tables, coffee tables, side tables and dining tables were stacked on top of each other with enamel and ceramic jugs and bowls. There were old wooden wine boxes filled to the brim with bone-handled knives and forks, and the open drawers of mahogany dressers were overflowing with fabric napkins with red stripes. Street signs and house numbers all in blue were piled against mirrors of varying decay and framed, yellowed embroideries, and vases and plates of all shapes and sizes were nestled among all the crates and boxes, so you had to watch your step not to kick anything over. In one dark corner of the shop was a stunning winged chair, upholstered in the palest pink satin. I took a seat.

"The perfect reading chair," I said.

"It suits you." He looked at me for a long time, almost smiling, almost something else.

We bought bottles of water from a café and downed them, the lunchtime wine making us suddenly very thirsty.

"I'm going to see some friends this evening, not too far from you. I was going to go after I dropped you off, but I'd like you to come with me, to meet them. Would you like that, Charlie?"

The thought of being with Richard's friends, with him, sounded wonderful. It was still hours until dinner. What harm could it do? *This could be the day that changes everything,* I thought to myself. *Maybe. Just maybe.* I told him I had to be back for 8 P.M. and he said that was easy, no problem.

We drove for a while in what seemed to be the same direction as the villa, but then headed west when I was sure we were further east, but I didn't question him.

"Who are the friends?" I asked, trying to sound breezy. I had texted Ophelia, telling her I'd be back in time, and she'd replied with a single *x,* which felt like progress. Eddy had then texted me to ensure that I would indeed be back by then.

"Old friends. Lewis Chalk and his husband, Tim, who I don't know as well. Lewis—Chalky—is a director; he works in the theater mostly these days, but he did a lot of films in the nineties. I've known him since I was in my early twenties, even before my first book came out. They have a rather luxurious villa. Though it isn't my taste."

I knew well who Lewis Chalk was—he was very famous. He had directed the film adaptation of *The Road Goes Only Back* in the early nineties. It had been a huge success and even been nominated for an Oscar for best screenplay.

"Are you not worried that they'll tell Elaine?"

"Tell Elaine what?" he snapped. I wished that I could unsay her name. "Anyway, I warn you now. Chalky is an alcoholic. High-functioning, but a mess."

It was a very elaborate and expensive modern villa hidden in the forest-covered Pyrenees. Huge black iron gates opened slowly as we approached. Chalky and Tim were walking through the gardens toward us as we arrived. I was feeling typically self-conscious, which wasn't helped by the look of surprise on their faces when they saw me. I felt very uncomfortable as they took turns to embrace Richard, sharing a glance between them as they did.

"I hope you don't mind, but I've bought my friend, Charlie. We've been spending the day together, as we both happened to be in the area at the same time. Charlie, this is Chalky and this is Tim."

I kissed them both on each cheek, thanking them for having me, saying I wouldn't be staying long as I had to meet my friends for dinner in a few hours. When I told them where, they looked a little confused and checked the time on their expensive wristwatches.

"You'd need to leave now to get there for eight, dear girl—are you not familiar with the area?"

I looked at Richard, but he didn't meet my eye.

"We'll have a glass of wine, then I'll drop you off. You won't be late."

We walked through the house, which was all marble and white and designed with features that were meant to feel older. There was a terrace at the back, which overlooked a stunning turquoise swimming pool, surrounded by perfectly manicured trees. Shocking-pink oleander was in full bloom, framing the view perfectly. Chalky poured sparkling wine and we toasted our glasses. I noticed Chalky and Tim catch each other's eye a few times, no doubt questioning who on earth I was and what the hell was happening. Chalky was a similar age to Richard, but Tim was younger. They were both in much better shape than Richard, although nowhere near as handsome. They were so tanned and sun-damaged that they looked like a pair of walnuts.

"So, Charlie, what brings you to France?"

I explained that I was on holiday with friends, just for a week.

"And what is it that you do?"

Richard jumped in on this one, sensing that I wasn't sure what I could and couldn't say.

"Charlie works at Winden & Shane. She's a very talented publicist. She's working on the book."

We were seated around a table, Richard and I on one side. He took my hand in his, which was such a surprise that I jumped. We talked a little about the book, about London in the nineties, and I loosened up with the wine. Chalky went inside to get a packet of cigarettes and we all smoked them. They were such interesting people. Tim was an actor and I'd seen several of his films, once I'd placed him. They kept mentioning people by their first names, telling stories of hedonism and madness and creativity. Richard would clarify who they were talking about by confirming the surname to be that of someone equally or more famous.

As well as *The Road Goes Only Back,* another of Richard's books, *Little Blood,* had also been adapted into a feature film by Chalky. It had dominated Cannes and Sundance that year and been a big box-office hit even as an indie. He had never said much to me about this era of his life and I loved hearing him talk about it. I was having a lovely time, but the anxiety of getting back to the villa and my friends was rising. Richard didn't look like he was going anywhere and was on his third glass of wine. With all we had drunk at lunch, I was surprised he could stand.

"Richard, I'm really sorry, but I have to get back. I told them I'd be back for eight."

"Nonsense," said Chalky. "Make your excuses. You must stay. We've got a room made up and ready for the both of you. Richard can't drive now anyway. It's well over an hour away."

I panicked, which wasn't a good feeling as my brain was working sluggishly from all the wine and food and sun.

"I really do have to get back. Do you have a number for a taxi?"

"Darling, you can't get a taxi around here. It isn't London. Relax, call your friends and tell them you'll be back first thing. I'll drive you myself in the morning if you need a lift."

I felt suddenly trapped, here in the mountains, caught between two worlds—my life with Richard, which had expanded tenfold in the last twelve hours, and my life with my friends, where I was a twenty-something publicist who owned nothing much bigger than a chest of drawers from Ikea. I wanted to stay with these important people and the man I loved, experiencing this other world I'd never imagined I could be a part of—not even in my wildest fantasies—but I knew that Ophelia would be furious if I didn't come back for a whole night. I wanted to stay and I wanted to be back with her and Eddy, and I wanted the choice to be mine. I had nothing with me, no toothbrush, no medication. But there was absolutely nothing I could do about it. If I couldn't get Richard to drive me, and there were no taxis, then I couldn't get back. I looked at him, imploring him with my eyes, but he either didn't notice, or ignored it.

"Come on, Charlie, it's just one night. I really shouldn't drive. I haven't kept track of what I've had to drink today. I'm sure your friends will understand."

I went back into the house to call them, finding a sitting room with a long white leather sofa and closing the door for privacy. They didn't understand, which I knew they wouldn't. Ophelia answered her phone after just one ring and from her tone I could tell that she knew why I was calling before I'd said a word. She was cooking and I could hear music playing and laughter. She didn't want to hear my reasons and simply said she'd see me tomorrow, that she couldn't talk as she was about to serve up. I'd not even realized it was after eight.

My phone buzzed. A text from Eddy.

Leave it for this evening x

I tried to call him but it went to answerphone after two rings.

Can't talk. Having supper. See you tomorrow

I hadn't intended for this to happen, but it didn't seem to matter. My eyes felt prickly with tears and although I did my best to blink them back, a few escaped. The rising feeling of claustrophobia made me long for safety, to be back with Ophelia and Eddy. As the panic pushed upward, I started to feel my control of it slip and I knew then that I had to make the best of the night, to throw myself into it like it was a choice I was making to be there. I couldn't change the situation. I couldn't seem to make Richard, Ophelia or Eddy understand what I needed. I couldn't break down here, in the middle of nowhere, like a child. This was my chance to show Richard and his friends how fun, how easygoing I was. How mature I was for my age, and that it didn't matter that I was Richard's junior by thirty years. So I stood up, let my shoulders drop from my ears, wiped my eyes with the hem of my dress and walked back onto the terrace with a smile, telling them that everything was fine and that I needed a refill.

Richard got drunk. We all got drunk. Chalky and Tim felt like great friends and were warm and welcoming, showering me with attention and compliments and not asking any questions about our relationship. They seemed to absorb it all without a second thought, and for a moment I wondered if he had brought women other than Elaine here before. As the daylight faded and the sky turned pink, we walked the grounds of the villa, Richard with his arm around my shoulders. Chalky and Tim smoked a spliff and then later brought out cocaine, but when Richard declined, I did, too. At some point, I ended up in the pool. It was a strange and dreamlike evening that could only be recalled afterward as a series of freezeframes and vignettes, like a montage, like a mirage.

Our room was on the opposite side of the house to Chalky and Tim's. There was a huge four-poster bed with white linen sheets and curtains and cool pillows. We'd fallen asleep in our clothes and I woke early, before Richard for the first time. I was very hungover and startled from a dream in which I'd been trying to drink from the carved mouth of a stone fountain. I was extremely thirsty. I looked over at Richard, asleep and snoring, his jaw slack and his mouth hanging slightly open. He looked very old.

Chalky was on the terrace already, stretched out on a lounger in tiny neon-pink swimming shorts with very large sunglasses on. I was a little shy after such an evening of throwing all inhibitions so far out of the window they were probably back in London by now. I wasn't sure if he was asleep or not.

"Morning, darling. Help yourself to anything. I'm too hungover to be a good host."

I took two bumpy glass bottles of Orangina from the fridge and sat on one of the other loungers. Chalky threw me a packet of paracetamol and I swallowed two. The sweet, cold, fizzy orange tasted so good as it hit my stomach, I groaned.

"Last night was so much fun. We should get together in London sometime," I said.

He tilted his sunglasses down his nose and looked over them at me. He had a quizzical expression on his face.

"Dear, you can't really be as naive as to think that's going to happen. I certainly hope you are not. If you are, he's even worse than I thought he was."

My hangover had my insides in knots as it was. This bluntness from Chalky, who just hours before had been so warm and kind, felt so unexpected and cruel. I felt a jolt of nausea.

"I was his best man, you know."

"At which wedding?" I snapped back, and then smiled although I couldn't have felt less friendly. Chalky smiled back at me, impressed.

"Touché. His wedding to his current wife, Elaine. Whom you have met, I believe?"

I leaned back and rubbed my eyes, realizing I was still wearing yesterday's mascara.

"I have. Look. I know what you must think of me. But you don't know what he's like with me, the conversations we have. I don't pretend to understand the arrangement with Elaine and I know not to ask too much. Marriage is complicated; it's not all black and white." I found myself echoing Richard again and it felt just as hollow as it had the first time.

Chalky laughed at this, in the way you laugh at a child saying something they'd heard an adult say. I blushed.

"Arrangement is one word for it, I suppose. He cheats on her and she doesn't do a thing about it, because she loves him too much to leave him. And he's too selfish to do anything other than what he wants to, so she accepts it. That's how I'd put it. You are not the first and I can guarantee that you won't be the last."

At that moment, Richard appeared. He looked crumpled and broken, like an unmade bed. If he had overheard our conversation, he didn't let on.

"I have an absolutely dreadful hangover. I hope you are all suffering equally, or more." His voice was almost an octave lower than usual, which I'd not thought possible. I handed him my second bottle of Orangina and he took it. At some point he'd lost his hat.

"Is there any coffee?"

Tim was less hungover than the rest of us and, once he surfaced, made us all coffee and eggs, which I could hardly eat. Nothing about the day felt good. The house, which the night before had felt like a palace, looked ugly and garish. The sunlight was too harsh, the heat too much even at this early hour. I wanted to get away from these people, this place, and back to my friends, who I remembered then would not be pleased to see me either. My phone battery had died and they didn't have a charger that fitted, so I couldn't even text them to say I was coming back.

Richard showered after me. I was sitting on the edge of the bed in a fluffy white towel staring at my lifeless phone when he came back into the room. His belly was soft and bloated. He sat down next to me and stroked my back.

"You don't seem happy today, Charlie." I felt like crying again, so I didn't reply. "Did something upset you?"

"Chalky. He called me naive. Which I probably am. He was defending Elaine. He says she loves you too much to try to stop this. Us. I didn't think she cared about you at all."

Richard sighed in exasperation. "He was stirring, Charlie. Chalky likes to stir. He doesn't know what's going on in my life. He's an old friend, but not a close friend these days. I only see him a few times a year at most. And he doesn't have any relationship with Elaine that I'm aware of. I don't think you're naive. I think you are remarkably worldly for your age."

I leaned my head against his chest but felt no comfort from him.

"I'm going to drive south to the coast for a few days and clear my head. I'll take you back to your friends first. Shall we get moving?"

"My friends are furious with me. They don't want to see me."

He said nothing for a while, but kept stroking my back with his thumb.

"Come on. It won't seem as bad when you get there."

CHAPTER

Seventeen

The hour it took to get back felt like two. In the heat with my hangover, I felt motion sick and had to have the window open for the whole journey. We didn't really speak.

When we got to the village, Richard pulled up in the same spot he'd parked in just twenty-four hours before. It felt like weeks ago.

"Can you wait here? Just for twenty minutes? I might not be able to get in if they have gone out somewhere."

The clock on the dashboard showed that it was nearly 11 A.M.

"You could come with me, if you wanted. To the coast."

I shook my head. As wonderful as that sounded, I knew it was a fantasy. "I can't. We fly the day after tomorrow. I have to see my friends and make good with them."

He kissed me goodbye and I walked up the hill to the villa. The gate was open. I wondered if they had half expected me home and left it open all night. I walked around the edge of the house. It was quiet. I couldn't hear any voices or music. The doors were open at the back, but the terrace was deserted. I felt sick and uneasy. I didn't know what kind of welcome I was going to get.

"You came back!"

Finn had appeared, coffee in one hand, an enormous chunk of baguette in the other. Our kiss seemed to have happened in another lifetime. His cheerfulness and his lack of anger toward me was too much on my hangover, and I started to cry.

"Whoa!" He put his breakfast down and came to me, wrapping his arms around me. "It's OK, don't cry. Ophelia will be fine; we'd all had a lot to drink, a lot of sun."

"I'm so sorry."

"Oh, don't worry about *that*. I get it. Honestly, I do. There's no need to cry. I don't know what you have going on with this guy, but I get that it's a big thing for you. Hey, don't cry. Come on, let's go and sit by the pool; the rest of them are still sleeping. Do you want some coffee?"

We sat by the pool in the shade of the parasols. There was a breeze for the first time since we'd arrived. Finn got me to jump in, said the water would shock me out of my mood, and he was right. The cold, quiet blue below the surface reset me and goose bumps furrowed my newly tanned skin. He got out a pack of cards and made me laugh. I was so grateful to him it made me want to cry again.

Ophelia appeared a little while later and I hugged her tightly, although she felt tense in my arms.

"I'm so sorry," I whispered to her. "Please let me explain. I couldn't get back here. I tried so hard to get back here, I wanted to be with you all. Richard said he would drive me back for eight so I could be here like I promised, but then he took us to this villa his friends owned and I couldn't get him to leave and I couldn't get a taxi. I was absolutely sick about not being here with you. Honestly, Ophelia—"

"We'll talk about it another time. I don't want it to ruin the rest of the holiday." It was a weak excuse, and I don't think she believed my efforts, but she patted my back and gave me a little peck on the cheek as I broke away from her. Eddy raised his eyebrows at me and later called me an "absolute nightmare," but with some affection. He wanted to just enjoy the last few days with no more drama.

My hangover eased and the world softened at the edges. The sound of the crickets seemed to mix into the music from the speakers dotted about the house until I couldn't distinguish one from the other. The blue of the pool and the blue of the sky were so perfectly matched they must both have led to the same other dimension. I was exhausted and hungry and thirsty. Around two that afternoon, tiny bottles of cold, weak beer started to appear, but I was too broken from the previous night's drinking to be able to get drunk. We ate big bowls of pasta with anchovies and tomatoes, and I was in bed by ten-thirty. I fell asleep wondering if Richard had waited the full twenty minutes, if he'd considered coming up to the house and explaining to Ophelia that it hadn't been my fault.

I woke early again the next morning. It was the eighth anniversary of Mum's death, and I carried it with me like a millstone around my neck as I walked down the hill into the village. It was so quiet I questioned if anyone else was here, if the earth was still turning. All the shutters on the houses were still closed. I called Richard and he answered after one ring. Although I never called without permission, I knew he was alone and I had to speak to him. Had it all really happened, had that strange day been real? Had Richard really said he loved me? Had he meant it?

"It's very early for you, isn't it? Is everything OK?"

"You were right. Things weren't as bad as I thought. Or maybe they will be when I get home, but for now everything is forgotten. I think they just want to enjoy their holiday. Where are you?"

"A little place called Sainte-Marie. It's beautiful. There are flamingos. You'd like it."

"Did you talk to Chalky?"

"About what?"

"About what he said to me. About me being naive."

There was a long pause.

"What do you want me to say? It was wrong of me to take you there—we both know that. I have been reckless these last few days. I'm not quite myself. You know me well enough to be able to see that."

"I thought you'd explain to him how things are. That I'm not some wet-behind-the-ears child who doesn't understand the way the world works."

"Is that what you want me to do?"

"I don't know. I don't know what I want." I really didn't.

"Well, I know that I don't want to be challenged like this before eight in the morning."

There was a long pause, neither of us wanting to be the first to speak. I'd been out for an argument, I realized, and having got one I regretted it.

"When are you coming back to London?"

"I don't know yet. Maybe another week. I'd hoped to have some downtime to clear my head ahead of the publication and all of the madness that awaits. This isn't helping."

"I'm sorry. I just—I thought you'd defend me, defend us."

"And what good would that do?"

"It would make me feel better."

"Then I'll call him. As soon as we get off the phone. I'll call him and get into it, because that's what he'll want to do. I'll make a big deal out of it, and then it will be a big thing. We'll fall out and he'll call Elaine. Is that what you want, Charlie? Because it isn't what I want."

I was silent for a while, unsure what to say to this. I wanted to tell him about the importance of today. Maybe that was why I was calling him. But there was no comfort to be found in Richard when he was in a mood like this. "No, of course not. I don't know what I want. I want you, but I don't know how I want you. I don't know if that makes sense."

I could hear him sigh, deeply, as if hoping he'd find some more patience for me at the end of his breath. I thought about us walking through the grounds at Chalky's in the blue-pink twilight just a couple of days ago, dust clinging to the sweat on my skin, his heavy arm around my shoulder. That's what I wanted.

"The next few months are going to be very intense for me with the book. I'm obviously stressed about it; I'd expect you to be able to tell. I can't deal with these angry, challenging outbursts from you. I need you to be supportive right now, Charlie, and make my life easier, not harder."

"I'm sorry. I will. I'm being awful." I meant it. I was being awful.

"And I will always defend you, protect you, where it matters. Chalky is not where it matters. OK?"

I said I understood. He said he'd call me that evening. His words were gentler when we said goodbye, but there was a hardness to his tone that let me know how he really felt. He didn't say that he loved me, and I didn't say it to him.

Back at the house, no one was up yet so I got my book, a slim

Don DeLillo paperback that Richard had lent me as a part of the literary education he was giving me, and I tried to read. The words seemed to fall out of my mind as soon as I'd read them, so I folded the corner of the page and put the book down on the ground next to me. Swallows dived off the pool and the air buzzed with insects. I'd scratched at my mosquito bites and little scabs had formed in the trails of dried blood on my ankles. For a minute I considered calling Dad. But the date might have slipped his mind, and, anyway, I didn't know what to say. We didn't talk about her, ever; it had been that way since she had died and all of the practicalities had been dealt with.

I thought so much about Mum, about that day, but I didn't cry. The sadness was hard and cold and quiet. It was empty. I was empty. I had no one to even talk to about it. I had cursed the holiday with enough drama, and I didn't want to bring Ophelia and Eddy down with it. I considered calling Richard back to apologize, hoping I would feel his warmth and affection again if I did, but I knew it would be too much.

When everyone was up we drove to a town on the coast, but nowhere near where Richard was staying. There was a market by the beach and we bought more fruit and vegetables and strings of smoked garlic. It wasn't like I'd imagined the beach to be. There was no clear, tropical water and palm trees; the sea was choppy and dark, and the shore covered in sharp stones. Ophelia spent the whole day no more than a meter from Oscar, careful not to be alone with me. I knew that I deserved this, and I was too exhausted for confrontation, so I gave her the space she was quietly asking for. Any chemistry with Finn and me had been replaced by a lovely feeling of security and friendship. I spent the day locked into him, Ciaron and Eddy, and I greatly appreciated the distraction their company brought. I took photos of the three of them together on the beach, shirtless and tanned, under a street sign with a digital display showing the temperature. It was thirty-nine degrees. I posted it to my Facebook page, something I never did.

On the way back to the villa, we stopped at a supermarket for more wine and steaks for a last-night barbecue that Finn was going to cook for us. We all got in the pool when we returned, sticky and stiff from our hot cars. Even Ophelia seemed more relaxed with me by then, but still I couldn't bring myself to tell her that today was the day, all those years ago, that I'd lost any chance of ever being happy.

There were a million ways I would have done things differently that week if I'd had the chance to do it all again. But there was no point dwelling on the impossible. When we got back in London, summer would be almost over. Work would consume us for the last three months of the year, as it always did from September. Leaves would be raked in gardens and parks, and the smell of bonfires would drift in through windows that had been cracked open for months, reminding us to close them. It would soon be time for tights. Denim jackets would go from the coat pegs in hallways back to wardrobes, and wool coats would come out to replace them. Evenings would be short and soon it would be Christmas, with all the excitement and feverish hope of comfort and coziness, and the intimacy of lovers, best friends, and family. As I sat and watched my friends move around the table that last night, it became clear to me just how disconnected I had become from them, from my own life. I knew no way back, maybe because I didn't want one, maybe because I was so sick of myself and the inside of my skin that I could see nothing that would halt me as I moved further forward into inevitable self-destruction.

CHAPTER

Eighteen

Ophelia and I never talked about that day in France. Eddy suggested I didn't bring it up and I didn't. None of us enjoyed conflict and I didn't need to speak to either of them about Richard to understand how they felt about him. The distance that night had put between us was vast and more impermeable than I could have imagined. To them, I knew, it had been a choice that I had made. Either way you looked at it, I was in the wrong. I'd either let him take me away from them and not been strong enough to change the situation, or I had made the choice and blamed it on Richard. After that night I would see something change in Ophelia's eyes when I mentioned him, something so small that it would have been imperceptible to anyone else. So, as before, it just became easier not to talk about him. I became more secretive to avoid mentioning him and with it came a horrible feeling of isolation, stronger but this time quieter than I had felt it in France, sitting on that ugly white leather sofa, begging my friends to understand me.

In the week we'd been away, London seemed to have moved through time at a different velocity. The streets of Stoke Newington were suddenly lined with the dust of the first leaves to fall that autumn, and it seemed to get dark and chilly very early. Richard stayed on in France for another week and went straight back to Yorkshire on his return to England. We spoke every day, but sometimes not for very long. He was becoming more and more preoccupied by the upcoming publication and his mood had become darker. Even the news that *Altitude at Sea* had made the Booker shortlist didn't seem to cheer him up.

I busied myself without him. I ran each evening, read lots and even went home to see Dad, Laura and baby Noah for a long weekend that conveniently coincided with his fourth birthday. It was strange to be in my old room. I found it very hard to sleep. Dad had packed up my scattered belongings in boxes and put them under the bed. I pulled them out to look through them and, sitting with my legs crossed on my old bedroom floor, it was like opening a time capsule of an era of my life that had been the saddest, even sadder than now. The memorabilia of my teens consisted of cinema tickets from long-forgotten films, a mood ring that had turned from silver to green, several school diaries covered in doodles and stickers, a beaded purse filled with train and bus passes, and countless birthday cards with silly nicknames and in-jokes from people I no longer knew. I threw everything into the little woven wastepaper basket in the corner of the room, tied the bag and took it straight out to the bin at the front of the house. I didn't want to remember or recognize the Charlie I had been back then. I wanted to be free of her, to be a grown-up who had moved far beyond all of the misery and guilt and shame. But it was there, wherever I went. Even when I had Richard and he had said he loved me, I couldn't be happy. I was incapable of it and the thought depressed me a great deal.

They asked a lot about work. Dad said several times that he had no idea what my actual job involved me doing all day, despite me explaining over and over. This made Laura laugh, and wink at me in an overexaggerated way, knowingly, as if to say, *Silly old Dad,* like we shared him. It was a lot at the house with the baby, who wasn't really a baby anymore, although that's what we all called him. He still walked like a little drunk man, bumping into things. He always seemed to have a stream of snot coming out of one nostril or the other, but when he wasn't crying, he was very sweet. They kept calling him my "brother," but he wasn't. He didn't even know who I was when I arrived, hiding behind Laura's legs with the blue blanket he carried with him everywhere, like Linus from *Peanuts.*

When it got to be too much, I took Laura's bike out, cycling to the woods or the beach where we'd walked so many times at the end of the summer holidays and the beginning of the autumn term, like it was now. Some part of me looked for us as we'd been, the little family that we'd been back then. I hoped I'd bump into them, somehow, traveling through time like I could travel through memory. Everything certainly looked the same, but it didn't feel the same. My mother was nowhere to be seen.

I knew from social media that people from school still met up at a particular pub near the beach, the Anchor. I cycled past it, keeping a safe distance so I wouldn't be seen, but I didn't recognize any faces in the crowd sitting on the picnic benches outside. It must be nice, I thought, to have old friends like that to go home to.

By the end of the second week of September, it was like the summer had never happened, and not just because the weather had turned. The office was fraught and busy, and everything was needed yesterday. For all of fifteen minutes Cecile had seemed quite relaxed from her three weeks in Tuscany, but there was door-slamming and crisis meetings by 10 A.M. on her first day back. The new publicity assistant was terrified of Cecile and more than once I found her crying in the toilets. I tried to comfort her and offer advice, but she just looked at me like a rabbit in the headlights, seemingly terrified of me, too.

Altitude at Sea was to be published on the twenty-third of September. A number-one *Sunday Times* bestseller was inevitable, as this was a book that people had been waiting years for. This was what we called a publishing "event" and the last few days and weeks before it was released were critical. Even though all of the big interviews and photo shoots had been done earlier in the year, there was so much to do.

I'd been told to clear my schedule for publication week, which wasn't hard. Richard would be on the radio and TV, and the week was packed with interviews and appearances. He had been famous for a long time, but this was going to take him to another level.

Overall, we expected good reviews. Richard asked me every night about this, if I'd heard anything or seen anything early. He knew that he would be carefully managed by Cecile and Markus, with any news of bad reviews rephrased and softened and sandwiched between good ones. He hated it.

"They treat me like an infant. I want straight information delivered straight up, but it's always put to me like I need to be talked down to. Cecile especially speaks to me like a nurse. I can't stand it."

"You know I'll tell you the truth," I said, but I knew that I wouldn't. He didn't really want that from me, he wanted reassurance, and he wanted me to tell him that he was brilliant. So I did. As publication drew nearer and his mood grew darker, I wanted more and more to separate my life at Winden & Shane from us, fearful that he couldn't see me for me. If the book didn't do well, I didn't want to be panned with it.

We spent a night together just before all of the madness started. I'd not been to the flat for some time and, I realized, not had sex with him for a month. When I arrived there that Saturday morning, he was on the phone and finished the call in his office with the door closed. He emerged some thirty minutes later, distracted and clearly angry. I took him to the bedroom, undressed for him slowly and gave him everything I could that I knew he liked, and after he was much happier.

"You are wonderful, Charlie, you know that? You are made of gold. I'm sorry I've been such hell lately. I've hated being away from you. Look how you've transformed me. You are exactly what I need."

It felt so good to hear him say it. We had sex three times that day and night, which he told me was pretty good going for a man of fifty-six.

We talked a lot about the weeks ahead. He warned me that he would be difficult, and that I must be wary of that. His writing was everything to him, and these few weeks would determine the success of the book he had worked on for years. We'd be under the microscope, too, and any little slip-ups or over-familiarities would be noticed, not just by Cecile and Markus, but by Elaine, who would be in London for much of the coming week. It seemed that they had had a reconciliation since France, enough so, anyway, that she would be with him.

I was disappointed by this, and I internally chastised myself for it. What did I think would happen, that he would just up and leave her? I had allowed myself, after that day, to imagine a future with him. But my usually overactive imagination didn't really know what to do with this new permission and there was no pleasurable feeling to satiate, no sweetness there that would carry me into sleep at night. Just visions of bitter feeling everywhere I looked. Of Cecile's disappointment in me, our dynamic switched so that she would have to tread on eggshells around me like she did with Elaine. I imagined myself going with Richard to some press interview, me wearing Elaine's Burberry rain mac, the whole team from Winden & Shane on edge with me. All confidence and camaraderie lost with my betrayal. Bringing him home to meet Dad, Laura and the baby, parking the Land Rover outside on our little cul-de-sac; how he might greet my dad, to whom he was so close in age. How he would have to stoop at the low doorways, how uncomfortable he would be at our small dining table in the corner of the kitchen. I even imagined a dinner party at the flat with Chalky and Tim and John Cormorant and Markus, all of them cold and quiet, sharing looks of disapproval as I walked through Elaine's flat holding a steaming casserole dish, which would be revealed to contain plain pasta with cheese because it was all I could cook. I daydreamed, sometimes, about the practicalities. Would he move me into the Covent Garden flat? How long would we wait after he left her before we went public? Would we get married after the divorce went through? I *was* naive, even if he couldn't see it, and I hated myself for it.

I was dreading spending time around Elaine. Most of all, I was dreading the publication dinner, which was to happen on the Thursday following the release of the book.

"You mustn't be jealous, or over-familiar. Don't forget that she knows me better than anyone. So, you must promise me you'll be very careful, as this is not the time for her to learn about you. Do you understand what I'm saying?"

"Do you mean to say that there will be a time?" I shouldn't have said it, I realized, the moment the words were out of my mouth.

"This isn't a conversation for now."

The subject was closed.

The week the book came out was a blur. We were between television studios, radio studios and bookshops from before dawn until late. I was given permission to make any and all journeys by taxi on our company account, and I took full advantage of this luxury. My shoulders ached from the tote bags of books I carried everywhere.

Cecile and I worked together like clockwork. I was able to anticipate what she needed before she had to ask and I felt competent, capable, professional. Richard seemed taller than he ever had before, and he looked tired, but his focus was incredible. For every question he was asked, he had a perfect and interesting and articulate answer. People gushed about the book wherever he went, asking for him to sign their copies, which he did with a quick flourish of a Sharpie. He bent down to hear their names, or the name of the husband or brother or boyfriend he was signing it for. I took it as testament to the strength of our relationship that we could switch off from each other in company. I didn't slip up once.

Elaine didn't come to any of his interviews with him, but she was to join us for his publication day event at the Southbank, a huge venue on the bank of the River Thames. Richard was to be interviewed by a famous British actor who had become a Hollywood A-lister after he had appeared in the film adaptation of *The Road Goes Only Back*. The event was sold out, with nearly three thousand tickets bought, all with a copy of the hardback included. Backstage that afternoon, Cecile and I hovered in the production office. It was a few hours until the event started and after months of preparation, there was nothing to do now but wait.

"Oh, shit, Charlie, can you go and collect Elaine from the stage door and take her down to Richard's dressing room? I've just had a text come through from her. No idea how long she's been out there. She won't be happy. Good luck."

In the moment, it was a flutter of excitement I felt, rather than dread. We had patchy phone signal in the venue's bowels, so I'd been given a walkie-talkie, which made me feel important.

When I greeted Elaine at the door, she seemed to have no memory of me whatsoever. It was raining and she was under an umbrella, looking very cross. She was wearing her usual rain mac and skinny jeans, which today were tucked into black boots with a thin, spiked heel that looked like a murder weapon. Her clothes were so expensive and stylish. Again, in her presence, I felt dowdy and poor. It didn't matter that I was working all hours on a book campaign as big as this. I was still broke.

"Finally."

"So sorry, Elaine, have you been waiting long?"

She looked at me, confused that I knew her name. She shook off her umbrella.

"Long enough. I can't get hold of Richard."

I hated hearing her say his name. "There's no phone service in the dressing rooms."

"Are you from Winden & Shane?"

"Yes. I'm Charlie. We met in Sheffield?"

"Oh. Sorry, I don't remember." She was so obnoxious.

I walked her through the fluorescent-lit corridors of the building to Richard's dressing room and knocked on the door. I turned to leave.

"Actually, could you hold on," she said, pushing past me and into the room without waiting for an answer. The door slammed closed behind her and I could hear a muffled conversation. Then it opened again.

"Sorry, Claire, wasn't it? Can you go and get me a soya chai latte and a salad from somewhere? I think there's a Pret nearby."

"For goodness' sake, Elaine, she's busy enough as it is."

"I don't mind," I said. Richard appeared at the door and, with Elaine's back to him, he allowed me a look that said, in the most infinitesimal way that you could detect when you were in love with someone, *I'm sorry.* "Any particular salad?"

I went back to the production office to get my coat and told Cecile where I was headed.

"That woman . . ."

I smiled knowingly and shrugged. I went and got her salad, and her latte, and got soaked in the process. When I knocked on his dressing room door, she seemed to again have no recollection of me or any idea why I was there, sodden and holding a box of lettuce and a steaming paper cup. I was glad she was so abhorrent. It cemented in my mind what I already knew; he was unhappy with her, and I had nothing to feel bad about. Chalky had been trying to stir up drama, just like Richard had said.

The event went brilliantly. Richard was flawless; everyone said so. Cecile and I sat in the front row with Allegra, Elaine, John Cormorant, Markus and a few other people from Winden & Shane who had been invited. Everyone on the team who had worked so hard on the book for so long wanted to come, but there were only a few spaces for staff. When the event finished, the room erupted in cheers and Richard was given a standing ovation. Cecile and I went to speak to a few journalists and quotes were checked ahead of copy being filed for press the next day. Then we went backstage to Richard's dressing room, where we'd arranged for drinks to be served for his friends.

By the time we got there, the party was in full swing. The room was full of actors, writers and a host of literary editors. In the corner, deep in conversation with Elaine, was Chalky. He looked drunk. I couldn't see Tim anywhere. I tried to catch Richard's eye, but he was oblivious. Had he known he'd be there? Surely he would have warned me.

Cecile poured us champagne and clinked her glass against mine. "Good job, Charlie. You've been brilliant."

"Brilliant is right, isn't it, Charlie!" Chalky had made it across the room to me without me noticing. He smelled strongly of alcohol and kissed me wetly on both cheeks. "How are you, dear?"

In shock, I looked at him blankly. Cecile looked at me, and then back at Chalky, and then back to me.

"You two know each other?" She looked confused.

"Oh, darling Cecile! It's been years."

"Indeed it has." She looked back at me, confusion on her face. Not knowing what else to do, I smiled and rolled my eyes, then mimed smoking a cigarette and grabbed my bag, running out into the corridor. It hadn't been my fault, but it had happened. Cecile had seen something amiss.

I stood in the doorway smoking for a long time. I wanted to be sure that the party would have finished by the time I got back. Freezing fog had descended on the city but my coat was inside—I'd left it in my panic. It was so cold that I was shivering, my teeth chattering uncontrollably. The London damp seemed to have seeped into my bones and I thought I would never be warm again. I played it all over and over again in my mind, wondering how I would explain it. I could say I'd met him earlier in the evening if she ever raised it.

After about an hour, I went back inside. The dressing room was empty. Half-drunk glasses of champagne were littered about in front of the mirrors with their surround lights like something from an old film noir. I found my coat and called a taxi to collect me from the stage door. When I got outside my phone pinged with a text from Cecile.

> We've gone to the Groucho. Not sure where you went?? Come and join us if you want, my name on the door. If not see you tomorrow. 10 a.m. is fine. Well done again.

I thought about it, but I knew it wouldn't have been right. I wanted Richard to enjoy his night and not worry about me. I wondered if Chalky had said anything else to anyone. I wondered if Cecile had caught on more than she was letting on, or if she would just forget about it. She could be absentminded like that—she was always so chaotic with a million things going on both at work and at home that she would often forget conversations she had had with me or someone else. In part, that was why being her assistant had been so hard—she was all over the place.

I fell asleep in the taxi and woke up on my street with the driver knocking on the glass divide. For a second or two I had no idea where I was, or who I was. I went to bed without brushing my teeth or taking my makeup off, wanting to go into Ophelia's room and sleep in with her like we used to. I missed the heat of a body next to me. I missed being with Richard as he celebrated his glory, the glory of a publication I had been a part of and worked so hard on. He'd be with his best friends, drinking and telling stories. It would be an evening that people would talk about for years to come. I wondered if he had his arm around Elaine, if he had thought of me at all. I thought that probably he hadn't.

Probably he hadn't thought of anyone at all, anyone except the great Richard Aveling, the living literary legend.

CHAPTER

Nineteen

The book was a number-one bestseller and sales were beyond what had been expected. Richard was on the television or radio every day, it seemed, with many more requests coming in than he had time for. Before this, he was often quietly recognized but rarely interrupted. Now, though, he was being approached everywhere; in cafés and restaurants, getting in and out of black cabs, in the corridors and green rooms of the BBC's White City headquarters. We were all so busy that it was hard to find a moment to stop and absorb what was happening.

The reviews were, on the whole, very good. Several of them mentioned the ending as being particularly strong. I wondered, wordlessly, if I had been in any way a part of it, but I had never even wanted to bring it up with him; it seemed a step too far to presume that I had had any influence on his writing. I'd tried to remember exactly what I had said to him all those months before, studying the last chapter, certain that the suggestions I had made were in there, clear as day.

The week after the book was published, Richard came into the Winden & Shane offices for an hour to have a glass of champagne with staff. Markus made an awkward speech, standing on a lopsided sofa, his Grensons kicked off and red Christmas socks on full display. It was full of the usual affectations masquerading as eccentricities, complete with a handwritten script and a forgotten pair of reading glasses meaning that Richard had to lend him his own. Markus thanked all of the team by name, including me. Richard nodded and raised his untouched glass in my direction as he did with everyone who got a mention.

The night before, we'd had a long call, him in his office in the flat and me in my dark bedroom in Stoke Newington. He was full of it, the high of the week and the success of the book had him feeling elated, but there was a lot of uncertainty there, too. Much of this was about the Booker Prize night, which was a week away, but also about his upcoming trip to America to promote the publication there. He was leaving at the end of October and would be gone for a little over a week. The book had done well and hit the *New York Times* bestseller list, but it wasn't at the top of the charts and there had been some less favorable reviews. One journalist had called it *self-indulgent, overtly, tiredly masculine* and then worst of all, *far too long and pretentious to the point of farce.* Cecile's equivalent at his American publisher hadn't fared well in the conversation that followed, and they were "regrouping" to "reconsider strategy for the fall." Elaine was due to fly out with him and they'd spend a few days in New York doing publicity and book signings before he'd be off on a four-city book tour, which was to end in Los Angeles. He had some meetings to take with studios and various producers about the film adaptation, which was progressing quickly and now had a big name attached to play the part of Seb.

I felt like I was being left behind. I had no place in any of this, and I missed him terribly. He was slipping away from me and with every new venture or opportunity that materialized, I felt him slip a little further. Every new reader who approached him took something from me. There would be nothing left for me at the end of this, and things couldn't ever be the same because his life would never be the same. Any small anonymity he had enjoyed would be lost. But the last thing I was going to do was to put that on him. All I could do was be enthusiastic and supportive, even though I felt sick with sadness and jealousy. I wanted to be next to him on the plane, next to him everywhere he went. And not as his publicist, but as his partner.

Richard's status in the world as a celebrity beyond the confines of the literary world, and my love for his work, had made his affection for me all the more validating. This was my first proper relationship and until now, I'd managed to contain the feeling that it wasn't enough to be loved by him in private and private alone. But the romance of the secrecy had faded to nothing, and it was clear now that I had done a bad job of trying to convince myself that he alone was all that I needed. That I was a mess. I wasn't oblivious to the fact that I was looking to Richard for the security I so badly needed and missed since losing my mum. I knew enough of myself, too, that my grief had been overwhelming, and had disrupted something in my formative brain. That I was painfully vulnerable as a result. I didn't like to think of myself like that, although I knew that I was.

It wasn't just Richard who was leaving me behind. I would let self-pity engulf me at night when I was alone in the house, unable to sleep, crying silently into my wet pillow as the realization of just how alone I was submerged me completely. Although Dad had always been my dad, when Mum died, the fact that he was not my blood was laid bare. As he had moved on and found a new partner and they'd started a new family, I had been left completely detached from the intimacy of our lives during my childhood. I'd felt like I'd had no family. I had felt, beyond anything else, entirely lonely, as I did again now.

Bursts of closeness with people had always been intense and unsustainable, messy and passionate, and without the roots and foundations that meaningful connections needed. But those roots had been growing with Ophelia and with Eddy. Those friendships had started to become truly meaningful, transcending transience, but again they seemed to be slipping away from me and I had no idea what to do. I didn't know how to talk to them about it, how to bring them back to me. So I told myself in those moments that it was OK. That friends moved on.

But with lovers—well. You hope that there will be one, one day, who doesn't move on, who instead moves with you through your life. Ophelia and Eddy—they had everything they could ever want. They didn't need me. And it was starting to look more and more like Richard didn't, either.

The next week was the publication dinner, which was taking place in the private dining room of the Savoy hotel in the West End, not too far from Richard's flat. It would be small, just Allegra, Cecile, Markus, me and a few others from the marketing and sales departments, as well as Richard, Elaine, her sister and John Cormorant. I hadn't really expected to be invited, but Cecile insisted as I'd worked so much on the book.

Richard said he loathed these types of events and only went along with them out of politeness. He said the dinner was more for the team than for him, which I suppose was true. I did offer to make my excuses, but he said it would look odd if I did.

We were all seated at a long table. Cecile seated me to her right, opposite Elaine and her sister, Pamela. To Cecile's left was Markus, and opposite him, next to Elaine, was Richard. Allegra was at the other end, opposite John Cormorant.

Conversation was stilted at first, and it was evident to everyone that Richard and Elaine were on bad terms. She was as unfriendly as usual. She remembered me, at least, but still called me Claire, even though I corrected her. She didn't take much notice of me; I was of no consequence or use to her. Pamela looked so much like Elaine I wondered if they were twins. They had the same meanness, the same absence of anything gentle or kind. It was clear that Pamela was also furious with Richard and there purely to support Elaine. She kept wordlessly checking in with her with a squeeze of her wrist, a raise of an eyebrow or a crinkle of her nose. She didn't speak to anyone else. Elaine sat with her hands clenched together in front of her mouth, her elbows on the table. She didn't eat any bread, so I didn't either. I noticed her long, slim fingers and her wedding band. There were no diamonds and no engagement ring. She didn't even speak to Richard, who was leaning back in quiet conversation with Allegra and John Cormorant about something or another. I carried on chatting with the marketing manager sitting next to me, who was actually called Claire. I knew her from the pub on Fridays and I liked her a lot.

Cecile was very skilled in these types of occasions and, like our captain, she ordered champagne, then wine for the table. We were eating a set menu. She tried to engage Elaine and Pamela a few times, but she didn't get much back. Elaine wasn't even trying to hide her displeasure at being here.

"Have you been in France for the summer then, Elaine?"

"I got back a few weeks ago. I've been in Yorkshire. It's already horribly cold."

"Yes, we don't see you in London as much these days."

"Well, I'm hardly interested in staying in his love nest. He's got another spate of young girls coming round, you know." Pamela put a sympathetic hand to Elaine's shoulder. Neither of the women seemed to be concerned about being overheard by Richard. Claire kicked me hard under the table. This was just the kind of gossip we'd normally take to the pub with our co-workers for endless speculation on who those young women might be. I gave her a look that said, *Stop*.

Elaine had almost spat the words, her glacial veneer faulting for just a brief moment. Young girls? What did she mean? I felt like I might throw up, right there at the table. My pulse was so loud in my ears I was sure that other people must be able to hear it, too. I moved my chicken around my plate with my fork, suddenly disgusted by it.

"You know the flat was gifted to Pamela and me in my aunt's will back in the seventies? She was my godmother, too. But London is Richard's territory; he has made that perfectly clear. I'm not welcome in my own flat."

Cecile smiled sympathetically and nodded, unflinching but clearly unsure how to respond. Pamela went back to her chicken, subtly shaking her head as though in shock at the unfairness of it. Fortunately, Richard hadn't heard what had been said because he was still deep in conversation with Markus, Allegra and John Cormorant.

"The French house is so wonderful. I remember that trip well." Cecile was trying to change the subject. Elaine sipped her wine and said nothing, looking down at her untouched plate. "Have you been having some renovations done? I think Richard mentioned you were planning some work to be done on the pool . . ."

At this point, John Cormorant, by quite fortuitous timing, tapped his glass with a butter knife and had us all raise a toast to Richard and the book. All of us, except Elaine and Pamela, murmured our agreement with his praise for both the man and the work. After the toast was over, Cecile moved her attention to Markus, sensing that Elaine wasn't in the mood for conversation. It was clear that she had brought her sister with her so that she wouldn't have to engage with any of us. The tension between her and Richard was uncomfortable for everyone.

Elaine left with Pamela before dessert was even served, whispering something inaudible into Richard's ear and thanking Cecile with nothing more than a wave. Allegra left shortly after. We carried on drinking at the table while Richard and Markus had coffee. Claire took Elaine's seat next to Richard, and I felt a stirring of resentment toward her for being so close to him. Although she was really very pretty, much prettier than me, he didn't seem interested in her at all. Things felt much easier without Elaine in the room, but I couldn't stop thinking about everything she had said.

"Great news about the US," Markus said. "Good to see they are stepping up."

"God, I'm dreading it. It's nearly a month. I thought those sorts of backwater, backbreaking book tours were behind me."

I tried not to look surprised by this news. Cecile, noticing us for the first time in a while, brought Claire and me into the conversation.

"The US team want to tour the book through November, rather than just doing a few big cities. I think it's exactly the right strategy, to get back out there meeting the readers. I know it's a slog, but it will pay in dividends."

The wine had loosened me a little and I looked at Richard, who was careful not to make eye contact.

"A month. That's a long time."

"It's a big country," said John Cormorant knowingly. He'd spilled some of his chicken on his tie. "We'll make sure you are looked after. I've asked to see a schedule next week . . ."

We all left together. I took a taxi with Cecile as Islington was on the way to Stoke Newington. I was still in shock at everything I had heard. Elaine knew someone younger was coming around? Another spate . . . Why did she think there was more than one, and had this happened before? And then, a whole month away. He hadn't said anything to me last night. I wondered if that was why Elaine was so angry, too. But then they spent so much time apart, it wouldn't matter to her where he was.

"She wasn't always like that," Cecile said on the way home. She was a little drunk and seemed to forget herself, because she never usually spoke so openly about Richard's private life, even to me. "I remember about five, six years ago, they invited us out to France for a few days, to relax and have a bit of a break, as well as to plan for publication for the last book. As if you could relax staying with an author! Ha. But she was quite good fun back then, really. They seem miserable, now, don't they."

"I don't know why they stay together. They don't seem happy. And what was that about a love nest and young girls coming round?"

But Cecile didn't bite.

"Oh, I don't know. The two of them are always falling out about something. They seem to feed on drama. He used to stray a bit, I think, when he was much younger. Maybe he's misbehaving again. You will learn this, Charlie, but older men have certain appetites. You need to watch out for people like him—they don't think twice about taking what they want if it is available to them. You know, they say that marriage is a mystery, but with these two it really is. They both have their own lives, and it works, or it doesn't . . . Regardless, they have their reasons for staying together. Although God knows what they are."

The taxi dropped Cecile outside her Georgian townhouse. I couldn't believe she lived there. I'd never seen it before. It was one of those London houses that you walk past and wonder what people do to be able to live in such a place. Cecile seemed to spot me rubbernecking out the window.

"It's all Matthew," she said, digging about in her Chanel handbag for a key in the glow of the streetlight. I'd hoped to get a glance inside the hall, to see if the portrait was real.

When we pulled away, I looked at my phone. I had a missed call from Richard, which surprised me. After a night of being ignored and discovering he'd be away for a month, and that his arrangement with Elaine might not be as mutual as I'd been led to believe, I didn't feel like emailing him to tell him to call back as I usually would. When I got home, some half an hour later, the house was quiet; Ophelia was staying with Oscar a lot, and Eddy was out somewhere or another. It was a Thursday night, and Thursdays were bigger than Fridays these days. I was taking my makeup off in the bathroom when he called again.

"Hello, Charlie."

"Hello, Richard."

"Well, that was quite the evening. You looked lovely, by the way." He was being totally charming, which was very annoying.

"A month? Couldn't you have told me that?"

"I wanted to tell you face-to-face. I've only just confirmed it in the last few days. Elaine is fucking off back to France tomorrow morning, thank God. I'm in the study now so I can't speak for long. I was hoping you'd come here tomorrow so we could spend some time together, talk properly. I feel like I've not seen you for a long time, which is odd, isn't it."

"I feel like that, too. Everything feels strange at the moment." I decided not to raise what I'd learned from Elaine until I saw him.

"Will you come by then after work?"

It was busy for a Friday, and I couldn't get away before seven. As well as tying up loose ends on *Altitude at Sea,* I was now planning for our spring books as well as working with Cecile on a contingency campaign just in case Richard did win the Booker. Everyone had their head down in their own overwhelming workload. No one even mentioned going to the pub, which never happened. At 3 P.M. on Fridays, without fail, someone would start taking an inventory of who was coming for post-work drinks.

I was utterly enervated, and happy when Richard suggested I take a bath and we order food in rather than cook. The flat felt familiar and cozy. There was no real evidence of Elaine anywhere, but the sheets were fresh on the bed, and I could feel something of her, which put me on edge. A hint of perfume in the air, two coffee cups on the draining board, a carton of soya milk in the fridge that I knew he didn't drink. I put his caramel jumper on after my bath. He'd resigned himself to the fact that it had been adopted by me. It felt like autumn was close to over, although it was only just October.

We sat on the sofa eating pizza from the Italian place a few doors down, big chunks of congealed cheese sliding off the base and sticking to the box. I could see that Richard was exhausted, too. His eyes were slightly bloodshot and rimmed with dark circles. There was a faint sourness to his breath and his tan had faded. His shoulders slumped a little and he was unrecognizable from the man who had commanded the Southbank the week before. He kept rubbing his face and pushing his hair back. He was distracted, as he had been for weeks now, really since before France. I didn't know how to bring him back to me, or if I could. I knew that any mention of Elaine and what had been said the night before would not be well received, so I decided to leave that for now. I could contain it, I had to, or I would push him away even further. Although he was quiet, his mood was volatile and felt like static electricity. I didn't know what to say, so I said nothing. The longer we were quiet, the more it was like he wasn't really next to me, like he was some stranger in Richard's clothes, in his flat.

As if he'd read my mind, he said, "I'm sorry I've been so—absent. I have been consumed by the book, obsessing over it, really. And at the same time trying to start writing again. Dealing with everything that goes with it, traveling . . ."

He paused. I didn't dare look at him, instead focusing on my food, hungry but unable to eat.

"It hasn't been fair on you. I can see you slipping into a melancholy mood, Charlie, and I know you are prone to this sort of feeling. I'm not really sure what to do about it."

"I'm OK, don't worry about me," I said quietly. "My moods are far beyond the control of anyone. I've been busy, too. Work has been crazy. And with my friends. I do have a life outside of you, you know—you just don't really see it."

I was lying. I had hardly any life outside of Richard, hardly any thoughts, even. Ophelia, Eddy and I were moving away from each other slowly, our universe was expanding and we were being thrown outward in different directions.

"Well, that's good. I don't want things between us to end. You know that."

I needed to hear him say this to me more often.

"But, look. I'm going to be away, and busy, a lot over the next few months. As well as this American tour I expect a few more trips to

Los Angeles, and then there will be international festivals. Australia, I expect, in the spring. I don't want—I can't—think of you waiting for me. You need to live your life, Charlie; it won't change that I am here."

"I don't understand what you mean by that."

"I just think . . . you should be having fun, meeting people. Sleeping with other men—men maybe more of your own age."

Tears burst before I could think to stop them. Richard was shocked by my reaction and went to comfort me, but I pulled back, overwhelmed with that awful, familiar feeling of rejection and loss. I had to look at his face, to see what he was really saying.

"But I don't want that—I don't need that. I have you."

"And you still will have me. But, Charlie, you must realize—you must see that this, this thing that we have, it's not straightforward. And I don't want you to miss out on your own life, the experiences you should be having at your age. I'm not going anywhere. I'll always be around. Well, not always, but I hope for a long while yet."

"How can you bear to think of me with someone else?"

"Well, how can *you*?"

"I don't!"

"But I am married. It must have occurred to you." His words hit me like a fist in the stomach.

"It hasn't, it doesn't. I know next to nothing about your marriage, other than that you can't seem to stand the sight of each other."

He sat back. Whether he was frustrated or bored by my anger, it was hard to tell.

"I don't like the thought of it. Of course I don't. But it would be selfish of me not to put this to you."

"Is this coming from you or Chalky?"

"Chalky? Why on earth would it be coming from Chalky?"

"He saw me at the Southbank event. He was so drunk, he seemed to forget that we shouldn't know each other. Cecile clocked it."

Richard rubbed his eyes again. "I didn't know that. But, no. This has nothing to do with Chalky."

"Are you trying to end things with us? But do some reverse psychology thing where I end it with you?"

He smiled and pulled me into him. I resisted at first, fighting against him, but then I gave in, putting my head on his chest and listening to the dull hammer of his heart.

"No. I want you all to myself, whenever I can have you, but, Charlie, that's selfish of me. I'm trying very hard to be good to you, despite it being bad for me. I live independently from anyone, really, even my wife. And I want you to have that same independence. Do you understand?"

I felt in that moment like the abyss of sadness that lived inside me was shaken wide open, and that I was upside down, falling into it in slow motion. Strangely, it was a relief to feel it again so completely, a relief from holding it back, trying to stop myself from looking at it. Without him I would die, and he was moving away from me, like Ophelia and Eddy, like Dad, as his own universe expanded. Everyone always had a different direction to go in, away from me. I couldn't speak, I couldn't really move. It was like my body no longer belonged to me. If I called for it to move, it would surely refuse to do so.

Richard held my face up to his and kissed me, and as he did more tears fell and he wiped them with his thumbs. We stayed like that for a little while and then in my desperate state, I pulled him on top of me and we had sex there on the sofa, the curtains open and the windows lightly misted with condensation as the warm air of the flat greeted the cold air of the London night through the glass. I wanted to climb inside him, to tether our souls together somehow so that wherever we were in the world, I'd be able to feel him, to see him. To never be alone again, no matter what happened, or how much time passed.

I loved him that much.

CHAPTER Twenty

If I'd had anyone to talk to about what was going on, they would have pointed out to me that he was trying to take a step back from me and that this might be signaling that things were coming to an end.

But I didn't. The only person I had was Richard.

The relationship had isolated me almost completely from my friends, and certainly from my dad. I couldn't possibly tell him that I was involved with a married man as old as he was, let alone an author that I worked with. Dad would always worry that I'd lose my job for taking a sick day. This would probably kill him. Sometimes I tried to imagine what my mum would say to me, what guidance she would have for me. But I drew a blank. I couldn't bear to think of how she would react to me being with Richard. I wasn't sure that I would be able to make her understand, if she'd been here for me to tell, and that made me feel very sad.

Richard didn't win the Booker, which he said was a relief, but I didn't believe him. The award ceremony was broadcast on the BBC and the camera panned to him as he clapped and smiled at the success of another of his contemporaries. I could see Cecile, Markus and John Cormorant at the table. We had a drinks party that night at a private members' club in Soho, all the publishers of the respective nominees did, but he didn't come by after the ceremony as expected. I knew his ego would be bruised, even if he said he didn't care.

We saw each other even less over the next few weeks, although I knew he was in London almost constantly because of publicity engagements and various meetings. He called me less. I started to feel that same panic that I had felt in the spring at the start of the affair, that it could come crashing down at any minute. He gave me just enough hope to believe that it wouldn't, lending me precious copies of books I knew needed to be returned, talking vaguely of things to come next year.

All I could think about was the month he'd be away. My every day was a countdown to it, as I knew that every day he was gone would be a countdown to his return.

He was flying out on a Tuesday, and so I stayed with him the Saturday and Sunday night before he went. He spent a lot of time taking calls and working in his office while I read on the sofa. There was an easiness to us that weekend, a domesticity that suggested we'd been together a long time rather than that this was an affair that was coming to an end. I worked very hard to please him not just sexually, but by being cheerful and good company. I wanted us to part on the best possible terms and for him to pine for me.

On Monday morning, I woke up early with him as I did on weekdays. We drank coffee together and I did my usual job of ensuring I'd left nothing behind while he stripped the bed; Elaine was arriving at lunchtime and they'd be flying out together first thing the next day. I was always tempted to leave something and say it was an accident. A pair of knickers under the bed, an earring by the bathroom sink, something that would blow up his marriage and leave him available to me. But I didn't. In my heart I knew it would just cause an argument between him and Elaine, and he'd be furious with me. I wasn't powerful enough to break up their marriage. It was already broken. They were choosing to keep it.

"No goodbyes, OK?" He was standing in the kitchen drinking from his mug, leaning on the kitchen island. It wasn't completely light outside yet, and it was raining so much the sky seemed to be sagging low enough for the tops of the buildings to touch it.

"No goodbyes. Got it."

"I'll call you in a few days. Don't call me, OK?"

"I never do, do I? I know the rules. Look. I hope it goes well. I know you'll be busy, too. So just call me when you can."

I kissed him goodbye as breezily as I could and left. As soon as the doors to the lift closed, I felt the curtain slip and had to work hard not to fall to the floor. I felt unwell, not myself. The Tube was packed and when it came to King's Cross, I found I couldn't get off. I couldn't move. I just sat there. When the Tube got to the end of the line half an hour or so later, I didn't even notice.

"All change, please. All change," said the muffled voice of the driver over the speaker. A cleaner moved up and down, picking up old newspapers and coffee cups and stashing them in a bin bag. She didn't acknowledge me. My phone beeped in my bag.

You OK? You not coming in today?

It was Cecile. I realized it was after ten in the morning.

So sorry. Not well. I thought I'd texted but didn't hit send.

Don't worry—everything all right? Will you be back in this week, do you think—just need to know if I should prep cover.

We had a busy week of events. The thought of being around people, smiling and serving Prosecco, seemed impossible. I put my phone away in my bag without replying. The train crept back along the dark blue of the Piccadilly line, returning toward central London. Little red shapes danced in the corner of my vision, but no amount of rubbing my eyes could make them stop. I felt peculiar, disconnected from my lower body, and my head was hurting. I knew a migraine was coming. I got off at Manor House station and walked home in the rain, the water seeping through the worn soles of my boots.

At home, I was horrified to find Ophelia on the sofa under a pile of blankets. She looked dreadful.

"Oh, no, not you, too! Have you got this cold as well?" She was so ill her consonants were all flat. I wanted to get into bed, to cry, for the ground to open up. Instead, I found myself cheerfully saying yes, I was coming down with something or maybe it was the beginning of another migraine, and that I just needed to go to bed. I wanted to get away from Ophelia and every single other person on the whole of the planet, to be entirely by myself. I had nothing for anyone, I realized, no words, no part of me to share, no kindness, no real thoughts, even. I was as hollow and empty as anyone had ever been.

"Sure you're OK, Charlie? Have you got your migraine meds? I could run you a bath—you're soaked."

"Yeah, fine! And I've got them; I'll take one now! Just feel rotten and this rain and it being a Monday aren't helping!"

"But you love the rain. I've literally never heard you complain about the rain once."

"Yeah, but I don't love getting soaked through by it on a Monday morning, eh! Best enjoyed from the inside!"

I sounded completely mad, I knew it, taken over by some mania. I closed my bedroom door and got straight into bed in my wet clothes. The rain was striking the window, or maybe it was hail. My head was thumping and I was freezing. My sheets smelled musty, damp and unfamiliar after a weekend away. I couldn't remember when I'd last changed them. My tights were soaked, and I thought of all of the mess and detritus of London life that was washed, foaming, into the gutters and puddles, and how it had seeped through my shoes and now into my bed. I thought of the sheets at the flat, swirling in the washing machine, washing out all traces of me, my sweat and hair and all other remnants of the most intimate parts of me. Elaine would be arriving soon. Would he kiss her hello at the door? Would they have sex today? Cook a meal together or even go out to eat? Would her passport be packed with his or would they carry their own, separately? It would be at least a month until I'd see him again, but I knew even that was hopeful.

Sleep with other people. He wanted me to *sleep with other people,* feel hands other than his on my body.

The headache was now definitely a migraine. I didn't have the strength to find my medication. I was somewhere between the sleeping and waking worlds. Patterns danced across the insides of my eyelids, little auras changing colors. It didn't occur to me that I could call out for Ophelia and she could find my medicine now, before it got worse, that there was help there if I needed it. Instead, I fell further into a feverish, sickly sleep, where the viselike grip of pain on my right temple tightened intermittently.

I woke with a jolt what felt like hours later, but it must have only been minutes. I had to get that medicine; the pain in my head was so intense that I was convinced I was going to die, probably like my mother had. It must surely be the same thing. I thought of her elbows, and her wrists, so like mine. We must be built with the same faulty veins and arteries running through our heads. What a relief, to die without having to even do anything, with no guilt. Maybe this was it, the pain telling me it was over.

I fumbled blindly in the drawer of my bedside table, trying not to move my head, and found a cartridge of medicine. I had left one in there just in case. I pulled the cap off and sprayed it into my nostrils, one after the other. Almost at once I felt the veins in my head tighten. It was like being pulled upward in a sudden jerk. The change in how I felt was immense, but then the taste of the medicine started to drip down the back of my throat, tasting worse than any of the cheap drugs I'd ever snorted. I managed to get to the bathroom. I drank deeply straight from the tap, but the taste wouldn't shift. I was sick, noisily.

"Charlie, are you OK?" Ophelia was tapping on the locked door.

"I'm fine, Fee. It's just a migraine."

"Can I come in?"

I was lying on the floor and reached an arm up to turn the lock.

"Oh my God, Charlie." She went to a cabinet and got out a fresh, fluffy white flannel, which she ran under the cold tap and placed on my head, stroking my hair out of the way. She sat next to me on the floor. "Where are those spray things you have?"

"I took one. I'm honestly OK. The pain is easing. It was the taste of the spray that made me sick. Do you have any gum or mints? I can't get the taste out of my throat."

She returned with a packet of chalky white mints. I ate one, then another, then put two in my mouth. I felt very peculiar. Ophelia put a glass of cold water next to me and felt my forehead with the back of her hand.

"You feel freezing. You're absolutely soaked, Charlie, you're filthy. I'm running you a bath, OK?"

The tiles of the floor felt cold on my cheek. We needed to dust the skirting boards. I nodded.

"Do you need me to message Cecile and say you aren't coming in?"

"I did it already. I'm so sorry, Fee."

"What are you saying sorry for? For being ill?" She was so congested that "ill" sounded more like "dill."

"I don't know. For everything." I was crying now.

"Oh, Charlie." She smoothed my hair and turned over the flannel. "What are we going to do with you?"

I had a bath. Ophelia had changed the sheets on my bed and replaced them with a set of hers, which seemed to have been ironed and smelled of lavender. She helped me into bed, my wet hair wrapped in one of her towels. I took some paracetamol and lay down. My alarm clock showed that it was only 1 P.M. I'd been apart from Richard for less than five hours. The medicine made me feel sleepy and I drifted off back into the strangeness of my unconscious. I slept for twelve hours, waking in the dark of night confused and sad. I drank some water and fell asleep again, not waking until the following day.

The migraine left me raw both in my body and in my mind. It was hard to be sure for a few days if what I was experiencing was down to being ill, and what was down to feeling Richard's absence from both my present and my vaguely imagined future. He didn't call, as I knew he wouldn't. I'd told Cecile I was sick with the same flu that had taken out half the office, and Ophelia said she wouldn't say a word otherwise. A migraine didn't feel like a reason to be off for a week and every day that I thought I'd be back to work the next, I woke with such a feeling of heaviness and dread that I could barely make it to the kitchen, let alone central London.

Clemmie came by that week to stock the fridge for sick Ophelia.

She went to Whole Foods and must have spent the equivalent of a month of my pay on organic fruit and vegetables, kombuchas and tonics and teas, essential oils and supplements and homeopathic remedies. She arrived armed with green smoothies and pots of turmeric-and-ginger-infused broth for both of us. I had the smoothie, but the soup, in its cardboard tub, sat uneaten with a layer of grease congealing on the surface in a reflective skin that turned my empty stomach even more. From my bed I could hear them speaking in hushed tones in French, which I knew meant that they were talking about me. Why they were trying to whisper when I couldn't understand a word of what they were saying baffled me.

Ophelia knew that Richard was going to be away for a while. She tried to talk to me about it, asked me if he had upset me and what had happened, but I just shook my head and said everything was OK.

By the Friday, Ophelia was much better. She tried to encourage me to go with her to a "gentle" yoga class that afternoon, but I couldn't face it. When I declined, she asked me if I might instead call my GP and get an appointment.

"I have a repeat prescription for the migraine stuff."

"But that made you sick. Maybe they have another option. I've been reading up on it online. There are lots of different migraine meds you can try."

"Maybe next week."

On Sunday night, she came into my room again. She was feeling better and going back to work the next day.

"Are you coming in tomorrow? Shall we get the Tube together as a treat?"

The Tube was so much quicker but so much more expensive than the bus that, unlike Ophelia, I only took it to work on occasion. I'd been in bed all weekend, watching TV shows on my laptop and sleeping. I didn't smell good, and I wasn't sure I'd brushed my teeth today or even yesterday. There were piles of plates with half-eaten slices of toast and half-drunk glasses of water that I had no energy to clear away. She was being kind, and cheerful, which made me feel even worse.

"Yep, I'll be going in. Not sure what time. Let's see in the morning."

But morning came and I was filled with such panic, such blind fear and anxiety when I woke up, that I couldn't do it. I had wanted so much to feel better, so much. Instead, I stood in the bathroom, not showered and still in my dirty pajamas, unable to even look myself in the mirror.

"I don't feel well," I told Ophelia as she bounced down the stairs from her room. "I'm not going in. I'll message Cecile."

Ophelia put her handbag down and perched on the stairs by the landing. She was very quiet.

"I think you need to call your GP and get an appointment. I'll call them if you want. I can do it now."

"No, I don't need that. It's not a migraine. I just need to take another day."

"Charlie, I think you are very depressed." She was being firmer with me than I had ever heard her. "I love you so much. So does Eddy. And that's why I'm—we're—saying you can't go on like this. We can't let you. I don't know what has happened but, darling, you must go and speak to your doctor about how you are feeling, see if they can prescribe something else."

I wanted so, so much to go into my room, put on my work clothes and makeup, brush my hair and join her. I wanted to go to work, I truly did. But the Charlie that worked at Winden & Shane, that did the job, she was someone else entirely. I started to cry. Ophelia took off her coat and hung it on the banister. I heard her go upstairs, and then her talking to Eddy, who came down and sat with me on the bathroom floor.

"You'll be late for work," I said.

"Don't worry about that. I work seventy hours a week at the moment if you count reading hours and when the stuff I'm reading is as dreadful as it is right now, I count reading hours. I can be late one day." He rubbed my shoulder gently. I felt so embarrassed, so less than him, less than Ophelia. Less than everyone.

Ophelia made me an appointment with the GP for 11 A.M. that morning. Eddy went to work, but Ophelia insisted on staying home to take me to the doctor's. We sat on the grim plastic chairs in the waiting room for nearly an hour. There weren't many of us. An awkward-looking middle-aged man. A young mum with an inconsolably screaming baby and toddler fast asleep in a buggy.

"Charlotte Turner," called a voice from one of the rooms on the adjoining corridor.

"Do you want me to come in with you?" Ophelia squeezed my hand. I shook my head.

It was the same doctor that I'd seen a few months previously. She seemed harried and short today, reading my notes as she gestured to the chair next to her desk. I sat quietly, wondering what to say, while she caught up on my history.

"How can I help you today, Charlotte?"

I was stuck for what to say, unable to look at her. She bent her head thoughtfully, seemingly catching herself, suddenly aware that I needed to be handled with much softer gloves than she had offered me. She checked back to her screen. Her tone changed.

"Have you had any more migraines since I last saw you? Which was . . . Ah, yes. Back in May. Then I prescribed you a triptan nose spray. Have you had to use it?"

"Er, yeah, I had a bad one, really bad. About a week ago. The spray stuff helped the pain, but it made me sick."

"Migraines are very commonly accompanied by nausea." She was talking to me like a schoolteacher, which was extremely irritating as she couldn't have been much, if at all, older than me.

"Yes, I know, but it wasn't like that. It was the taste of the spray when it dripped down my throat. I'd like to just have the pills again, if that's OK."

"That's no problem at all, Charlotte, whatever works for you." She didn't go back to her computer to start the prescription as I had hoped. I'd fixed my view on a curling lino tile in the opposite corner of the room. The fluorescent strip lights and the dark winter day gave the room an artificial brightness that made me feel all the more uneasy. I wondered how she could spend her whole day in here.

"I had hoped you'd come and see me to chat about your antidepressant medication. But now is as good a time as any. How has your mood been? Do you mind if we have a little chat about it?"

I paused. "Well, I think, lately, maybe not so good. Actually, bad. I've not felt right for a while really, but now it is really bad. My medication doesn't seem to be working. I've not been to work all last week. I need to be at work. I find this all very uncomfortable to talk about. But I need to get better so I can get back to work. So, if there is something else you can prescribe, then I can try that?"

"Can I ask if there is anything going on that might have brought this on? Stress at work? A relationship ending?"

I shrugged, swallowing hard to stop from crying. "All of those things. Can't really get into it without getting even more upset." My hands were shaking in my lap.

"OK, Charlotte, I can see you are having a really hard time. I'd like to start by referring you for some talking therapy. That's something we mentioned last time. In terms of your medication, I can see you have been on a very high dose of sertraline for a long time. So rather than mess around too much with that, I think it's best that I get you in to see a—a specialist, to look at this. We have a psychiatrist who works with this surgery. He's coming in this week actually, on Wednesday. What I'd like to do is to see you again myself this Thursday, by which time I will have had a chance to speak to the psychiatrist about the best course of action, and we can talk then about next steps. In the meantime, I'm going to write you a sick note for this week. I can put on it whatever you'd like, I don't have to say it's because of . . . well. We can say migraines. Does your boss know you suffer with migraines?"

I left with a sick note, a prescription for migraine tablets, a higher dose of my antidepressants at my own insistence, and some diazepam at hers, which was just for the short term, she stressed, given my "high level of distress." I found that phrase odd. I didn't feel like outwardly there was anything much to see other than my greasy hair and lack of makeup.

Ophelia waited with me at the pharmacy while they dispensed everything. The pharmacist lectured me on the addictive nature of diazepam loudly enough for the entire queue of customers to hear.

"What an absolute joke," Ophelia said angrily once we were outside. "You'd think discretion would be pretty high on the list of required skills for being a fucking pharmacist. I'm going to write a complaint as soon as I get home."

But, after much arguing, Ophelia went off to work rather than coming home to look after me. I walked slowly, every part of my brain and body running at a much-reduced speed. I caught sight of myself in the window of a coffee shop. I looked like a ghost. When I got home, I messaged Cecile to say I was off for the week because of a seemingly never-ending migraine, telling her I had a doctor's note. Then I took a diazepam and fell into a wonderful, dreamless sleep.

When I woke up, it was nearly five. I had a text from Cecile telling me not to worry and that she'd see me the following week, and to get in touch if I needed anything.

And then, there it was—a missed call from Richard.

CHAPTER

Twenty-One

I spent the week in a haze of diazepam, rocking between the waking world and some other strange and dull place where there was nothing really, just grayness and echoes of voices that I couldn't make out. I had another few missed calls from Richard, but I was always asleep when he rang. I didn't even check my email.

By Thursday I was feeling a little less sad. Each missed call strengthened me. I started eating again, small and bland meals cooked by Ophelia or Eddy, who came straight home after work each night. I showered, changed my sheets and cleaned my room up a bit. I was drinking red wine again with the season change, but not much, just a few glasses a night. Mixed with the sedatives, it created an even more expansive and deep sense of sleep than without. Although I knew it wasn't sensible and probably even unsafe, I didn't really care enough not to. I kept a bottle of wine in my room as I knew my well-meaning housemates wouldn't like it.

I went back to see the GP and told her I was starting to feel a bit better. She'd spoken to the psychiatrist, and he wanted me to be seen in his clinic. She said I'd get a letter with those details. There was a bit of a delay, and I couldn't be seen as quickly as they would like. Even though this was urgent it could be a few weeks before I would get an appointment. I told her I didn't need it, but she insisted I go so I said I would, although I thought I probably wouldn't.

I was given various crisis phone numbers in case things got really bad out of hours and I promised to call if they did.

By that weekend, I started to taper down off the sedatives as my supply was dwindling and I needed to keep some in reserve. I forced myself to go for a run on Sunday morning, just a short run, around the park. My muscles felt flat, like there was no power in me at all. After a while I just walked. It was raining and the grit and dirt from the concrete sprayed up at me, soaking my leggings. The park was quiet, almost deserted. It looked so different from the summer days just months before when you couldn't find a patch of grass free to sit on.

I went back to work that Monday. Cecile took me out for a coffee as soon as she saw me. She seemed concerned, and I wasn't sure she bought my two-week migraine story. She offered to introduce me to a friend of Matthew's, who was a neurologist at King's. I said it was fine—I'd been checked out, all was good. She said I was to take it easy and not work any extra hours, to go home immediately if I didn't feel well. I genuinely appreciated her kindness. It was odd that this woman whom I really knew so little about had become such a big part of my life.

Emails had built up over two weeks and it took me most of the morning to go through everything, decide what to delete, what to keep, what to check had been followed up on. There were a few from Richard that I had been copied in on, press requests, declines and acceptances of festival invitations for the following year, nothing much of note. I opened my own personal email account, keeping the window minimized in the bottom corner of my screen. There were several from him, asking how I was, telling me times he would call, and then telling me to call as Elaine had flown home. I opened each, reading every word, savoring his attention with a little flush. But I didn't reply. As long as I didn't reply, and didn't see him, then it couldn't change, it couldn't end. I had little control over anything but this.

Ophelia came to my desk every day to take me to lunch, although the weather was so bad that we couldn't sit outside. We'd go to Pret, or one of the other cafés, or sit in the break room in the basement. I'd watch her pick open her sandwich and eat the little pieces of chicken or prawns or whatever protein was in it, and then chuck the rest in the bin. Neither of us had much of an appetite. Everyone was tired, ready for the year to be over, for the long Christmas break. I remembered the excitement of Christmas the year before, when Eddy still worked with us. It seemed like that whole time belonged to other versions of ourselves.

That Saturday night, it was to be Oscar's twenty-sixth birthday party. It wasn't going to be a big thing, some drinks in a bar in Peckham with some of his friends. Eddy and I were invited. Our friendships had been cemented that summer in France. I was looking forward to seeing Finn. I hadn't felt that feeling of looking forward to something for a while. We had kept in touch, texting when we saw something that reminded us of the other, checking in, that sort of thing. I got the feeling he knew I'd been unwell, because he'd texted me the week before just asking how I was, with extra little *x*s at the end. Ophelia must have told Oscar, because she'd been home with me rather than at his for over two weeks. Oscar would have in turn told Finn.

Ophelia was happy I wanted to come, but I also sensed that she was nervous that I'd get drunk, or upset, or somehow it would be too much and cause a setback. I promised her that I was OK, that I'd take it easy.

"It's not going to be a crazy one, anyway. Just some drinks. The pub closes at one. And Oscar is going to stay here, so we can all share a taxi home."

We got ready together and then took the overground line down to Peckham Rye. We'd had a glass of wine as we'd got ready, but not the usual bottle.

It took so long to get to south London that it might as well have been a different county. I was nervous walking from the station to the pub, suddenly anxious and self-conscious, wondering if I had made a mistake coming. But when we arrived, Finn was outside smoking a cigarette and he lifted me up in a hug, which made me laugh out loud. He looked gorgeous, even more so than I remembered, and he was drunk and happy. I immediately felt better in his company, like the version of myself that I had been in the summer, before that strange day with Richard. That day that had, I now realized, changed everything.

There weren't too many people, a group of about fifteen that fluctuated throughout the evening as people joined and left to move on to other parties. Ophelia looked beautiful in a skintight, asymmetric dress that just covered one of her slender shoulders. She'd made a lot of effort to look good, which of course she didn't need to do because she always looked amazing. Finn stuck close to me, and I completely forgot about how bad I'd been feeling and slipped into another skin, a carefree and happy one. Everything was fine, after all. People kept ordering Prosecco and I lost count of how many drinks I'd had, only realizing I was drunk when the cold air and nicotine from another of Finn's cigarettes hit my lungs in the cold of the winter night. There were fairy lights up outside and although it was too early for Christmas, it had some of that feeling that London gets at that time of year.

Finn and I slipped off at about midnight, back to his place, which was just around the corner. He lived alone in an apartment in a converted warehouse and although Peckham was a bit rough back then, he must have had more money than I'd realized, because it was big.

Sex with Finn was so different from anyone else. He was beautiful without his clothes and there was still the heat, the physical memory of the summer's attraction. I didn't feel guilt, or sadness, or outside of myself. For a moment I was able to get completely lost in him and the comfort of his body, connected wordlessly as we moved against each other. When we had finished, I lay back, naked, thinking that feeling nothing much at all felt really, really good. I spent the night with him, his warm body hooked around mine. In the morning we had sex again, and it was slower, sweeter and more self-conscious. He walked me to the station and kissed me goodbye right there on the street. He knew it wouldn't happen between us again. That I wasn't in that place and never would be. We didn't have to talk about it.

"See ya later, Charlie."

I had texted Ophelia the night before when we'd snuck away. Even though I'd left without saying goodbye she didn't mind, she was just happy I was with Finn, or anyone other than Richard.

When I got home, what felt like a lifetime later, she was in the kitchen with Eddy and Oscar eating bacon sandwiches. They all teased me, and Oscar winked at me. We took turns showering and went to a pub near the park for a roast and a few bottles of red wine, spread out hazily over a full afternoon.

That night I had a text from Richard, the first ever.

> I've almost given up wondering what I have done to upset you enough for you to ignore me for the three full weeks that I have been on this hellish tour. Anyway. My mother died yesterday. Cutting the trip short. Back to the UK Tuesday night. Can you come to the flat. I'll be back by 11.

CHAPTER

Twenty-Two

Richard flew back to the UK that Tuesday and landed late that evening at Heathrow. I was at the flat ready to meet him just before 11 P.M. I waited in a nearby pub for a while when he said he'd be late and then when they closed, I stood outside in the cold until his black cab pulled up just before midnight. He looked old, like he had aged ten years in less than a month. He put his arms around me there in the street. He kissed my head and then my mouth, holding my face in his hands. I could feel him breathing in the smell of my hair. I hadn't believed I would ever feel this again and I was overcome with emotion, but only inwardly. He was wearing leather gloves and a beautiful black coat that he must have bought in America.

The flat had the feel that a home does when it has been empty for a while. It didn't smell bad, exactly, just a little off. Usually, I'd arrive and he'd already be there, the right balance of table lamps and overhead lights and windows open or curtains drawn, and it felt bizarre to see it like this. It felt sad, like Richard did.

"I'm glad to see you. I can't tell you how glad. I didn't want to be here alone tonight. Thank you for coming. I know it's late."

The "thank you" caught me off guard. He went to the sink and poured himself a large glass of water, which he gulped down before refilling his glass again.

"Charlie, I don't know what happened or where you have been

the last few weeks, but I'm too tired—really, truly tired in every way—for an argument. Is that OK? Can we not do that?"

I went to him and put my arms around him, and he put his around me. He smelled the same, even if the flat didn't. He was familiar and warm. I didn't want to argue with him. I wanted to comfort him, to be what he needed, to give him everything I could. It was all I had.

He was, really, all I had.

Any power or distance I had manifested in the previous few weeks had gone, because he was grieving and I had grieved for my own mother for so long, so deeply, that I couldn't ignore him. For the first time I had something that I could offer him, other than my body. My experience could help him through this loss, like his writing had helped me with mine. I couldn't withhold anything from him. Again, I surrendered, utterly powerless to him.

He told me that his sister had already started arranging the funeral and she was taking care of the paperwork. He said there was a lot of paperwork. I didn't remember any of this from when Mum had died, but I supposed there must have been. Dad would have just sorted it all. I thought for the first time about how lonely that must have been for him.

Richard's brother, from whom he was estranged, had been informed of the death by the family solicitor that morning. There was no money to be inherited; it had all been spent on her care. I asked if his brother would be at the funeral, but Richard said he doubted it very much. It wouldn't be for another few weeks. Apparently it had been a bad flu season and there was a backlog. He didn't mention Elaine. I took a lot of hope from that. I'd have thought in such a moment as this that he would have wanted his wife, his history, standing by his side.

He took a long shower, and I walked the flat, turning on the lamps, picking dead bluebottles from the windowsills in bits of tissue and discarding them along with a forgotten carton of milk which I had found in the fridge. The use-by date on it was just two weeks ago. So much had changed in the weeks we had been apart. Yet everything was exactly the same.

He wanted to go straight to bed, so we did. He said he didn't want to have sex, as his mind was preoccupied with unhappy things and he was tired in a way he hadn't been in years. He fell asleep almost immediately with my head on his chest. He must have had a few drinks on the plane, it occurred to me.

The US tour had been hard on him. His schedule had been packed out with events, interviews and signings, and it had taken its toll. Richard loved to perform and to be adored, but he didn't have a lot of time for people, especially sunny Americans, and to an even greater extent, sunny Americans on local radio shows early in the morning. He could have finished the last week of the tour as she was already dead, he told me, but he had wanted to get home as quickly as possible.

At around four in the morning, I woke and found him reading in bed, jetlag getting the better of him. I rolled over and climbed on top of him, and, although it took him a while, he got hard and I lowered myself down, feeling him inside me, where he should be, where we fitted together almost perfectly.

Afterward, he said, "Thank you, Charlie. I'll be able to sleep now."

The next morning, I called in sick again and we went out together to get a takeaway coffee, walking through Covent Garden in broad daylight, side by side though not hand in hand. No one approached him that day. But then Londoners rarely did, it was almost always tourists that interrupted him to say hello or ask for a picture or an autograph. I noticed each glance of recognition, and that there were more than there would have been before *Altitude at Sea* was published. I noticed, too, that everyone who saw him didn't really see me. We were more on show than we had ever been, but, still, next to Richard, I was invisible.

I wanted to tell him that I'd done as he had said and slept with someone else. I wanted to show him a picture of Finn, to show him how gorgeous he was. I wanted to tell him I'd had a small mental breakdown and that I was going to start seeing a psychiatrist, and that I was on even more psychotropic drugs, which were helping my mood.

But I didn't. Instead, I let him talk about this grief that was so heavy on him in the hope that it would lighten. It seemed that it was the dividing of his life to have lost his last remaining parent. He was now next in line for the grave, as he put it. This was, for him, a before-and-after moment.

"I can't be an orphan at fifty-six, so why do I feel like one? Why do I suddenly feel like there is no one to take care of me, when I have been taking care of myself since she shipped me off to boarding school when I was nine?" I had no answer for him. I just leaned in, intently, and rubbed his shoulder. He didn't cry, not once. "I feel like I've got so much I need to tell her. She was gone, really, years ago, but she was my mother. You only get one mother. But you know this; you've been through this," he said, and I thought, *No, I've been through something a hundred thousand times worse.*

He was so changed from the man I had imagined all those years ago. The man who had carried me through my own grief with his writing, who had seemed to understand more and better than anyone—he was gone. Because in the face of his own grief, he was a child again. He understood no more of death than I did and that realization made him more human. As time passed between us, I was able to see him more and more clearly. The creases in his face first thing in the morning, when he caught his toe on the edge of a step and stumbled, when he forgot his PIN buying coffee, all of these little details of Richard brought him closer to the mortal world where he was nothing extraordinary, just a man with a remarkable talent.

Watching him wrestle with the loss of his own mother was so humanizing, but also disappointing. I don't know what I had expected, but it was not this inelegant, almost petulant state of grief. His mother had been seventy-nine years old when she died of Alzheimer's in a warm bed in a nursing home, with her daughter and her two grandsons at her side. It had been years since she had recognized any of them. Richard was a fifty-six-year-old man with three properties and two marriages when his mother died, surrounded by people who loved her. *This is the way it should be,* I thought. *This is a good death.*

He had hardly talked about her in all the time we'd been together. Yet it was a huge blow to him.

But everyone knows you shouldn't compare grief.

The next night he did sleep. He was still asleep even when I woke. I got ready as quietly as I could. I kissed him goodbye and he stirred, seemingly confused at where he was, that I was there.

"I've got to head back today. I have a lot to sort out. I'll try to get back soon. Charlie—I missed you."

The appointment with the psychiatrist happened the following week. It was at his own clinic rather than at the GP surgery, which was in a building that I must have walked past a hundred times but never really noticed, hidden around the back of a car park on Stoke Newington's busy Church Street. There was a plastic Christmas tree in the reception area, and decorations up around the pinboards, which were full of advice and adverts for help services and support groups. I waited for a long time because they were running late. When I was called in, it was by an energetic and handsome middle-aged man who, I saw from his lanyard, was a consultant. He introduced himself as Dr. Harding. I liked him immediately. He took me to a side room and we talked for an hour about my life, my upbringing. I understood after this meeting, from the lengthy letter he had written detailing our conversation, that this must have been him taking a history.

The conversation was very helpful and allowed me to put the events of my life in order. I found some place of truth between the story I had told over and over, and the story as I had told it to Richard months before. Everything had been on a fairly good path despite the problems I had managing my emotions, which the doctor said were likely due to the upheaval in my early life, and then things had been broken, shattered. He asked a lot about my memories and my family before my mum had left my real dad. He told me that the first five years of our lives are probably the most important, that in these early moments we form all of our understanding of attachment and safety, and disruption then can go on to cause all sorts of problems later in life. That I didn't have any memories of these years seemed to interest him even more. We talked a lot about my mum and I cried a great deal in a way that felt cathartic.

Then I told him about Richard. He couldn't tell anyone about that, I checked before I did. He knew Richard's writing very well, he was a big reader himself, with aspirations of writing fiction one day. He asked me a lot about the relationship, and I told him everything.

I told him about Lee, and how Richard had been the one to explain it to me, how safe and loved he had made me feel, how good he was, really. That none of my friends understood and that they couldn't ever understand being with someone older, someone like Richard.

He wanted to talk more about the "sexual assault" and it took me a moment to understand what he meant. When I told him I didn't have much to say about it, he didn't press the matter. He asked me why I thought I put so much of my value into Richard's affections, why I felt like my life would be over when the relationship ended. He wanted to know a lot about that, about the finality I had placed on it for myself, the end of my story written and me just waiting for it to unfold in absolute, Shakespearean tragedy.

I asked him what was wrong with me, and he said that I was suffering with depression and anxiety, but not to place too much on a diagnosis because I was a whole and complete person with a lot of thoughts and emotions and complicated trauma. He referred me for some psychotherapy at the clinic, which I would have to wait a bit for, and added another medication to my prescription to help stabilize my mood. Until my therapy started, I was to download an app for my phone that would give me some breathing exercises, try to keep up the running, eat three regular meals a day and try to avoid alcohol. He said I'd see him again in two months, that we would work together, and that his secretary would make an appointment and send me a letter. Something about his care and attention made me feel better. No one had ever really asked me about my life in a way that made me feel listened to. Not even Ophelia or Eddy. He hadn't judged me or offered a word of advice and yet I felt more understood than I had ever felt before.

A week later, a copy of a letter he had written to my GP arrived at the house. In it, he detailed our conversation. Over four typewritten pages, he had referred to me as *highly articulate* and *extremely bright,* and I wondered again why older men were so daft about me, because I was neither. I was wholly, completely, unexceptional. Some other phrases and things I had said were noted word for word, although I couldn't remember saying them.

The sudden death of her mother when she was sixteen was extremely traumatic: "I lost everything, my entire world was torn

> *apart"—a significant factor in her subsequent depression, although the patient states she was "born with it, something is wrong inside me that always goes toward darkness." And then, later: Fears her lack of a biological connection to her father means that there is no bond between them. This is inconsistent with the warmth of her account of him. At the end: Fatalistic attitude to her relationship—"I don't want to be ordinary. I can't stand myself, the ordinariness of myself. I want the opposite of that, and he makes my life extraordinary." This idea of dying is tied to her unhealthy attachment rather than to any active intent. She remains at least in part oriented to her future. Nevertheless, I think it will be wise for me to see her again in a few months. Meanwhile, I have given her the contact details for the Hackney Crisis Line and she has agreed to use this if necessary . . .*

I folded the letter back into the envelope and hid it in the drawer of my bedside table. There was a part of me that wanted to show it to Ophelia and Eddy, to share with them that things were OK and that I was getting better, but I'd not seen either of them for days, and in disappearing back to Richard at his first call, I had tested their patience. They had taken such care of me, nursed me back to health, eased me away from him while he had been in America, and I knew they were frustrated and had told me as much. They blamed Richard entirely for my lapses in mood. Repeatedly, Ophelia had tried to remind me about how I'd been when I had met her, how I had been happy. This sadness that she had seen come and go over the previous ten months must be down to my relationship with Richard, a married man over thirty years my senior. A man she knew I had idolized since I was young. But things were not that clear-cut, as I tried to tell her. You never knew what someone had going on inside, or in their past. What Ophelia really didn't seem to understand was that when terrible things happened to us, especially in those formative years where we are nothing but soft, wet clay spinning on a dizzying wheel, they change the shape of our insides forever. Only people who have experienced such a thing can understand such a thing; our foundations have fault lines even before they have been built on. But they just blamed Richard. They saw all of my problems as being directly related to my relationship with him, and I think by this point they had accepted that there was nothing either of them could do to change my mind about him. It would have to run its course.

None of which changed the fact that I knew, but would never admit, that the relationship was tearing me apart, because it really was. It's just that I was so fragile that I was tearing more easily than any of us could have ever predicted.

When Ophelia messaged me asking me if I would be home that evening, I expected another lecture on Richard. Instead, I found her at home, pacing the kitchen, nervous to tell me that Oscar had asked her to move in with him the following spring. I was pleasantly surprised to find I was nothing but happy for her. Her life was moving onward and upward. She was doing well at work and had acquired a book in a highly competitive auction, with the author choosing her over many other more experienced editors based on her talent and personality. She'd had a decent pay bump and title change as a result, and an article with a picture of her had appeared in the publishing trade paper, *The Bookseller.* Now she was moving in with her boyfriend. She'd be married in no time, I thought to myself, although I didn't say that to her.

I told her I'd be able to find a new place no problem, but she looked confused by that and said of course Eddy and I could stay as long as we wanted. There was no mortgage on the house and her parents didn't need the money. I couldn't imagine living there without her, but at the same time I couldn't imagine finding anywhere even a quarter as nice for twice the rent. I guessed I'd just stay there indefinitely. My life was not moving in any direction.

CHAPTER

Twenty-Three

Suddenly, it was December and it was Christmas again.

The streets of central London were packed with shoppers, and vomit littered the pavements. The late-night Tube was full of drunk people in tacky party clothes and cheap-looking Christmas jumpers, and everywhere you went the same old songs were playing, reminding you of better and happier years. *One Christmas is going to be my last,* I thought. *That is a fact. It is inevitable.* I wondered if it would be this one. If next year would be the year that finally killed me.

After the funeral, Richard had stayed in Yorkshire for a while to write. It did him good and he came back to London in mid-December feeling more cheerful and hopeful. I'd spend most of the week staying with him. He wrote during the day while I was at work, and when I got back to the flat in the evenings, he would let me read little bits of what he had been working on. He was writing using a typewriter—he wanted to go back to where he had started and he found computers full of distractions. He'd hand me the odd page of text, the words pressed into the paper by those little keys hit by his own hands. He said he wanted my honest opinion, but he didn't—he wanted reassurance and praise, but not too much. As always, I gave him what he needed, peppered occasionally with a little of my opinion which he would frown at, usually, before changing the subject. I wanted a repeat of that moment, just ten months previously, when my suggestion had wowed him and made it to the page, but that moment didn't come. We hadn't ever even talked about it. Nevertheless, it was wonderful to read his words like that, untouched by editors or proofreaders or even his own second thoughts.

My change in medication seemed to be working well and I felt more level. I was glad to have Richard back, even though the world had a bigger piece of him now. He was still appearing regularly on the radio and television, and he had even been photographed walking down a Soho street with a director and some of the cast that were going to be in the film adaptation of *Altitude at Sea*; the actor playing Seb had a colorful private life that was the subject of much speculation. The pictures appeared in the tabloid press, mentioning Richard by name, which, as Cecile expected, he neither liked nor really understood. He hadn't acknowledged his change in status directly. He loved being famous, but not fame.

At the same time as this change in his anonymity, he was much less worried about us being seen together and we now often walked around Covent Garden together.

"I'd just say we were at an interview and you work for my publisher. I don't know why I was so concerned otherwise. And if it's anyone from Winden & Shane that we see, well, what are they going to say to me about it? They work for me, not the other way around."

I longed to feel the weight of his arm on my shoulder, as I had in France, but I was happy just to be out with him. I did hope to bump into someone I knew, maybe someone from school or university. To introduce him to them. But although we were right in the center of London, one of the most populated places on the planet, we never did.

One Friday, just before Christmas, I arrived at Richard's a little drunk after a work party. He covered my eyes and guided me into the living room. There, in the middle of the room, was the chair from the *brocante* in France, the one that I'd sat in and loved on that day all those months ago. I was confused, wondering why he was showing it to me as a surprise.

"Happy Christmas, Charlie."

He had it sent to my house that weekend. As we stood looking at it on Sunday afternoon, I could tell that Ophelia was impressed. We were sipping on wine that Eddy had mulled with brandy and cloves, filling the house with a warm and familiar smell.

It was a rare thing for just the three of us to be together on a Sunday. We'd been out and bought a tree, which we'd carried home up the high street in fits of giggles, and had decorated it with the strings of lights and ornaments that had been stashed in the unused office for a whole year.

We'd had a lovely afternoon, playing old Christmas standards from the 1950s and 1960s, which I much preferred to the Christmas hits that were played on the radio everywhere you went. We hadn't talked about our relationships, or the future, or anything like that, and just focused on the task at hand.

The chair was too big for my room, which Eddy and Ophelia had predicted before we'd maneuvered it up two flights of stairs. I was disappointed, I had loved the idea of it being just for me, but we decided to put it in the dining room instead, in a corner by the French doors that opened into the side-return and the garden. It looked out of place among the modern furniture, which was all pine and plastic, but it didn't matter.

"It must have cost a fortune." Ophelia winced. "You could always sell it. I mean, what use does anyone renting in London have for a giant antique chair?"

But I would never sell it. Every time I looked at it, I told myself, I would remember that he loved me. Since Oscar had asked her to move in with him, Ophelia had been less interested in the car crash of my own love life. She was undoubtedly glad to be getting away from me and my mess, and had given up the fight, resigned to the fact that I was going to be with Richard until it all fell apart.

Only it didn't fall apart that Christmas, not for Richard and me, anyway. In fact, things between us felt better than ever. He was softer, more open and more vulnerable than he'd ever been and he was aware of it, even curious about it. And I in turn felt good.

Ophelia was taking Oscar with her to Switzerland for Christmas. Eddy was going to Sri Lanka with some friends from university, and, with no other options, I was going home to my dad's for a few days. I'd get the train down on Christmas Eve after work, and would stay for a few nights, coming back after Boxing Day. I had a huge reading pile that I had accrued and I was planning to spend the period between Christmas and New Year's at the house, working my way through it. I was quite looking forward to having it all to myself. Richard would be in Yorkshire with Elaine, and he was planning to write. He was seeing his sister over the holidays, and her grown-up children, which surprised him as much as it surprised me. His mother's death had continued to bring a marked change in him.

On Christmas Eve, the office was deserted and with Cecile's blessing I left at eleven in the morning. I had bags of gifts for Dad, Laura and Noah, many of them books that I had exchanged with people in different departments, and some that I'd swiped off people's desks after hours in the preceding weeks. Some I had actually bought. The handles of my tote bags dug into my shoulders as I walked to King's Cross station, which was alive with flustered, stressed travelers trying to get home for the holidays. A storm was forecast, and the worry was that trains would be canceled that afternoon as a result, so everyone was trying to get ahead of it.

When I arrived at Victoria station, I bought two miniature bottles of red wine from Marks & Spencer for the journey, but the train was so busy that I couldn't get a seat until I was half an hour from home. Dad came to meet me at the station. He had a new car. I thought how odd it was that I didn't even know what kind of car he drove anymore.

Dad wanted to stop at the big supermarket to pick up some last bits on the way home. I wondered if I'd see anyone from school, but I didn't. At the house, Noah was initially wary of me and hid behind Laura's legs, but after a little while he seemed to forget his fear and insisted that I help him with his Lego project. Laura was preparing food for the next day. We watched *The Snowman* on Channel 4 before dinner, as we always had done when I was little, sitting in that same spot a meter from the screen. I watched the animation reflected in Noah's thick glasses; he had appalling eyesight even at four. I wondered if he knew it was about loss and death, and not just a flying snowman. I hoped he didn't.

After dinner, Laura insisted that Dad and I go for a drink, which was a bit uncomfortable for both of us. I'd not spent time alone with him for what was probably now years. He asked me where we should go and I suggested the Anchor. I don't know why. I didn't want to see people from school, yet I did, in the way you can't stop yourself from looking at a car accident. Perhaps they would have forgotten about everything. Perhaps seeing them would make me happy that I didn't have them in my life. I felt extremely lonely being back at home with no friends.

It was a bit of a walk to the pub, but it was dry and cold in that way that cities can't be. We chatted about work, Laura and Noah, but mostly about Noah. There was some concern that he was too sensitive, which Dad said was funny because I had been the same. I wanted to remind him that it must have just been a coincidence because he hadn't known me when I was Noah's age, and we weren't of the same genetic stuff for it to be inherited. We didn't talk about Mum. He asked me if I had a boyfriend, but again I could tell Laura had told him to ask me. Dad would have never come up with such a personal question about a subject he clearly didn't feel comfortable hearing about.

The pub was heaving, and Dad asked if we should go elsewhere, but there was nowhere else nearby so we decided to just stay for one, even though there were no seats free. He went to the bar to order for us, and I stood awkwardly by a fireplace, which had no fire in it. Instead, it had a small plastic Christmas tree and a creepy-looking Santa doll posed in the empty hearth. I looked at my phone, rather than look up, but I could see a few faces I thought I recognized from school. They weren't people I was close with, or even friends with on social media.

"Here you go, love. Happy Christmas." He clinked his glass against mine. He was drinking a pint of something dark, flat and bitter. "Anyone you know from school here? Do you keep in touch with anyone?"

He was either completely oblivious to the events of my last year living at home, or he had forgotten.

"Yeah, a bit, on social media." I did have social media accounts and did spend time looking through people's photos, relationship statuses, news updates. Hours, sometimes. But I didn't post anything, or message anyone, and no one messaged me. "You know how it is, I'm just so busy with all my friends in London, and work and stuff. And uni. My uni friends."

Just then, Cassie and two others that I had been friends with that awful year walked past us, arm in arm, from the toilet. I recognized them instantly. Cassie looked at me for a second, but her face didn't change. I looked different now—I had different hair and different clothes. At first, I thought she hadn't recognized me, but she whispered something to one of the others, who glanced back at me and shrugged. They carried on to a table on the other side of the bar out of my sightline.

"Look, Dad, I know you hate it, but I need a cigarette. I won't be long. Do you want to come out with me?"

"Are you mad? It's freezing out there. I'll wait here. This fire can keep me warm." He mimed warming his hands on the nonexistent fire and smiled, pleased with his dad-humor. I would have usually had a lecture on my smoking, but not today.

It was very cold outside, and the smell of the sea filled my lungs between clouds of smoke and nicotine. I could hear the roar of the ocean somewhere ahead, invisible in the darkness of the night. There were picnic benches around the edges of the old white building and a few heaters on, which people had crowded around, laughing and in good spirits. How many were coming home, and how many had never left? It was impossible to say.

As I was going back inside again, a group of men were coming out. They were about my age. I stood out of the way of them and held the door open.

And there he was. Lee.

I didn't know how I would react to seeing him. I had created this situation, as I did with all of the messes in my life. I had come here, I knew, partly hoping that I would see him. But now that it was happening, I couldn't think why.

Everything had slowed down. I could see my hand on the edge of the door holding it back, his next to mine, pushing it open, but it didn't feel real.

He had an unlit cigarette in his mouth and was with a friend that I didn't recognize. "Thanks, love," he said, moving past me, outside. He had looked right at me, but he hadn't even recognized me. He probably didn't think about me at all, not ever. My ears were ringing and my hands were shaking, but I didn't feel anything that I had thought I might; there was no fear, or anger. Just more emptiness. I went back inside, moving on autopilot, hoping that nothing of the moment that had just passed could be seen on my face.

Dad was where I had left him, pint in one hand, the other in the pocket of his jeans.

"You all right, sweetheart?" he asked me when I returned to him. So I wasn't keeping my composure as well as I'd thought.

"Yes, I'm fine! I just bumped into some people I knew from school."

"If you want to stay and join them, don't let me stop you—just one for me or Santa Claus might forget to visit little Noah."

"No, I'm so tired. Let's just finish these and go."

I drained my large glass of red wine in minutes. I wasn't doing a very good job of being my normal self, whoever that was. Dad, who hardly drank these days, abandoned his pint before it was finished, sensing I wanted to get out.

Outside, Lee and his friends were laughing at something unknown to me that must have been hilarious. I looked at him, willing him to speak to me. But he didn't turn around or catch my eye. He didn't even know I was there.

We walked home in almost total silence. Laura was waiting up. Noah had optimistically left a carrot and a mince pie on the mantelpiece above the gas fire. Dad ate the mince pie, leaving the foil wrapper crumpled on the plate, and took a bite of the carrot. I could tell this was a special ritual for them. This would be the first Christmas that Noah would really understand, they told me.

I went to bed ahead of them, but I couldn't sleep. I remembered the miniatures of red wine in my bag and sat on my bed, in the darkness, drinking them. I didn't want Dad or Laura to know I was awake, so I didn't turn on the light. I was still trying to comprehend the enormousness of what I couldn't feel, but the wine didn't help. *There must be something so wrong with me,* I thought for the millionth time in my life. *Normal people aren't like this.*

Christmas Day was nicer than I'd expected. Noah had been up since dawn opening his presents and playing with them, delighted that Father Christmas had delivered. There had been some worry about him not being able to get in, given that we didn't have an open fire.

He'd eaten the mince pie! There were actual teeth marks in the carrot, from the reindeer! Noah's happiness was very sweet to behold, even to me and my dead insides.

The living room floor was covered with empty foils from chocolate coins and scraps of wrapping paper. Noah was running around from one toy to the next, so happy and excited that I thought he might lose his mind. When I came downstairs, he immediately wanted me to come and see what he had got, which was an electric train set, a digger and a rocket that you used a foot pump to propel into the air. He climbed into my lap as I sat next to him in my pajamas, talking excitedly and making noises for each toy. The smell of his baby shampoo and chocolate, sweet on his breath, were comforting and familiar.

Laura had got me a necklace and matching earrings from a shop in the village. They were not at all my style, but it was thoughtful, and I knew she had tried hard to get me something I would like so I put them on. Dad, Laura and Noah had bought me a mini Polaroid camera like Ophelia's, which was an excellent gift and one I was thrilled with. I gave them books, mostly, which they liked. I tried to explain that I had even bought some of them myself as we didn't publish them, but I was pretty sure they thought I'd got them all for free. No one minded, though. I gave Noah a set of Play-Doh, which he loved but I knew Laura was already thinking about how she'd get it out of the carpet.

We ate a big Christmas lunch and then later went for a walk on the beach. It was bright but freezing cold, and the narrow path, which was overgrown with sea kale, was packed with families so that we had to keep stopping to give way. Everyone said hello to us and us to them, which Laura said wouldn't ever happen normally. I liked her. She was kind and she was a great mum to Noah, steering him on his little balance bike the whole way, always with one eye on him.

Richard called me late that afternoon when we were back at the house. I slipped out the French doors into the dark garden, still in my slippers, hoping to agree on a time for him to call me back. I could tell straight away something wasn't right from his voice.

"Charlie, darling. Happy Christmas."

"Happy Christmas, Richard. Is everything OK?"

"You always know, don't you?" A pause as he smoked his cigarette. "It is, and it isn't. The inevitable has happened, and Elaine has left. We are separating."

I didn't know what to say to this. He didn't exactly sound happy. More maniacal, almost. My thoughts turned immediately to what this would mean for us.

"Are you there?"

"Yes, yes, I am. I'm sorry, Richard."

"No, you're not, and that's fine. Please don't pretend otherwise. You know I hate falseness." He was drunk.

"It's not that simple. I am sorry, of course I am." There was another long pause.

"Anyway, she has gone. And this means that I have space and freedom, and I wondered if you would like to come here, to Stone Heap House, and spend the week with me. When you've finished at your parents', of course."

Parents, I thought. *Parents?*

"I'm staying until the day after tomorrow. There are hardly any trains on Boxing Day."

"Well, the day after then. You can get the train from London, and I'll pick you up. Would you like that? To see the house?"

"You know I would. But isn't it a bit soon? Shouldn't we give it some time for things to settle down?"

"Time, Charlie, is not something I have as much of as you do. And anyway, she has left and will be on the first flight back to France that she can get. I thought you'd want to come here. I didn't expect to have to persuade you."

"I do! You know I do."

"Then do. You can call me whenever you like, now. So let me know what time you'll be getting in, and I'll come and get you. Whichever station is convenient."

It was only when I was back inside that I realized how cold I was, and that he hadn't asked me how I was or how my Christmas had been. But he was dealing with a lot—that much was clear. And I had, so very badly, wanted to go and stay at Stone Heap House. As hard as I tried to think differently and more maturely, their separation was the greatest gift I could ask for.

"Who was that?" Laura was alone in the kitchen scrubbing the burnt remains of roast potatoes from a dish, a Christmas compilation CD spinning on the player next to her. I could have told her. I felt almost like I wanted to confide in her.

"Oh, no one, just a friend."

CHAPTER

Twenty-Four

Richard met me at Sheffield train station, which wasn't far from the university campus that we'd been at earlier that year when things between us were just starting. It felt like a different lifetime.

My heart fluttered joyously as I walked from the platform into the station looking for him, trying not to let on that I was excited beyond reason to be here and see him. Our eyes met and I went to him, but I wasn't sure how to greet him. He kissed my cheek, his mouth lingering there for just a moment. People stopped and looked—everyone recognized him here. He took my little suitcase from me and we walked to the car, which was parked just outside with the taxis. He was not inconspicuous, this giant man and his muddy old Land Rover. I enjoyed every double take, feeling their eyes on me. They really could see me. They were probably wondering who I was. *His daughter? But he doesn't have children—maybe a niece? But that was not a kiss you'd give a family member—maybe a girlfriend?* I smiled to myself as we swerved around the cars outside the station and took the road out of the city.

It was nearly an hour's drive to Stone Heap House, through Sheffield and out into the Peak District National Park. I'd never been before. I had imagined it to be barren, and on higher ground, it was. Skeletal, lonely trees leaned into the relentless wind, which sang across the gorse and fern and brown brush that gave way, suddenly, to forest and valley and houses. We slowed down, driving through a silent village untouched by modern architecture, perfectly preserved as though the world outside the national park had not been allowed in. Protruding corners of dry-stone wall and buildings lost to time lined the roads, never stopping, sometimes falling deep into disrepair but always there, coated in lichen and moss and hugged by thistle and nettle. Snow had fallen and in places it was quite thick, like a dusting of icing sugar on a sticky cake.

We made small talk, a little shy of each other in these new circumstances. He asked about my dad, Laura, Noah. I talked about Christmas, about the train journey. I remarked again and again about the landscape. I understood him more, seeing it. It was almost desolate, but then abundant. It was so changeable, and so wild and cold and isolated that I couldn't think of anything further from Covent Garden.

Stone Heap House was far grander than I had expected it to be. Parts of it dated back to the seventeenth century, he told me. It was built in pale stone and positioned on a private road where it couldn't be seen by anyone unless they knew to look for it. The main house was three stories high. It looked like it had had other additions on many different occasions over the centuries, with some parts of it shaped differently and covering two stories. The windows and doors were small, and all of the woodwork was painted a deep, sea-foam green. I immediately thought of Richard's height and how incompatible he seemed with such a house.

We parked in the gravel drive but, rather than go to the main house, he walked me around the side to an area to the left. At the back, there was a series of connected outbuildings that were more like cottages, arranged in a L-shape against the house, with a large, cobbled courtyard. When he had said he lived mostly in the stables, I'd imagined a single room.

He let us in through the front door in the center of the longest building. It opened into a dark sitting room with a kitchen area to the right, and a heavy door which must have led to the main house. I followed him to the left and into a narrow corridor. I stopped at the doorway of his office. Here, the windows had been knocked through to create a thick wall of glass, giving an uninterrupted, panoramic view of the surrounding countryside. His desk sat in front of it; a typewriter, a cup of pencils, a box of paper and a pile of yellow legal pads covered in his handwritten scrawl were neatly stacked next to it. There was a stove burning in the corner, and a red sofa.

"This way," he said, leading me on down the corridor. "Bathroom . . ." He pointed at another room, which had a white bathtub with an old Victorian-looking shower over it. "And bedroom."

I felt inexplicably nervous as I followed him into his bedroom. He put my suitcase on the floor and motioned a hand at the bed. "This is where I live, when I'm here." In this most intimate of spaces, he felt as unknowable as a complete stranger, and I couldn't understand why. He seemed self-conscious, something that I had never seen in him before. His accent was stronger than I'd ever heard it. I sat down on the bed, but he gestured to follow him back into the living room.

There were wood-burning stoves in each room, all alight and glowing, and condensation on the inside of the small windows. The ceilings were so low that he had to duck as he moved between rooms, but he moved in such an instinctive and graceful way that he probably didn't even think about it, having done it for so long. Each room was full of beautiful, sophisticated old things in various states of disrepair. A copper kettle sat on a small red Aga next to a stained Italian percolator. An armchair with stuffing creeping through the leather at the seat stood next to a side table with a fold of card supporting a single leg. Oil paintings of what I took to be the Peaks hung mismatched in gold, chipped frames, and piles of typewritten paper sat under stubs of pencils, which had been crudely sharpened with a knife. And there were books—everywhere there were books. Bookshelves and then just shelves with more books, books on the tables and sofa and even a small pile of books on the floor. The whole place was dark and smelled richly of woodsmoke mixed with cigarettes and coffee. It was so incredibly Richard, it was like he embodied every lovely corner, every space. I saw now that the flat was all Elaine; this was all him. I thought of Dad's house, the curtains from Next, the DFS sofa set. I thought of the fairy lights in my bedroom in Stoke Newington, the floral Ikea bedspread, and I felt very small.

I didn't know what to say to him about the place that would not make him feel uneasy. He was so quiet that I feared he was regretting bringing me here.

"Coffee? Or something stronger?"

"Something stronger. Definitely."

He took a bottle of red from a wine rack in the kitchen, inspected it and then replaced it, choosing another one. He wiped off the dust and opened it with a pop and poured out two large glasses. I could hear the radio playing from his office.

I realized I was still wearing my coat and shoes, almost at the same time he did. He took my coat from me.

"Please, make yourself comfortable. I want you to feel at home. Are you warm enough?"

I nodded and went to the sofa. He brought over the wine and sat next to me.

"So, this is it, this is Stone Heap House. These are the stables."

I sipped my wine, noticing the glass was a little dirty. I had imagined this place so much, and so differently. How had this come to be? I let my shoulders drop and stretched my neck with a crack. He put his hand there in a surprising gesture of tenderness. It was nearly three o'clock and the light was fading.

"Do you want to see the rest of the house?"

"Maybe tomorrow, in the daylight—is that OK?"

"Whatever you like. You are my guest. I'll roast a chicken this evening, if you aren't sick of such meals after Christmas."

"It's still Christmas and I'm not. You don't have a tree."

"There is one in the house. I have no interest in pageantry, you know that."

"I love Christmas trees."

"That doesn't surprise me about you."

"There must be fewer and fewer surprises now. It's been almost a year. Aren't you getting tired of me?" I was being playful, goading him into reassuring me. But he didn't bite. He looked instead at the wineglass in his hand.

"I'm bored with myself, Charlie. I'm sick of myself. Absolutely sick. But when I'm with you, I feel better. I see myself differently. I'm not dreadful anymore. I'm happy you are here. Things are messy. I think I should probably explain everything to you so that you understand the situation. Is that all right?"

And so he did, finally, explain to me the part of his life that I'd not been privy to at all—his marriage. And it was something like this.

Elaine and Richard had lived very separate lives for the last fifteen years or so, with that gap widening over time. Stone Heap House and the house in France were his. His money paid for everything. All Elaine really owned was the flat, the place that I thought of as ours. He had suspected she had been unfaithful some time ago, with someone in France. They had never really discussed their arrangement in detail. He had always, even from the very beginning, told her that he was unlikely to be satisfied by her alone, but that he would, when it came to it, come home to her and no one else. After her infidelity, he had told her that he was going to live his life as he wanted to. He had had the odd affair over the years, short-lived ones, both in New York and London, and even while he was a visiting professor at Sheffield University. The women had for the most part been around his age, or, perhaps, a little younger. But never as young as me.

Meanwhile Elaine had set up her life in France. She hadn't written much after they'd got married and he found that deeply unattractive, that she had just switched off and lost the creative part of herself that he had fallen in love with. In the last few years, their relationship had become more strained. She was unsupportive of his writing and wanted to be in France, whereas he preferred to be in England, here at Stone Heap House, or, if he needed to be, in London. She hated the cold and he hated the heat. She was less interested in sex, and he was only more so as he got older. They were left with no common ground, except the world they inhabited publicly, and it wasn't enough for either of them. She had been unsympathetic to his sadness at the death of his mother, frustrated by his affair with me (although he made it very clear she didn't know who I was) and his refusal to break it off, and, in a fit of rage over a burnt turkey, had announced she wanted a separation, maybe even a divorce. She had packed a bag and called a taxi and left two days earlier.

I listened in silence, taking it all in with curiosity and an almost morbid fascination as we worked our way through the bottle of wine. With every revelation I tried to think about the next steps and where it left us. He seemed calm, but used his hands more than he usually did as he talked. I couldn't detect any anger in his words, or bitterness, or even sadness. He said it was unlikely she would actually want a divorce, because as long as they were married, she was quite wealthy. A divorce would be messy and public and mean selling Stone Heap House, maybe, or even the house in France that she loved so much. I didn't have to ask if that meant we wouldn't have to keep our relationship a secret anymore. I knew that wouldn't change, certainly not for the time being.

As the darkness had crept across the land, the room had grown even dimmer without us realizing, like frogs boiling in a pot. When he had finished talking, he turned on a series of floor and desk lamps and brought the room into focus again. We went to the door to smoke. The air outside was damp and cold. There were no stars.

I had nothing to offer Richard on these matters; it was far beyond my lived experience or real understanding of how a marriage longer than my entire life had broken down. I didn't want to say something stupid or naive. Instead, I sat next to him on a stool in the little kitchen as he prepared a chicken and potatoes, and put them into the Aga, which radiated a soft heat through the room. I talked to him about books, I asked him questions about books, and this cheered him. We had another bottle of wine and by the time the chicken was cooked, I'd lost my appetite.

The bedroom was warmed by the little wood-burning stove that sat glowing in the corner of the room. The bed was soft and comfortable, and built big enough to accommodate Richard's frame. After three nights in my childhood bed, it was delicious to spread out, to feel him next to me, on top of me, inside me, which was exactly where he should be.

In the morning, Richard made me a breakfast of eggs and toast and coffee, and then we went for a walk. He had to lend me some wellies and a coat because it was so wet, but I was the same shoe size as Elaine and he had an old Barbour that fitted me, which I wore over one of his scratchy wool jumpers, so it worked out OK.

We walked for miles. It was very windy, and the sky would move quickly, turning from brilliant blue to black, and then shake itself off, dappled. The sunlight would suddenly illuminate a valley dark with heather far in the distance, changing the spectrum from brown and gray to almost turquoise in places, and when that same sunlight fell on the path we were walking, it felt warm enough that I took off my coat for a few minutes. Hikers with dogs would pass us and we would say good morning to each other and move on. The path wasn't always easy—it was so uneven and rocky and steep that downhill was more difficult than uphill—but Richard knew the area well and that made it feel easier.

Every few miles he'd ask if I'd had enough, and I'd say no, and we'd go on. He talked to me about the landscape, about the earth and the grass, the birds and the rabbits and the foxes and the flowers and the moss. About the trees, executed by disease or lightning, decapitated, strange and sad, standing defiantly in the brush, thickening to forest as we went to lower ground. We stopped at a stream, which would, in summer, be caressed by fingers of the ash and sycamore trees that watched over it, but in this deep winter ran untouched by anything but light and snow, clean and clear as glass. We then walked to a pub a short distance away, where Richard said we wouldn't be bothered.

It was a very old pub, which smelled so strongly of cigarette smoke I wondered if people did indeed still smoke in here in the evenings. The walls were all wood-paneled and the ceilings were even lower than at Stone Heap House. There was a Christmas tree by the open fire, covered with slowly flashing colored lights. We ordered pints of beer and beef sandwiches, and sat by the fire. There were two liver-colored springer spaniels roaming the pub floor, hunting for crisps or other scraps. One put its muzzle on Richard's leg, looking up at him submissively with its big, dark eyes. I was embarrassed to be reminded of myself. Richard held out a bit of fat from the meat in his sandwich and the dog wolfed it gratefully before falling asleep under his chair.

Even dogs couldn't resist Richard.

The barman seemed to know him but made no comment about us, and I said nothing. I was enjoying taking in every second of his world, of being with him.

We got back late that afternoon. Richard needed to get food from the larder in the main house and I joined him as I'd not been inside yet. It was a magnificent house. The ceilings were much higher, the corridors wider. It was less cluttered and cozy, but the décor was undeniably tasteful, and, more important, Richard explained, sensitive to the age of the place. The larder, as it turned out, was a cool room that you walked into next to the kitchen, which was itself huge and had obviously been added within the last hundred years. It wasn't modern like ours in London. There was no white marble. There was another Aga—this one pale green and much larger—and there were long wooden surfaces. The windows were bigger than in the stables, too, and there were big Crittall-style doors that framed a dining table and overlooked a kitchen garden.

On the side next to the sink was a bowl of clementines that still had their leaves attached. I loved those little leaves. I took one without asking and peeled it, the smell of Christmas bursting as my thumb pushed through the skin. When Richard came back into the room, he surprised me by kissing me, so much so that I had to swallow a whole segment of orange and it made me choke. He laughed and took a piece from the skin on the side.

"Take off your jeans," he said.

"Here?"

"Yes, here. There's no one else here. No one for miles. The housekeeper is on holiday."

I did what he told me, taking off my thick wool socks and jeans in as dignified manner as I could. He lifted me onto the kitchen counter and kissed me again, and then loosened his belt and undid his own jeans and we had sex there, in his kitchen, next to the bowl of clementines, a piece of orange still stuck in my throat.

After, I got dressed and he showed me the house. On the ground floor were two living rooms, a snug and a grand dining room, as well as a boot room and an office. Upstairs were five bedrooms of various sizes, two with ensuites, and an elegant bathroom with a huge copper bathtub. There were two attic rooms, but they were just being used for storage. Richard clearly had more money than I'd ever realized.

"Elaine dominated the main house. I've always been in the stables, although it started out as being just for my writing as the view from the office was so good. I don't know why I let her push me out, or why I've stayed there. We should cook here tonight. There's more room."

We did, although we still slept in the stables. The next day we drove out farther south to Derbyshire, to a reservoir edged with forest and a shore of smooth gray slates. The sky was dark and the air damp and cold and still. We parked up and walked across the top of the dam, watching the water fall into the two sinkholes that had been built on either side to manage the overflow. The water roared, sucked down into nothingness, and for a reason I couldn't put my finger on I felt truly scared by this sight. But I said nothing, experiencing this feeling, and silently trying to understand it. We watched them for a very long time. Richard pulled out a hip flask filled with whisky that tasted like the earth, and we drank from it and it warmed us. We walked for miles around the edge of the reservoir. Sometimes Richard held my gloved hand in his.

When we got back, we returned to the main house to cook. I sat on the surface where we'd had sex the night before and drank his expensive wine, while he cut carrots and celery and onions to go with whatever meat we were having that night.

"Ophelia's moving in with Oscar in the spring. I think I told you that, didn't I?"

"You did."

"She says I can stay in the house, though, which is great because I wouldn't be able to afford anything that nice. It will be odd without her. I feel like everything is going to change in 2011."

"Do you want to stay there?"

"I guess. I don't know. The house is great and I have a good room. I don't know if Eddy will stay. I hope so."

"Remind me which one Eddy is?"

"Eddy, who works at Penguin. He's an editor. You saw me with him that night in Wilton-upon-Avon. He knows about us, by the way. He has since then. I didn't tell him; it just all came out when Ophelia found out."

He paused and raised an eyebrow at me before going back to the vegetables. I picked a piece of carrot from the chopping board and inspected it before popping it in my mouth.

"I don't know if we'll be able to meet at the flat anymore, as we used to."

My heart sank. "I'd guessed that might be the case."

"But I'll need a place in London. I'll probably rent somewhere for the time being. I can't see any reason for you not to live there. I won't be there all the time, as much as I have been. I would pay the rent; you wouldn't need to worry about money or bills or anything as banal and domestic as that."

"Are you serious?"

"I am always serious." He put the knife down. I leaned over and kissed him.

"I'm not saying we're moving in together. I want to make that clear. But you always stay when I'm in London, and if your friend is moving on, you don't have much reason to stay so far out in the sticks. This way you'd have a place nearer work, and all that happens in the city. There is no point in living somewhere as exhausting and difficult as London if you aren't really in it. Don't you think? And I'd really like to be reunited with that chair. It cost a fortune."

He could call it what he wanted if it made him feel better, but he was asking me to move in with him, I knew that. I thought about texting Ophelia right then to tell her. She would be happy for me. But I didn't. I wanted to keep this news to myself for a while, to feel it with all my being. Plus, I couldn't be sure that she wouldn't spoil it with probing questions about the practicalities, which I didn't yet have an answer for.

CHAPTER

Twenty-Five

I ended up staying with Richard for New Year's, only returning to London on the fourth of January, the day before I went back to work. We welcomed in 2011 with an expensive bottle of champagne, and lobsters, which I'd never had before. Richard had to teach me how to eat them, and they hadn't agreed with me. This had been embarrassing but he had been very nice about it, and I'd felt some new closeness with him once my insides and my dignity had recovered.

Ophelia, Eddy and I had a long catch-up that first night that we were all back in London. Eddy had also had some trouble with his stomach while away, and was even thinner than he had been when he'd left. Ophelia, on the other hand, had a flush to her cheeks from skiing and even a little more in the way of cheek than before Christmas, which I knew meant she was happy. I let them both talk about their Christmases before revealing my news, that Richard and Elaine had split up and we were going to get a place together in London.

Their jaws dropped when I told them. Although they tried very hard to feign excitement, I could almost feel them trying to speak telepathically. Little *what the actual fuck*s were flying silently across the room. I caveated everything with a knowing, "We'll see," because I was truly torn. A part of me didn't really think it was going to happen. I had accepted months before that things wouldn't end well with us and that he would eventually leave me. Even before that, long before I had even met him, I had come to understand things in my life were never going to be happy or work out well, and that because of this I should take the good I could find day to day, wherever I could find it. To think that this was going to happen seemed impossible, yet there it was, happening. He surely wouldn't say it and not go through with it.

Regardless, I appreciated Ophelia not making any plans for the house or living situation.

January wore on as it always does. Richard was in Yorkshire, writing. We spoke every day. He was more attentive than he had ever been, though he didn't mention anything about looking for a place to rent in London, and I didn't bring it up. He said that he couldn't go to the flat with things as they were. I told him that he could come and stay with me, but he didn't like the idea at all, and I understood that for a man like him to stay in a house share with people more than half his age was not appealing.

He'd come down to London in early January. He'd booked a suite in an expensive hotel in Mayfair for a week and I'd met him there, staying with him over the weekend and returning to him after work on the Monday, but it hadn't been the same as having the flat or being at Stone Heap House. He'd missed his office and had found it hard to write in the clinical cleanness of a hotel room. After four days, he'd returned to Yorkshire, telling me that I was welcome whenever, and handing me three hundred pounds in cash for the train fare. He would sometimes hold my hand in public now, and he would kiss me on the mouth when we met or said goodbye even if it was on the street or at a train station. I wasn't sure if his guard had dropped because he no longer cared, or because he felt that no one was watching him. He told me that he had not heard a word from Elaine since Christmas Day.

It was a Thursday in February that I realized I'd missed my period. I went out on my lunch break to buy a pregnancy test. I didn't have the patience to wait until I got home, so it was there in a stall in the toilets at work that I discovered I was pregnant. Some basic maths led me to conclude that I was about seven or eight weeks along. I'd been a bit lax with taking my contraceptive pill over Christmas, and I had been ill from the lobster, but I had forgotten to take it many times over the years and nothing had ever come of it.

It was immediately clear to me that I didn't want to continue the pregnancy and that I would get an abortion as soon as possible. I was furious with myself for getting into this situation and briefly considered having it done without telling Richard. But I couldn't do that. I was going to see him for the weekend and would tell him then.

I called my GP and explained to a sympathetic receptionist that I needed to arrange an abortion as quickly as possible. She gave me the number for a clinic at Homerton Hospital, and I called to make an appointment for the following week, which was the earliest they could see me. It wouldn't be done then, they told me. They'd have to do some tests and a scan, and I had to speak to two doctors to get it signed off. I said that was fine. I had no sentimental feelings about the situation whatsoever. I felt claustrophobic in my own skin, suddenly, like I was trapped. It couldn't happen soon enough.

Out of interest, I googled the names of the medications I was on to see what it said about pregnancy. It said there was no evidence to say if they were safe or not, and they should only be taken under the advisement of a doctor.

I was far too ashamed of myself to tell Ophelia, who was eternally sensible, and it wasn't the kind of thing I'd tell Eddy or that he would know what to do with. I certainly wasn't going to call my dad or Laura. So I just sat alone with the information at work, opening and closing emails, sending out books and flicking through the day's newspapers. At lunch I bought a sandwich, but I couldn't eat it. I couldn't tell if it was because I actually felt nauseous or because I was imagining I was nauseous. It felt both unreal, and invasively real, all at once. Cecile asked me what my weekend plans were. I said I was going north to visit a university friend.

I spent the two hours on the train the next evening thinking about how I'd tell him. I'd be straight up, straightforward. I had an appointment already booked for the next week. I was just telling him for his information. I was so worried it would spook him. I never wanted to be a bother or a hassle, and I knew this was both.

I told him as soon as we got to the house. He was in a great mood. Writing was going well and he was in a flow with an idea for a new book that he was excited about. We were in the kitchen of the main house. He asked if I wanted some wine.

"Richard, don't freak out, because I am sorting it. But I think it's important that I tell you. I'm pregnant."

He froze. The color faded from his cheeks in a cartoonish manner, and he put down the two wineglasses he was holding.

"What? How?"

"How?" I asked indignantly.

"Is it mine?"

"Of course it's yours. I'm not sleeping with anyone else."

"You've not been with anyone else at all?"

"No. Well. Once, when you were away. But it's not from then." He didn't even blink at this revelation. He just went to sit down at the dining table.

"Are you sure?"

"Yes, Richard, I'm sure."

"And when you say sorting it—"

"I'm not keeping it, if that's what you are asking. I have an appointment next week for tests and scans and stuff, and I guess I'll find out then what happens next."

"I just don't understand how this has happened when you told me you were on the pill."

I was getting really cross now.

"Yes, as I remember it, I did tell you that, after you were already inside me. But yes, I am on the pill. I guess when I got ill at Christmas it didn't stick or something. It's not one hundred percent effective. This happens to people all the time. It's not my fault."

He wasn't looking at me. His eyes were fixed on some point across the room. He was completely knocked by this information, this man that I again and again mistook for being unshakeable. I picked up the wine and poured us two glasses to show him how serious I was about the abortion.

"Should you be drinking that?"

"I don't think it matters if I'm not keeping it." I didn't feel like drinking, but I did anyway, to make a point. "It's just a microscopic clump of cells. There is a good chance it will go away on its own anyway; it's super early. That might even happen before I even get seen." I was trying to minimize the seriousness of the situation, which was only making me realize how serious the situation actually was. He was as spooked as he could have been.

He took a sip of his wine and buried his head in his hands. "And you are sure it is mine?"

I gave him a look that shut down that line of questioning for good. We sat in silence for a few minutes, sitting opposite each other at the long table, drinking our wine. I felt like crying out to him that this was happening to me, to my body. I didn't want to be dramatic.

"So what does it involve?" he asked, finally.

"I don't know really. I've looked it up online and you can either take a pill, or have a quick procedure under anesthetic. I think if I get the choice, I'd do that, rather than go through it at home. I don't want Ophelia or Eddy to know."

"I've never been in this situation before, Charlie. I know it's partly my doing, but it's a big shock for someone of my age. I'd long ago given up the idea of ever having children."

There it was. He'd never even thought about a future with me. Or if he had, it had been a childless one, and me not consulted in that. He seemed to realize what he'd said had bigger implications almost at once.

"Do you want to have children? Is this something that you want?"

"I don't know. Not now. I guess—yes, one day, I see myself having or wanting children. But not now. I'm too young. You know the most expensive thing I own is that chair you bought for me?"

He nodded his head, but he didn't make eye contact, and I wasn't sure he had heard what I had said. It sounded right, all of the words in a good order. It sounded like what someone normal would say about their future. When I thought about my future, I could see nothing. It was like trying to look through thick, frosted glass.

"Look, Charlie—"

"Richard, I don't want to talk about the future with you if that's where you are going with this. I want to stop thinking about all of this, drink my wine and go to sleep, and tomorrow I want us to walk a long way in the cold, and come home and eat nice food. On Sunday, I'll go back to London, and I hope by this time next week all of this will be done and dusted, over, and we never have to talk about it again. Can we just do that?"

We didn't have sex that night. He didn't gesture for me to roll onto his side of bed as he usually did. I woke at eight the next morning, hoping, as I had every morning, to find the pregnancy had ended on its own. But it hadn't. Richard was already in his office, writing. He was deep into an idea, so I made coffee on the Aga top and took my cup back to bed. The stables were freezing cold even with the stoves, and the weather was miserable, with sleet clumping on the windows. He emerged at around midday and we went for a walk, but it was so wet and windy we had to turn back after a few miles. I took a long bath in the main house while he wrote. He was so deep in thought that weekend, I wondered if I was intruding and should leave. I was almost glad when we got in the car on Sunday to head back to the station, which was usually a moment I dreaded.

When we got there, he didn't turn off the engine or get out of the car.

"Should I—come with you? To this appointment. Is that what you want?"

"No," I said flatly, meaning yes. He was the only person who knew what was going on. I wanted him there with me.

"OK." He didn't move. His knuckles were white from gripping the steering wheel so tightly. "OK. Well. You can call me after and tell me what they say. You can call me whenever you like. You know that. Look, I'm sorry this weekend has been . . . I have been, that is, distracted."

I nodded, feeling the gulf between us that I thought we had closed for good opening again, deeper and wider than before, like a wound. I had ruined everything with my carelessness.

He kissed me goodbye and left. It was still twenty minutes until my train, but he didn't offer to wait with me like he usually did. I sat on the platform trying to read. Richard had lent me a Cormac McCarthy novel that I had been looking forward to reading, but the words floated out of my mind as soon as I had read them, leaving no mark of the story at all. I gave up and bought a disgusting, overpriced coffee. I felt sad all the way home, watching the green fields turn to concrete. I imagined the lives of the people that lived in the houses we rushed past, and how many of them had unwanted pregnancies, affairs and broken hearts.

I told Cecile the age-old lie of having to miss work for a dentist appointment. She looked at me with slightly narrowed eyes that said, *I don't believe you,* but she was fine about it. I felt very lonely in that waiting room in an outbuilding of the Hackney hospital. In the toilet, there was a laminated piece of card on the wall above the sink that said:

IF YOU HAVE MISCARRIED OR LOST YOUR BABY, WE ARE VERY SORRY. PLEASE ALERT ONE OF THE TEAM BEFORE YOU LEAVE THE HOSPITAL. THEY WILL BE ABLE TO PROVIDE YOU WITH SUPPORT NUMBERS.

I waited for a long time for my appointment. When I was called in, the sonographer asked me to pull up my top, and to undo my trousers and roll them down so she could get to my belly. She asked if I wanted to see the screen, but I said no, and told her I wasn't keeping the pregnancy. She didn't flinch, or ask me why. She was very kind about it. I stared up at the ceiling tiles as the cold jelly moved across my body and she made a series of clicks to take photos of what she saw. When she was finished, she handed me a load of rough paper towels to clean up with.

"It's very early. I can see you are only about eight weeks. Just take a seat in the waiting area and a doctor will call you to talk through your options. OK, love?"

And so I sat and waited, again, watching other people arrive, get called, come back and go again. Women of all ages and walks of life. Women with children and women without. Women who looked more like children, and women who looked too old to be mothers. But here we all were, sitting, asking for the same thing, to make the same choice. A choice that was ours and ours alone.

The doctor that I saw was a woman of about Richard's age, I guessed. A nurse took blood and did my blood pressure, measured my height and weight, and checked my urine, while the doctor talked to me about my options. I was surprised by her kindness, by the overwhelming absence of any judgment. I told her I was judging myself more severely than anyone else seemed to be. She said that I should remember that in this very moment, there were rooms full of women in my situation. All over the country, in many parts of the world where we were able to decide for ourselves, women were making this same decision. That she wouldn't ever judge a single one of them for doing what they needed to do with their bodies, with their futures. I bit my lip hard and wanted my mum more than I had in a long, long time.

I chose to have the abortion done surgically, which would mean coming back in for a general anesthetic, but it would only take ten minutes or so and I could go home within a few hours. She asked about my partner and sexual history. She asked me if I was sure. Then, another doctor came in and asked me the same questions, and signed a form saying that I could have the procedure because a pregnancy would be a risk to mental health, which I then signed. They explained that the only way they could legally perform the procedure was if they had both signed this document stating as such. There was no law that allowed you to simply ask for an abortion because it was what you wanted.

I was to go in the following Wednesday. There was no earlier appointment. Despite their reassurances that it would be minimally painful, I was very nervous. As well as leaflets and a photocopy detailing how to prepare and what would happen at the procedure, the doctor gave me a printout with some numbers for support groups. I said I didn't need it, but she made me take it anyway.

When I got outside, it was dark. I took the bus home and called Richard from my room to explain what would happen and what I'd been told. Because of the general anesthetic, I needed someone to collect me and stay with me after. He asked if it would be better for Ophelia to do it, but I told him I didn't want her to know. That was the reason I was having it done in hospital, and not going through it at home. I didn't ever like to push him, but I did on this. I couldn't face telling her. He said he'd come down, but it sounded like a bother to him. I was a hassle, suddenly, and I'd never wanted to be.

I was so disappointed in him. In the situation. We had a big press event the following Wednesday, a showcase of authors for that coming autumn. We had been preparing for months. I would have to tell Cecile I wouldn't be able to work. The doctor had suggested I return to work the following week if I possibly could.

After I got off the phone, I felt so sad and restless that I knew I needed to go for a run, even though it was dark and stormy outside. The streets were wet and busy, the roads blocked with traffic. The rain was coming in sideways and got in my eyes. I slipped on a leaf and fell, landing on my knee. No one stopped to help me up. I could feel it bleeding under my leggings. I limped home, feeling very stupid and very alone.

To make things worse, neither Ophelia nor Eddy came home that night. I didn't want to speak to anyone, but I longed to hear the comforting sounds of them shuffling about the house, Ophelia's electric toothbrush buzzing to signify she'd be going to bed, Eddy's elephant-like gait on the stairs, bounding up and down to get water or snacks from the kitchen. Ophelia would be gone soon. She was going after Easter, which was a little over a month away, but spring seemed impossibly distant.

The next day, I told Cecile that I had to have dental surgery the following Wednesday and that I wouldn't be back in until the Monday. I apologized and explained that it was the only time they could do it, but she just flopped back in her chair and sighed with relief.

"Thank God for that! I thought you were at a job interview. Dentist appointments are almost never real, especially with people your age. Sorry. I hope it's nothing too painful. What are you having done?"

"Er, root canal. Triple root canal."

She raised one perfectly plucked eyebrow.

"And you need three days off?"

"General anesthetic, and they said the swelling would be bad. So I won't be able to talk. I think." I was making this up as I went and hoped she had as much knowledge of dental surgery as I did.

"Well, it is what it is. I'll be very sorry not to have you at the showcase." I stood up and turned to leave her office. "Charlie, if there was anything wrong, or going on with you, I hope you know that you can talk to me."

I blushed bright red. "Yeah, of course. I'm really fine, though. Just need to get this tooth sorted. Thanks, Cecile."

CHAPTER Twenty-Six

I spent all of my spare time on the internet over the following days, looking up all I could about abortions. I watched medical videos showing the surgery, meant as teaching tools for students, and read first-person testimonials about how it had been straightforward and easy, and how life had been normal afterward, as well as articles about how it had impacted people's lives in other ways. I wanted to read everything I could about botched procedures and all the ways it could go wrong, and stories of how horrific and painful it had been, of anesthetic sickness and heavy bleeding and all sorts of other terrible things. I started to feel very nervous about it. After I had exhausted that, I went down a rabbit hole of "pro-life" groups, reading website after website, and digging through Reddit threads and Facebook groups to read diatribes of angry, unforgiving rhetoric about dead babies. I thought maybe it would make me feel something more about what I was going through, but it didn't. I didn't feel pregnant. I had no sickness, and, although I felt tired, I suspected that it was probably because I felt so emotionally drained.

On Sunday night, Richard called me. It was the first time we'd spoken since the Wednesday of my appointment, the longest we'd gone without speaking in almost a year. I expected he was calling to say he couldn't come down after all, that I'd have to go it alone or tell Ophelia. I almost didn't answer.

"Hello, Charlie."

"Hello, Richard."

"Charlie, I've been awful to you this last week or so. I know I have."

He cleared his throat. I could hear that he was outside, and smoking. Probably outside the stables. He sounded hoarse and, I thought, it was likely that he had been drinking all day.

"The thing is, it shocked me. It shocked me to the very core. These last few months—year, really—have been a lot. And I went inside myself, and I've not been fair to you. I'm sure you hate me right now."

"I couldn't ever hate you."

"I know you couldn't. Even if I deserve it. You are too good to hate anyone."

My face was wet with tears.

"Charlie, I'm going to come to London first thing in the morning. I'm going to stay at the Covent Garden Hotel, not that atrocious place in Mayfair. Will you come after work? I feel very strongly that I need to see you."

I said I would. I had to hang up then, saying I'd call him back later. I was a mess with emotion and I didn't want to cry on the phone. There was a good chance I was more hormonal than I thought I'd been. After I'd sobbed, really sobbed, I felt much lighter. I called him back and made him laugh with some comment about hormones, and fell asleep.

I made it through Monday, somehow, clock-watching so much that I stuck a Post-it note over the corner of my screen to stop me looking at the little digital display counting down. I was out of the door at one minute to five. As soon as I got above ground at Covent Garden Tube station, Richard called to say he was in a meeting that was running over, and I should come to meet him at the restaurant he was at on Old Compton Street.

As I walked around the corner, I saw him shaking hands with a group of people, some of whom I recognized. There was the famous actor who was playing the lead in *Altitude at Sea,* and the director. There was also another woman with them, who I took to be a producer or maybe an agent. I hung back a little but as they parted, Richard stood where he was in the middle of the road, looking out for me. There were a few seconds when he didn't see me, and I didn't wave. I just watched him. Richard Aveling, this man I loved, that the world loved. Who maybe did really love me. He was wearing the black coat he'd bought in America and he looked great. I went to him, then. He kissed me hard on the mouth and picked me up.

"I'm so very sorry, Charlie," he said into my ear. He put his hands on my cheeks, cupping my face, and kissed me again. I kissed him back and we broke apart for a second. He was smiling at me, and I had my arms around his neck. We walked back to the hotel, hand in hand.

In those few minutes, another of those momentous moments in my life happened, although I didn't know it yet.

We didn't see the photographer.

That night we ordered room service to his suite, which was much more in keeping with his tastes, opulent and dark with velvet curtains and antique tables and bold, patterned wallpaper. We ate burgers and fries and cheesecake and ice cream in bed. I wasn't supposed to have sex in the forty-eight hours before the procedure, so we didn't, but that was fine. We watched an old Hitchcock film, and I took a long bath. I felt less scared about what was to come because I knew he would be with me. He would be there to pick me up and to take care of me. We talked about the pregnancy and that it was the right thing to do.

"You never know, Charlie. Maybe a little way down the line . . ."

"Maybe. But not now."

"Not now. No."

I don't remember how we parted the next morning. Richard walked with me to Covent Garden Tube station and kissed me goodbye, I remember that, but not what we said to each other. I'd left some clothes and a book in his room as I was coming back straight from work, so I doubt it was anything more than a breezy farewell. I do remember walking through the ticket barriers with him behind me and thinking that finally, at last, things were good between us. All of our dark corners had been revealed to each other. We'd looked deep into them and still, even after that, we were together. And as long as we were together, everything was going to be OK.

CHAPTER Twenty-Seven

It was mid-morning Tuesday when I started to realize something was going on. Cecile was called upstairs to a meeting, and I saw Markus on the staircase on his phone, looking very worried. I presumed it was a standard publishing emergency, which would be of no consequence to the wider world but would cause a huge amount of stress and aggravation internally. I went to get lunch and came back to eat my salad at my desk.

"Charlie, can you come with me?" Cecile appeared next to me, looking pale and very serious. I put my fork down.

"Of course. Let me get my notebook."

"You don't need that. Come on."

I could suddenly hear my heart beating in my ears. Something was very wrong. On the stairwell I asked her what was going on.

"Let's talk when we get upstairs."

The warmth of her tone from the previous week had all but evaporated. I followed her to the fifth floor, the executive level of the building that just had meeting rooms, and our one-man IT department. We were going to the boardroom. The room where we'd had that first meeting with Richard, over a year before. Allegra was walking toward us along the corridor like it was a catwalk, but she looked down at her phone when she saw me and passed by without even glancing up.

In the boardroom was a woman I knew to be Janet, the head of our human resources department, and Markus. As we walked in, he left. Like Allegra, he didn't look at me. He didn't say anything at all.

"What's going on?" I wasn't even trying to hide my anxiety now.

"Sit down, Charlie," said Cecile, and I did. Janet looked at me in that awkward, robotic way that HR people do.

"Charlie, we had a call from the Showbiz desk at the *Daily Mail* earlier today, asking for comment on some photographs that were taken yesterday that they will be running online later today. The photographs show Richard Aveling in a—a compromising position, with someone that they know very well not to be his wife. It seems the paparazzi were following the cast of *Altitude at Sea* and caught these afterward. I'm surprised they think there is enough interest in him to publish, but they do, probably because the photographs are very suggestive. Anyway, Charlie." She looked down at a piece of paper in front of her. She was playing with the rings on her left hand and was, for the first time ever, without some of her composure. I knew what was coming.

"They have sent over the photographs and the woman he is with is very clearly, to us, anyway, you. They don't know who you are because, fortunately, your face isn't really in view. But for anyone who knows you, as we do, it is obvious. We won't comment. I doubt that they will follow this up. But they will run the story today and that puts you, Richard, and Winden & Shane in a very difficult position."

It felt like the walls of the room were moving. Panic like I had never felt before was rising, obscuring my vision. My mouth was dry, and I thought I might pass out. I couldn't get enough air into my lungs. They wouldn't expand. My chest hurt.

Cecile seemed to realize that I was having a panic attack, as did Janet, and they both rushed around, Cecile telling me to put my head between my knees as Janet shakily poured me a glass of water.

"Breathe, Charlie," Cecile said, her cool hand on the back of my neck. She counted in for four, out for four, and I followed her, my eyes screwed up tightly. After a few minutes, I got my breath back and Cecile stepped away and brought her chair around next to me. She held my hands in hers. I sat up and looked at her and shook my head. I didn't know what to say.

"Does Richard know?"

"I called John Cormorant about an hour ago. He has been in touch with him. Like I said, we won't comment. The story will go away in a few days. But, Charlie, it's going to be very difficult for you. You can't imagine how difficult. I've spoken to Janet and Markus and Allegra, and the decision has been taken that you should take a leave of absence. It's the best thing for you, for everyone. I know you have this dental surgery thing tomorrow . . ." She looked at me, searching my face and imploring me to tell her the truth. I looked at Janet and shook my head. "Janet, can you give us five?"

She took her phone and went out into the corridor. It was just me and Cecile now.

"Charlie, I've suspected this has been going on for a while now. Certainly since the autumn. How long—"

"Over a year. I didn't push myself on him or anything, I swear it wasn't like that . . ."

"It's OK—I don't think that. And tomorrow . . ."

"It's not dental surgery."

She nodded.

"I've been stupid and sloppy and I'm pregnant. I've not told anyone except him. That's why he's here in London this week. He's picking me up after."

She looked surprised. "He's here because he has meetings with screenwriters about the film all week." My shoulders dropped and I switched my eyeline to the floor, feeling even more stupid. He hadn't told me that. I thought he was here for me. "Anyway," she said gently, "that doesn't matter. Does Ophelia know?"

"About Richard and me? Or that I'm pregnant?"

"Both. Either."

"She knows about the relationship, but not that I'm pregnant. I don't want her or anyone to know. I'm so ashamed of myself." I was crying now. I could see my life falling away, everything I had dared to hope for. And I could see how foolish I had been, how foolish I looked to Cecile, to the world. I had been warned. I had known it would end badly, yet it still felt like a surprise now that it was happening. I had never considered it would end publicly.

"Look, Charlie. We're going to talk a lot more about all of this, you and me, OK? But right now, what I need for you to do is get yourself together enough that we can get you out of here and into a cab and home. This story is going to break this afternoon and you don't want to be here when it does. Do you understand what I'm saying?"

I knew that this was it. This would be the last time I'd be in this building.

"I'm going to pop downstairs for a moment, OK? I want you to wait here."

When she came back, she was with Ophelia, who looked very worried. When she saw me, she ran to me and put an arm around me. Cecile mouthed, "I haven't told her anything."

"Charlie, what on earth is wrong? Is it your dad?"

I shook my head. "Someone took photographs." Ophelia looked at me, and then at Cecile, unsure what she knew. "Cecile knows. Everyone will in the next few hours."

Cecile explained what had happened. Ophelia immediately went into crisis-management mode. She was brilliant. She kept a firm hand on my back as I sat slumped forward on the chair.

"Ophelia, can you go and get Charlie's things and bring them up? Are you OK to head home with her?"

Cecile called a taxi, which was to collect us from the back door and take us home. Once Ophelia had left the room, Cecile took the chair next to me again.

"Charlie, I don't know how things are going to play out in the next few days, but there is one other person in all of this who is going to feel it hard, and that is Elaine. Regardless of them being separated, or fighting, or whatever it is now, she is going to feel humiliated. I don't think you can count on him to be with you tomorrow. So, you either need to tell Ophelia, or you need to let me pick you up, and you come and stay with me while you recover. I've had this procedure. You will need a lot of love and care over the next few days. You can either have that from me, at my house, with my seven-year-old boys and my husband up in your business, or you can have your best friend."

"I can't tell her."

"Then I will. You have nothing to be ashamed of. Nothing at all.

And not just about the pregnancy, but about any of it. He is a much, much older man and he shouldn't have ever let this happen. You're not the first person, you know, that he has done this to."

I looked at her. She pulled her hand from mine and patted at her curls.

"Years ago, when I wasn't much older than you. Yes. But also, there were two students when he was teaching. I know for a fact that there are more. It will all come out, eventually."

"This is different. It's been a year. He's getting us a place. He said he would always defend me, us, where it matters."

She looked frustrated with me. "Charlie, you have to be realistic about what is going on here. Can't you see? He's been married to Elaine for thirty years. This is what he does, what they do. This is the worst of it, and goodness knows what will become of them after this, but I don't think that anything except death will ever part those two. They have separated and threatened divorce more times than I can remember."

It all made perfect sense. She softened her tone again.

"He isn't defending you, Charlie. I don't want to upset you more, but it's over. He will be on the phone to Elaine now, I would expect, begging her for forgiveness. I've known him for a very long time."

Surely not. Surely he wouldn't let this happen to me.

"Now, are you OK for me to tell Ophelia?" I nodded, numbly. "Good. Now I'm going to go and do that, and then I'm going to come back and get you. While I'm downstairs, I'm going to get Janet to come in and talk to you about the terms of your leave of absence. But don't worry if it doesn't all go in. They will send everything in writing."

The terms were that I would be on full pay, but I wasn't to come into the office until an agreed date and that would be based on an evaluation of "business needs." I wasn't to access my email, and I was to give them my security pass.

Cecile and Ophelia came back up to get me. Ophelia had clearly been crying. She looped her arm through mine and whispered, "You silly sausage," in my ear, and then bumped her head against mine. We made a quick exit down the back stairs, which were thankfully empty, and out into the waiting black cab. As we drove away, I looked at the door where I had first met him, and wondered, had I not gone for that cigarette break, if any of this would be happening now. So many things had had to happen for me to be where I'd been in that moment in time, and for him to have been there, too, that it seemed impossible that it had worked out as it had. And although it was awful, it had, at times, been magical. It had been transformative beyond my wildest dreams. In that moment, I wouldn't have taken a day of it back.

We didn't talk for the whole drive. I stared stupidly out of the window, my forehead against the glass as the tears fell freely, wondering if I'd see him somewhere on the street, looking for me. Ophelia sat refreshing the *Daily Mail* homepage on her phone again and again, but the article didn't appear.

When we got home, Ophelia took my phone and my laptop and put them in her room with hers.

"We won't need those today. Today we are making pasta."

I wasn't sure I'd heard her right. But she marched me into the kitchen, and tied up my hair. She put an apron on me and then one on herself, and pulled a giant bag of flour from the top cupboard. It landed heavily on the marble surface in a cloud of dust.

"Ophelia, I can't—I just want to curl up in bed and . . ." I could hardly stand up.

"And die? Yes, I imagine you do. This is a very, very bad day." She sniffed, trying not to cry. "But none of this is your fault and I won't let you go into that dark place, Charlie, not yet, not until you have tomorrow over and behind you. Then you can do what you want. But today we are going to make pasta, and tomorrow I'm going to take you to hospital and then I'm going to bring you home and take care of you. How you could possibly think I would be *angry* with you—I thought you knew me better than anyone."

She went to the fridge and poured us each a very large glass of white wine.

"Just one to take the edge off."

And so we made pasta. Or, Ophelia made pasta and I watched dully as she mixed golden yolks into flour, forming a ball of dough before splitting it and handing me half to knead. I knew what she was doing, that she remembered what I had said about how my mum used to distract me when I was small, and it was smart, because Ophelia was smart. For a little while, my brain managed to stay afloat. We rolled and stretched and rolled again, and then repeated the whole thing. Then she showed me how to roll the dough into little shapes that looked like ears. When this task was complete, she set me to making a sauce, and then to washing up. At some point Eddy came home and she closed the kitchen door and took him upstairs to explain what was going on, although by then the whole world knew. That night I took a diazepam I had left over from the autumn, but I didn't get the deep and dreamless sleep I'd hoped it would bring.

At seven the next morning, Ophelia packed us into a taxi which took us to the hospital. She had to drop me off at Reception; they wouldn't let her come in with me. She hadn't allowed me my phone so I had no way to call her when I was done, but she had arranged all of that with the nurses.

There were five women, including me, all there for the same procedure. I was given a pill to take and a little cup of water. We were all given hospital gowns and baskets for our clothes, and each went into a little cubicle to change. Then we all just sat there, waiting to be called.

There was another young woman who looked like me, and I wondered if she worked in publishing or something, too. I hoped we'd never cross paths out of here and that our secret would remain locked in this dimly lit corridor. There was a much older woman with a shock of white hair who had arrived at the same time as me with her husband, who I knew from overhearing their conversation was waiting for her in his car outside. There was a woman of indeterminable age with the most beautiful butterfly eyelashes I had ever seen, and then two other women. One couldn't have been much older than sixteen, and the other didn't speak much English, she said—she had an interpreter meeting her. She smiled at me, but the smile didn't reach her eyes. She looked very sad. We didn't make conversation. I wanted to know their stories, to compare reasons for why we were all here, in this place, at the same time. They all had their phones to look at. I wondered if any of them read the *Daily Mail*. They probably did.

I was glad to be called first. The anesthetist was dressed in blue scrubs and he was so kind and handsome, in that way that Nordic men can be, that I couldn't muster the energy to be sad with him. He spoke to me gently as a nurse inserted a cannula into my hand, which took two attempts and made me cry out with pain. Everyone worked around me so busily. Each person had a clear job to do, a place in the hierarchy of the operating theater. The doctor whom I had seen the week before was performing the procedure, and I was comforted to see a familiar face. She held my hand and told me not to worry, that it would only be ten minutes and that she would come and say hello later when I was in the recovery room. I felt a tear escape the corner of my eye for no reason other than that her kindness felt maternal in its softness. I wondered, briefly, if I would wake up again, and thought that it wouldn't be so bad if I didn't. Then the cold anesthetic rushed into my arm and I lost consciousness.

I woke up on a bed being wheeled into the recovery room. It felt like hours had passed, not ten minutes. I didn't feel different. I knew, though, that my last tie to Richard had just been destroyed forever.

I sat in a big armchair with a blanket over me and had some tea and a cheese sandwich at the nurse's insistence, even though I didn't feel like eating. It was such a surreal place, and I was so dopey with the medicine that I had been given, that the events of the day before didn't seem to have happened here. I watched the other women come in one by one, ten or fifteen minutes apart, until we were all reunited in the recovery room. My stomach was cramping, and the handsome anesthetist gave me some extra pain medication when he came to check on me. I felt very tearful, which he noticed. He said it was to be expected as a side-effect of the anesthetic.

The woman with butterfly eyelashes was in an identical chair in the bay next to mine. She smiled at me and asked how I was feeling. I told her I was OK, that it wasn't as bad as I'd thought it was going to be. She said she felt the same, that she had been racked with nerves about it.

"Do you have any kids?"

I was always so surprised when anyone asked me this. "Me? No." I paused. My head was foggy. "Do you?"

She nodded. "Ten-month-old baby girl and a six-year-old boy."

"You are lucky." It was the woman who had smiled earlier. She was sitting in a chair under the window to our left. Her English was heavily accented but still impressive. "This is my second I have had to say goodbye to. My second that would not have ever had a chance for a good life." She looked down into her lap. I could see the rise of her bump under her gown, a now empty shell. "It is the hardest decision to make." I wanted to go to her, to put an arm around her. It had not been a hard decision for me. I was lucky in this respect.

"It's the biggest act of love a mother can make," said the woman with butterfly eyelashes. "To stop your child's suffering even when it kills a part of you to do so."

"I was so scared I wouldn't wake up. But then I have been so sick from the pregnancy that I have not slept in weeks. And now I just want to sleep again, like I did in there."

The doctor that had performed the surgery came round to check on us all once she was finished. She took time and care with each of us.

"It's not like I thought it would be. It's not like in films or anything," I said truthfully, feeling the naivety of my words. "I think I'm just relieved that it is over."

"Now you can move on with your life," the doctor said, with a hand on my shoulder.

The young woman whom I thought to be sixteen was in fact much younger, so young that her mum was allowed in with her. She kept asking her daughter if she was OK, if she wanted anything, and the girl kept shaking her head silently. Her mum would stand and stroke her hair only for her daughter to brush her off. If only she knew how lucky she was to have her mother there, I thought. The older woman with white hair said nothing, but she smiled at me when our eyes met.

The three of us talked about who was collecting us. They both had partners meeting them. I told them that I didn't, that it would be my best friend, and they both agreed I was lucky to have such a good friend that I could rely on, and I knew it was out of sympathy.

They let me go home a few hours later. I was bleeding only as much as I would on a heavy period and the pain was fine after the extra tablets the anesthetist had given me. I went to the loo and wondered where the big pad between my legs had come from, which reminded me I had been unconscious and hoovered out, and how bizarre it was. The anesthetic had left me feeling woozy and I was tired and emotionally raw with the slow realization of my new reality, which was a darkness creeping in at the edges of my vision.

A kind nurse helped me get dressed and called Ophelia to come and meet me. Ophelia was standing under a streetlight that shone like a halo around her in the dark Hackney afternoon. She hugged me and helped me into the front seat of the taxi, which was waiting. It must have cost her a fortune, but she didn't say a word about that. She just took me home and made me some soup from a carton, and she sat quietly with me at the table while I slowly ate. I only managed a few mouthfuls before we both gave up and she helped me into bed.

I slept for fifteen hours.

CHAPTER Twenty-Eight

The depression that followed this was bad.

It was the worst I'd ever felt. It was worse even than when Mum had died.

Ophelia stayed at home with me. For the first few days after the procedure, which to my surprise left no lasting physical marks or symptoms beyond a regular period, I refused to get out of bed and move to the sofa. So she came to me with pillows and cushions and throws from her own room, and set up camp in my bed. She didn't speak much, knowing that I needed silence, but she petted my hair and put on film after film without asking me what I wanted to watch. She removed all decision-making from me, bringing me food and drinks and painkillers and sedatives when the allotted time between doses had passed. When we had tired of films we watched season after season of *Friends,* and then *30 Rock* and *Frasier.* When I slept, she would creep out of the room and I'd half hear her cleaning up and making calls. Once or twice I heard Clemmie in the house, the familiar sound of their hushed French soft through the walls, lulling me back into unconsciousness. It was as if my heart and my mind had been severed from my body. I couldn't cry, or really speak. I couldn't form thoughts or follow any train of thinking for more than a few words before I found myself lost and unable to find my way back. Or anywhere. I no longer wanted nor needed food, just sips of water.

Eddy would come in and take over from Ophelia for a few hours in the evenings. His approach was different from Ophelia's. He didn't expect a response, but he would talk. Not about publishing or about Richard, but about whatever we were watching. His preference was *Buffy the Vampire Slayer,* which he would sort of commentate. Somewhere, far away, where I now lived inside an atrophied corner of my mind, his voice and all of the silly accents he did could still reach me.

That Monday, I was dressed by Ophelia and taken, physically taken, to the GP. My usual doctor wasn't available and so I had to see a locum. Ophelia came in with me and explained what had been going on. The doctor called the crisis team there and then, and I was sent home with another prescription for diazepam and promise of a callback. Dr. Harding called Ophelia that afternoon and we went in. Again, she came in with me, but after a few moments he asked her to wait outside.

"Charlie, I'm very, very sorry to hear what has been going on."

I nodded mutely. I had bitten the inside of my lip so viciously that it was bleeding sickeningly into my mouth. I took a tissue from the box on the small table between us and spat into it. He didn't flinch. He asked to look at my tongue.

"Charlie, we're very worried about you. Your friends are, I am, the GP is. I can see how dehydrated you are. I'm happy for you to continue taking sedatives at the moment, but it is not a long-term solution. I really need to see you pushing yourself to drink a little bit or we might have to look at bringing you into hospital and you really don't want that. I wish hospitals were a better place to get well, but they are not. I wonder if you are hearing me. Charlie?"

"I don't want to go to hospital." These were the first words I'd said to him.

"OK. That's good. So neither of us want that. I'm going to arrange for our crisis team to pop in once or twice each day. Make sure you are drinking and eating a bit, getting showered, things like that. Would that be OK?"

I nodded again.

"OK. Good. Charlie, I know that right now it feels like the world is ending, but you have been through and survived worse than this. You are a fantastically bright and capable young woman, and I know that you are going to make a full recovery. But today, I need you to just focus on the next minute. Set small goals. Drink some water. Get in the shower. Go for a walk. Brush your teeth, if that is all you can do. Just find small things each day, even if it is just one, and make that your focus. I will keep in touch with the team and see you again next week."

Different social workers came to the house, sometimes twice, sometimes three times a day. They would ask me to stand while they took my blood pressure. They would talk to me, hover next to me as they made me make a slice of toast and take at least a bite, or wait in the hallway as I took a shower, standing under the freezing water, willing it to kill me or shock me back into my body. I did what they said because I was terrified of going to hospital, of being locked up.

Ophelia had a laptop sent to the house by bike so she could work from home, but I couldn't stand to even be close to it, so she worked in her room, popping down to check on me every half an hour as I sank deeper and deeper into the sofa. She'd not let me have my phone since she'd checked my messages and seen the streams of unanswered texts I'd sent Richard, begging him to call me. Eventually she had to give it back and I continued, in my worst moments, to try to reach him. But Richard didn't call, or text, or email, as deep down I knew he wouldn't. He'd probably never even turned that phone on again, as I was the only person he ever called.

The article was handed about by everyone at Winden & Shane, as well as the wider industry, and it became the greatest piece of gossip for years. Although you couldn't see my face straight on, anyone who knew me would, if told, recognize me. I was so embarrassed and ashamed, and all of Ophelia's or Eddy's attempts to calm my paranoia were in vain. Ophelia, especially, told me again and again that no one at work was laughing at me, that no one thought badly of me. That it was him everyone was judging. But that was almost worse, because it meant I had ruined his reputation. And that was the worst thing I could have done to him, worse than ruining his marriage. His private business, which he worked so hard to keep private, was out in the world for all to see. Ophelia would scream at me for defending him. For worrying at all about him when

I was so broken and it had all been his fault. But there was nothing but him. There was nothing of me left, not even at the edges. With Richard removed, I was an empty husk, devastated and beyond hope of repair.

I had lost my job, my career and my relationship, all in one go. Richard was gone from me forever. I'd never feel his hands on mine again, never set foot in the flat again, never hear him say my name again. His promise to defend me, like all his promises, had been hollow.

The following Monday, I went back to see Dr. Harding. I was more lucid now. Flashes of anger and crippling pain would sweep through me with waves of grief that bordered on hysteria, but I didn't tell him how bad it was, just that my anxiety and panic were so intense that they were causing hallucinations. In these moments, I couldn't tell what was real. This was true. I had seen Richard in my room. Heard his footsteps in the hall. Always when I was just between sleep and whatever this new state that passed for waking was. I would jump up thinking he was there, only to find nothing.

Dr. Harding talked to me about all that had happened. He was kind and supportive and measured, and seemed to understand what was going on. He reminded me a little of Richard, which made me want to put my hand on his knee, but I didn't. He said I was disassociating, like I had done when I was little, when my anxiety would overwhelm me so much that I would get lost and find myself staring at the wall. He taught me an exercise that took me inside my head, and allowed me to look at what was there and to really just look, without getting overwhelmed. I promised to try it out when I could and found some relief in some moments. But I couldn't find any way to make the reality of my situation feel better.

As much as people told me it wasn't my fault, I knew that it was. I knew what I had walked into and the damage waiting to happen. I had told myself I could always die if it hurt too much when it ended, and I comforted myself with this thought. It was my way out, if I really wanted it. Now that it had happened, it had ended, I kept the thought even closer, like a key in my pocket, ready to open the next door if this house did, as it threatened to, collapse around me.

Over the next few weeks, I spiraled. Ophelia didn't move into Oscar's as planned but stayed with me. Both she and Eddy looked after me, calming me down when I was hysterical, telling me things weren't that bad, that people weren't talking about it when they clearly were. I was paranoid and obsessed by this thought. Dr. Harding saw me again and increased my mood stabilizer, and he told me that weaning me off sedatives could wait for now. My grief for the relationship and the future I had imagined for myself was as consuming as the grief I had felt for my mum all those years ago, and I couldn't see how I could ever get better.

Somehow or other the article had been seen by my dad. Although I knew he wouldn't ever read the *Daily Mail,* I suspected that Laura did, out of boredom, sometimes flick through the Showbiz section when she was on the toilet or Noah was napping, or whenever else she found a moment to herself. Dad had tried to call multiple times and Ophelia had ended up speaking to him. He wanted to come and pick me up and take me back home, but I couldn't think of anything worse. I could tell that Ophelia and Eddy, and probably Clemmie, felt out of their depth with me and wanted me to go, too, but they didn't put that on me because when they broached the subject I would scream and cry, and it would take hours to calm me again.

Then it happened. Winden & Shane officially let me go, with an offer of a payout of over half a year's salary and a good reference in exchange for my signature on a legally binding non-disclosure agreement. My position had become "untenable." I felt furious and betrayed, an anger raging inside me that stuck in my throat, that I sobbed with until I couldn't breathe. The news came by letter, no doubt because I refused to answer my phone. It was worded with such formality, such a lack of heart or even an echo of feeling that I was sure for a minute that it was a mistake. I had given Winden & Shane absolutely everything I had for the last two years. I had worked every minute I was asked to and then more. I'd gone the extra mile at every opportunity, formed what I thought were real relationships with not just my contemporaries but with the senior staff like Cecile and Markus. But it was done. My employment was terminated effective immediately.

I had five days to sign the NDA or the payout offer and good reference would be withdrawn. So I signed it and sent it back. Ophelia was horrified when I told her, saying I should never sign a document without a lawyer's advice, but it was done. Cecile tried to call me maybe twenty times in the weeks that followed—she had been, up until then, speaking to Ophelia as I had said I wanted no contact with anyone from work—but I didn't answer. I didn't want to speak to anyone except Richard, the Richard of before. I couldn't stop thinking about what Cecile had told me. I told Ophelia and Eddy, omitting the part about Cecile's own involvement with him, and they balked at it, saying they weren't surprised at all and cursing his name over and over.

It had been three weeks since that awful day when Ophelia announced that she had to go back to work, full time, at the office. The crisis team had by then decided I wasn't really in a "crisis" anymore, and had stopped their visits, and, as with my housemates, I was glad to be rid of them.

While Eddy and Ophelia were at work, I slept, drank and chain-smoked. I walked around the house like a specter, into their bedrooms, through the halls. For the most part, I felt utterly empty and miserable. Sometimes I felt angry, or desperate. I wanted to die, for it all to be over, yet I had no strength to do anything about it.

Then, one day, I drank a whole bottle of red wine on an empty stomach and passed out on the sofa. I'd had a few diazepam tablets as well, and Ophelia found it hard to wake me when she got home, and in a panic called an ambulance. I woke up with her pouring a pan of water on me, screaming and crying, soaking both us and the sofa. The ambulance came quickly. The paramedics took my blood pressure, examined me and suggested I come in, but I was OK. I didn't want to go near the hospital. They let me stay at home but insisted I get some help, and re-referred me to the crisis team I had been seeing. Ophelia called Clemmie, hysterical, saying she couldn't do it anymore, and the next day my dad turned up on the doorstep. I had no energy to fight with him; we packed up enough of my belongings to last me a few weeks and he drove me back home.

CHAPTER Twenty-Nine

Nothing I imagined could be worse than being taken away from London and the ruined remains of my life. The very thought of going home to the abandoned, now derelict haven that had been my childhood home seemed enough to make me stop living. To have to face my dad, to have to face the absence of my mum; it was too much.

At first, being home was as bad as I had thought it would be, if not worse.

The house was always alive with unfamiliar noise and ruled by Noah's schedule, which started at six in the morning every single day, without fail. He didn't understand what was wrong with me or why I wouldn't come out of my room. They had told him I wasn't well, and he thought that meant I maybe had the flu. There was no alcohol in the house and Ophelia had told my dad I'd been overdoing it, so he had made sure that I couldn't get at any.

Dad took a week of compassionate leave from school and took charge of everything while Laura looked after Noah. With the help of Ophelia, he'd managed to get Dr. Harding to transfer my prescriptions and care to my old family GP in Hampshire. My diazepam supply was promptly cut off, despite my appeals, and I had to use my remaining stash to taper off it. A social worker from the crisis team started to visit me daily to see how I was. Unlike London, it was the same person every day. At first, I wouldn't speak to her. She insisted that I take a walk each day, which I flatly refused. But she was relentless, and eventually I did give in and go out for a walk with her, just to get her off my back.

She signed me up for group therapy sessions while I waited for one-to-one therapy to start; the waiting list was long, and they had no idea how much of a wait I would have. When Dad found out it could be months, he went online and found me a therapist locally who could start seeing me straightaway. We'd start at twice a week and see how we went from there. I knew that they didn't have the money for it and told him it was unnecessary. But he was resolute on it.

"This is non-negotiable, Charlie. For goodness' sake, I should have done this years ago," he said.

I reminded him about the payout from work and he agreed, if I wanted, we could go halves.

So, eventually, at my dad's desperate request, I went. It was easier to go than to fight him on it. The therapist, Nora, was a kind woman in her mid-fifties. She had a room at the back of her house that she used to see patients. It was a house me and Mum must have driven past every day when I was a kid, because it was near my school. I asked her how long she had lived there and she said about ten years. So we had.

That first session I didn't say much. Dad had arranged to have my notes sent to her so she read through those with me, asking questions and marking up the printout with her Biro. She had a warmth to her that I found so soft, I didn't dare be angry or sullen with her. The room we were in looked out onto her garden. It was raining, which I was glad of. A fat tabby cat jumped onto the windowsill, pawing at the window and meowing to be let in. She laughed and apologized, opening the window and letting the wet cat in. She asked me if I minded cats, and I said I didn't at all. It curled up at her feet and purred.

After that first session, I fixed all of my efforts on any therapy I could get. I went to group therapy twice a week, which I much preferred to being one-to-one—I found it was actually better to listen to other people's problems for an hour than sweat in my own. It pulled me out of my own misery for a few seconds to hear a room full of sad souls tell their own sad stories, though I didn't say a word. Laura drove me there and back while Noah was at nursery, waiting outside in the car for the hour I was in the session because no one trusted me to be on my own. I appreciated that she didn't press me to talk, or try to mother me. She was only fourteen years older than me.

I worked with Nora over those next few weeks and I started, bit by bit, to come out of myself, and stay out for longer and longer periods. We didn't really talk about Richard directly, or about what had happened. In some sessions we'd talk about nothing but the weather, or the news, or the cat. But the very act of talking about absolutely nothing seemed to be starting to reconnect me to the world.

I had looked at the article. Of course I had. I didn't have any other photos of Richard and me. I had never dared to take a photo on the little Polaroid camera in case he said no. I looked happy, I thought. He looked happy. We looked like we were in love. The photos were suggestive, sensationally so. The article itself was very badly written with scant detail; and they didn't name me. *Mystery younger woman,* it said. As Cecile had predicted, no one ever followed it up.

Why had they published it? For what possible good? Those photos had destroyed everything. It wasn't even news.

After I'd been home for a few weeks, Ophelia moved in with Oscar. She called me most days and some of the time I answered. She was careful not to talk about work. It would be a long time before I'd be able to talk about that place or our lives as they had been. Eddy texted me all the time, but he didn't call and he didn't expect a reply. He sent me a big bunch of flowers from our local florist, which made me cry every time I looked at them so I threw them in the bin. I had lots of messages from people from work after the announcement of my "resignation"—a term of the agreement—was made public. People said they hoped I was OK, they wished me well, wanted to meet up. I didn't reply to any of those.

The person I did reply to (although it was just with a few little *x*s) was Finn, who sent me a message saying:

> Fuck them all. Hope you are OK, babe. Always here. F.xx

Being away from London and publishing and all of my life was incredibly painful and alienating, but, as spring arrived, the darkest parts of my illness felt some of the light and warmth of the pale sun and started to retreat. I talked to Nora about it, telling her how fearful I was that by giving this feeling words, I would frighten it away. She nodded, and asked why I felt like that, and I told her that it was because I had stopped believing good things would happen for me, or that I would ever be able to recover.

It had been over two months since I had last seen Richard, last spoken to him, and I'd been sure that the pain I'd been feeling was permanent. But it wasn't. It happened so slowly at first that I didn't dare to feel any hope of being better. The world outside my bedroom was turning green again, and with such exuberance and optimism it was like the trees and shrubs and bulbs didn't realize it would be temporary, that in six short months the cold and dark would reappear and force them into a deathlike state, frozen and underground in the darkness. If they knew, they didn't seem to mind.

It was so different to experience the change of seasons in the countryside. Dad's modest garden was alive with tulips and lilacs, and the trees were soon thick with fluffy blossoms. Noah was totally obsessed with the clouds of frogspawn blooming in the pond, having learned about it at nursery, and I watched him hunched over the edge on his haunches watching the little tails wiggle out of the eggs. Sometimes, in the days that followed, I'd feel well enough to sit with him and watch their little legs start to form and so on and on until they were tiny frogs. A heron feasted on them mercilessly one afternoon, along with the pond's few resident fish, so only a few remained. He was initially very upset, but within half an hour he was shrugging and saying "the circle of life" in a knowing way, just like Dad had explained it to him.

Every day, that little boy whom I'd felt so distant from, whom I'd refused to recognize as being my family, brought me a little closer to life and the world that I now inhabited. He was so used to me being around now that I got to see his full self, not the reserved child that I'd known from my one- or two-night stays of the past.

Laura was home most of the day with me. She was really kind, making me food and cups of tea as I sat in the garden and chain-smoked, something I did only when Noah wasn't around. Her cooking was really good and my appetite started to return. She loved feeding me, making me sandwiches with soft bread and piles of crisps next to them, soups and stews, and, best of all, cookies and cakes, which she made with such care and attention I understood her better as a person, and as a mother. She insisted that I read some of the authors she loved and I found great comfort and solace in these stories by women, about women. They were writers I had never read before, presuming they weren't for me, but they became my new favorites. They were rich and dark and innately, beautifully human. I read almost everything by Marian Keyes on Laura's recommendation and wondered if perhaps some of my melancholy had come from the miserable lives of the men that I had been immersed in for the last year, trying to impress Richard by reading everything and anything he put my way.

What was most surprising was how quickly Richard became a memory, a part of my past. With the help of Nora, I adjusted to the understanding that he was not in my present, or my future. It didn't lessen the pain, but it gave me some better grasp of my reality to accept that I'd never see his initials pop up on my phone screen again. After a while, I stopped calling and texting.

I thought about him all the time, despite this. I had this new information about him from Cecile and some days I believed it and understood it was the truth, and some days I couldn't. I would cry silently in bed, mouth open, feeling the pain of being separated from him course through every bone of my body. I thought a lot about the pregnancy and how things would have played out if I had kept it. In group therapy I started talking a little, no specifics, but talking. The tiny connections I felt with the other people in the room felt good to me and I needed to feel anything that was good as much as possible, because as it turned out, I really didn't want to die.

On a Friday morning, about four months after that awful day, Dad came into my room and told me to get dressed, as I had a visitor coming. I immediately thought he meant Richard, but, sensing it, he shook his head and said, "No, not him."

I got dressed and brushed my hair. My fringe had grown out as

I'd not been to a hairdresser since I'd been here, and I couldn't remember what I looked like with makeup on.

I heard the doorbell and went downstairs to get the door. It was Cecile. I couldn't quite get my head around seeing her here, in this place, on the doorstep of my childhood home. I was suddenly aware of the size of the house, and the décor. I was ashamed for a second. But I realized with relief that I also wasn't angry with her.

Noah came flying through my legs, holding a toy Buzz Lightyear. Not much was more exciting to Noah than the doorbell or visitors.

"Hello!" He looked up at Cecile, blinking through his thick glasses. I'd not even had a chance to say hello myself. I ruffled his hair.

"Hello!" She bent down to get a little closer to his height. "Who's this?" She pointed at his toy.

"Steve!" he said excitedly.

"Oh, right! Steve, is it?"

He looked at her, suddenly bashful, and ran back inside singing, "Steve, Steve, Steve."

Cecile stood up. She was in jeans and a T-shirt and trainers. I'd never seen her out of heels, let alone in jeans. She was tiny. She looked great.

"Hey, Charlie. Shall we go for a coffee?"

She left her Mercedes parked outside our house and we walked into the village. I didn't know what to say and I don't think she did, either. We walked in silence for about fifteen minutes.

When we got to the café we were headed to, I sat outside in the garden while she went in to order. It was a beautiful day, not too hot but gloriously still and sunny, like it could be in June outside of the city.

"How have you been?" It was funny hearing her voice, seeing her. She was so familiar to me, but she came from a time and place in my life that felt distant.

"OK, I guess. Better lately, if I'm honest. I didn't want to come home, but it was for the best, I think. To be out of it all."

She shook a packet of sugar into her coffee and took a sip. She frowned.

"They can't do coffee out here. Sorry, I should have warned you."

"It's fine. I'm too French about coffee, as you know." She looked into her cup, thinking about what to say. I didn't know what I could do to make this easier for either of us, so I said nothing. "Charlie, I have been so worried about you. I tried to call, but I guessed you wouldn't want to speak to me. I've been in touch with Ophelia a lot, though; she has been keeping me up to date."

I nodded. The tables around us were all full, mostly with older couples. It was another month until the summer holidays, when the whole village and the beach and the forest would be overwhelmed with tourists. "I know. She told me. I appreciate it. I do."

"It wasn't my decision, you know. I fought for you. But it was the right decision, for you more than anyone."

"Did he fight for me? Did he defend me at all?"

She looked into the distance, thinking about what to say.

"He took Elaine's side, as I knew he would. And her position was that you went, or he left Winden & Shane. She made a formal complaint and that was the end of it. But everyone—Markus, Allegra, all of us know who is to blame and how this happened. I'm sorry that the company have treated you as they have, but, really, Charlie, it's just business. Publishing—especially Winden & Shane—pretends to be fluffy and eccentric and village-y, but it isn't. It's brutal and it's all about money, which is why there was never a question of siding with you over Richard, regardless of our responsibility to you as an employee. But no one thinks badly of you. Especially not me. I'm sorry I didn't protect you better. I didn't see it coming. I honestly thought that kind of behavior was far behind him. And it never even occurred to me that he would be so brazen as to do this to my own assistant."

"I didn't need protecting. That was never your job. I knew the risks of what I was doing. I knew, really, that it wouldn't end well. But I couldn't stop myself from hoping otherwise. I ignored my instincts because I did . . . I do . . . I don't know . . . love him."

"He's a very magnetic person. He is a very powerful person. More than that, though, he's a very selfish person."

I nodded. "I get that now."

We sat in silence. I drank my coffee and smoked a cigarette.

"I don't know if what I've told you about him and how he has behaved to other women has helped you or not. But I do think your relationship was different. It lasted a long time. He is having some kind of late midlife crisis. He used you horribly. But for what it's worth, I do think things were more real than with his other affairs."

I didn't know if it made it better or worse. I was quiet for a while, letting her words sink in and trying not to cry. I was still a way off from being better. I heard Nora's voice in my head. *Be gentle with yourself.*

"I think it's going to take me a long time to understand things for myself. There were moments that it was so real. But what I see now is that he lied to me, a lot. And he manipulated things. He was lying to himself, too."

Cecile nodded but didn't say anything more. "So, you feel . . . better?"

"I do feel better than I was, where I have been at some points in the last year or so. I've started some proper therapy and I'm going to stick to it. But I have no idea what comes next or where I go from here."

"That's something I came to talk to you about."

Cecile's husband, Matthew, was opening a New York office of his literary agency, Ridgebrook & Co., and Cecile had arranged for me, if I wanted, to start a new job in the new office as the team assistant. It wasn't a step up—in fact, it was a step down—but it was a chance to start afresh, somewhere new. New York was more than I could have hoped for. They'd arrange a visa for me, and I had enough money from my payout to get myself set up out there, but there would be a small relocation package to help with that, too. Cecile and Matthew owned an apartment in Manhattan that they rented out, but it was currently empty. I would need to find a place of my own, but I could stay as long as I needed to get settled.

I was sick of PR. I couldn't go back to that work. Even Cecile said I wasn't suited to it. She went on and on about me being clever and talented and having a bright future in publishing, and that she could see me doing brilliantly as an agent. I had, for a long time, envied Ophelia and Eddy for the jobs in Editorial, shaping the books rather than selling them to journalists, and working at a literary agency would mean being even closer to the writing than they were.

I still wanted to work around books, and had no other offers, so I said yes on the spot. It wasn't to start until late in the autumn, so I had time to get back to full speed. I thanked Cecile, and she gave me a hug as she got back into her car to drive to London. Noah waved at her from the living room window.

Ophelia was delighted for me. She came down to see me one Friday afternoon a few weeks later, with Oscar. They had packed up my things into a van, which she drove. I had rented a garage near Dad's for storage. Even when we had unpacked all of my belongings, they only took up a corner. I told them to leave my chest of drawers on the street for someone to take and it had been gone within an hour. Ophelia had asked me if I'd wanted her to bring the chair Richard had given me, but the garage wasn't secure enough for something so valuable and there was no room in the house for it. She'd suggested that we get her parents' friend from Sotheby's to value it, and I'd agreed. It seemed that it could sell for up to six thousand pounds at auction. I would use the money to pay my dad back, and keep the rest for New York.

As we unloaded the van, I saw all the evidence of my life in London laid before me. I was relieved to see my things again, but it was very painful. I wasn't sure if it was right to up and leave, but New York seemed so distant, so far away. It was like a dream, really, getting the chance to move to a new city and start again. I wondered if people out there would know about what had happened. I decided not. If they had heard about it, which maybe they would have, they wouldn't necessarily recognize me and put two and two together.

Ophelia and Oscar stayed for the afternoon. It was warm so we went to the beach. We drank Diet Cokes on a picnic bench outside the Anchor and talked about the summer, what they had planned. They were going to Italy together for a few weeks and I wondered if Oscar might propose to Ophelia. I hoped so. They talked to me about New York, which they both knew very well. They told me the good areas and the bad, the best restaurants and bars to visit. Ophelia had a friend from school living in the city who worked in fashion, and she was going to introduce me on email. I had never been before, but I felt like I had from books and films and pop songs.

They said I'd love it. When Oscar went inside to use the bathroom, Ophelia got up and sat next to me and put her arms around me.

"We'll come and visit. And email every day. I'm so jealous, really. Moving to New York at twenty-five. What an adventure you're going to have. You do feel ready, don't you? It's a big step."

"I know. And it will be hard, I'm sure, but I honestly think it's for the best. I don't know what I would do if I stayed. Everyone in publishing in London knows about me, knows what happened. And don't deny it, it will have been gossiped about everywhere. I'm unhireable. I know it. You know it. Ophelia, I am so sorry for how awful I have been, how I behaved after it all happened. You and Eddy—you have been nothing but good to me. I don't really know how I can ever thank you."

Ophelia was crying. "I'm so sorry I called your dad to get you. I didn't know what else to do. I know how angry you were about that."

I tilted her face to mine. "You did exactly the right thing. You have always done exactly the right thing, and you have always wanted only the best for me. I know that." She nodded, unable to speak. "And now I'm doing better, thanks to you, and I can start moving on. And you are moving on, too, and I'm so excited for you. Hey, do you think he'll propose in Italy?"

Ophelia choked on her drink and snorted, something I'd never seen her do before. It was loud enough that the people at the next table turned around to look. I started to laugh, and then she did. By the time Oscar came back we were both recovering, but there were tears in our eyes that were not, for once, tears of sadness.

They said they'd come and visit soon, and get a hotel or something so they could stay the night. I hugged Ophelia for a long time before they left. They offered me a lift back to the house but I wasn't ready to go back. I walked on the beach instead. The tide was out and the familiar smell of seaweed drying in the sun filled every part of me with memories from my childhood. I thought about the version of me that had, aged eleven, searched the rockpools for crabs or fish or pearls as my parents sat on these stones, watching me from a distance. I thought of Noah doing the same in a few years, Dad and Laura maybe on that very spot, those very stones. I checked my phone. No emails, no missed calls. I knew it was really over.

When I got back to the house, Laura was in the garden with

Noah. They were sitting by the pond. He was crouched in his shorts, glasses on the end of his nose, looking in the water for fish or frogs or newts. Dad was in the kitchen making a salad to go with dinner.

"Hello, love. Did you have a nice time with your friends?"

"Yes, thanks. How was your day?"

"Ah, it was OK. Tiring. I'm always tired these days. I'm ready to retire. Only a bit more to go now. Did you tell them about New York?"

"Yes, we talked about it. Ophelia has a friend out there she's going to introduce me to. They told me about all the best places to go."

"And you're sure you are ready?"

"I am. Don't worry about me, Dad."

"I will always worry about you, Charlie. You can come home if it gets too much."

I stole a piece of cucumber from the chopping board.

"That used to drive your mum mad. Do you remember?"

He didn't usually mention her, so it was jarring to hear him do so. "No. I don't remember. There's lots I don't remember. I think there's far more that I don't remember than I do remember."

He carried on chopping. "She'd say, 'You'll ruin your supper if you keep picking.' She always said supper, not dinner."

"I remember that."

"You know, I've always . . . worried about you. When it comes to relationships." I could tell that he felt awkward. I looked out of the kitchen window. Laura was still by the pond with Noah. "Your mum was vulnerable when she was young. She lost her parents in her early twenties as you know, and it was hard for her. I think that's why she fell in with your dad."

"What do you mean?"

He put the knife down and looked at the ceiling as if hoping to find inspiration there.

"He was abusive. Coercive, they'd call it now. He didn't like her having friends. And he had a really nasty temper, to put it mildly. He drank too much." He clearly regretted saying this, knowing it was a sensitive subject for me. "And when I say too much, I mean he was an angry drunk. She was scared of him toward the end, very scared. You are so like her, you know. Inside and out."

"Am I like him?"

"You are absolutely nothing like him. You really don't remember him? Or that time?"

"No. I mean, I have some memories that don't fit into the timeline of my life with you so I think they must be from then. But I don't think I have any memory of him specifically, or any of the stuff you are talking about that happened."

He nodded, then started chopping little red tomatoes in half. I said nothing, hoping he would go on.

"Did he ever hurt her? Or me?"

"I think he came close. It was a bad time. When she came to live with me, he would get drunk and come to the flat. We had to call the police more than once. You don't remember that?"

I thought really hard. I tried to dig through any memories that would fit that event. "No. Nothing."

"Good. We were so concerned about how it might impact you. I thought maybe that that is why you'd ended up involved with—with that man."

"Richard didn't hurt me."

"Didn't he?"

"He was never violent." This was the most intimate and personal conversation I'd ever had with Dad, and I didn't want to frighten him away. "I think I'm understanding more now about that stuff. That he isolated me, and made me completely dependent on him. And that he wasn't always kind." I was starting to see what I'd been blind to before.

"You should be with someone who is kind to you, Charlie. You should have good people in your life. Those friends of yours from London are absolute crackers."

"They are, aren't they?"

I smiled, and he smiled back. Then he pointed at the chopping board and winked. "Go mad. Your mum's not here to tell either of us off."

Home. It was, for the first time in a long time, starting to feel like I had a real home. It wasn't London. It wasn't Stoke Newington or the Covent Garden flat. It wasn't Stone Heap House. It was here, the house I had grown up in. The people had changed, but those who had left were in the walls, the bricks, the mortar. Noah and Laura, they were there, too, now, with Mum and Dad and me. Something had shifted inside me in the last few months. Being forced to sit still had had the effect of making me see what was right in front of me, not behind me, and not ahead somewhere in the future; she was unknown. So much was unknown.

As we stood in the kitchen that summer afternoon, I was hit by something that I recognized as being hopeful in how it felt. There was a long way for me to go to get better, I knew that, but I saw that there was a path ahead of me, maybe for the first time since Mum had died. I wasn't exactly sure where it would take me and who would be by my side, but it was there, ready for me. Waiting. In a few months' time, I would pack up my things and I would go to New York alone, not knowing anyone, and I would build a life for myself. I would work hard. And one day, maybe, just maybe, I would finally find a place for myself in this strange and surprisingly beautiful world.

Now

When I saw Cecile's name appear on my phone, which was buzzing on the kitchen table, I knew that she was calling to tell me that Richard had died.

It was a warm Friday morning in May. I was alone in our little house in Oxfordshire, working on an edit. She told me that Richard had passed away the night before from complications relating to pancreatic cancer. He was seventy-one. He had been diagnosed just weeks before, and although he'd known that it was terminal, they'd thought he would have more time. A few months, at least.

I listened and then asked all the usual questions—was he alone? No, Elaine and John Cormorant had been with him. Was he in any pain? No, but they always say that. And then, when would it be announced? Later this afternoon—they were preparing a press release and giving the obituarists time to get copy together. It would say: *following a short illness.* I thanked Cecile for letting me know and hung up.

Although I knew myself better than I had ever done in my twenties, I was still surprised by how I reacted to things sometimes, and this was one of those times. I couldn't feel the familiar, feathered hands of the depression that I knew still lived inside me. I waited to feel it stir, to rise up from where it had been sleeping, to put its cold fingers around my neck. I expected it to come, but it didn't. For now, it stayed quiet, curled up and motionless.

I called my husband. He was in London at an academic conference for the day. He knew what had happened with Richard, but we had met nearly seven years after I'd moved to New York and it had been less raw by then. I had made a conscious decision not to talk about it too much with him. I didn't want the sharp, broken pieces of that relationship anywhere inside my new, happy one.

He asked me if I wanted him to come home, but I said not to. Then I called my dad, and told him, because he would see the news later that day and worry.

I'd seen Richard once more, after everything happened. It was about three years after I'd moved to New York. I'd been at a publisher's office for a meeting. As I was leaving, he had just arrived. He was standing at the security desk with someone I didn't recognize. He had slowly lifted a hand to wave at me. I didn't wave back. Our eyes had met for a moment, a barrage of memories flashing through my mind. He'd looked so much older. His hair was more white than gray, so different from how I'd remembered him.

I couldn't settle in the house. The news of Richard's death hung quietly around me. I decided it was best to go for a walk. We lived in a lovely red-brick terraced house with a yellow front door in a small village in the countryside just outside of Oxford, far enough from the rush and noise of London, but still close enough for me to commute in a few days a week. My husband worked at the university; he was an age-appropriate, true New Yorker and a prominent academic. I had met him in a dive bar in Brooklyn on a night out with my friends; he had been to college with one of them. We had quickly fallen in love, and then quickly fallen pregnant. After the birth of our daughter, we had packed up and moved back to England to build a life for our little family.

I still missed New York—we both did. It was the first place that I had ever really felt like I fitted in. It had been a haven for me after everything that had happened, and had offered me the anonymity and fresh start that I had hoped for. I'd loved the work and had flourished at Ridgebrook & Co., moving up through the ranks quickly to become an associate agent in less than a year. I'd stayed single for a long time, but I'd made friends, really brilliant friends, through work and apartment shares and running clubs. I'd run almost every morning through Central Park or along the Hudson or the East River, depending on where I was living. Running had kept me healthy, given me a reason to get up each day, a reason to eat well and to go to bed at a decent hour. Watching the city wake around me had connected me to it and to the people that lived there, and I'd soon found that I felt less alone, and less like I was living on the edge of everyone else. By the time we left New York, there was a group of us who were so bonded it had felt like it might be impossible to ever leave them, to unpick the beautiful tangle of our lives. But we had, and I knew it was right for us and our daughter to finally come home, to be nearer to Dad, and Laura and Noah.

The trees that Friday in May were suddenly full and green again after a slow, cold spring, and the world around me felt lush and clean in the sunshine, like a postcard from a long-ago time. The earth, the sky, the flowers, even the tarmac, none of them seemed to know the news about Richard, or if they did, they didn't care. While I walked, I called Ophelia. She was worried about me. Any mention of his name always concerned her. Over the years we had talked about this day. Given his lifestyle, we'd have been surprised if he'd made it to a ripe old age, but this was still sooner than we had expected. She couldn't talk for long and promised to call me back that evening. Her children were all off school with colds, the nanny was also ill and Oscar was away on Finn's second stag do; his first marriage to an Australian supermodel some ten years earlier had not lasted three months. It sounded chaotic. Ophelia had three children, whereas I had just the one.

I texted Eddy telling him the news, but the text went green, so I presumed he was somewhere abroad or off-grid, writing, as he often was these days. I'd not heard from him in months, which meant that wherever he was, he was likely happy.

There was so much unsaid between Richard and me that would now remain that way forever. I hadn't hoped for any absolution or reconciliation. It had been a very long time since I had wanted to have any contact with him at all. A lot of intensive therapy over the years had helped me come to terms with much of what had gone on with Richard, and to understand why things had gotten as bad as they had. I'd faced what I had been through in my teenage years, with losing my mum, even with Lee. I wasn't cured of my sadness, that wasn't going to be possible for me, but I knew it well enough to know what it needed. I knew it intimately, and what I had to give it in order to keep it contained, and how fragile that balance was and always would be for me.

But you can't ever really get over loss like the loss I'd experienced.

You just learned to live with it, to grow around it.

If you were lucky, you could even maybe find something good in it.

I stopped at a very old church about a mile from our house and sat down on a bench in the shade of a yew tree among the ancient, moss-covered graves. Some were tended beautifully, and others long forgotten, their family lines either stopping or moving on to a different place. It was hard to imagine Richard's cold, lifeless body on a metal tray in a dark cupboard somewhere in the depths of a London hospital. It was hard to imagine that such a man could simply cease to be, but there you had it. He was only human, after all.

When I got home, I went to my laptop and logged into my old email account, feeling compelled to read our emails, to see what they would make me feel. I'd not logged in for months, maybe even a year, and it took a few goes to get the right password. Scrolling through the newsletters and spam and notification emails, there it was. An unread email from Richard Aveling, dated the previous week.

Dear Charlie,

I don't know if this is an email address you even use anymore, but I have no other way to reach you. I daren't ask Cecile.

I have, rather unfortunately, much less time left to live than I had hoped. I have pancreatic cancer, and they have only just found it. The news is dire. This is not a good cancer to get, and they always get it too late, I'm told by the doctors. I have months, maybe a little more.

I am in Guy's and St. Thomas's at present, but I am focused on getting home in the next week or so. I want to die at Stone Heap House, in my own bed. Do you even live in the UK? Last I heard, you were moving back. If you are here, and you feel able to, I would very much like to see you. There are many things I need to say to you and there is rather a rush now for me to say them. The biggest of all is that I am sorry, and I'm sorry that it has taken this to happen for me to tell you that.

You can visit whenever you like.

I hope to see you, Charlie, just one last time. I really did love you, despite what you might think.

Yours,
Richard Aveling

I read the email several times. I felt something but it took me a while to realize what it was. It was pity. It had been close to fifteen years since it had all fallen apart and yet there, in a hospital bed in his last days, he was trying, finally, to say he was sorry.

Had I seen it in time I would have gone to see him. That's what I told myself then and I will tell myself that every day for the rest of my life. That I would have shown him the mercy he needed in his last days. I didn't have to test that theory—he was dead and gone; there was no one to see. I closed my laptop and put it away. It was only early in the afternoon, but I decided to go and pick up my daughter from nursery.

She was surprised and delighted to see me. She was as scruffy, sticky and generally grubby as she always was after a day at nursery, her strawberry-blonde hair teased from its ponytail and clips, and sticking up at all angles around her sweet face. Her hair was red, like my mum's, which I loved. I took her backpack and her warm little hand in mine, and we went to a nearby café for cake, as a treat. She told me all about her adventures that day, what they had read, played with, eaten. *Oh, to be five,* I thought. Then, suddenly, *I will protect you. You will never go through what I went through.*

As I watched her carefully lick the icing off a cupcake, I was hit by a wave of sadness.

"Are you OK, Mummy?" She was so small, but so sensitive that she often noticed the tiniest shifts in her adults. You could get nothing past her, so we were always as honest as we could be.

"Someone I used to know has died. I'm a bit sad about that, but I'm OK."

"Like Socks?"

Socks was a little cat that we had lost to the road a few months before.

"Yes, like Socks."

"Well, he's in a better place now, so we don't have to worry about him. With the blackbirds. With Socks."

I smiled at her and wiped at a tear forming in the corner of my eye before it fell. It would be the only tear ever I gave to Richard's death.

"Of course. You are right."

After I'd fed her and bathed her and tucked her in that night, I poured myself a glass of white wine, not something that I did that often, and found a packet of cigarettes that had been left behind by a colleague of my husband's from the university after a party the previous summer. I went out into the garden and lit one. The taste was familiar, but I didn't enjoy it as I used to. I'd rebuilt myself very slowly after my breakdown that awful winter, and in doing so I'd let go of a lot of habits that were so destructive. I started to look after myself, to eat properly and to drink much, much less. Quitting smoking had taken longer.

The garden, which I cared for in any small moment I had that wasn't consumed by motherhood or work, looked finally like it was coming together after years of us owning it, or it owning us. Hydrangea bloomed pink and blue, and the scent of star jasmine mixed with honeysuckle in the warm night air. I walked around the little garden, snipping the dead heads from the roses and cosmos as I went, tending these plants as I did with whatever care and attention I had left in me by the evening. I had never imagined this life for myself. A house, a husband, a daughter, a career. Under Matthew's guidance I had become a literary agent. When he retired a few years ago, he handed over the reins to Ridgebrook & Co. to me and another colleague, and, between us, we were making a real success of it. I had never even thought I'd make it to thirty, yet here I was. Well. Happy. Alive. And now, maybe, just maybe, I was finally free.

I reached back for any memories of my time with Richard that I could find. Although they were just out of reach, my mind unpracticed now in thinking of him, I did remember something of how it had felt to be with him. Remembering was bitter, and it was sweet. And it was something in between. I tried to remember his face, his voice, his hands, his body, but the details weren't there. I thought back to that afternoon in France, to the first time that he told me he loved me. I thought of him in his panama hat, his arm heavy on my shoulder in the pink evening. Him next to me, real and warm. But it was like looking at an image reflected in rippling water; he was just out of focus, shifting as I tried to look closely at each part of him. All I could see was that old black-and-white photograph of him from his book jackets. I could still see that clear as day.

I thought instead of my mum. How she would have loved her granddaughter, who bore her name—Elizabeth. I could remember all the details of her. The lines on her neck, the shape of her fingernails, the softness of her belly, the white threads in the red of her hair. When I heard the front door click, the catch turned by my husband's key, I put my cigarette out and went inside, back to my life, to the quiet domesticity in which I had found happiness, far from where I was ever looking for it.

Acknowledgments

Enormous thanks to my agent, Juliet Mushens. You are the most patient person on the planet (along with Charlotte, and I guess my husband) and I couldn't have hoped for a better human to have in my corner. Thanks also to Kiya, Alba, Catriona, Emma and Liza and all at Mushens Entertainment.

I feel very lucky to have Charlotte Mursell at Orion as my editor. Thank you, Charlotte, for believing in this book and giving it such *life*. You have made me a better writer, and I am so grateful to you for your kindness, tenacity and care. Thanks to everyone at Orion who has worked so hard to bring this book into the world—what a team! To Carina Bryan, Sandra Taylor, Sam Eades, Jess Hart, Charlotte Abrams Simpson, Suzanne Clarke.

Thanks to Caroline Weishuhn for starting this journey with me at Penguin Random House US, and to Hilary Teeman for continuing it. Thanks to Cindy Berman, Elizabeth Eno, Jennifer Hershey, Kim Hovey, Emily Isayeff, Kathleen Quinlan, Emma Thomasch, Kara Welsh and Katie Zilberman. Thanks also to Becca Rodriguez at Grandview LA, Jenny Bent at The Bent Agency, Monika Boese and Tabea Horst at Ullstein, Federica Gracefa, Leo Teti, Crina Draghici, Ana Babovic, Tatyana Fedorenko and to all of the international agents, publishers and their teams, to the cover designers and the translators and booksellers that have given their time and energy and expertise to this book all over the world.

A. J. Finn and S. J. Watson were among the first to read *Bitter Sweet* and I am eternally grateful to them for giving me the push I needed, as I am to all of the wonderful writers that have offered support and advice. A very special thanks to my friend David Headley, and to Emily Glenister, at the wonderful bookshop Goldsboro Books in London.

There are elements to this story that I had some help on; Dr. Helgi Jonasson and Miss Vinita Nair at St. Mary's Hospital spent time with me talking about the incredible work they do with women, and Helgi was instrumental in getting the detail right on the page. To the women that I met at St. Mary's, if you are reading this, thank you—it was a privilege to speak with you. Dr. Mark Salter was very generous with his time and energy ensuring that the mental health elements of the story are accurate. Thank you for this, and indeed for everything.

Jeff Mangum of Neutral Milk Hotel kindly gave me permission to use lyrics from his extraordinary song "In the Airplane over the Sea." Thanks to both Jeff and to Brian McPherson for arranging this.

Thank you to Bubba, Tómas and Dagný for inviting us to stay at the remarkable house Andahvilft in Bíldudalur, West Iceland, where this book began. Thanks to Kerry Ryan at Write Like a Grrrl (this is a great place to start if you want to write) and to Jon Harley, whose teaching at Angmering I have never forgotten.

Thanks to my beloved friends: To Amy Carolin, whose friendship, guidance and belief in me has shaped everything I have ever done and will ever do. To Chloe Healy, who was the very first person to read this book and whose encouragement, love and loyalty have persisted for more than a decade. To Gill Heeley and James Mackay, Richard Bravery and Katrina Mason (what a holiday), Christa and Biff Bloom-Burrows, Suzy Aspley, Suzanne Azzopardi, Rachael Clark, Jack Cregan, Laura "Curly" Davidson, Teague Emery, David Fennel, Rhi Griffiths, Tom Harris, David Harrison, Rebecca Ikin, Philip Jones, Bethan Moore, Birta Diljá Ögmundardóttir, Miriam Robinson, Yrsa Sigurðardóttir, Óli Þórhallsson, Jillian Taylor, Pétur Valsson, Liz Vater, Nuala Watts, Annabel Wilson and Erin Young. Thanks also to Sam and Billy Beech. To Lin and Tim Brown. To Marianna, Mark, Sinead and all of our adored Emery family. To Edi.

To the Street family. To Alex College, and the Chevallots. To Christine.

To my parents-in-law, Jennifer and John Bentham, and to Laura and Dan Aston.

To my dad, Christopher Robin, my brother Toby and to Marta.

To my late mum, Diana Williams (1943–2003), who never got to read this, but is very much alive in the pages of the book.

Thank you to all of the Ophelias and Eddys and Ceciles I have met over the years working in publishing—you know who you are.

Greatest thanks, though, to Chris Bentham and to Astrid Snow.

About the Author

HATTIE WILLIAMS began pursuing a music career in her teens and toured Europe extensively, making three studio albums and working as a composer before finding her way to book publishing (quite by accident). She spent the next twelve years working with some of the biggest authors in the world and is the former producer of the Iceland Noir Literary Festival, which takes place in Reykjavík every November. Williams continues to feed her creativity through her writing from her home in East London, where she lives with her partner and daughter.

About the Type

This book was set in Fairfield, the first typeface from the hand of the distinguished American artist and engraver Rudolph Ruzicka (1883–1978). Ruzicka was born in Bohemia (in the present-day Czech Republic) and came to America in 1894. He set up his own shop, devoted to wood engraving and printing, in New York in 1913 after a varied career working as a wood engraver, in photoengraving and banknote printing plants and as an art director and freelance artist. He designed and illustrated many books, and was the creator of a considerable list of individual prints—wood engravings, line engravings on copper and aquatints.